D1706383

LOOKING FOR LEO

A NOVEL

PATTI CAVALIERE

ISBN:1493671375
ISBN-13:9781493671373

PATTI CAVALIERE

DEDICATION

This book is dedicated to my beloved cat Rudy.
It was out of grief over his loss many years ago that I began to write.
And to my parents, **Joe and Lee Cavaliere**, an Aries and a Taurus,
who have loved me all along.

PATTI CAVALIERE

With Heartfelt Gratitude To:

Barbara Gingold, a social worker and a veterinary client who became the inspiration for Ingrid when she showed me that smart women believe in astrology. She left me her library on the subject when she died in 2004. **Tom Connor** and fellow members of the **Trumbull Writer's Group** who helped me to grow as a writer. Fellow **Members of CTRWA** (Connecticut Chapter of the Romance Writers of America) who share their knowledge and experience generously. They gave me the courage to realize the dream of publication. **Carol Kennedy,** my loyal high school friend to whom I owe the credit of my title. **Letha (Logan) Dardani,** my childhood friend who loves me in spite of my eclectic taste in fashion, and who inspired the character of Logan. Readers of my earlier versions of this novel who provided the kind feedback that kept me believing in this novel: **Gail Andreyka, Linda Cirillo, Gretchen Fry, Judy Kantor, Marylou Roof, Patti Schott**, and especially **Lexi Bone**, a Leo, whose thoughtful suggestions inspired scenes that shed new light on Leo. My sister **Sue Jamieson**, a Master Gardener and avid reader, who understands the need for conflict in novels and never complained about my false portrayal of her family. My brother, **Bob Cavaliere**, a witty Gemini who never borrowed a penny. **Shirley Goldberg**, my writing partner, a Scorpio whose keen edits helped me bring this story to life. **Joyce Maynard**, whose workshop, Write by the Sea, on Star Island, taught me the beauty of the beats. Her story telling is as warm and honest as her friendship. **Clients of Spring Glen Veterinary Clinic** during the years of 1986-2002 who left me with fond memories of themselves and some of the pets immortalized in this novel. **Brian J. Silverlieb, V.M.D,** a Virgo who was fun, loving and generous. We remained friends for thirty years until he died of cancer in February 2011. Brian saw the possibility in a neglected Connecticut farm when he purchased it in 1980 and created the legacy of Amberfield. Lastly, to the pets that tolerated my annual Christmas card photo shoot, kept me company in my garden, and enriched my life with unconditional love.

Special Acknowledgement

Anita Jacobs, Editor of *Listen Magazine* in 2003 who gave me my first publishing thrill with my teen story, "Breaking the Chain."

Anna Katz, Editor, Girl Friday Productions and **Judy Roth**, Editor, who believed in this story.

Tim Ditlow, Grammy award-winning audiobook producer, Vice President of Content and Member of Advisory Board at Epic! Creations Inc. who is my music friend. Thanks to Tim's insight, I wrote a better ending.

Victoria (Vicovers at Fiverr) for her exceptional talent and endless patience in capturing my vision for this book cover.

I would especially like to express my gratitude to **Deb Werksman**, Editorial Director at Sourcebooks, for her continued gentle replies to my queries. It means so much to unpublished authors when an editor takes the time to give detailed personal feedback, and she did.

Special Note

The character of Dr. Bob is fictional, as is his wife Pam, however, the personality of a dedicated, caring, sometimes humorous mentor was inspired by the many wonderful veterinarians I worked for during the period of 1975-2002.

Although many of the situations were based on reality, the places and people in this novel are the product of my imagination.

~1~

I watched Ingrid unfold the dog-eared paper with a perfect circle in the center. It was sectioned into twelve pie slices and there were strange symbols scattered inside the astrological chart wheel. She pointed to the right side and called it the House of Relationships. Then she proceeded to tell me everything I knew about myself, and something I didn't want to hear. She told me to look for Leo.

At the brick Tudor building with a carved sign posted on the front lawn, I drive into the lot and park my Honda. *Mount Pleasant Animal Hospital.* A shadow of myself settles into my bones. Then out of the corner of my eye, I see a woman lean into her back seat and tug the end of a dog leash. I grab my tote bag and run to the door before she does, because my job makes it impossible to stay away.

Jeannie's hands are tucked like pistols into each pocket of her white cotton sweater when I step inside the office. The A/C is cranking. My legs feel like they're made of wax when I stop beside her reception desk to check the appointment book.

"What's the boss' mood like today, corny or cranky?" I say clearing the nasal tone in my throat.

"You have a little breather. The first appointment cancelled. Turns out the puddle on the floor was from the dishwasher, not the cat."

Jeannie chuckles and spurts out a cigarette cough. She squints at my long hair as if she can tell why I never brushed it this morning. I turn to do just that before appointments start.

"Pretty soon you'll be taking over the practice, Jill." *She knows something is up.* Last week, that comment would have made me happy.

First comes marriage, then comes the house. Next comes ownership of a veterinary practice I've loved since I was a kennel girl— at least in an animal doctor story. At least until now. Jeannie doesn't know my marriage plans got spayed and neutered last night. I was the "right age," as Mom says.

"I brought some of my streusel," Jeannie yells as I'm almost out of sight. *Words from a woman who solves problems with a piece of pie.* "It's next to the coffee."

"Thanks, Jeannie." I smooth my hair and look back at Jeannie's. It's brittle and gray now and her make up is a little too beige for her sallow skin tone. It wasn't like that ten years ago. *Is that what I'll look like in a ten years after keeping up these ten-hour days?* I walk past Jeannie's homemade pastry, and close my office door.

Rows of colored notes are lined up on my desk. I lift a stack of patient's charts that I need to call back. Then I notice the local newspaper that Jeannie has left on my desk. There's an article about the Amberfield property being for sale.

The kitchen cabinet handles were missing and the enamel stove was smeared with black grease when Tim and I went to see the house. That's not at all how it once was. I swipe through my phone photos again. I picture the bedroom decorated with the new comforter and drapes I've bought, Tim standing at the gas stove, barefoot and blue jeans, frying Sunday morning breakfast—bacon sparking in the frying pan, golden egg yolks fluttering with lacy brown edges. This wouldn't be his place or my place. It would have been ours.

And after twenty years I could have closure for what happened there with Petal.

I flip pages to the astrology section— maybe a million other Pisces like me are miserable, too. Yes, despite eight years of animal medicine, I still read my horoscope.

PISCES: You now have the ability to eliminate the things in your life that you think you cannot live without. It's time to reinvent your life.

I start to close the paper, then glance up the column to read Tim's.

SCORPIO: You have the unique ability to tear things down and rebuild your life from shreds. It's time to make a fresh start by standing alone on your own two feet.

I've known since high school that Tim was the man I wanted to marry. We never dated back then, but a few years later one night we ended up at the same concert and I thought to myself, *some people are just destined to be together*.

And now, it must be someone else.

I pick up the phone and leave a message for the realtor to call me.

~2~

I squint at the time when the phone rings. No one except the answering service calls me this early, and I know from the number, it isn't the service.

"Hi Jill. I hope I didn't wake you." My head tips, like a hungry dog to the rustle of a food bag.

"No. I'm up." I walk into the bathroom, disrobing. "How are you?" I clear a panicky soreness in my throat and turn on the shower.

"A builder contacted me about seeing the Amberfield property after you and Tim saw it."

My hand snaps back from the scalding water.

"You've always been good with my animals, Jill. I realize how much the place means to you. Are you and Tim still interested?"

You and Tim. I feel my cheeks flare. "Yes, I'm still interested."

"Okay, I'll get back to you."

I aimlessly turn the faucet and finish my shower, feed the cats as I get dressed, then head to work. Now, I have to talk to Dr. Bob.

Before heading to the clinic treatment room, I stop off at the cat ward. The blind tiger cat I love swivels his ears toward my voice. I scoop Chrissy's marshmallow belly in my arms and carry him back to my office.

Jeannie pokes her head inside and catches me talking to Christopher Patrick. The marionette lines of her mouth sag into a sympathetic frown.

"I know appointments are starting, but I need a minute," I say, my arms full of the fat cat.

I was still paying off my student loan, and then, there was my little credit issue. The only way I could swing buying the Amberfield place now was to hurt the one person who loved me like I was family. He'd expect my change of heart about as much as I had expected Tim's.

"Isn't that your friend's old place?" Jeannie asks when she spots the picture of the house.

I nod. "It's finally for sale now that Petal's father died. When I saw the kitchen again I wanted to grab a scrub brush and paint the cabinets—maybe the color of daffodils, like the ones that pop up along the driveway in May. But there's a builder interested in the property."

Jeannie's eyes seek the floor trying to avoid mine. *I'm sure she's sorry after what she said when I told her Tim and I were getting married.*

Jeannie knew my long history with Tim. But she didn't know me when one week after my thirteenth birthday, my mother drove me to Petal's funeral. Chrissy starts purring, as if he senses my need for sympathy.

"It would be a sin if a builder buys it." Jeannie raises her voice as if she's angry, not about the house as much as that she was right about Tim. Jeannie has never been known for being subtle. Sometimes I think that's why Bob keeps her around. Bob is such a softie, and not just with animals. Jeannie's a natural for cracking the whip with the young staff, or the clients that expect service for free.

"Maybe that house is bad luck."

I shake my head and lift my water bottle to wet my lips. I have begun to wonder. *You can come back to visit anytime,* Petal's mom had told me after the accident happened, but I never did.

"Someday you'll have a cute house like that," she says.

She doesn't get it. I don't want *any* cute house any more than I want *any* cute man.

"It's run down, but it still has so much charm, Jeannie--the big bay window in the kitchen, and a white-painted brick fireplace in one bedroom. The bedrooms are small with sloped ceilings, one with bureau drawers built into the walls, and another papered with tiny antique flowers."

"It sounds adorable," Jeannie says with a tone of disenchantment. We both know the place isn't what it once was after Petal's mom left.

I reposition folders and drug samples that I've arranged alphabetically on my desk. Then I smooth the astrology prediction about reinventing my life.

"Petal's mom used to sit cross-legged and braless crafting shadow boxes or peeling potatoes from her garden. She wore airy vintage skirts without panties!" I laugh into my hands as if I'm thirteen again. "Petal's mom always talked about astrology."

Jeannie stops smoothing her hair as I transfer Chrissy into her arms. I grab my stethoscope. Jeannie follows me back to the exam rooms clearing her smoker's voice. It's what she does when she's holding back from saying something that will eventually come out, like when she said that she knew Tim would "never settle down." I was so sure then that she was wrong.

We're at the door of a closed exam room. There's sniffing noises from a fifty-pound Newfoundland puppy, then a crash as the dog biscuits hit the floor.

"Better hurry. Before you know it, the Smiths will be here with Cooper," Jeannie says puckering her face at the checkerboard of treats when I open the door. "He's been vomiting since he got into some Easter candy, and you know they only want to see you."

Jeannie hands me a chart and wiggles into her swivel chair. When I bend down the pup rolls his tongue across my skin. For a second, his chocolate eyes catch mine. "*I love you,*" that look tells me. This is the reason I became a veterinarian.

As for love, I never expected it to be as simple as with a puppy, but loyalty like I'd seen from my parents was on the top of my list, and I wonder if I'll ever find it.

After morning appointments, I head back to the treatment ward and peek in at the delicate feline patients, most of them curled and sleepy. I flick a thin tube hanging from a saline bag into the vein of an emaciated Siamese cat.

A vet tech in pink scrubs and scuffed white clogs approaches with a clipboard in her arms.

"Quincy's temperature was 100.2 this morning, but I couldn't count his respirations because he was purring."

"Sounds like Quincy's ready to go home. Have you seen Dr. Bob?"

I click the cage door shut and the rattle of cold metal vibrates inside me when the tech points toward the radiology darkroom where Dr. Bob stands viewing x-rays. I start toward a white-walled room fluorescing with metal gurneys, stainless anesthesia machines and chrome lights. Despite the sterile appearance, it always felt like family here. Now I'm twisting my neck in my collar when I spot Bob.

"Hey, Bob. Are those the hip films on the Fidelco dog?"

I try hard to sound as if the only thing between us is the daily agenda of sick pets. I am his first choice as co-owner of this hospital when he retires at the end of the year. In fact, I have always been his only choice. But that was when I thought my life was going in a whole other direction.

"I haven't seen the films yet. Owners left a message that the dog was doing better today." He doesn't look up from the manila card he's jotting notes on, but I know his mind is multitasking, and my chest feels wormy anticipating what he'll say. Then he looks up at me, and his crescent eyes flicker with enthusiasm. "So, I thought we could sit down later. I've worked out a financial plan."

My eyes dart towards the skeletal film on the x-ray viewer.

Bob's leaning on the metal gurney dressed in khaki pants and a polo shirt. He hasn't aged since the day I started to work for him as a kennel girl. Looks like he just got his hair trimmed, his sideburns have that clean edge and his slender nose and chin make him appear years younger. He isn't a tall man, but he has the proportions right.

"I'm sorry, Bob. I can't meet tonight." My temples tighten when I look back at him. Because of him, I became a vet. But I can't buy both places, and between the two, I've made my decision. Somehow, I had to buy Amberfield.

"Okay, well, maybe tomorrow." He winks.

Just then Jeannie struts towards us from her perch at the front desk to where she listens to the young help gossip.

"There's a new client that just called named Dr. Stevens. Her old cat is drinking a lot of water. She sounded worried so I squeezed her in later."

"Isn't that the ridiculous woman that's into astrology and calls herself a psychologist?"

"Her latest book has to do with dreams and post-traumatic stress," I answer. "I know of a client's daughter that she treated. The mother of that child with post-traumatic stress didn't think Dr. Stevens was ridiculous." My head starts to feel like a balloon. Did Bob think I was ridiculous? Does he think like Jeannie that Tim would never settle down?

"People like that woman think everything has something to do with the stars," Bob says, as if astrology were the equivalent of voodoo.

I ignore him. When the day comes that he's not around here anymore, I'll miss his cheesy sarcasm. I chuckle under my breath at the dumb jokes he tells kids.

How do you know if your dog's got fleas? Start from scratch!

Do you know what Purranoia is? The fear that your cat is up to something!

He rolls up his sleeves and leans his tanned biceps on the gurney, his face illuminated by the light of the x-ray viewer. He squints at the light before he shuts the viewer, slides his glasses back on and winks again. This affection I've known for so long will change if I back out of our deal.

Dr. Bob and the technician have left for the day, but Jeannie and I don't mind tying up loose ends until the last client arrives. In fact, we've never been so excited to stay late. Dr. Steven's was something of a celebrity in Mount Pleasant.

The last hour drags, and yet not long enough until I break the news to my family. They liked Tim.

I'd told my sister, Suzanne. She'll undoubtedly spill the beans to my parents— better that she breaks the ice, spare them my melt down.

Jeannie knocks on my office door, then knocks her knuckles together with playful enthusiasm. "She's here."

When I step inside the exam room, I help settle the cat carrier on the exam table and wiggle the cat out of it. The pinched-in face of this ancient cat is one I've seen too many times before. I didn't need a blood test to recognize the look of failed kidneys.

"Let's see if we can do something to help Olga, Dr. Stevens," I say. The weight of my will power is behind my words because I'm hoping for Olga's sake, my diagnosis is wrong.

"Please, call me Ingrid." She leans over her frail tabby, cooing to the cat in a tranquil voice, but her smile is flat lining. Her hair is loosely bobby-pinned, no make-up, and she's wearing a faded *Race For The Cure* sweatshirt. On her feet are drab Birkenstock sandals and her fingernails are lined with soil as if she'd stopped in the midst of gardening to run to this appointment. I remember seeing her once— petite and elegantly dressed in an emerald green satin tunic embroidered with zodiac symbols, her silver hair French-twisted, a not-so-translucent dusting of beige foundation applied to bony features of her cheeks and nose.

My sister's warning about living alone pops in my head. *"Don't end up like some of your single clients, Jill, the ones who settle for the companionship of an animal. I'd start dating right away if I were you."*

The chink of Jeannie's keys on the reception desk counter signals that she is ready to leave.

"I'll lock up, Jeannie," I call out.

"Okay, see you tomorrow," Jeannie says. The click of the deadbolt lets me know Jeannie secured the door.

After I finish the examination, I collect a blood specimen and administer warm subcutaneous saline. Then I walk Ingrid out to the reception room.

"I'm interested in your work, Ingrid. I knew someone years ago that loved astrology."

She looks up and for the first time tonight, she is in control of herself again.

"I see you have a gifted touch. My old girl likes you. I'm closing my practice for personal reasons, so this would not be professional, but please call me. I'd love to give you a reading. Find out your exact time of birth so I can prepare your astrological birth chart. We'll meet for dinner." Her eyes smile for the first time tonight as she hands me her card— *Dr. Ingrid Stevens, Ph.D. Practical Astrology.*

"I'll call you with the results of Olga's lab tests tomorrow. Start these antibiotics tonight," I say, handing Ingrid a small blue vial. Like always with these terminally-ill animals, I've sealed in a prayer.

I unlock the door for Ingrid. She walks to her car toting the cat carrier as if she has weights strapped to one foot. I turn off the desk light.

On my drive home, the sun's heat seeps into my skin from the leather seats. At least it feels that way as I dial my mother and leave a message.

"Why do you need your birth time?" Mom says when she calls back on my home phone. Her tone sets my age back twenty years.

"It's for work," I say. I stoop to pick up my cat and listen to Mom's soft soles squeak down the hallway to where she keeps old photo albums and the satin-covered book that she has kept details of each of her children. My fingers move over my cat's spine, tracing his small bones with my fingers like a young mother might do to her baby's toes. Obsessive Compulsive Disorder. I never admit the number of times I recheck to make sure the alarm clock is set for the same awake time every morning, or the way I need to organize groceries in the refrigerator, or my teeth-brushing ritual after I eat. All that started after losing Petal.

"It was March 3rd at 12:40P.M.," she says. "It was snowing that day."

"Thanks, Mom. I haven't eaten yet. I promise to call tomorrow."

"But I haven't heard from you lately, Jill. I hope Dr. Bob hasn't talked you into buying his business. It's too much for a woman to take on herself."

Although I've made my decision not to buy Bob's practice, that's not why. My empty stomach cramps like a dry sponge.

"You didn't say that to Rob when Dad wanted him to stay in the family business. After Dad spent years teaching him how to run the repair garage, he relocated out of Connecticut when he finished mechanic school and started his own place."

My brain freezes the second I say it— Dad had groomed Rob just like Bob had groomed me. The whole Rob thing is a sore subject. He never paid me back. My credit was ruined.

"I can't walk away from Bob like that," I say, mumbling to myself.

"Jill, you know what I mean. You're thirty-two years old."

I bite my lip. *So she does know about me and Tim.*

"You'll meet someone else and want to get married and start a family,

Jill." Her voice softens, soothing me like a lullaby. "How would you keep up with kids and that busy practice?"

There are now black scribbles on the paper next to my birth information. If it weren't for Dr. Bob, I probably would never have become a vet. But the only way I can buy Amberfield is if I don't buy Bob's practice.

After I end the call with Mom I call Ingrid's phone number and leave the details she requested for my astrology chart. I kick the overhead fan into high gear, then try to swallow the dried-out turkey wrap that I never ate last night. Sometimes I wonder if I was born under a bad alignment of planets. I guess I'll find out.

The next morning Jeannie is busy answering phones and I hustle through appointments to get patrons in and out on time— makes me wonder if the moon has something to do with pet problems like with humans. But being here, especially when I barely have time to eat lunch, helps the day pass. I never lose my focus when it comes to helping animals.

"I'm stepping outside for a ciggy break," Jeannie says, pinching an unlit stick in her fingers. "Mind picking up the phone if it rings? The tech ran across the street to the bank."

"Sure. Has Dr. Stevens called? I left a message for her about Olga. Her BUN is high and her crit is low, but treatable." Jeannie has no veterinary background, but she's been around the office long enough to know what abbreviations like BUN and PCV and V/D(vomiting/diarrhea) means. She leans on the door frame and takes a drag. When the phone rings, she gives it a dirty look and snuffs out her cigarette.

"Did I tell you, I'm meeting with her? She said every person's birth chart is like a blueprint of their life."

Jeannie picks up the phone, one ear listening to the client on the other end. She points to the *Love Signs* webpage she's bookmarked like she's dangling the carat of love. "Don't you want to read yours?"

I pretend I didn't hear her.

I drop my head to my phone and scroll my recent calls. The last one from Tim gave me no warning for what happened that night.

"I'm really sorry," Tim had whispered before he leaned over and kissed my cheek the day he left me. I'd walked in my house wondering why his Land Rover wasn't parked in the driveway as usual when he'd spend the night. No sound of the sports channel, no silky guitar riffs from his acoustic guitar. I'd called to him as I stepped past his stuffed duffle bag on the kitchen floor, carrying the groceries I'd bought to make dinner. When I saw him sitting on the couch bent forward, elbows resting on his knees, I knew something was wrong. He'd lifted his blond head and looked up at me, his eyes shining like glass.

His mouth quivered and tightened as he told me "he wasn't sure about us anymore." Then there was a whoosh as he picked up his duffle bag, the clatter of a key left on the counter.

The crease of my eyelids had felt sticky at some point after he left. Upstairs before the bathroom sink, I'd pressed a cool towel to my puffy lips to stifle a gag reflex, afraid there was someone else. At least he never said that.

Ingrid calls me back later.

"I can meet tomorrow." she says. "I looked over your birth chart. This year is a turning point for you."

My chest cavity feels as if my heart has been replaced by nothing. *Turning point. Wasn't that what they called it when I turned thirteen?*

"Oh, one thing," she adds, "would you mind picking me up? My old Volvo's on the fritz. I live in the Colonial at the entrance of Red Rock Park. I think everyone in town knows my house."

"I know it, Ingrid," I say. How could I not know that house? They were alike, Ingrid and the mansion—out of place among quaint Arts and Craft bungalows of Mount Pleasant.

~ 3 ~

Palo Alto, California

James Chamberlain had just shut his office door when his administrative assistant caught up to him at the elevator.

"Dr. Chamberlain, Attorney Chamberlain is on the phone. He said he really needs to speak to you."

James tightened his lower lip and managed a smile. "Thanks, Stacy. Can you tell him I'm not here?"

She canted her head and pouted. "I've tried. He's called three times because he said you don't answer your cell."

James shook his head gently. "Alright. I'll call him. I'll be back for my five o'clock meeting with the oncology resident. Can you send me his resume again?"

She sighed. "What should I do about your Biosketch? Grants and Contracts emailed about your proposal." Her expression froze in a state of mild panic.

"I'll update it over the weekend."

"But they need it by tomorrow afternoon." Her eyes softened. Keeping up with Assistant Professor Chamberlain was a challenge. Not because his chaotic schedule made her head spin, but because despite his accomplishments, he was humble, and appreciative. That made her want to keep him happy.

"I promise I'll have it back to you today."

The elevator opened. He hopped on, multitasking on his phone to search for his latest publication. Publish or Perish—the university's motto. He had nothing to worry about. Not even forty and he already had twenty-five peer-reviewed publications on his resume. He was on track for his next faculty promotion. But he wondered if this was all worth the price his life had paid. Being here wasn't the same now that Amy had left him. Lately, all he cared about was Dizzy.

The vet had squeezed him in for an appointment at noon. *If I can't make it back in time for the telecall at 2PM, I'll call in.* That would be easier than the call to his uncle.

James jogged past Hoover Tower and down the bisque-colored concrete to the small university lot reserved for faculty. He put the top up on his BMW, shutting out the California sunshine, and slid a thick manila envelope containing another health policy grant next to his seat. He dialed Chamberlain Law.

"Hi Mary, it's James," he said before the receptionist finished her phone greeting. "Can I speak to Jake?"

"James, how are you? We miss you," her voice warmed like butter in a hot pan. "You know your uncle would love it if you'd move back here." Her formality returned without missing a beat, "Hold on. Let me get him on the line." James accelerated down the long elegant university drive. The engine hummed past tropical Royal Palms he loved. They were a fair trade-off for the lush New England landscapes where he grew up.

"James. You never answer your cell. I'm getting to know your secretary quite well."

"Sorry, Jake." He knew better than to bother making excuses with his uncle. "And Stacy's my administrative assistant. They don't call them secretaries at Stanford, or anywhere else. Your dating yourself." James enjoyed ribbing his uncle. He'd earned that right. He wasn't the lanky teen that crashed his dirt bike into Uncle Jakes's Mercedes after his dad's funeral. Maybe it was a little on purpose, and Jake knew it. James' dad was Jake's younger brother— too young to have a fatal heart attack. But now their relationship wasn't based on sympathy. James had earned Jake's respect. "So what's up, Jake?" As if James couldn't guess. There was one reason why Jake would be so persistent.

"It's about your mother. I'm worried about her."

James was more worried about his dog, Dizzy, but he didn't admit that. He didn't want to have to listen to another story about Ingrid when they hadn't spoken in five years.

"You know I have no control over what she does."

"Listen, James. She's not well. She closed her practice."

James swerved the car. His mother would rather die than stop working.

"Are you sure?" *This had to be a ploy.* "Come on. She wouldn't do that. You know how much she loves giving advice and fixing other people's lives. Maybe we'd still be speaking if she hadn't done that with me."

"No, no. She's out, and she doesn't look well. You know your mother is an attractive woman, but she's let herself go. I think she's sick again, James. She's been on that herbal chemo stuff and doing yoga for years, but the last time I saw her she looked pale, and she was limping. I think you should call her."

James gripped the steering wheel, pulled into his condo complex and headed for the shady corner spot. Charcoal leafy patterns from the birch tree draping the asphalt would keep the leather seat cool. He didn't want the car to be too hot for Dizzy. The A/C made her sneeze. He got out of the car holding his phone to his ear.

"I'll think about it," James said to his uncle.

"Now you know it's in both of our interest. Your father would have wanted you to have the house, and if it's up to Ingrid, it'll end up in the hands of some animal fund."

James didn't mind. Sometimes he wondered why he hadn't become a veterinarian. He donated generously to the Morris Animal Fund. They did good research. James was all about research, not with animals, but when it came to his animal, he wanted to know he'd done all he could.

"I need to run, Jake. I'll be in touch," His tone of voice deepened. "Thank you for letting me know." As far as Ingrid's money, James wanted no part of it. But he loved the house where he grew up as a boy, hiking the park trails and swimming in the river with his dog. He hadn't been back to Connecticut to see it since before the estrangement. But the last thing he wanted was for it to end up in the wrong hands.

~ *4* ~

I circle into Ingrid's driveway and park beside a garden of dark pine chips and blue-green foliage, the kind I'd seen in exotic gardening magazines. If the huge white Colonial were a white circus elephant, it would be adorned with a crown, without the gaudy jewels. There's a low curved rail along the balcony that sits above the front door, and two pillars, like giant tusks, framing the entrance. The elegant house was definitely one I'd seen the likes of before in my book of early 1900's historical homes.

Ingrid appears through the stone path and stands beside a tall bamboo grass plant with plumes that resemble the fireworks that will light the night sky in a few weeks.

"Ready, Jill?" she says when she ducks her head inside my car. Her arms are holding a sloppy folder of papers "I'll give you a tour of my house some other time. I'll bet you're sentimental about old homes."

My eyes dart away from staring at her beautiful home.

"How did you know?"

"You have Cancer on your Ascendant. That aspect is also one that makes you hold onto the past."

I feel a breeze pass over my shoulders, though the air is still. Was this the reason for my attachment to a run-down farmhouse?

Ingrid is dressed in a white flowing top with a yellow sun symbol on the front. Her silky pants are cinnamon color, and she's wearing a necklace, a jagged charcoal stone attached to a piece of rawhide. "It's from Kazakhstan," she tells me. "You might go there some day." She settles an oversized canvas tote and a tapestry bag at her feet as my Honda creeps along the cobbled driveway. I wanted to know where my life was heading and I'm pretty sure it didn't include a foreign country.

We pass the new assisted living complex and Ingrid appears to notice that my eyes have left the road. I remember when there were dozens of dogwood trees instead of a brick building. *If that happens to Amberfield, I'll never have closure.*

"Let's park near the church," Ingrid says. "I love the ornate stained glass windows."

It was an odd similarity that those dark windows resemble the photos in the tattoo parlor on the next block. We continue to walk down the sidewalk dividing the park green into geometric shapes, the scent of fresh-cut grass lingering in the June heat. Ingrid waves to a homeless man sitting on the bench near the bus stop amidst the whirr of prancing pigeons. He appears dazzled by them and barely notices.

"I did some counseling at the health center last year. It's frightening how people's lives can change."

My head drops as my flip-flops slap the lopsided sidewalk. I point out the pub that serves free Irish stew on Thursdays to musicians. In my head, Tim is playing his song. "My ex-fiancé and I used to go there. He'd wait his turn for hours to play guitar with a local band. The first night he got up on stage, he strummed with his head down. He was terrified to look at the audience, but soon as he finished the song—"

I stop talking, my words consumed by the hollow feeling of remembering Tim's eyes, how they looked for me in the dark crowded room, how he used to hold me like his beloved guitar.

Ingrid looks at me. "Is he a musician?"

"No, but if Tim didn't have a mechanic tool in his hands he usually had his guitar in his arms." I smile but my brow tightens— the thought of Tim giving up engineering to be a "rock star" like he joked about. I was quietly relieved that his father pressured him to stay in the family business. When Tim dressed in worn Levi's and some dark-colored tee shirt of band tours, with his talent, he could have been a rock star.

"We knew each other since junior high, but started dating in college." For a moment, I let myself drift. "Tim loved restoring old things, cars, furniture."

We reach the historic restaurant and step inside a narrow room with dark tin ceilings and dusty Tiffany lamps hanging over a glossy mahogany bar. The atmosphere feels heavenly haunted, the leather creaks eerily when I walk my thighs into the circular booth framed by hazy blue mirrors. I set my phone down on the table.

"Is that Tim?" Ingrid asks as she points to my phone.

My hairline feels damp. I still hadn't changed the photo. I slide the phone towards her and a mesmerized expression clouds her face.

"He's very handsome. A kind face." She slides the phone back and smiles gently. "Do you believe things happen for a reason?'

He's very handsome. A kind face. It takes me a moment to answer. "I do, Ingrid. I just didn't expect things to be so complicated. When I was a kid, my friend's mom bought a Ouija board at a tag sale. Petal asked it how old she would be when she died. It spelled out the next year."

I rub a spidery tingle on my arm.

"When I asked about marriage, it spelled out my own initials."

"So you're wondering?"

I know she's testing me. "Yes, I'm wondering if it's true. If I'll end up alone. It was just a game. Until Petal died."

"Well, astrology doesn't have anything to do with the supernatural, but it can predict the energy surrounding us at any time. Your birth chart reveals what you're dealing with in the coming months."

"Can you tell the future from a chart?"

"In a way. The planets are constantly moving through the twelve zodiac signs, and they create angles to where they were at our time of birth. Think of the heavens as a reflection of the opportunities and obstacles each of us will face on earth."

When she tugs my astrology chart out of her book, the onion-skin of Ingrid's hand distracts me. It was hard to tell her age. At times she looks like a Turner classic actress with cheekbones like plums and sheen beneath each eye that looks as if she's coated them with Vaseline. She's got an age spot on one cheek, but her complexion is white as a pear, her translucent eyes are her most captivating feature.

Ingrid stares at my chart as if she's stuck in another dimension. Then she looks up at me.

"You have the same birthday as my sister," she says, her lips part for a second as if frozen in thought. She blinks, then starts to continue.

The young waitress with pierced brows and a cat tat on her wrist sets down two glasses of water. Before she takes our order, she crooks her head at the fantasy-like figures of Ingrid's astrology book, and I at the gaudy images pierced into her skin. This suddenly feels strange. I came to learn something normal about my life.

I wedge my hands, prayer-like, between my knees and lean in.

Ingrid smooths the creased paper with a diagram that looks like hieroglyphics. I can't imagine how it's possible to predict anything meaningful from the circle of pie slices and symbols scattered on the page. But she does. She tells me quite a bit about my closeness to family, my healing hands with animals, my biggest fears. Then Ingrid flicks her gaze clockwise and points to the right side of the birth chart. "This is the House of Relationships," she says.

"You have the sign of Capricorn on this cusp." With her finger tapping the chart she says, "Capricorn has a connection to learning lessons. People are going to come into your life for this purpose." She glances at my phone again, as if she can still see the photo of Tim even though the screen is black. "Within one year you'll find what you're looking for, Jill— if you look for Leo."

"Leo?" All I knew about Leos was limited to my experience with a high school drama teacher who choreographed our every move. "I never thought Leo was a match for a free-spirited Pisces."

"I've taken the other planets into consideration of your chart. You should look for Leo." Her silver spoon tinkles against the glass of iced tea and my gut swirls. Ingrid isn't telling me what I'd hoped to hear— that Tim might change his mind, or that someone would be around the corner to change mine.

"How about the veterinary clinic? Do you see anything?"

As the waitress arranges our food on the table, she consults her ephemeris again. "A Mars transit coming to your Midheaven would definitely influence your career. It's complicated to explain. Let me study your chart a little more and I'll tell you the next time we meet. She folds my birth chart and tucks it back into her satchel.

I feel as if my body has shrunk inside an empty room. I've always thought I was as uncomplicated as my four-letter name. The invisible strap binding my forehead tightens.

"Did I tell you what Olga did yesterday?" Ingrid says, poking at her salad. There is lightness in Ingrid's voice that her cat is better. "One of my teenage clients was having difficulty expressing himself during his therapy, so I let Olga role-play during the session."

"I'm glad the medication is helping," I say gently, because Olga's prognosis is inevitable. Or is it my own prognosis that sounds shaky? How can I move forward when I hadn't confronted my past? I needed to know why I was starting over again in the first place.

~ 5 ~

I haven't heard back from the bank about the HFA loan even though I've called twice. My head feels like exploding when I think why that might be so. The "builder isn't totally out of the picture," the real estate agent had said. "How much do you think you can put together for a down payment?"

Not much. Not without Tim. And asking Dad for a loan at my age? He'd do it, but Mom would want to know why. And then I'd have to explain about my brother, Rob.

"There's been a change of plans, but I'm working on it," I say.

Two summer dresses are bunched in my lap as I remove the shoes I'd put on a half hour ago.

"It's not a date," Logan, tells me over the phone for her weekly pep talk. Logan has been dating since she started high school and has only gone out with three men. She's a professional screener, and proof that someone as selective as Logan eventually finds someone to marry.

"Why don't you come with me?" I ask, since she's the one who put me up to this.

"Yeah well, I'm sure Greg wouldn't like that."

"I can't get past the Leo thing."

"Why don't you just date one man of every sign?"

"That's more men than I've dated in my life. It would be nice if it happened naturally, like the way I met Tim. Not that I'd want to take a chance at getting killed." Of course I was busy watching a dog wiggle away from its owner and run across the street toward me. "Next thing I remember is Tim crouched over me to help me up, then he knelt down to help the dog."

I look at myself in the mirror and click my tongue.

"What's wrong," Logan asks.

"I can't wear this dress with my leg." I unzip the summer dress.

"I'm pretty sure no one will notice your bowed leg during speed dating."

I hang up the phone and paint my lips misty mauve, sweep fresh mascara across my lashes, slip into something uncomplicated — white slacks and a black blouse that I wore at the last vet conference. Color opposites, like the yin-yang I'm feeling as I head out my back door. I know I've already waited too long for Tim. He'd said so himself.

"If you're here for the speed dating, follow that corridor," the hostess says when I arrive at the Mexican restaurant. I hope every woman here doesn't look like her because I can't remember being that tiny since fourth grade.

I pay the fee, take my ticket for a free drink, then head for the Ladies Room to check that I don't have cat hair clinging obscenely to my slacks. The woman primping at the mirror pays little attention to me when I smile at her. She checks her face and hair and leaves.

As I swing open the powder room door, my phone chimes. I know it's the answering service by the theme song and this is probably the first time I'm eager to hear their voice.

"Dr. Christie, a call came in about a dog that was hit by a car."

Brain Freeze. I forgot to tell Jeannie that I'd switched On-Call service with Bob tonight.

"Should I refer them to the emergency facility?"

"Tell them I can meet them at the clinic in fifteen minutes," I say. The jitters in my chest disappear. Unlike dating, saving animals is what I'm good at. I toss my drink voucher in the wastebasket and swing open the Ladies Room door.

I jog through the parking lot and hop in my car. The wet road hisses at my tires as they spin down back roads to the clinic. A couple is standing at the clinic entrance cuddling their terrier and the ground around them is speckled with blood.

"I'm Dr. Christie," I say assessing the shoulder wounds as I twist the key to unlock the door. "Follow me," I say heading toward the exam room. I grab the thermometer from its holder and my stethoscope from the hook on the wall. As I listen to the lub-dub of the dog's heart, he rests his small head on his front paws and exhales. After I clip and clean a peach-sized area, I draw up a cocktail of antibiotics and cortisone and prick the dog's rump area gently.

"The technician will stop in later to check on Reggie," I say, smoothing his ruffed coat. Then I touch the wife's arm, hoping to do the same.

I settle Reggie in a cage with a fluffy blanket. As the owners leave and walk back to the parking lot, they argue. Then she throws the leash on the ground. He picks it up and without a word, slides into the passenger seat. *So relationships aren't perfect.* I know I'm not alone to feel as though something is missing from my life without one.

I prop my elbows on the reception desk. It's too late to go back to the speed-dating event. My heart wasn't in it anyway, and I know why. I don't need a psychologist to tell me why I'm not ready to move on. I need to say the things I was too stunned to say to Tim when he caught me off guard.

I grab my purse and re-apply lipstick. I lock the office door on the way out and my face breaks a sweat— not because I'm sprinting to my car, or because it's raining and my umbrella is locked inside my car. It's because I don't know *what* I'll do when I see Tim.

When I turn the key in the ignition, the radio is playing that song about a guy being scared to think he was *always on her mind.* Tim had admitted those same words to me. I reach up to the locket he had given me for my birthday last year and slide the silver heart between my fingers. Did he know then that he wouldn't marry me? Was he having second thoughts, or did something, or someone, change his mind?

The rain sounds like pebbles as they pelt my hot windshield. At Tim's place, I park in view of his kitchen window. The second-floor light is on at the top of the long wooden steps. I open my car door and step onto the wet pavement. From the stairs to Tim's apartment, the laughter of television voices swells from his living room. My hair is wilting, my stomach squeaks because the last bit of nutrition I've had was Trail Mix in place of lunch. *Low blood sugar has probably starved my brain—* I step back and turn.

At first it feels like levitation--palms slipping down the rail, arms flailing like a chubby toddler. Then my heel catches the step. My body lurches. In seconds, my hip slams the patio deck that Tim had built last summer. My lips bubble from the pain. I purse them to muffle my cry, but when I untwist my legs and try to stand, the pain shoots like a bullet. This time I do scream.

Tim's thumping footsteps pound inside my chest. Then the door cracks open and time stops.

"Hey, Jilly." Tim's mellow voice resonates like ancient chords inside me, as if we had this calling to be together before we were born.

I crawl up to stand, my toe pointed to take weight off of my leg. Tim probably can't see me very well at the bottom of the stairs in the dark. But I can see him standing in the porch light. He feathers his bang with his left hand like he does when he's caught off guard.

"Oooowwch!" Pain stabs my leg again like a prick of Novocain when I shift.

"What happened, Babe?" Tim races down the stairs when I cry. He hasn't shaved and his stubble is a golden halo on his chin. He's barefoot, dressed like he doesn't have a care in the world, except his eyes look worried.

"Take my hand." His voice is deep and sleepy, his sandalwood strands brush my cheek when he leans toward me.

Upstairs in his apartment, Tim helps me onto the couch and turns to grab an ice pack from the freezer. My eyes follow him. All around me are the things that make his place like my own— the same earth tones on the walls I helped him paint, the same sage green tiles he put in my kitchen, an odor of fried food seeping from a take-out dinner sitting on the dining room table. A stack of bills and magazines is piled to one side. It's the same as my place, except for the two beer cans on the table and the guitar propped against the coffee table.

I grab the fuzzy throw from the back of the couch—my wet pants will soil his camel-colored couch. But I stop. I was always cold at his place in the winter because he kept the heat down low. I push the blanket aside remembering the last time I'd slept here.

"So what's up?" he says, walking back with ice wrapped in a towel. He yawns, then smiles, not like he's tired as much as utterly comfortable with me. I stretch my toes into the carpet, cat-like.

"I remembered that Zippy's birthday was coming up. I can't believe he's going to be five years old." Zippy hears my voice and jumps on the couch beside me. "I could take him in to the office for his vaccines." I twirl a tassel of fur near Zippy's ear, unable to look at Tim. *I don't know where I'm going with this.*

"You were always thoughtful like that, Jilly. You know that I never meant to hurt you." He says it with the decency I love about Tim. His slender eyes turn hypnotic— the way he'd look at me when he was exhausted, but not planning to fall sleep yet. His dress shirt is unbuttoned at the neck and sleeves crumpled around his tanned forearms. I lean closer to him but he looks down and rubs his hand across the back of his neck. I can feel my heartbeat in my ears, then it gushes out of me.

"You told me you wanted to get married when you turned thirty, Tim. So I was patient with you. And then another year passed by."

He lets out a sigh, the one I loved waking up to when we were in bed, but not now.

"We were together for so long," I say in a monotone because this ending feels so wrong.

"Maybe that's the problem." He mumbles into his clenched hands, and those four words force my crushed spirit to life. My fingers tighten into a fist position.

"Are you seeing someone else?"

"No. I swear, Jill, I'm not."

Jeannie had said that she knew Tim "would never settle down." I thought *I was the one* who knew Tim inside and out. Like how I knew how to touch him to get him started. I know how, like I have for years. Before we'd had dinner, or the chance to shower after work, Tim's long torso would be lying over me, like a bridge tying us together as he intertwined his fingers through my hair.

All the times we had differences over his sloppiness or my tardiness—this is way past that stuff now. The metal picture frame I gave him is missing the photo of us. I have the same photo, but I never need to look at it to remember his blue denim eyes. They're staring off somewhere, anywhere, avoiding me.

"When did you know it was over between us?" I can hardly believe the calmness in my voice.

His arm is propped on the couch, the full length of his hand pressed to the side of his face. He has that look on his face, like when I used to tell him how much better off he is being an engineer than a musician.

"I don't know. It's not you, Jill. It's me."

The passive cop-out.

"You should have told me, Tim," I say, lifting myself off his couch.

His shoulders hunch. I know who I must sound like and I hated that he'll think of me like his father. *You Should blah, blah, blah, Tim.* But I wasn't his father. We are like a broken leg, and even a perfect alignment of two broken bones isn't a guarantee they'll heal. We are one of those times when amputation is the best alternative.

My nerve endings are bristling—I'm so angry I didn't see this coming. How did I believe he "needed to hang onto his apartment for the extra garage space" when I asked him to move in with me last fall?

I limp the first couple steps, then suck back the pain.

"Are you okay to drive?" he asks.

I nod without looking back. He gets up, follows me to the door and opens it. Then he grabs my arm. "Listen."

A crystal of hope swings like a pendulum from his hand. *A change of heart.* His eyes settle on mine for the first time tonight.

"I feel bad that you can't buy the house, Jilly. I thought it over…"

The strap of my pocketbook digs into my shoulder.

"Maybe I could let you borrow the down payment."

My eyes hold his as I let go of my last hope. "I don't need it," I snap.

I hobble onto the deck and grip the handrail. My ankle burns, but the rest of me feels like I don't exist.

Good luck, I want to yell back, so he'll know this time, *I'm really done.*

By the time I drive home, my ankle is hard as cement. It's puffy and the skin has a sunburned color that is sure to ripen into a gorgeous purple by morning because the flat shoes I'm wearing feel tight as duck tape.

In my bathroom, I turn the latch to open my medicine cabinet. The door sticks a second from layers of paint. It has a beveled glass mirror on the front, a replica of the one in the Amberfield house that I'd picked up at an antique store.

The shallow cabinet doesn't hold much stuff, but I know I have something in here for pain. The bottle of Tylenol is expired. I pick up a vial of Vicodin prescribed with Tim's name, surprisingly left over from his skiing accident. He'd stayed out of work for three weeks, until he couldn't take the phone calls from his father who was going nuts running the business without him.

I take one pill, just for tonight.

I limp into the kennel room the next morning holding a cup of coffee, the sweet scent of French Vanilla trailing like the good mood that is lost behind me. I slip on a clean lab coat since the one from last night is soiled. Reggie is wagging his tail today, thanking me with his amber eyes.

"The owner's have each called to see if he can go home this morning," Jeannie says, handing me two sheets of lab tests. "How was that speed dating thing?"

My brows tense as I cross my ankle.

"Jill. What happened?"

My cheek quivers from pins and needles. At the sight of my leg she grips my elbow to steady me.

"It wasn't from speed dating," I say, rolling my eyes up to the ceiling when the pressure slams my sinuses. "I'll be okay." She can't possibly know the details of my accident at Tim's, but she knows enough to let it go.

"Don't get discouraged. I talked to my niece last night and she offered to help you set up a profile for a dating service. Here. Read this."

"Jeannie, I don't need computer help and I don't feel like setting up a dating profile."

Jeannie's mouth opens but nothing comes out.

I drop my chin. My face must be the color of raw beef, the opposite of Jeannie's.

"I'm so sorry, Jeannie. I *am* going to set up a profile on a dating site." The surprising part of hearing my own words is that I start to want to do it. "What were you going to show me?"

She clicks her computer screen to an astrology site. When I lean over her and rest one hand on her shoulder, she turns toward me. Jeannie doesn't treat people like they are fragile, and I wasn't about to be.

"Hey, we're both Pisces, right? We fish let things go and swim off on our happy way." She opens the icon with the two fish swimming in opposite directions.

PISCES: Although you may be known as a peace seeker, sometimes you have to rock the boat. You are good at changing direction once you decide which way you need to go. Let your heart show you the way.

"See? It's a good time to make a change," she says, as if she wrote the prediction herself. This doesn't surprise me as much as how someone like Jeannie feeds into this stuff, because Jeannie is as particular with work as she is with her appearance. She's wearing a pressed white dress like she wore years ago as a nurse and white stockings that she practically wears year round. Of course she thinks it's her job to organize my life as well as hers.

"You're right, Jeannie." Maybe I should date one man from every sign of the zodiac like Logan suggested.

She pushes her readers farther up on the bridge of her nose and pulls out her assortment of highlighting pens. She color-codes client's charts, blue for Dr. Bob, green for me, red for clients that give her a hard time— they never got Saturday morning appointments. "This is not a bad idea for dating men," she says with a dirty laugh.

"You know, I thought you and Tim made a great couple— maybe someday he'll change his mind and want to settle down. Don't waste your life like I did. I had kids right away, so I put up with things that I wouldn't now. At least my kids turned out good."

Kids.

"Tim wanted to have two or three kids," I blurt. "I've hardly held a baby. My sister tells me all the time that some of the women she ultrasounds at the gynecological office where she works are holding off until their thirties to start families. But the problem was never my biological clock."

I fold my arms over my chest. "Even as a baby-sitting teenager, I couldn't wait to put the kids to bed so I could play with the puppy."

Jeannie's shakes her head. I know she thinks like Mom does— *once you have one of your own.* I don't expect a dedicated mother like her to understand how I can't bear to hold a baby.

By the end of the day my ankle is throbbing from hobbling around all day. When I get in my car and tap my toe on the gas pedal, my skin feels mummified, and crowned with thorns. The radio station takes my mind off the pain, until I get home.

There's a call from Mom on my answering machine. "Suzanne and Lee are coming into town for Fourth of July weekend." *Great*—questions about dating from Suzanne, a married sister who knows everything about being single from the gynecological office where she works. Not to mention teasing about *not* dating from my brother-in-law.

Beside the phone is a framed photo of my family. The photographer had taken care to make sure it was balanced— Mom and Dad, Suzanne and Lee, me and my younger brother, Rob. Rob is witty, fit and happily un-married. He's my brother and I love him, but Rob's series of shallow relationships make me wonder if I can ever trust a man to commit.

I dial the phone while flipping through pages of the AVMA veterinary journal. When I see the article with a photo of a dark bay thoroughbred, my shoulders drop like they do when I sink into a warm bath. Maybe I should have become an equine vet. Petal and I talked about it enough. We spent all day Saturday in the barn, braiding manes or wrapping her horse's sore leg. We talked about the animal practice we would have together someday.

The small animal medicine route had been one of those choices I made in vet school. No one knew I'd had so much experience with horses. It was better that way. I remember the last time I saw Petal's mom. She'd rested her forehead against mine as I cried when they loaded Petal's horse onto the trailer. *It'll be better this way, Jill. He's going to a good home*, she'd said. But I was so afraid Petal's pony would stop eating, like I had, out of sadness.

My eyes slam shut—even a helmet wouldn't have saved Petal. Her horse was charged up with the winds of a nor'easter, and I was too spooked to get on. Then Petal tossed her helmet to me. *'Come on, Jill. We won't go far,' Petal pleaded with me.* The wind lifted her shiny hair from her shoulders like angel's wings. I watched her squeeze a hard gallop out of her pony and tear down the path alone. I was still holding her helmet.

Maybe if I'd gotten on with her, she'd still be here.

The phone rings when I try to call Logan. No answer. Voice mail. By now my friend Logan's evening is surely wrapped up like a pretty package with her beau. I text a message: *R U free Friday night? Let's do Girl's Night.*
I limp over to the antique cabinet that holds special mementos. There's a periwinkle blue tea pot with gold trim from my Czech grandma and an Egyptian horse from Logan's trip to the Middle East. On the second shelf is a rosebud china vase from Mom and Dad and an iridescent bowl, signed by the artist, from Rob. Alongside this is a quarter-sized piece of smooth green glass that I found while walking at Hammonasset beach with Tim. It is a simple piece of glass that I keep among my most precious possessions—one that brings me back to the days lying on Tim's windsurfer in my bikini as his sandy feet straddled my body and he steered the board into the breeze. But make up and break up has lost its magic. I rub the tender bruise, which has consolidated like a lump in my throat, then slide the glass out of sight.

At the foot of my bed when I awake the next morning is a soggy towel and a melted ice pack. My ankle feels better after the long night of rest.
"Friday night's good for me," Logan says when she returns my call. "You can tell me more about the astrology dating thing." A bag rustles in the background— knowing Logan, most likely from Nordstrom's. "Listen, I'm on my way to my facial appointment. I'll see you at 7PM."
Logan and I are as opposite as Yin and Yang. Just who I need to pull me back into the single scene.

The Wharf Restaurant atmosphere is casual with a brackish smell of beer and fried seafood. Standing at the entrance, I scan the crowded bar room for Logan. I rub my arms, unsure if the chill is from air conditioning or the group of guys laughing in the bar.
When I turn back outside, Logan is parking her ice blue Mercedes. She's Manhattan material from head to toe. Her sable hair is wedged asymmetrically with copper highlights, her swan-like shoulders are covered in an Ann-Taylored layered look. She starts toward the restaurant with a Prada handbag tucked in the crook of her elbow. Her beige Rockstud Valentino pumps and her bare summer legs cross the asphalt with a chalk-on-a-blackboard sexy scuff of her heels.
I would have no idea who most of these designers are except that Logan has told me (more than once). Of course, I have heard of Ann Taylor. I

exchanged a gift that Bob's wife, Pam, gave me one Christmas. And Tim bought the leather jacket I love from that store. He probably walked in and pointed to it on a mannequin, because I couldn't imagine he actually shopped there. All Tim needed was a pair of boat shoes and faded blue jeans to look good.

Logan rolls her eyes at my ensemble of clothes— a mixture of consignment finds and T. J. Maxx, configured in my own funky style and exposing a modest sliver of breast. "I'd never think of wearing that top with jeans and strappy sandals. Didn't I give you that pocketbook a few years ago?" She tips my leather bag and pokes inside it for a label, dispersing a subtle whiff of fragrance that leaves me craving chocolate.

"What can I get you ladies?" the bartender asks, reaching back toward the register with his hands in constant motion.

"Cosmo and a diet cola for my daughter," Logan jokes, scissoring a wedge of hair from her cheek with her fingers. "So, have you set up a dating profile yet? Most people list their astrology sign." With a pinch of her manicured nails, Logan adjusts a silver tassel on her David Yurman bracelet—an impromptu gift from her boyfriend, Greg. Her eyes flit at my short fingernails, the whites barely grown out.

As if he's overheard Logan, one of a group of guys looks over at us and smiles. Logan peers over her martini glass, her peripheral vision working the room. "I would have never met Greg if not for online dating, and we both rode the 7AM train into New York. Maybe you should go out with Dr. Bob. I always thought he was good-looking." Logan takes a delicate sip, leaves a lipstick stain on the rim of her drink.

"In case you forgot, he's married." I ignore Logan's nonchalant shrug, even though I still remember the starry feeling the first day I saw Bob, when he was the handsome new veterinarian in town. Fifteen years was a big age difference back then.

"So I take it the astrologer didn't say anything about you and Tim getting back together?"

I'm grateful that Logan doesn't look me in the eye when she asks me this question.

"That guy over there's been staring at you. Do you want me to get his number for you?" Logan asks.

My clothes feel transparent and evidently so is my expression.

Logan squints at me, then her eyelids lift, exposing a shimmer of taupe powder. "You didn't see Tim did you?" She massages her temple as if the thought of this has given her a migraine.

"Yes, but we aren't getting back together." I press my icy drink to my lips.

"Do you know that when a woman makes love to a man, oxytocin is released in our brain? It's the hormone that is released when a woman gives birth, very maternal and makes us feel bonded to a man." Logan knows as much about hormones as she does about dieting and fashion from reading women's magazines—not that they don't contain some solid medical advice, but she also reads the National Enquirer.

"I didn't sleep with him," I say, but I remember the first night I did. We'd walked back to his college apartment and listened to CDs until we fell asleep on his couch. When morning broke, we spooned, then Tim.... I blink back to Logan, who never noticed I'd slipped away. "I thought Tim broke it off because of the house, but he's obviously moved on."

"And you should, too." Logan's diamond catches the overhead light.

We climb up the stairs to the entrance of dimly-lit vacuous room with windows overlooking the ocean.

"My neighbor's band is playing tonight," I tell Logan and wave to the vocalist. Logan picks out a table draped in aqua fabric and a candleholder made of seashells. The rustic floor is vibrating with drum beats. Just as I position my chair, a man appears beside me.

"Will you dance with me?" he shouts politely.

I glance at Logan. It's a slow song. A callous ridge presses against my palm when he takes my hand in his. They are like my father's hands, like a man who works hard.

My ankle feels numb from a surge of endorphins when his sunburned face grazes my cheek. I lean back and lose my balance.

"What's your name?" he asks, bracing my fall.

"Jill." I lift my lips to his ear so he hears me.

"I'm D.J. — I'm a friend of the band. The drummer's my brother. I'll come talk to you later," D.J. says when the song stops. He quickly pecks my cheek and disappears.

"Pretty *friendly*, isn't he?" Logan says.

"It was a kiss, not a hickey." I blot perspiration from my forehead with a cocktail napkin. When D.J. returns Logan watches him like a suspicious state trooper.

"I can only dance the slow songs," I say as I twist my foot to expose my bad ankle.

"That's okay with me." He slowly guides me to the dance floor and lifts both my arms around his neck. His shoulders feel firm and fit, and all wrong for some reason until I remind myself that it's perfectly fine to feel him.

"I'd like to see you, again, Jill," he says while we dance. "It's hard to talk here."

I bite my lip, practically tripping on his question.

"I'll probably come here again next time the band plays."

The bridge of his nose creases. He thinks I don't understand that he's asking for my number.

"I should get back to my friend now. She's been alone most of the night."

I walk back to Logan mentally kicking myself. Wasn't my visit with Tim enough to move on?

Logan stops twirling her watch and crosses her arms when I return to the table. "So why didn't you give him your number?" she says with a tinge of sarcasm.

I know better. This isn't jealousy. Logan is the oldest of her five sisters. When her mother died from cancer, she and her younger siblings were left with their workaholic womanizing father.

The band plays their last song just before midnight. It's a slow song, but no sign of D.J.

"Finally. I've been ready to leave for the last hour," she grumbles.

I wave good-bye to my neighbor, an attractive brunette who's been divorced twice and is only my age. Logan gathers her purse and hands me my pocketbook that has been looped over the back of the chair all night. I haven't needed to dig into my purse once to buy myself a drink, even if I do only drink soda.

We walk into the dark parking lot.

"Wanna join me and the band at the diner for coffee?" D.J. swings an amplifier onto the open van and slams the door.

"I think I'll call it a night," Logan says.

"Maybe some other time?" I slant my eyes in Logan's direction to let D.J. know that I need to leave with my friend.

"I had a good time with you tonight, Jill." His gentle voice draws me to him.

Logan rests one hand on her car door. I reply with a non-verbal gesture of *Lighten up Logan, I'll be fine.* She gets into her car and stares at us.

D.J. hands me his business card. "Call me anytime, Jill."

I stare at the card. D.J Builders, Inc. I was right about the calloused hands. He works construction, and I like that he owns his own business. He walks backwards a few steps as if it's an effort to leave me, smiles and turns his back.

Logan pulls up her car beside me and lowers her window.

"Call me tomorrow. Don't forget to ask for his astrology sign when you talk to him."

The lukewarm ocean breeze swirls around me as I sit in my car too preoccupied to start the engine. I'm pretty sure D.J. Builders is the name that the realtor had mentioned in connection with Amberfield.

At home I find a new message on my phone.

"Hi, Jill. I hope you don't mind that I got your number from your neighbor. I wanted you to know that I had a great time with you tonight. I'll be up for awhile if you want to call me."

As soon as I listen to D.J.'s message, my worries about Amberfield melt. It makes no sense why, except that now that I've met D.J., it makes the possible Amberfield competition less threatening. He's polite and reasonable, not someone who wouldn't care about one of the town's most natural resource of beauty. Although, he doesn't have a problem crossing onto my turf.

It's 12:30A.M., but for some reason, I call.

"Have dinner with me tomorrow night. I'll bring my dog, Shep, with me," D.J. says when I call back.

I laugh at his playful persistence. "How old is Shep?"

"I rescued him from one of the job sites. Someone tied him to a tree and left him, so I'm not sure of his age."

"What kind of dog is he?"

"He's a mixed-breed. About eighty pounds." He hesitates. "You know, I don't usually go out to hear my brother's band play. I'm usually tired after working all day, but something made me change my plans. I'm glad I did."

D.J. has stacked the odds in his favor that I'll see him again. Plus, there's more on my agenda now than dating D.J. Builders, Inc. *This could be like killing two birds with one stone.*

I tell D.J. that I look forward to seeing him tomorrow, and mention nothing about our mutual interest in Amberfield.

"I don't care what his astrology sign is," I tell Logan the next morning. "He's into the environment and green construction. He's also got a mixed-breed dog that he saved. I like him."

"Great," Logan says, but her voice lacks sincerity. "Just remember, you've got eleven signs to go."

~ 6 ~

"You're a good boy, aren't you?" I say to the Papillion pup, retracting the thermometer from beneath his magnificent tail. He raises his ears up and down like silk flags, eyes absorbing my excitement as if I'm sunshine.

"Dr. Christie!" A male voice yells from the other exam room. I excuse myself and start to run, which turns into a limp from my sore ankle. But the pins and needles evaporate when I reach the room and spot the cat with blood trickling from its nostrils. I recognize this patient, my patient, the cat that I've known since he was a five-week-old kitten.

My eyes are fixed as I feel for P.J.'s pulse, then position my stethoscope to find the erratic rhythm of his fading heart.

"Epinephrine, stat," I call to the assistant. My fingertips guide the needle through chest muscle. "Let's start an I.V." I squeeze the cat's ribcage with CPR, flutters rippling across its chest. My breath grows shallow because I don't dare to use more room air than I need.

Finally, P.J. expels a raspy breath, his cyan gums fade to violet and then to pink. I cuff a bath towel to his head like a turtleneck sweater.

"Keep him warm while I talk to the owner," I say to the tech. "That was a close one. Great job." The tech's expression reminds me what it was like to hear those words from Dr. Bob.

When I walk down the hallway to the reception area, the cat's owner is bent over and hiding her face with shaky hands. "P.J. is such a good cat," Mrs. London says in a dignified lament. "The kids are so upset."

I drape my arm around her shoulders. "I think he's going to make it, but we'll need to get some x-rays once he's stable."

"Oh, thank you, Dr. Christie. My kids and my husband will be so happy."

As I turn back to the trauma room, I hear Mrs. London bubbling with the good news to her husband. Funny, how the word, *husband*, stops me now. Same might be true of the word *baby*, or *mother,* to someone who didn't have one.

"Is Dr. Bob here yet, Jeannie?"

"I'm here," Dr. Bob says, coming up behind me. His jogger's physique is as sleek as when he was in his twenties, though hidden most of the time by his lab coat. Before stepping inside his office, he checks his watch and twists his expression, hinting at my tardy arrival this morning, but it's a comical frown that makes me want to be on time. I feel myself blush at Logan's comment about dating Bob.

"We had a little excitement this morning," I say, following Bob into his paneled office. Bob smoothes his hair, not as if he's grooming himself so much as soothing his busy mind. He lifts dark eyes from his briefcase, his skin glows of outdoor activities like golf or coaching his kids at Little League baseball. I can tell that's where he'd rather be now, because each day he's here, less of him actually shows up. If I didn't know why, I might lose respect, but we're alike when it comes to pleasing everyone else first. He arranges himself behind the Jacobean desk that his wife bought to replace the ratty oak desk that was left here. It had been Bob's father's desk and he loved it.

Bob picks up the call that Jeannie has transferred to him.

"The London cat was hit by a car," I whisper before he starts his call.

"I heard. The tech said he looked dead when they ran in with him. Nice job, Jill." He holds up one finger, phone pressed to his ear, still looking at me. I'm glad to be past a time when I could barely look at him. Back then, I thought he was so much older. His words of praise still make me feel like I'm fourteen years old. "Jill Christie? *Doctor* Jill Christie sounds like it would make a nice name," he'd said when Jeannie introduced me. Those words had felt like a pat on my back. Often his words still did.

How can I ever disappoint him when he retires?

I settle into the winged-back chair as he takes his call. He lifts a pile of journals, shuffles a stack of lab reports, and peeks under his laptop for a pen. I dig into my pocket and hand him mine. *I hope that's not the real estate lawyer on the phone with him again.*

Bob scribbles financial figures along the margin of a pad. My mouth goes dry.

He never let me believe I'd finish my career as only a vet assistant, and because of him, I didn't. It made it complicated to think of letting him down.

"I'll get chest x-rays of the London cat later," I blurt when Bob cups the phone to speak to me. "I suspect P.J.'s got a diaphragmatic hernia."

"Why don't you tell Jeannie not to book any more appointments in case we need to do surgery," Bob says, in between the lawyer conversation when he sees me shift in my seat and start to leave. At the thought of doing a complicated surgery with Bob, my hands grip the chair. Scrubbed in, head to feet with sterile garb in the 8' x 10' surgery suite gives him every opportunity to corner me about my fear of performing surgery. The simple stuff like dog neuters and lacerations are no sweat, but cutting into anything like a chest is as bad as having my heart ripped out— a paralyzing fear that I might be responsible for another death.

No one but Dr. Bob would ever hire a vet that didn't pull her weight with surgery. And worst of all would be explaining to any new boss why. Had I accidentally tied the ligature with a Granny knot, or had I tied the vessel with a surgical knot—*three throws of the hemostat, right, left, right?* I'd done that hadn't I?

Bob wouldn't be around forever. Then what? My career as a vet depended on getting past this.

That night D.J. shows up at my door holding a ginger-jar candle, a scent called *Beach Walk.*

"Thank you, D. J." I pat his back when he reaches for a hug because the intimacy of dancing last night now feels like a distant dream. "I guess it's safe to invite you in since you know my neighbor."

"Yeah, plus I've scoped you out here a few times before."

"What?"

"Calm down. It was harmless," he says, and winks. "Just a little flash of you running from the house to your car, no window peeping, I promise."

Even if he isn't intentionally flirting, his ocean-blue eyes make me feel as if I'm the center of his world for just this moment.

"Okay, that is pretty harmless." I would be guilty if I didn't admit it was flattering to be noticed by D. J. He's wearing shorts and a casual dress shirt with sleeves cuffed to his muscular tanned arms. He crosses his athletic calves and leans his backside against my kitchen counter.

"I hope you're hungry, Jill. I picked out this great little place on the beach. I remodeled it."

I'd been to the old place— with Tim. "I'm starving," I tell him with a slight lump in my throat. We walk outside and he opens the passenger door to his Silverado pick-up truck.

"Where's Shep?" I ask.

"I decided to leave him home."

"I was looking forward to meeting him, though these black Capris are a pet hair magnet."

"We can stop to see him on the way back. My place isn't far from where we're going."

My belly snorkels and it's not because I'm hungry. I press my purse to my abdomen. But at the shoreline restaurant, everyone knows, and likes, D.J., so I get the notion that I know him better too.

The hostess walks us out to the patio and hands us two menus, one with a list of exotic drinks as long as the list of entrees. D.J. slides back into the wicker chair and the setting sun radiates in his eyes.

"I know what I'm having already. Order whatever you'd like, Jill." I browse the menu, but D.J., the salty air and salmon-colored sky are distracting. It's a recipe for summer romance, except this was my opportunity to find out about Amberfield. He orders "two Picnic Bar-B-Qs" when the waiter returns.

"You mentioned that you did some remodeling here. Are there any other places you're planning to remodel?"

He gives me the blow-by-blow details of the sheetrock, floors, and counter work he's done here at the restaurant. All I want to know about is Amberfield, but I'm not good at playing detective. And it shows. It starts with my clumsy attempt to stick a scoop of guacamole in my mouth.

D.J. reaches over with his finger to wipe away the smudge on my chin, just when "Amberfield" was on the tip of my tongue. He hands me a napkin as I lick a green spec of dip from my finger.

"When's your birthday, D.J.?"

He gulps the chip he put in his mouth as if its poison.

"You're not going to tell me I have to be a certain sign to date you, are you?"

"It's too late for that," I tease.

"I'm a Capricorn," D.J. says, like he knows what that means and he's worked hard to earn it.

Although Ingrid told me to look for Leo, she said something about Capricorn— that sign being on the cusp of my 7th House, the Relationship House.

"So is that a good sign?"

I shrug one shoulder as if it doesn't matter when I know it does. What matters is that he's confident, polite and responsible. "Water and earth signs are supposed to be good together," I say. "Although I wouldn't judge someone by their sign anymore than by what shoes they wear."

"So I guess you're not like your friend? I could tell she would never have danced with me."

"You're right. No offense but she's picky. And she's engaged. Our friendship works although we're so opposite." I can't help but feel protective of Logan.

"I wasn't the least bit interested in Logan." He squeezes my wrist as if to make sure I understand. This doesn't make things easy.

After dinner, D.J. pays the check with a hundred-dollar bill that he sorts from a neat stack in a silver money clip. *Wonder how many more of those he can dig up? Enough to scoop up an old farmhouse on four acres of prime pasture?*

He holds out his hand for me.

"Come on, Jill. I wanna show you my place on the beach." My breath freezes for a second. *Just to meet his dog, then we'll leave.*

D.J. turns his pickup down a dirt road lined with pastel beach cottages close as eggs in a carton. In place of a lawn is sand with thin patches of grass.

"I used to ride with my dad in his tow truck as a kid," I say when the truck bucks over a dirt mound.

"Cool. I should have let you drive."

"I don't remember how to drive a stick." I grab onto the door handle.

"It's like riding a bike."

D. J. pulls into a sandy clearing and the engine decelerates. Even in the dark, his home puts me at ease. There's an antique scrolled plaque with brass street numbers posted on freshly-painted clapboard, and new casement windows are cracked open. The dewy scent of the ocean surrounds us as D.J. pauses at the door to check his key rings. A nightlight glows through the glass of the oval window, and a shadow of a large dog appears on the other side.

"Your hair is beautiful," D.J. says when the wind weaves my dangling earrings into my curls.

"Thanks, D.J. Look at those stars," I say, tugging my sweater to my shoulders.

D.J. looks up at the sky and turns the key, then a rambunctious black Lab mix shoves his face into my crotch. *It's like the dog knows what I'm afraid D.J. is up to.* I scruff the dog's ears and nudge him off of my thigh.

"Awwwe, be a good boy, now, Shep," D. J. says. "I know he's not a German Shepherd, but my nephew named him," D.J. says apologetically.

"I see a ton of cute pet names— a Siamese named KitKat, a gray cat named Dante, a tiger named Dallas, Bootsie, Einstein, Kihn, Ozzie, Pumpkin, Spike, Skimmy Mud, Ghost." My rambling tapers mid-sentence to admire his cozy living room.

D.J. clicks a remote for the overhead fan, another for the surround sound system. He hands me an iPod device. "I've downloaded thousands of artists. Pick out whatever you like to hear." I skate my finger down the endless list. "Want something to drink, Jill?"

"Water is fine," I say snuggling into his plush couch.

He returns from the kitchen and hands me a glass of ice water. Soft rock is playing. He takes a slug of his beer and slouches into the sofa beside me. D.J. stares at me for a second, the way a man does when he's talking with his eyes. Then he leans toward me.

I close my eyes when his tongue brushes across my lips, as if he's asking permission and I don't have an answer. He can't read my mind. Like Tim could. D.J. can't tell that I'm thinking, *this is nice, but it's only my first date.*

He slides deeper into the couch and takes me with him. My waist flinches when his hand reaches the handle of my hip. His unfamiliar touch feels taboo.

"This is too soon, D.J." I scoot back, blotting my lips of his beer.

He grabs a pillow and slides it over his crotch.

"Sorry." His head tilts back. His dreamy eyes turn sleepy. "I haven't been with a woman since my girlfriend left. I miss intimacy."

For a second, I feel the loss, too. But a deeper need clouds my passion tonight.

"D.J. I need to ask you something," I say softly.

He reaches for the remote and shuts the music. Then he sips his beer and it's as if he's forgotten how to blink.

"Are you the builder who bid on the Amberfield property?"

He swipes his lips with his thumb. "Yes. I heard there was a veterinarian that was interested, so when your neighbor pointed you out to me last night at the Wharf and said you were a vet, I kind of figured it was you. Then I saw how nice you were and it didn't matter that the realtor said I'd lost to a stronger buyer."

I narrow my eyes. "It's not me, D.J. So there's another buyer?"

"I don't know. I don't really care." Shep raises his crouched haunches and nudges D.J.'s arm. With a lazy sweep of his arm, D.J. rests it on the dog's shoulder. "The land is awesome, but that house and barn is a mess— abandoned for five years after the owner left. He never did much with the place besides tinkering with lawn equipment. The farmhouse needs so much work. The roof needs to be ripped off. And the inside is out of date, especially the kitchen."

My hand catches my heart. The old Hoosier cabinet, the built-in shelves and drawers in the bedroom, the stone fireplaces that are likely too caked with creosote to be safe. I don't mention how I planned to knuckle down on the woodwork with Murphy's Oil soap, paper the plaster walls, and lots of T.L.C. I can tell D.J. thinks of the place like others in town— Amberfield, the town scab. "The guy who owned it was my friend's father," I say.

D.J.'s face sobers and I can tell he's made the connection.

"I heard my friend's mother left because of her father's drinking. He lived there alone all these years until he finally lost it. He might have neglected the place, but at least all of it was still there," I say.

"That's why you want the place?"

I nod. "I was supposed to buy it with," I hesitate, "someone."

"It's no job for an amateur carpenter, Jill. Anyone smart will buy it for the land." He shrinks after he says it as if he's read the horror written in wrinkles across my forehead. "That place is more than I can deal with now." His sigh sounds exhausted. "I killed myself to give my girlfriend whatever she wanted. Then she dumps this bomb on me that she doesn't love me anymore." A look of defeat changes his face. "I feel like there's a reason why I met you, Jill." His eyes flicker and they are so soulful. It's impossible to turn away.

"I started therapy for depression," he explains over the next half hour.

If I was anxious after making out with him, now I'm restless as a girl in a men's restroom. Until age ten, I'd never seen a man cry. That was when I saw the uncle I loved become hysterical one day for reasons I never understood. I can't let D.J.'s weakness be our strongest bond.

"D.J. it's eleven o'clock. Maybe you'd better take me home."

"Why don't you stay, Jill? We don't have to sleep together." D.J. blinks as if he can't keep his eyes open. His glass of beer is almost full, yet when he tries to get up from the couch, his legs collapse like mine the time I got dizzy from watching my first surgery. My mouth goes dry. Minutes later, D.J.'s out cold.

I wander into the kitchen and rummage through D.J.'s cabinets for coffee and filters and spot a pill vial of anti-depressant medication on the counter. Shep trots over and wags his tail as if I'm getting close to his dog treats. I toss him one, then brew four cups of coffee, checking the living room to see if D.J.'s moved. A cab ride home will cost $60. It's too late to call anyone for a ride— not that there is one person I would want to know about this. I want to scream!

"I made some coffee," I shout over the zzzzzzs of D.J.'s dozing. I try the remote, all three of them lined up on the coffee table. There's a snapping sound but the television doesn't go on. The medication on the kitchen counter tells me D.J. could be out cold until morning, and I'll be out of my mind.

Outside the surf crashes on the beach. I count each wave, rubbing my hands repeatedly. I push back the curtain window— the silver monstrosity in the driveway looks like a metal dinosaur. It should have a lift for people my size. Earlier in the evening I had to crawl into the front seat using both arms. It feels like decades ago that Dad taught me to drive a stick shift. *Like riding a bike, Jill.*

"You won't feel a thing," I say to D.J. as I manipulate two fingers around his key ring and tug it out of his pocket.

After I write D.J. a note where to find his truck when he awakes in the morning, I toss Shep another treat, lock the door behind me and step up onto the chrome running board. Once settled inside the cab, mirrors and seat adjusted, seat belt fastened, I turn the key in the ignition. My chest rumbles from engine thunder. One glance back, then I feed the choke and lurch into reverse.

I back the truck out of the driveway and steer off toward the highway. The whole forty-minute cruise home, I embrace the foolhardy persona of being in total control of my life.

"I took my medication too early," D. J. explains when he calls me Sunday morning. "I can be down in a half hour to pick up my truck." The hopeful heart he showed me last night sounds absent from his voice now.

D.J. rubs the stubble on his chin when he shows up on my front porch and rings my doorbell. I can see him from where I'm standing inside my kitchen.

"I hope you didn't have too much trouble driving home," he grins and says when I come to the front door. With the screen between us, and my cat in my arms, it feels safe to smile back. As I open the door, Rudy jumps down. I angle my body in case D.J. doesn't realize that I'm not interested in starting where we'd left off last night. But cutting ties doesn't come easy to me with a decent person like D.J.

"You know I could fix this in no time," he says about the cracked window pane that my landlord had promised to fix months ago. I know he's not looking for work so much as another chance. It's what I'm looking for, too—except I know he's not the one.

D.J.'s split is too new, and so is mine from Tim, not to give myself time.

After D.J. backs out of my driveway, I head out the door for Sunday mass service where I'll likely see Tim's mom, Maggie. She's there every week, a devout Catholic, the kind of woman that stays with a man like Tim's father and never complains. She can't tell him that brow-beating your son or withholding affection is a form of abuse when she's felt it too.

Ever since grade school, I've believed religion was like a seed rooted deep inside me. So it may be odd that I want to believe the stars can help me find love. Only now, I'll need more than an astrology sign.

~ 7 ~
Palo Alto, California

James held his breath as he opened his condo door, not because of the sour odor emanating from his normally spotless floor. At first he didn't see Dizzy, only the pink amoeba-shaped puddle on the floor. Her food dish with the special diet was still topped with kibble.

"Dizzy?"

At the rustle of Dizzy's nails on the tile floor, James turned, then squatted down. The bulldog had squeezed her compact body beside the dishwasher. He lifted her chin so her marble eyes met his. "It's okay, Dizzy. Come on girl."

James tucked a small rug beneath the dog's taunt belly and lifted her into his arms.

At the Palo Alto veterinary office James sat on the floor next to Dizzy with his laptop on his knees awaiting the results of her ultrasound. She was still groggy from the light sedative, but the urinary catheter had been removed.

James emailed another Biosketch back to Stacy with his latest publication. This week the telecall only lasted fifteen minutes. The statistician hadn't finished analyzing the data, which meant the funding agency for the grant wouldn't be happy. Why had he gotten into this career?

A middle-aged man in blue scrubs entered the exam room. He shook James' hand then turned to Dizzy.

"Well, Dizzy, the antibiotics cleared the infection, but it doesn't look like you'll pass those stones."

James swallowed. "So what's the plan now, Doc?"

The vet ruffled his bed-head and looked at James. "We'll put Dizzy on the surgery schedule next month. Let's keep her on the antibiotics a few weeks until then. I'll rerun the culture."

"How about a stone analysis?"

The vet's head snapped up as if not many owners would think to ask. "Oh, that's right. You're a physician."

"No. Ph.D. Public Health, which just means I research everything. I was hoping the diet would dissolve the stones, but she's not crazy about it. Guess I've spoiled her a little with …," he hesitated, "table scraps." *More like a cheeseburger and fries at the beach stand when Dizzy came surfing.* "So what day do you want her back for surgery?"

"Let's see." He checked the computer screen. Tuesday. That's August 7th, right?"

"Yep." There was no doubt about the date. August 7th was James' birthday.

~ *8* ~

Late Sunday morning, the sky is bleached clean of sunshine, streaky clouds cover it like a gray sheet, and my mood is low as rain on a holiday. It was too good to be true, meeting a man that looked like D.J., and to top that, a builder with ties to Amberfield. Now I'm wondering who the other buyer is.

Facing my family today will be tough. They loved Tim, but sometimes I think Mom and Suzanne just want me married. *Did they really think I needed someone to take care of me?* That would be Dad. He also wants to look tall and handsome when he walks me down the aisle. "Don't wait till I'm using a walker," he'd teased Tim last Christmas about wedding plans.

So what shall I tell them when they ask about my current dating status? An astrological dating plan? Better than listening to advice from a married sister who knows everything about being single from the gynecological office where she works.

Downstairs in my basement standing beside my laundry basket of clothes, I sort out darks from whites until I get to a wheat-colored crocheted top. It's a consignment shop purchase I love. Yes, it was used, but that meant I'd take extra care to preserve my one-of-a-kind find. Why couldn't men think of women that way? I guess that invisible label on my heart hasn't washed away.

I load the washing machine and pour in some new green detergent, fill the kitchen sink with wool wash and immerse the fabric in suds. I tie the laces of my sneakers and thump down the deck stairs with my cell phone in hand to call my sister.

"Hi Suzanne. What time are you and Lee coming for dinner?"

"Early afternoon so we don't get back to New Jersey too late. I left you a message, about bringing more allergy pills for Champ. He's really itchy."

Suzanne has her own business, two kids, a husband and an allergic dog to care for, while according to her, I only have my two cats and a job where I get to play with animals. I break into a slow trot when I reach the wooded path.

"Make sure you bring Champ so I can take a look at his skin."

"Lee put the dog carrier in the car. We'll see you in a few hours."

My breath grows shaky from jogging, but the melancholy coo of a mourning dove, a crackle of dead branches under my feet—beauty in nature always reminds me I have no excuse to be depressed.

I loop around the pond before I return home. Sitting on my deck overlooking the yard, I sigh at the sweet gardens I'd made from the saddest specimens. It felt like I'd rescued those plants that sweltering day at the tree nursery. I feel a trickle of sympathy for D.J. He's a sweet guy.

"How was your date?" Logan asks when she answers my phone call. I loosen my laces.

"Well, the short story is he fell asleep."

"What?"

"You heard me." It would be shallow discussing D.J.'s depression when one hike is all it takes to shake off mine.

"You realize my wedding is coming up soon. I was hoping you'd have a date."

"It's not like I scared him off. Listen, I need to jump in the shower and stop by the office. I was wondering if you could ask Greg if he's heard anything about the Amberfield sale."

"You aren't still interested in buying that place alone?"

Alone. "I can't stop thinking about it."

"I'll ask Greg. Keep me posted on your next date."

I take a detour before stopping at the vet clinic.

I hadn't been by Amberfield since the night I saw it with Tim. But when I pull up, the For Sale sign is lying on the ground. A utility vehicle is parked near the house. I squint toward the barn, picturing sunlight shooting through cracks in the hayloft where I'd hid the Ouija board years ago. No living soul knew about it but me and suddenly I feel as if I'm one of those earthbound spirits that can't move on.

My only chance for closure now is to retrieve the very thing that started all the trouble— that damn Ouija board. My own initials. Was it proof I'd end up alone?

In the living room window there is a shadow of activity. I throw the car into reverse and jam the pedal as my thoughts accelerate— the bank loan officer's promise to call me, my last conversation with the real estate agent. *I never got back to her about the down payment. Guess I was embarrassed... and hoping for a miracle.*

It's getting late and I still need to get Champ's allergy meds. But when I pull into the clinic parking lot, Bob's car is there. He's never here this late on Sunday and that could only mean one thing.

I enter through the back door and walk toward Bob's office. He's sitting behind his desk with his business ledger and the file cabinet drawer slid open behind him. His dark hair, brows and eyes have a stunning effect on his face when he wears black, like today. Not difficult to understand Logan's comment about him.

"Hey, what are you doing here?" he asks me.

"I was going to ask you the same thing. I didn't think there were any medical cases left in the hospital. Just a few boarders."

"Yeah. I know, but I had a little book work to take care of."

I back away from the doorframe and turn toward the room of pharmaceuticals and pet food. "My sister's in town. Her dog's having trouble with allergies again."

"Well, I don't have to tell you what to do. Stop back before you leave," he calls out to me.

My shoulders snap as I open a cabinet and stretch for the vial of cortisone from the top shelf. I count out Champ's pills, twice, because I lost track thinking about Bob's plans for me and his veterinary practice. I grab a bag of venison and potato prescription dog food from the rack and the vial of Champ's prednisone.

"So, Jeannie mentioned something to me yesterday that surprised me," Bob says when I walk past his office.

The bag of food slips from my hip. *Jeannie said something to Bob?* My eyes burn with anger at Jeannie, which sickens me because I love Jeannie.

Bob taps his pencil on the leather ledger. "I thought I'd organize a breakdown of the clinic expenses so you'll feel more comfortable about the whole deal." One corner of his mouth dimples.

I freeze like a startled deer. "Thanks, Bob."

"We'll sit down and talk next week."

Out in the parking lot, I dump the bag of dog food in my trunk. How do I explain my reluctance to Bob—once his father's practice, then his? It's an honor he's asked me.

After a thirty-minute cruise down the highway, I turn onto a pear-tree-lined road that curves left and right and ends in a Belgian block cul-de-sac. Suzanne's new hybrid vehicle is parked in our parent's driveway when I arrive at the three-bedroom, fifty-five-and-over retirement home my parents moved into five years ago. All the houses are painted in pale primary colors with New Englandish landscapes cut like a birthday cake, brick walks and porches with flower boxes. Mom loved this feature. One of the first things she did was arrange purple petunias and baby's breath in the planters.

"We just sat down to eat," Mom says when she sees me. My family is seated at the dining room table when I walk in and greet Mom with a peck on the cheek, avoiding her pity look that I'm not with Tim. I don't want to see it any more than hear her answer for everything that ever turned out badly—"*It was meant to be.*"

"You look nice, Mom." She's wearing her size 8 black Gloria Vanderbilt jeans with a royal blue shirt that I haven't seen on her before.

"Oh, thank you. I got these Esprits at Costco." She twists one petite foot to show me the fine quality of her latest shopping coup. "I'll pick up a pair for you next time I go."

I help carry a steaming platter of penne to the table. A dish of sausage and meatballs is being passed around the table, set with mom's heirloom china and crystal, like always, even on these casual get-togethers. So opposite from Petal's mother. "The ex-hippy chick," dad called her, with her homemade herb breads and jams. She made curtain rods out of wild grape vines that she dragged out of the woods and decorated them with chandelier crystals and swigs of dried lavender. I'd hoped to decorate those rooms one day.

"Hi, Dad." I lean over the teak wood salad bowl I'd given Mom last Christmas and kiss my father. Although it's early afternoon, his deep-set Italian eyes look tired. His once dark wavy hair is stiff as steel wool. He's still handsome though.

"Hi Jill," my sibling and her husband says.

I turn toward a clatter of silverware.

"Hello, Rob. Haven't seen you in awhile." My words are meant to sound like daggers—the toy plastic kind that pinches a second then bends like taffy. It was hard to be mad at Rob. He'd tried. What if it were me that failed?

"Hey, Jill. Good to see you. Pass me the bread, please." I reach for the basket of thick bread slices and shove it playfully towards my younger brother. He and Suzanne look like my father. Their brown eyes and olive complexions are distinctively from the Christie side of the family. Even their noses, prominent but not over-bearing, are unmistakable.

My brother-in-law, Lee, hands Suzanne a glass of Pinot, then meets my airy kiss with his lips. I jockey into the empty seat next to Suzanne and spoon pasta and meatballs dripping with red sauce onto my plate. One mouthful makes my mouth juicy. *It tastes so good to be home.*

"Did you get Champs pills?" Suzanne asks.

"Of course."

"Thanks." Suzanne's short curly hair is the color of burgundy wine. She's wearing a pair of dangling earrings and I don't have to ask— I'm sure she's made them. She colors her own hair and bought a kiln to fire the pottery collection she works on when she's not at her job, or volunteering at the community garden. "Mom said you went to some astrologist?"

Lee interrupts with a kind chuckle. "I heard about you looking for a Leo. Isn't Leo the sign of the cat?" I pretend to be annoyed, but Lee knows me—a little too much. I look away when he slides into a seat on the other side of Suzanne.

"Ingrid uses astrology as a professional therapist. It's amazing what she can tell from looking at someone's birth chart."

"I bought you a book," Suzanne says. "*My Life as an Internet Dater.* My friend wrote it. Have you had any dates yet?"

"I met a guy last weekend when I went out with Logan," I say.

She looks up from her salad. Her expression reminds me of when we were kids, as she held one of my stuffed animals as a hostage and threatened to tell Mom if I didn't tell her my secret. Even then, she knew my weak spot.

"He has issues." I whisper, "he's on medication for depression."

Suzanne's face changes. Maybe today with medication and therapy the uncle we lost from suicide would be alive. Suzanne and I had witnessed our uncle fall apart one Christmas. Evidently, the tragedy of our mother's brother is not lost on Suzanne.

"You mean he couldn't, you know—"

"No, Suzanne. I'm sure he could." I moan quietly at how dumb I feel now—going back to D.J.'s house to meet his dog. "His cottage was right near the restaurant. It was no big deal." *No one needs to know.*

"Hey, first date sex worked for Suzanne and me," Lee says under his breath.

"He passed out on the couch," I say in a softer voice.

Suzanne smiles, but it's not a friendly smile.

Lee rubs his hand across Suzanne's back, smoothing her blouse. I reach for my water glass and take a sip. *Am I embarrassed, or crushed with longing?*

I put down my fork. I haven't tasted a bite since Suzanne started this conversation. *Really, Jill, what were you thinking? That a little affection would erase Tim's rejection?*

Mom butters a slice of bread that she places before my father, as if she's trying to ignore Suzanne's comment. There is not a flicker of contact between our eyes.

"Pour me another glass of milk, please, Jilly," Dad says, as if he's in another world. The pitcher is sitting right in front of him on the table, but I reach over and pour milk into his glass. He hasn't asked me about Tim, even though he'd started calling Tim his "son." My brother, Rob, doesn't play their pretend game.

"So, what's going on with Tim?" Rob asks. "I miss that guy."

Dad looks up from his meal. I avert my eyes so they don't give me away. "It's totally over between us," I say. I pick up my dinner plate and walk over to the dishwasher, scraping the last bits of food into the disposal. *Thump.* My silverware dives into a tub of soapy water.

Mom gets up from the table for the third time to clear dishes, start a pot of coffee, and unwrap the sour cream cake she made for dessert.

"So what about you, Rob? No girlfriend yet?" My tone of voice rises, one octave shy of sarcastic. Maybe the money I'd lent him bothers me more than I thought. Or maybe the issue wasn't about the money.

Rob leans his back into the chair, holding a glass of milk in his large hands. With his looks, he doesn't have to work hard finding women.

"Oh, I have girlfriends." A sly grin dimples one cheek. If he wasn't my not-that-much-younger brother, that comment could make me hate him. I exhale and try to shake it off.

By the time we finish dessert and I check Champ's skin, its eight o'clock. The guys have drifted outside with their coffee mugs to check out a comedy program on Sirius in Suzanne's new car, except for my father who has retreated to the den.

Suzanne and I clean up the pots and pans like we used to when we grew up, she washed and I dried. We each pack up leftovers to take home. I rag on Suzanne about hoarding most of the Rice Krispies dessert, until she says they're for her kids who stayed home in New Jersey for a neighbor's party.

"I'm leaving. Call me if Champ's skin isn't better in a few days, Suzanne." Our good-bye hug is like touching a hot stove.

Before I leave, I walk into the living room where Dad is slouched on the couch staring at FOX news.

"You feel okay, Dad?"

"Sure, Jilly." There is only one other person that calls me that. By the time I swallow the lump in my throat he's no longer looking at me and for the first time in a long time, I see a fine line of resemblance between us. His pride when he has something to hide.

"Okay, Dad." I start to turn away, the unspoken pact.

"Dr. Bob still treating you well?"

"Yes." I start to say more but notice he's turned back to the news again.

"Good," he says with uncharacteristic disinterest that makes me realize how age has changed him. I'd always pictured my father walking me down the aisle some day. What if by the time I get married, he can't?

On my ride home, a second shift of energy kicks in from mom's coffee. I pass a billboard with a sky blue background and a good-looking couple.

When I open my back door, I squeeze the plate of food between the other leftovers already piling up in my refrigerator. I pop a cat food lid, feed the cats. Rudy's feet patter upstairs beside me to the landing between two bedrooms of my home. One is where I sleep, romantic in a Bohemian sort of way. It has a platform bed low to the floor and is decorated from curtains to cat tree in an eclectic design where nothing matches, but it works. I picture it in the bedroom at Amberfield, with my antique dresser along the wall papered with cream magnolias and ivory trim. Some people need a beach at dusk, others a quiet golf course, I only need a clean pretty room to make me happy.

The other room upstairs is a baby-sized room. When I moved here, I had turned it into an office.

I undress and toss my clothes onto a blue velvet chair, then turn down a quilted coverlet of peach-colored trumpet flowers that looks like the bed wears a prom gown. I button my pajama top and walk barefoot into my office.

The glow from my computer is barely enough to illuminate my keyboard. Sitting in the dark, I type the words C-o-n-n-e-c-t.c-o-m.

The website fills the screen and I feel a curious joy dawn on my face.

Before I leave for work the next morning, Sunshine, the stray cat, flops on his back for me to knead his belly. He belongs to the family down the street, but lives part-time at my house. It warms me up to see him lounging on my sunny porch, paws flexed, eyes shut tight as a reverent monk. I like to think it's my love that keeps him showing up at my house—a romantic outlook that usually colors my outlook. At least most of the time. Not today.

Fifteen minutes into my ride, the street becomes polished with sheen from light drizzle. Rainy days are Jeannie's worst nightmare—white tile floors smeared with muddy footprints.

I hop-scotch wide puddles in the parking lot of the veterinary clinic and trot along the brick walk toward the entrance. Before stepping inside the crowded reception area, I shake out my umbrella. The phone is crooked to Jeannie's ear as she gives change to a client. She is too busy to notice my stern look for mentioning something about my indecision to Dr. Bob. It doesn't feel right being mad at her, but I'm in one of those moods— the mixed emotions yesterday with my family makes me want to blame someone for something.

When I walk through the door, Mrs. Miller is to my right, sitting with her cat carrier beside her. Inside it is her crinkle-eared tomcat.

"Good morning, Dr. Christie." Mrs. Miller tips her carrier when she greets me, and two glaring cat eyes catch full view of a Great Dane named Tiny. Suddenly the walls explode from a caterwaul that's loud and long as a police car siren, the carrier rattling from the hailstorm of spitting, eighteen-pound feline.

Tiny hops back, then he spots me and lopes toward me like a moose, jowls dripping with slobber, paws wet and sandy. The owner's leash unfurls and one hundred pounds of Dane knocks me into the counter.

First I let out a weak moan from the blow to my ribs, then something more fragile snaps.

"Bad dog! Bad. Go away." I shake my fist with one pointed finger.

Lifting my ribcage off the counter I spot Tiny crouched with his tail tucked down so far it looks cropped off. A horrible hush fills the reception room. Even Mrs. Miller's cat is silent.

Jeannie's brow lifts, her forehead looks pleated.

"Are you okay, Dr. Christie?" Mrs. Miller asks in a pitiful voice.

I'm smeared with mud and dog spit, my side splints with pain, but that isn't what hurts most. "Yes. Thank you." I make eye contact with Tiny. "I'm sorry, Tiny. You're a good boy. You're a Good Boy," I repeat over and over as I smooth my hands from his head to his tail. Tiny's blues disappear, but not mine. And I know why.

The smile that usually comes so easily is too much of an effort when I walk into this place lately. Mount Pleasant Hospital's blue and silver awning has begun to feel like my backpack, and it will be my backache when Bob retires.

"There's a minor emergency in the first exam room, Jill." Jeannie is nearly out of breath from the tizzy.

"I'll wait, Dr Christie," Mrs. Miller says. "You take care of that poor dog. Zeus and I don't mind."

Jeannie's bug eyes switch from Mrs. Miller to me. Her fury fizzles like a worn-out puppy as she rubs down the counter with disinfectant. As I walk away to the exam room, the air smells like mouthwash. I exhale and open the exam room door.

"What happened to Cinnamon?" I tickle her snout and her fancy tail thumps the metal table. This is what I love— the animals, not the business.

"We don't know how it happened, Dr. Christie," the owner explains. "All of a sudden, my boyfriend noticed the blood on the carpet."

Jan's boyfriend bends over the golden pup, his sleeves tarred with blood and feathered with dog fur. *There is something very attractive about a guy that isn't afraid to get his hands dirty, especially when it concerns animals.*

I remove the makeshift bandage. "Looks like her toe needs a few sutures. Leave Cinnamon here with us and I'll have her stitched up in a few hours."

The boyfriend scoops up the small Retriever and follows the kennel boy to the medical ward. Jan's eyes well up with tears.

I was the first person to lay eyes on Cinnamon the day Bob performed an emergency C-section on Jan's older dog. "There's only one pup that we can see on x-ray," Bob had told Jan last year as he pointed to the delicate S-shaped skeleton in Lady's belly. "I don't think I can save the pup, but I'll try." When Bob finally removed the hamster-sized puppy, its lips were purple. I remember squeezing that puppy's chest, blowing into its nostrils, and praying.

"Lady's doing fine and I think the pup's going to survive too, thanks to Dr. Christie," Bob had told Jan over the phone. Since then she's trusted Bob as if he were a beloved pediatrician. The whole office knew Jan's husband had left her for another woman when she couldn't have kids— of course Jeannie blabbed to everyone. Six months later we hear Jan met a widower, and they made one solid couple out of two broken people. Everyone loved hearing their story.

As I stand here with Jan, I envy her now, especially when her boyfriend returns with the dog leash looped around his neck and secures Jan to his side with a bold hug.

Before afternoon appointments start, I pull up a chair beside Jeannie.

"Well, my first date was a disaster." I fill in details between mouthfuls of turkey sandwich from the deli across the street. I've decided to let go of my animosity about Jeannie's big mouth, because, well, that's Jeannie and

I love her.

"Sounds like he has too many problems, Jill. At least you saw it before it went very far. You don't need to rescue these men like you do animals."

"I know," I say in the monotone voice I use when she patronizes me.

"Best way to get over an old love is to find a new one." Jeannie taps her finger at the magazine she's reading— this week's tabloid hook-up. She reads *People* magazine cover to cover.

By 6:30PM, the last of the clients have left the office.

"Everybody's all fed, cleaned and watered," the vegan kennel boy says.

"I'm leaving, too," Jeannie says. "Dr. Bob left while you were seeing the last patient, so lock up when you leave."

I call back to Jeannie. "He left early?"

"One of the techs got bit by Mrs. Miller's cat. He drove her to the emergency room and called to say he wouldn't be back today."

Great. As if there isn't enough on Bob's plate already. It'll all be on my plate soon if I let it. I have to talk to Bob.

I shuffle back to my office and slump in my chair. My mind is overflowing with hematology values, antibiotic doses, x-ray images, and I still needed to make a few calls.

This used to be the hour that my mind shifted from caring for animals to my night with Tim— ordinary couple-type things, that's what I miss most. Simple things like picking up a couple of steaks and making mashed potatoes. I haven't made mashed potatoes since we'd split. My tongue curls with the thought of my secret recipe— butter, milk and a dollop of cream cheese for stick-to-the-roof-of-mouth flavor.

I pick up the phone to return a call to the woman who came in earlier with a lethargic kitten.

"Hi, this is Dr. Christie. I'm calling to—"

"Can you hold on a minute, Doctor?" I feel like I'm inside a candy wrapper as she drops the phone. "I told you to stop that. Now finish your supper! Yes, hello?" she yells in a harried voice.

"I'm calling to let you know that the blood tests on Pussywillow are fine, so—"

"I'm sorry, Doctor, can I call you back some other time?" Click.

"Okay," I say to no one, gathering things to leave. I glance at the horse painting I'd picked up at an estate sale last year. It reminds me of Amberfield with its gray barn and electric green countryside. Amberfield. The last horse property left in the town of Mount Pleasant.

D.J. has called and left a message on my cell. He was right about another buyer, and although I hate to encourage D.J., I'll call back to see if he knows who it is.

I look up at the sky as I close the door to leave. Everything fades away when I look at the marbleized moon tonight. Its changing shapes and color and size has mesmerized me since I was young. Ingrid tells me the moon is part of the mystery that has everything to do with how our life plays out on earth. According to Ingrid, the sign of my moon in my birth chart can indicate the type of person I'll be attracted to.

Wednesday is my day off, and Bob will be doing surgery all day. I'm glad I won't be around after hearing his phone conversation earlier.

"Yes, I know she is," he was saying to the client who owned the cat named P.J. "I agree. If not for Dr. Christie, P.J. wouldn't be here."

How do I disappoint a man that respects me like that? Me, the colleague that's never performed any serious surgery. I know there are others like me, but they are vet associates that never own practices. Every time I think of doing surgery beyond a simple laceration or cat neuter, my throat feels like I've inhaled cotton balls.

The image of the stiff white body in its bloody cage flits to mind. It wasn't a lab rat. It was a pet I'd raised for three months. Even when my classmate suggested the rat had chewed its sutures out, I knew it was my fault he died.

When I get home, I change into a tee shirt and shorts and reheat Mom's leftover pasta. Half of this gets covered up and goes back in the refrigerator. Instead, I grab the pint of Haagen-Dazs and head to my computer.

With three clicks of the mouse, I'm back to where I left off last night— the dating website with a photo of a couple, and a woman who could be me.

~ *9* ~

After filling in age limits and zip code, I click SEARCH. In seconds, endless pages of men pop up on my screen—men of all ages, sizes, lifestyles—and astrology signs. So far, there's not one I picture myself with.

I cross my legs, pausing for a closer look at *BlackDiamondRacer*— doesn't look much like a skier. And *tony111* is in a tux with his shoulder cropped off, as well as the bride originally in the photo. I think about some of my own photos. Most of them are with Tim.

TrueBlues1002 mentions his grandfather, how he'd taught him about love and respect and why nothing was as important as family. I grab a tissue. His words hit me more than expected.

It is one o'clock and I am only on page ten when I log off and walk into my bedroom. Rudy and Sadie have assumed positions, at least for the first hour or so, then they'll hop off and on and off again to tend to important cat duties. Before I slide my toes into bed I grab my pad and pen and jot down a few things. *Set up Internet profile. Call D.J. Ouija board.*

When I awake in six hours, my head is off the pillow and my legs are twisted in sheets. I can't remember if I actually watched a television movie of a bride showing up to an empty church, or if it's an ominous dream. On my To-Do List, I add: *Call Ingrid.*

"Jill, didn't you get any sleep last night?" Jeannie asks when I walk into the clinic.

"Any coffee, Jeannie?"

"Just made a fresh pot."

"Did you make any goodies?"

The tech walks by with a pudgy dachshund and nudges her onto the scale as I stuff a piece of crumb cake in my mouth.

"Thirty-two pounds, Chloe," I say. "Your owner is going to hear it from Dr. Bob. A dog, no bigger than you ruptured Bob's vertebral disc last year." Mug of coffee in hand, I step on the walk-on scale after the tech heads back to the kennel with Chloe and her sister, Isabella.

What! How can I be five pounds more than last week?

I cut another sliver of Jeannie's cake and cover the rest. Guess it's true about sex burning off calories. I grab a Post-It from the counter and scribble a note: *Gym with Logan.*

When I get back to my desk, Jeannie pages me.

"Jill, Dr. Stevens for you on line one."

I pick up the receiver. "I just wrote myself a note to call you last night," I tell Ingrid. This synchronicity is not something I've started to take for granted since meeting her. The connection feels like déjà-vu.

"I have a gift certificate to that wonderful Asian restaurant I mentioned to you, Jill. I'd like to discuss something with you."

"Sounds great, Ingrid. So how is Olga doing these days?"

"You can see for yourself. She's comfortable and eating. All anyone of us can ask at her age."

"I'll see you tomorrow."

I walk out of my office and pick up the chart of the next patient. The mother and a daughter with a metal bracelet on her front teeth are in the exam room. They've adopted an exotic kitten and the eye is closed and runny.

"We'll dispense some triple antibiotic ointment for Willie," I say after the eye exam. The girl watches with wide eyes as I medicate the tiny golden eyeball. I retrieve my ponytail from Willie's baby cat paws before I hand him back to the teen.

I remember when I was her age. I never thought I'd want to revisit that time. It wasn't until now that I realized I had to.

"There is a wormy Husky puppy in the next exam room, and the lethargic pug that devoured a bacon and sausage pizza is on the way down," Jeannie says when I exit the exam room.

It is going to be a late night— too busy to talk with Bob. But the dating site is open all night.

Before I get home, I call D.J. back. No answer, so I leave a message. *No harm in being friends.*

"Hi D.J. I drove by the Amberfield place. You're right. The *For Sale* sign is down."

Next to my home computer monitor is the Haagen-Dazs container I'd left on my desk last night. The container is flipped over and licked clean. I had to have been pretty tired to leave it there when I hadn't finished the ice-cream. Two sticky footprints trail away from the desktop.

I clear my desk and re-open the dating site.

Ingrid can size up a person once she knows their astrology sign. Every sign has good and bad traits, she's told me. But I do have a list of basic criteria that needs to be met, and that has to include a man who would tolerate sticky footprints. How could a veterinarian think of dating someone who didn't love animals?

I click on the next page, and stop at the profile of a man crouched down with his arm hugging a Golden Retriever. His hair is the same color as the dog, a long bang dusting his forehead, and eyes the color of sea glass.

I scrunch the collar of my bathrobe and check his astrology sign. Cancer.

If I were going to date every sign, it doesn't matter where I start. I drag a hair clip through my hair, letting it cover one shoulder. What if we were perfect for each other and I got this dating thing right from the start?

Gullible, Logan calls me. I think I'll leave that part out of my profile.

Logan's expression sags like wet clay when she spots me saunter into the gym the next morning. She's pedaling a stationary bike with a cardiovascular monitor built onto the front of it and the television screen is tuned in to Judge Judy.

"Where's your gym bag?" Logan's brow ripples, like her brain is working harder than her long legs.

"I don't have time for a work out today."

Logan's eyes drop to my hips.

"I know I've put on weight, but losing weight is not big on my agenda lately. Besides, I heard that Heidi Klum said she's TIRED of holding her stomach in?"

"Yes, but Heidi Klum has had a litter of Seal puppies. You're not even married yet."

"Pleeeease don't start on my diet."

"We Virgos are big on that stuff, you know."

I slouch my butt down to the carpeted floor and hug my knees to my chest. "I saw someone I'd like to meet on the dating website."

"Did you email him?" Logan's cool within seconds of stopping her exercise routine, but its low impact and I'm not impressed.

"Not yet."

"What does he look like?"

He looks like the boy I had a crush on in tenth grade, the one that dated Alysha Mills. *Are any girls named Alysha ever ugly?*

"He has a nice smile," I say, because it doesn't matter if I say his eyes are round or slender, if his face is long, how his hair is cut, or not cut. "Nice-looking, but not perfect," I say. I didn't want perfect, but I can't help but think how much I wanted to look like Alysha Mills when I was in high school.

She brings up the dating website on her phone. "Show me his profile."

I navigate to the page, then hand Logan's phone back to her.

"Nice. Why haven't you contacted him yet?"

"I haven't finished setting up a profile yet," I say.

"Is he a Leo?"

"A Cancer. I'm going to leave Leo for last."

"Why?"

"I don't know." I did know. "Sometimes I buy new clothes and let them sit in my closet for that special occasion. You know what I mean."

"No, I never do that with my clothes, Jill, but whatever helps you get your feet wet."

I lean back against the bench press and exhale. "What if I don't click with any one?"

"Is that what you're afraid of?" She hands me her phone to check out the funny email that her fiancé, Greg, sent her. I do one of my snort-laughs, like a kid that's heard their first joke.

"Do me a favor. Don't ever laugh like that when you're with a man until your married to him! Even your looks won't get you by with that dorky laugh," Logan rifles through her Coach bag for a tissue.

"Isn't that the point of finding someone who likes me for myself?"

Logan holds out a package of tissues and her face softens as if she's thoughtfully considered my question.

"Greg and I would never have met if it wasn't for the Internet and we lived within in the same town. You would have thought we would have run into each other on the train to New York."

"I'm not like you and Greg. You both like traveling to places where the biggest attraction is the golf course, and drinking bottles of wine that cost as much as an annual vet bill."

"There are all kinds of guys out there, Jill. If you still want a guy that has you sleeping in a tent listening to skunks rustling through stale groceries instead of on a king-sized pillow top with room service, those guys are out there, believe me."

"Camping with Tim was some of the best times we had together," I say, thinking out loud. "Tim was organized with stuff like that, had all the gear and could make sleeping on an air mattress in a canvas tent more sensual than a Marriott suite." *And I used to think our relationship was as grounded as the earth beneath us.* I never pictured myself with the high profile, aggressive types Logan liked, though I did think her Greg was a great guy.

"What if clients see my profile?"

Logan does one of her eye rolls. "You're totally anonymous until you decide to give your name or number to someone. You can leave out your photo, but to tell you the truth, I never bothered with any of the guys who didn't have a photo."

Logan sneers at a man eavesdropping in our conversation.

"Just don't ever go back to Tim, even if you have to come to the wedding alone."

My cheek twitches. Tim had made our midnight stop at the Mediterranean Restaurant our secret place. He was the guy that filled a cat cookie jar with a hundred chocolate kisses on Valentine's Day. My head spins thinking maybe I dismissed his fear about marriage as something one of his disgruntled divorced buddies started. Maybe I should have listened to him instead of telling him that his doubts didn't mean he didn't love me. Or maybe I should have moved on a long time ago.

"By the way, I asked Greg to let me know if he hears anything about the Amberfield property." If anyone would know, Greg would. As Vice President of Harbor Bank, his connections included everyone in the real estate business. "He said it's not a done deal yet, but you'd better save your pennies. You have to put down at least 3.5% with an FHA loan, and more if you're credit isn't good. I'm sure it is, knowing you."

I swallow hard. "How much more?"

"With all that property, Jill, just 3.5% is going to be a lot. You always pay your bills. Don't worry about that."

My cheek twitches again. I was worried, plus I didn't want anyone in my family to find out Rob screwed up my credit. "So, it's still for sale?"

"Yes, but you'd better start looking for someone with lots of money. So hurry up with that profile. All Greg's friends are married. I'd hate for you to have to sit at our wedding without a date."

With half the day spent, I scale the stairs to my home office. But when I click on the Registration tab, my hands freeze above the keyboard.

Okay Jill, this isn't hard. You've made it through vet school. Fill in the blanks: Favorite Hot Spots, Favorite Things, Interests, Hair/Eye Color,

Best Feature. That one was easy. I hadn't cut my hair short since high school. Jeannie calls it the color of maple syrup.

Pets I Like, Pets I Have. *These are questions I like.*

Ethnicity, Height, Body Type, Religion, Sports and Exercise, Diet, Education, Occupation, Politics and my second favorite question: Your Astrology Sign.

They say Pisces can have chameleon-like personalities. I am able to adjust to a wide variety of personalities and situations, I write.

The hardest section is where I have to write about my life, but once I type, the words find their way onto the page.

I have many special people in my life and animals are a big part of it. Animals are non-negotiable. The feel of fur through my fingers probably does to me what the feel of a silk blouse does to Logan.

My favorite music is on an alternative rock station. I love crowds, jazz concerts on the town green, artsy flicks at the trendy cinema downtown, and souvlaki at 2A.M. I want someone who thinks a candlelit bedroom of second-hand furniture is dreamy, who loves patchouli incense and believes kissing can be a spiritual experience.

I re-read what I've written. *I tend to live like a bachelor with at least one or two take-out containers in my refrigerator at all times, because I hate to cook.*

I'd never said this before to Tim. It's so easy now. Not only the cooking. Everything. Every truth is easier to admit because I have no preconceived expectations to live up to.

~ *10* ~

Ingrid's estate is located on ninety acres of property once owned by Ingrid's late uncle.

I don't see a door bell, so I clap the bronze door knocker.

"Door's open. Come in." Ingrid is sitting at the bay window in a tall upholstered chair looking out at Lake Whitney. The room is cluttered with old furniture— a humpback couch and clunky cherry buffet, a marble coffee table with curvy wooden legs. On the floor is a thin Oriental rug. It's obvious the room hasn't been updated, in years. Maybe never.

"I was about to walk through the pine forest to watch the swans," Ingrid says. "Five cygnets were born Father's Day." Luckily I've kept the ace bandage on my ankle. Ingrid reaches for a floppy-brimmed beach hat and grabs two walking poles to help with her balance. She has never addressed the nature of her illness.

As we start to walk up a slight hill, despite the mellow Connecticut August weather, Ingrid's color changes to putty and she becomes short of breath. Was this why she told me she was closing her practice for "personal reasons?"

At the lake, green reeds are succulent from rain and a majestic procession of white birds flows like a bridal veil over black water.

Ingrid lifts her face to the weak daylight. "This reminds me of when I visited my uncle here as a young girl. The lake is as it always was, and yet the planets have continued to turn like clock gears, the working of all change in the world."

The birds move out of view as I turn to sit on the grass beside Ingrid. I can't imagine how the planets have something to do with my life.

"About every thirty years, the planet, Saturn, returns to the same sign it was at our time of birth. It's happening in your life now, Jill, because it occurs at about age thirty, and again at about age sixty. It gives us a chance to revisit our past."

"Is this why, after all these years, I need to go back to Amberfield?"

"Yes, and revisiting the past will open doors. Let's go. I've got something important to tell you."

Ingrid is limping when we make our way back to her home. Inside is a wall-length bookcase where she has a mixture of psychology, astrology and New Age books, and one on spontaneous healing. Ingrid grabs her satchel and slips like a cat through the narrow aisle of faded magazines stacked in the hallway.

"I think I've got everything. Do you know the way to Mica's Restaurant?" Ingrid crooks her arm and lifts her canvas bag.

On the drive to Mica's Restaurant, Ingrid is quieter than normal. It is difficult to tell if she isn't feeling well, or if this is a mood that I haven't seen. I don't know her that well, yet when she looks at my birth chart, it's as if she knows everything about me.

Ingrid points to a reserved parking space behind the establishment. When we enter, the owner greets Ingrid with a respectful nod. "I saved your special table," he says, leading us past four tiny rooms separated by rice paper partitions to a low lacquered rectangular table with benches. We're practically sitting on the floor. I stretch my legs and prop my sore ankle.

It is a dimly lit room and the buzz of adjoining rooms makes it like a hive, one surrounded with scents of teas and oil, prickly spices, and though I can't smell it, I imagine, honey.

The waiter enters with a smooth ceramic flask of warm sake. Ingrid pours some into a miniature cylindrical cup. With her book in her lap, she scans my birth chart, then she compares it to an ephemeris which lists the position of the evolving planets. She pages forwards to months from now.

Chinese bells tinkle faintly in the background. I sit quietly, watching Ingrid's eyes travel up and down the page of symbols and numbers that signify the position of the planets.

"Ahhhhh," she sighs, and by the sound of it, my spirits lift.

"Anything interesting?" I ask. A bubbly churn flips my insides, only partly from warm sake.

Ingrid thinks I'm asking about the menu. "I never know what to try," she says. "The recipes are original creations of food, flowers and exotic spices."

I look up from the menu, too preoccupied to appreciate the unusual culinary experience Ingrid has planned for me. "Ingrid, how much can you tell from my birth chart?"

"I can tell you that Einstein and Newton and NASA believed in astrology, not to mention a few Presidents. I can tell that you're heading for a crossroad. And so am I." Ingrid tugs at her silk shawl and pours more sake.

The waitress brings two seared oily rolls called *Tulip Shrimp,* and a tropical fruit drink called *African Violet Punch* for me. After four sips, my head feels as if it is swelling from the rum that I don't usually drink.

"I don't know what to do about the hospital. Dr. Bob is counting on me to fill his shoes when he retires. But everything depends on whether I can buy Amberfield. I know it's a long shot." I sigh. "My credit isn't good." I grab my drink. "I also had my first date and it didn't end well."

She glances at the geometric lines on my chart. The cedar-like scent of sandalwood spirals toward the ceiling. "That's what dating is all about. Finding what you don't like so you'll know when you meet the right person. Each person will show you something important. I like your idea to leave Leo for last. In fact, I think you should."

Crimson lanterns hanging from the low ceiling make Ingrid's skin look like wax, her face look mysterious.

"There's something that I neglected to tell you, Jill."

The sticky teriyaki roll I'm holding crackles. I slide forward, closer to Ingrid.

"I know you still have doubts about Tim. You and Tim were destined to be together, but it doesn't mean that you should be together now." Ingrid's chin drops as if she just nodded off. Then her lids flutter like she is watching a movie inside her head. "You and Tim knew each other in a previous life." Her voice becomes slow and deep.

The bewitching power of rum oozes from my armpits. If she could see other lives, could she also tell me about my friend, Petal?

Ingrid is still in her trance. "I see you with a thick braid down your back."

A braid. Mom used to braid my hair for horse shows. I scoot closer to Ingrid.

"You're wearing a long skirt with ruffles," she says. Ingrid walks her fingers like a spider from her chest to her knees as if recreating a flowing dress. "The boy has blonde hair, messy, sweaty," Ingrid's lids tighten. "His work has something to do with tools." My breath catches.

Ingrid massages her hair with fingertip lightness. "The boy's wearing a fur cap. His clothes are those of a peasant. His hands smell of linseed oil from chores." She presses her palms to her nose. Her eyes twitch open. "You both needed time to grow up. You would never have been able to do that if you'd stayed together."

My mind darts. Tim's hands never look clean, always tweaking his boat engine or one of his cars.

"Sooo, Tim and I were together in a previous life?"

Ingrid holds me back with one finger.

"Your time together was unfinished business between you two, Jill, your chance for closure."

Closure. My body feels as if it has become a puddle. Was she telling me that I have a haunted past? If only there was a way to go back in time and fix it.

A long minute passes before either of us speaks.

"Pisces and Scorpio are both water signs. I thought signs of the same element are good together," I say.

"That's true, but your other planets are scattered in the fire, air and earth signs."

I squint to convey my confusion.

"It means you can relate on some level to many people. Trust me. There is someone you are destined to be with, only the timing isn't quite right yet. Within the year. Just look for Leo."

It is as if Ingrid spoke in code sometimes— a book of knowledge, yet her explanations are vague. The waiter serves two miniature portions of food, a light fare that suits my knotted intestines.

"It's time for my special tea," Ingrid announces after we finish. "Let's go back to the house and I'll look more closely at your chart."

On the ride back to Ingrid's home, my light heart feels as absent as the moon. I came to her for answers, and now, I had more.

Then Ingrid mentions Amberfield.

I tell her what Petal's mom had said to me the last time I saw her. *You can still come to visit me every day. Someday when you finish college, maybe you can own a farm like this.* "I remember her words like yesterday."

Ingrid's head rears back a few inches. I get ready to defend the soiled reputation of Amberfield, but it turns out I don't have to explain my fondness for a dilapidated farm.

"Years ago, my uncle tried to buy that property. Most all Mount Pleasant was farmland. Then, one by one, all the horse farms disappeared. All except that one."

When I tell Ingrid about Petal, my voice races— "we doubled-up bareback on her gray pony and cantered through wheat fields tall as his withers." Ingrid is smiling and wagging her head like she understands.

"Horses are such intuitive animals. My sister and I used to ride." She pauses. "Therapists are using horses with patients who reject the human connection."

Now I'm smiling, too, for this bond I realize with Ingrid. Amberfield was never about Tim. I only hoped he'd love it like I do. Like she does too.

The setting sun bestows an angelic quality to Ingrid's living room by the time we return home. I settle into one of the high-backed chairs, imagining the farm girl identity of my past. It sure sounds like it could be true. It makes sense why I can't let go.

In a small frame on the side table is an old gray photograph of two young girls with a pony. I can't make out much detail from where I'm sitting. Ingrid walks back into the room holding a cup of tea and a glass of water for me. "That was me and my sister on my uncle's farm," she says when she notices me looking at the photo. "She had your same birthday."

I take the glass of water. Her eyes look soft and far away.

Suddenly my taste buds contract at the bitter aroma swirling into my nostrils. Six generic-looking black and white vials are lined up on an antique brass cart where Ingrid has dissolved five capsules into a tea-colored broth. I pick one up to study the label.

"It comes from a gum tree that grows in the rainforests of South Asia. It hasn't been studied extensively enough to be approved by the FDA, but it has anti-tumor properties." Ingrid walks barefoot across the oriental to a wicker settee and plops down unsteadily as a tired dog.

She winces when she straightens her knee. The tie-dyed sunset is shining like candlelight in the woods. Ingrid flips the switch of a bronze table lamp, a two-foot tall figurine of the Botticelli goddess, Venus. Click 60 watts, click 75 watts. She opens her astrology folder and props my birth chart against a pile of unopened junk mail. On the table there's an open bag of trail mix, spilled catnip and dried candle wax.

"Ten years ago, an oncologist told me I should make out my will after he removed my breasts. But I found Dr. Bernard in Texas and his unconventional therapy saved me."

Cancer— the word summons a different reaction in me this time than when I saw it on the Internet dating profile. Cancer took the life of my young grandmother. Death had a way of putting perspective on time.

Ingrid massages her cat Olga, twirling her fingers as if shampooing Olga's head. The cat nudges Ingrid's hand with her nose then licks the tips of Ingrid's fingers. When Ingrid looks up, her smile is calm as the cat and her eyes look vivid.

"We are all given a blueprint for our life when we are born. Each of us is born with a unique set of talents and weaknesses. But every astrological sign has positive and negative energy and it's up to each of us to use that energy wisely. The chart of a saint is the chart of a sinner. No one is born under a bad sign."

"I'm feeling a little tired all of a sudden, Jill. Let's promise to do this another night, okay? I'm so sorry."

When we hug good-bye Ingrid isn't wearing her prosthesis. My chest caves in to Ingrid's as our arms encircle. Ingrid's ribs feel delicate as a birdcage against my breasts.

Once home, I open the trunk where I've stored an assortment of knickknacks, old paintings, a lace coverlet— treasures I've saved for Amberfield. Now I don't know what will happen. Ingrid validated my past-life, and with a cruel twist of fate, she validated ties to Tim— when I'm trying hard to break them.

~ *11* ~
Palo Alto, California

James picked up the vial of antibiotics and tipped his head at Dizzy.

"Just a few more days of these, Dizzy." He gave her the pill and filled her bowl with the special diet for urinary problems. Then he sat before his laptop with a bowl of Ramen noodle soup and booted his computer screen.

It bothered him less now that word was out that Amy was no longer on the faculty, so all the more reason he should get her picture off of his screen. If he could only remember how to do it without asking someone. Submitting an NIH grant he could do. Researching Dizzy's surgery? No sweat. Changing your screen saver on a Mac? Ah, Launch Pad, System Preferences. Done.

He should be working on his Power Point presentation for his lecture, but he was focused on Dizzy as she snorted down the last bits of kibble. He got up from his desk and grabbed her leash. There was an extra set of keys hanging next to the leash. She'd never asked for them back. She was never coming back. James shuffled the key in his palm before he opened his hand and dropped Amy's keys into the garbage pail.

The evening wind was balmy. Tonight his walk with Dizzy was at a slower pace as he took in the sights of his neighborhood. There was a bike store he'd never once visited. The car rental place he'd had to use once when his car was in the shop was closed, as was the book store, but the lights were still on at Starbuck's and the Farmer's Market where he shopped, when he shopped, for food. James crossed the street and walked inside Starbuck's. The coffee aroma smelled rich and earthy, complementing the terra cotta tones of the Bohemian decor. He was surprised how many people were in the place at this hour. There was a couple sitting across from each other in the deep leather chairs. *Had to be a date*, James thought. Her crossed legs and short skirt reminded him of some of his own, before he'd joined the faculty. Dating wasn't as easy now. One of his colleagues had told him about the messy situation he gotten into by dating a student he'd met online. James jimmied his shoulders and spun around toward the barista.

He ordered his coffee and walked back outside with Dizzy. Then they found a seat at an outdoor table, a hammered metal of some sort with moon and stars cut outs. No surprise that he was drawn to that table. The table and chairs were cool to the touch from the night air. The hot coffee tasted smooth.

James turned back to look inside again. Three young women were talking to the barista, an Asian man was alone, and his fingers moved like butterflies on his keyboard. Another couple came outdoors with their coffees and in the course of the hour, the place was a swinging door.

Then a voice pleasantly startled him.

"Nice night," said a woman starting at Dizzy. "I had a bulldog when I was a kid. Is she friendly?"

"Yes, you can pet her. She loves people."

The woman stooped to pet Dizzy who licked her hand as if she were candy. James watched them. Then to his slight disappointment, she smiled and walked away. The small talk he wasn't used to was still in his brain. But watching Dizzy indulge her attention, made James realize how much he missed the sweetness of female affection.

~ *12* ~

One hand rubs the head of a mixed-breed Shepherd, my other skims over her swollen limb the next morning at work.

"Easy, Princess. We'll get you fixed up," I say to the panting dog. Her brows are pinched, her worried eyes resting on her owner. Pain has immobilized the dog's leg with a torn knee cartilage. Luckily, I'm feeling the opposite effect after sleeping on the information from Ingrid.

"Guess what I did yesterday?" I say to Jeannie after the client leaves. My eyes tear with a strong stretch.

"Whatever you did must have kept you up late. I hope you had fun, Darlin," the part-time accountant, Marlene, says, turning away from the coffee pot, mug in hand. Jeannie stops fiddling with a balloon valance that she asked the kennel boy to put up for her after Dr. Bob's wife, Pam, designed the hospital during Bob's remodel project. Although Pam's presence has a lip-biting effect on the staff, her stark architectural suggestions are quite an improvement. Luckily Pam rarely stops by. She'd never approve of Jeannie's cozy taste in window treatment.

"Didn't you get together with Dr. Stevens last night?" Jeannie straightens a reception room chair, assessing the magazine assortment.

"Yes." I don't bring up the past-life conversation with a Southern girl like Marlene. "I finally set up a dating site profile." I bite into Jeannie's pumpkin muffin and swallow quickly. "I'm going to date one man of every sign of the zodiac."

Marlene pours half-n-half into her mug and adds three heaping teaspoons of sugar to her coffee. She loves daytime soaps and can turn the most mundane gossip into a scandal. After talking to Marlene on the phone, clients expect to be greeted by a blonde wearing a red check midriff blouse and denim shorts. There's always a sheepish look on their faces when they meet her. Her cheeks are chubby, as is the rest of her body. She is wearing her navy blue shirt jacket that gathers at the waist she doesn't have, and her feet are crammed into pumps that she wears for comfort, not style.

"That's great, Sweetheart. You know that's how I met my husband." Marlene tosses her head back slightly to move her long hair from her face. She's perfected the maneuver, holding her full face tilted to keep a curve of bang draped over her brow. Her hair is as silky as a Spanish mantilla and Marlene gushes with pride when clients tell her she reminds them of Cher. "Each man you meet will be a stepping stone to something better. Take your time before you give your heart away."

My mind flits to D.J. He's called again and offered to fix the broken glass on my back door.

I think of Ingrid's one-year prediction. "There's so many different types of men on the dating site. Some are on their boat, or skiing on a mountain, or underwater in scuba gear. Some are with children, some with pets. Others post photos of things like an antique car, musical equipment, trophies. One guy actually put up a picture of his living room," I say.

"Really?" I turn around when I hear Bob's voice.

"Oh, hi Bob," I say, as we pretend to check the appointment schedule.

He runs the tap water at the sink and fills a glass half-way. I expect he'll mention our meeting.

Out of the corner of my eye, I notice him pop something into his mouth, raise the glass to his lips and swallow. He stands there facing the wall for a second, stabs his chest with the heel of his fist and excuses a soft belch. Blotting his brow, he walks back to his office and closes the door.

Headache? Something he ate? I've never seen Bob like this before.

Jeannie passes a chart to me and directs the next client into the exam room. The tech hands me two syringes of pre-filled vaccines. Preoccupied with Bob, I count the floor tiles and walk inside the lines of each one on the way to the exam room— ten, eleven, twelve. I continue my neurotic process after the appointment when I pass Bob's office door and it's still closed.

On the way home from work I stop at the Dairy Mart to pick a quart of milk, also Pecan ice cream. Once home, I make Ramen noodle soup for dinner.

My ankle feels better. My confidence feels strong as bone after my talk with Marlene. Only one detail left to finish before posting profile photos. I find one of me with my sister's dog and dial her number.

"What are you up to?" I ask Suzanne.

"Trying to finish a pottery project." Her brevity makes her sound preoccupied, or probably in a bad mood.

"How's Champ doing on the new diet?"

"He's still itchy."

Yep. Bad mood.

"Any more dates?" she asks.

"I'm working on it," I tell her, hoping to avoid advice from someone who hasn't dated in fifteen years.

Naturally, she mentions her favorite saying, 'Use it or lose it.'

"Thanks, Suzanne," I say in a snotty tone. "Now I have to think about having sex before it's too late?" I lower the television and hear the sizzle of sauté in the background on Suzanne's end of the phone. Lee must be cooking.

"It's true, Jill. I hear problems from women at the gynecologist's office when I'm doing their pelvic scans. And you know how Mom always wanted more kids before she had to have a hysterectomy."

Mom's hysterectomy.

"When she was only in her thirties," Suzanne reminds me.

"I'm not sure I want kids." I rest my hand on my cat's head when he looks up at me from where he's curled at my side. This endearing gesture comes so naturally to me when it's an animal, but I've never come close to patting a kid on the head.

"What if you meet someone who does?" She's snotty this time.

I look over at my computer— dozens of potential daddy's are staring at me.

"I can't think about that." But I will every time I look now that Suzanne brought it up. Losing the option to have kids— a problem from Mom's side of the family— and it's hereditary.

"I've got to get off the phone, Jill. Lee and I are meeting friends to see that new movie everyone is talking about."

I knew the movie. Two clients have seen it with their husbands.

"Let me know how it is. I'll probably end up seeing it on DVD." My tone is tinged with self-pity because the time I'd walked into a theater alone I felt like a pariah.

Self-pity. A Pisces trait, so I've read. And one I can change, according to Ingrid.

"Aren't you finished with that profile yet?" Logan says when I call. "It doesn't have to be perfect. Half of these guys aren't going to read it. They're going to look at your photo and hit that *Wink* button."

I have no idea what a "*Wink*" is, or how this thing works, but Logan tells me it is intuitive, if I can only tell my mind not to think so much.

"What about a user name. Did you think of one yet?"

"Something with the word butterflies," I say. "You know, the feeling you get when you fall in love."

"You don't still believe in them?" Logan asks, as if romance is no longer in style. Sometimes I wonder if Logan ever knew how it felt.

The night I ended up at the concert with Tim, I wasn't drinking, so I knew the intoxication wasn't from liquor. His arms were tucked inside his leather jacket. His body swayed as if it were an instrument and the bass chords were a connection to his soul. But I could tell he was switching his sights from the stage over to where I was standing— guitar strings, heartstrings and me. He leaned his head close to mine to talk and his long hair fell against my cheek. If a heart could have an aura, this would be how it felt.

It's ten o'clock. All I need to do is upload photos. I feel as though I've crossed the bridges of Madison County.

I scan through my pictures and pick out four fairly recent ones. One is the close-up that I took for my passport when I went to the veterinary conference in Canada last August. I was wearing my favorite necklace, scrolled silver with a single pearl dripping down like a tear. Tim had bought if for me on our trip to Florida.

I find one photo of myself standing by the ocean that shows my spiritual side. I choose another hugging my cat in which Mom says I look like her mother. I never got to meet her, but I'd been told of my resemblance—cheekbones and almond-shaped eyes that often brought up mention of the actress, Jane Seymour, in conversation about my grandma.

The last photo was taken at a Christmas party two years ago. My friend's husband took the picture. I'm standing at the entrance of the lawn club. My ankles are crossed to hide my bowed legs. They barely show in the photo, but what the photo does show is an elegant side I rarely see in myself.

I'd worn a tea-length gown with sheer black sleeves that clung seamlessly to my curves. Any man with imagination might guess how feminine I felt in those open-toed heels. But I'm only half-smiling in this photo—a melancholy look that no one would understand but me. The first Christmas party I'd attended without Tim because we'd had an argument. His foul mood started at work because he didn't measure up to another one of his father's expectations.

No nostalgia with this photo. I upload it and fill in my birth date.

Your registration is almost complete, the message flashes across the screen. The User Name prompt winks for me to enter a title. I don't need to give it much thought: *Butterflies303.*

I remember a question my college professor once asked of our psychology class.

"Is love a philosophy, or a feeling?" he'd challenged his freshman.

There was no question in my mind. Love was something I *felt*. Dumb as I sounded I'd told him it felt "like butterflies." I never forgot the look on his face—I wondered if it were envy or pity. In my essay I'd explained why I believed it was true.

"The solar plexus is a network of nerves located in the mid-abdomen that stimulate involuntary responses like increasing heart rate and blood pressure. So as our bodies tune in to emotions like romance, the nerves of the solar plexus become excited. This fluttering sensation creates the butterfly effect. Love isn't philosophical, it's a real physiological sensation."

My professor had given me an "A" for Psychology 101, although my brother, Rob, suggested that my professor was probably seduced by my answer. It made perfect sense to me why love was tangible. Even Tim had told me that he'd felt "butterflies," except he wasn't sure that he still loved me when he stopped feeling them.

I look over at my zodiac calendar. It posts the sign of the sun and moon as it travels through the twelve signs of the zodiac during each month of the year. There are times that are best for planting, times that are best for surgery, times that are best to make purchases, times that are best to begin projects. The date is August 4th. The Sun is officially in the sign of Leo.

"Leo is the natural ruler of the 5th House. It represents Love Given," Ingrid explained the day she told me to look for Leo. "Each zodiac sign also rules a part of the body, and Leo rules the heart." No accident the Leo sun is setting the stage to start my search for love.

Except something is holding me back.

I pick up the astrological calendar to take a closer look at the progression of the moon. The moon has been in the sign of Pisces the last couple of days— Pisces, the sign of two fish swimming in opposite directions. *Indecision.*

~ *13* ~

While I'm sleeping the moon moves from Pisces into the courageous sign of Aries. Ingrid tells me when the moon is in Aries, it's hitting my Venus, the planet of love. I'm awake an hour early, energy surging inside me as if I've had caffeine. I tread to my computer like a kid running to the tree on Christmas morning, ready to tear open my presents.

Four presents. The first two are like getting a pair of socks. I read the generic message: *Someone thinks you're Special,* and the words punctuated by a blinking cartoon. I hate cartoons.

The next email may as well be a re-gift. I close it before reading as soon as I see the photo of him dressed in hunting gear.

Although the last message is from a guy that's smiling too hard, I like what he says. *Gemini69* has curly hair and rectangular black glass frames like Suzanne's husband, Lee. He looks like a "Brainiac." The Internet dating term Logan uses.

I joined to find one special lady, not to shop at a meat market. I'm one of the good guys. Steve

Shopping at a meat market? I'm not sure I still consider him a Brainiac.

I start a list, one through twelve for each zodiac sign and write Steve's name down next to Gemini.

I search for the page where I saw the Cancer man. The cursor blinks, I swivel back and forth in my chair, staring at his photo. There are other photos and one where he's holding a long-haired white cat. It has to be a female.

"I don't know how you do it," Dr. Bob says whenever I tell an animal's sex by its face. "Ninety percent of the time you're right without an anatomical check."

I snap my fingers across the keys and send a message.

I enjoyed reading your poetry and the photos of you with the dog and cat.

Wouldn't it be impersonal not to sign my name? I add, *Jill*, and hit the SEND button.

After I get dressed, I race down the stairs and grab my purse. That Aries ram energy that yanked open my eyes this morning is butting me in the backside. I'll feel better if I talk to Dr. Bob. He's been the one I could talk to about anything from finance to failures. He even knows about my loan to Rob, which is why he planned to hold the mortgage on the clinic. So it's killing me to tell him that I don't want to buy it.

On my drive into work, I'm trying out different versions of how to break the news when the traffic stops dead. Then I hear a fire truck and it takes a left turn. My hands grip the steering wheel. There's not much else on that street besides Amberfield.

I crane my neck as I pass by the cop directing traffic, but he waves me past him. I lean on the gas pedal to make up for lost time. Once I reach my parking space at the vet clinic, I grab my pocketbook and sprint past a mosaic of perennials that Jeannie planted beside the dog walk area.

"You're energetic this morning," Jeannie says, shoving blind Chrissy into my arms as I try to rush past her. "At least someone is." The cat purrs when he senses my touch and I become paralyzed. Jeannie is too preoccupied with her appointment book to notice. She scrunches her face like a jack-o-lantern as she points at Bob who is fiddling with the fax machine.

"Aaargh!" he shouts, slamming the top shut and storming back to his office blotting blood from his pinched knuckle. Bob's shoulders hunch, the peninsula of hair on his forehead flips up and makes him look like his ten-year-old son. None of the versions I've played in my head to talk to him are an option now. This isn't a good day— for either of us.

"Here's the chest x-ray report from the Boxer that you saw yesterday," Jeannie says nudging my arm. "They're faxing the lab results now, as long as Dr Bob's fingers are out of the way."

I'm still speechless. Jeannie keeps rambling.

"The animal shelter dropped off a cat neuter and he's a real scrapper— right ear's all bloody. He's right there in the Have-A-Heart trap. The techs covered it with a beach towel to calm him." Jeannie points toward a rectangular object with a bath towel draped partially over the cage. On the towel is the likeness of a shark.

"Jeannie?" Her head pops up from the reception book when she hears my wimpy voice. "Did you hear anything about a fire on Meadowbrook Road?"

"No!" The word shoots out of her mouth, which doesn't close until I shove Chrissy toward her.

"I need to call someone." I nearly trip over the cage with the feral feline scrunched at the back of it. One ear is folded down like a little kerchief. He shakes his head and lets out a mighty sneeze.

I dial D.J.'s number from my office phone. When he answers his voice is subdued until he hears me, then he perks up. *Now I'm sorry I called.*

"Hey, Jill, I didn't expect to hear from you."

I moan so that only I can hear me. I feel like a heel. "Hey D. J., by any chance did you hear any news about the Amberfield property?"

"I haven't checked."

"There's been a fire," I say, feeling my spine kink.

"That's too bad. Maybe I'll take a ride over there. Give me a call later and I'll let you know. Hey, maybe we can have lunch sometime."

Out of guilt, I make a "sometime date" with D.J. I could do worse than a guy who brought me a scented candle and rescued an abused pup. I shuffle back to the reception area.

"This cat will never get a home," I mumble when I pass by the cage sitting in the corner. Then I look over at Jeannie.

Her face looks pale.

"What's wrong?"

"The tech just came back from the bank. The teller's husband is a cop." I have a delayed-reaction when she says the word "Amberfield."

I press my chest to steady the lead ball that has replaced my heart. My thoughts ricochet. *Any developer might figure the land is better off without a run-down house.* D.J.? No. I push that thought back and duck into my office to make another call.

The woman who answers my call at the fire department tells me it was only the sagging barn that collapsed in the fire.

"I love that place, too," she says.

After expecting the worst "only the barn" consoles me. Maybe not all the barn, not the floor where I'd hid the Ouija board after Petal died. I remember when her father found us playing with it one day, and how he'd yelled at us to get rid of it. "Your mother better not have bought that thing," he'd said. My lips quivered in fear, but I couldn't open my mouth. We hustled off to the hayloft of the barn, and played with it there.

Out in the prep room I draw up a cocktail of anesthetic into a syringe. The techs have set the feral cat cage on a gurney. "It's okay little buddy," I say, aiming the needle through the wire bars of the cage. With a skillful prick, I inject through the cat's thick hide. After my surge of adrenaline from the fire, I feel sedated myself.

Jeannie stands nearby fastening a pile of reminder cards with a rubber band.

"I'll let you know if I hear anymore news on television while you're busy today, Jill. They flashed a news brief on the local news, but there's not much info yet."

I lift the limp anesthetized kitty out of the cage and place him on a clean towel for his castration. The busy schedule will help take my mind off of the fire.

Later, I take the alternate route home to avoid going anywhere near Amberfield. News photos showed the barn glowing like matchsticks, one side reduced to a black skeleton. I can't bear to see it. *I wonder what happens to the sale of the place?*

When I get home that evening, I feed my cats and reheat left-over pizza. I carry the plate to my computer.

Scuba62 asks if I'd be interested in a ride on his sailboat. *JPHMed* thinks we have a lot in common since he works as a male nurse— I hadn't mentioned that I am a vet, only that I work in the medical field. A few generic messages make me wonder if I should bother if a man can't write something personal.

It takes so little effort to send back a kind message. But of course this is the mentality that takes me half an hour to pick out one birthday card for a friend.

Yankeefan60 has only posted one photo, one where he is wearing a baseball cap and Yankee tee shirt. His entire profile is more of an editorial on batting averages than scoring with women. *Not my type and too much of a sports fanatic*, but he returns my ripple of kindness.

Thank you for your response, Jill. Most don't bother. Yankee Bill

His words stick with me as if he's someone I know. *Most don't bother?* Will some of these men feel that way about me?

I finish another email reply and check the news again for details of the fire, as if this time, it won't be true.

For a few moments, I'm thirteen years old standing up to my ankles in wood shavings. There's a string tied to the bars of the stall door with four ribbons—pink, yellow, blue rosettes. There's a red one too. Petal won them riding her gelding. Everyone knew that horse wouldn't jump like that for anyone but Petal. It made it all the more heart-breaking when he stopped trying, and Petal's mother gave him to summer camp for kids with special needs.

I'm lost in time when I notice a new email from the man I contacted—

one that makes me feel my age again. My computer mouse skates across the screen to open his message.

Hello, Jill. Your natural beauty is lovely and your profile is interesting. I will be at the fresh table restaurant called The Champagne Café at 7PM this Friday if you'd like to join me. Aaron Scott

Well, that psychologist on YouTube did say to set up a brief meet quickly and not waste time emailing. At least I know he likes dogs!

Hi Aaron,

Thanks for your nice compliment. Tomorrow night works for me. Jill

Aaron: *We should be able to spot each other by our photos. See you tomorrow.*

A Cancer man—what does it matter where I start this dating thing? I open my bedroom closet. My clothes look outdated, or should I say, dated by my time with Tim. Something tells me, more than my wardrobe needs to change.

In the news the next morning the building inspector reports that the barn is totally destroyed. The police suspect faulty wiring, but aren't ruling out arson. I rub my temples, feeling the way I do each time animal control brings in an abandoned pet. I flip the newspaper pages to the horoscope section.

PISCES: With the moon in the communicative sign of Gemini today, you're more apt to speak your mind. Be sure to choose your words carefully, because you may never be able to take them back.

I shut the page. I've stalled long enough. I walk over to where Bob's extracting teeth on an old greyhound. Although the dog's out cold and hooked up to an anesthesia machine, I pet the dog out of habit. The monitor beeps every time the dog's heart beats and the repetitious tone throbs in my ears.

"I know you've wanted to talk with me." I look over at the settings on the anesthesia machine and check the oxygen level, even though the tech is standing nearby and I know she's checked them.

Bob doesn't look up. His face is close to the dog's and he's wincing as he wrestles with the bad tooth. He sighs as it loosens and he straightens up, looking as if he's aced a hole in one. "We don't have to do it today if you're busy," he says, plopping the decayed molar into the stainless tray.

My astrology prediction— I'm better off speaking up today. I definitely don't want to do this on the day of my blind date.

"No. Today is okay. How about during lunch?" I say.

"All right."

"Where should we go?"

"Doesn't matter."

My feet fidget, my appetite is gone. *Doesn't matter to me either.*

Around noonish, Bob and I walk across the street to the deli. We sit at the counter, me twirling back and forth, back and forth, back and forth on the stool as he talks.

"I've got an easy payment schedule worked out for you, Jill. You know I'm planning to hold the mortgage and keep the interest low. Plus, I'm throwing in all the equipment, even the new endoscope I bought last year. I'll get the surgery light fixed, too, and the sign repainted," he says, patting the counter to reassure me he's not going to set me up to fail.

I keep nodding between bites of my corned beef sandwich though I've barely tasted it and I'm half done. I pick at my French fries because I forgot to tell the waitress to hold them. I don't eat French fries, but I hate to waste food.

Bob asks for the check. He's unpeeling Rolaids as he waits.

It's now or never, I tell myself.

"Take your time Jill, eating that is, not deciding to buy the clinic," he chuckles at his joke. "I have to hurry back." He tucks three dollars under his empty soda glass.

The sandwich I stuffed down is balled up in my throat, blocking words that I need to say. "Bob?"

"What?" he says, resting his hand on my shoulder.

"I appreciate everything you do for me. I just don't know—" The lump in my mouth stays stuck like the rest of my words.

He pauses, watching me chug my water. "Don't worry about it for now. It'll work out. You'll see." He smiles at me the way I've seen him do when Jeannie mouths off about the clients who let their dogs use her perennial garden as their toilet. "I'll see you back at the hospital."

How can I tell him this won't work when he's doing everything he can to make sure it does?

He's already turned away, and doesn't see my corned beef sandwich fall apart.

"Something came up suddenly. I'll be away for a few days," Ingrid tells me when she calls the office later. "I hate to upset Olga by having her sit in a cage. I know this is late notice, Jill, but could you help me out?"

After I agree that a pet-sitter will be better for Olga than boarding her, I remember that the only tech that will be able to give Olga her daily medication is on vacation. "It would be no problem for me to stop by. It's on my way home," I say. "I'll stop by later to pick up your house keys."

"I'm attending a New Age seminar in Colorado," Ingrid says when I stop by her place after work. "Then I'm flying to Texas for my annual visit with Dr. Bernard. I appreciate this, Jill." She hesitates for a moment. "You know Olga thinks of you as family."

I feel my temperature rise— Ingrid doesn't mean Olga. Ingrid's fondness for me is mutual, although our weekly dinners have only amounted to a handful of hours, our friendship could be measured in dog years, seven to one.

"I'll leave her thyroid pills on the counter," Ingrid says, picking up the ring of keys which is beside a marble urn. "My sister," Ingrid says, handing me her keys. The sister who she's told me shares my birthday. "I appreciate this, Jill. I don't have anyone else I can count on."

"I'm glad to help. You've helped me so much. I have my first zodiac date Friday night," I say pausing at the door before I leave. "It's actually the second, counting D.J." I lift one shoulder in a shrug as if I'm taking this in stride.

Ingrid's eyelids lift.

"Who is this first man that you've chosen?"

"His name is Aaron, he's a Cancer."

Ingrid nods. "I'm not the least surprised. Your Ascendant is in the sign of Cancer."

I'm bewildered and it must show.

"The Ascendant is based on your time of birth. It indicates our physical appearance and personality. It's how we are first perceived by the world, regardless of what sun sign we are."

"So what does that mean as far as Aaron?"

"Well, it has a lot to do with the astrological laws of attraction. We'll talk when I get back from my trip." I lean in to hug Ingrid and her breath hums lovingly as she holds me tight. When our arms drop, she stares at me with a sad smile. "I'll miss you, Jill."

"I'll miss you too," I say.

At home, I pack up clothes I've picked out for my date after work on Friday. I fold linen slacks and a lace blouse in my tote bag and set it by the back door so I won't forget to take it to work with me in the morning. I also stuff a pair of dress shoes and my Victorian choker. The antique jewelry and feminine blouse should make a good impression with a Cancer man, because if he's true to Cancer's profile, he'll have a fondness for history and tradition. *He might be sensitive and romantic, too.* I'll save the crazy print blouse and primary colors for a Gemini!

Ingrid has taken astrology beyond my understanding of weekly horoscopes. I can't help but believe that if the moon pulls oceans from high to low tide, if it orchestrates the ebb and flow of menstrual cycles, it just might help me find love.

~ *14* ~

Appointments are scheduled back to back on Friday afternoon. "I need to be out no later than six o'clock for my date, Jeannie." I toss the last chart on her desk.

Jeannie glances at the wall clock. "It's already 5:30." She looks me over and scrunches her nose at my stained scrub shirt and baggy scrub pants.

"I brought a change of clothes," I say. "I need to stop at Ingrid's to give Olga her medication. I can freshen up and change while I'm there."

"Is this the A-guy?"

I chuckle. "Yes, Aaron. If the zodiac plan doesn't work, I'll date one man from each letter of the alphabet. But don't expect the next to be named Bob!" I lower my voice in case Dr. Bob happens to be nearby.

When I ease myself away from the last client, Bob is in fact standing nearby.

"Are you finished with appointments?" He's opening a cream envelope with a scrolled letterhead, an inch of names that spells out the law firm he uses.

He looks up when I don't answer. "You didn't forget?"

My utterance comes out like warped music, because *I don't want to meet the landlord*, is stuck to the tip of my tongue. "I'm so sorry, Bob. I forgot." The air-conditioning is blasting, but I have to pull my shirt away from my sweaty chest. "I have a date."

"Oh, great. Have a good time. I'm tired today anyway. Let's try next week."

"Okay," I chirp. Next week sounds far enough away.

It's 6:10PM and I still need to treat Olga, change, and drive to the restaurant to meet Aaron. I peel off my lab coat and rush toward the back exit.

"I'll put the chart back on your desk, Jill." Jeannie sticks her head out the door and catches me sprinting away. "Have a good time."

I wave back while checking my cell phone for messages mid-stride. Maybe I should have texted Aaron to confirm, but we didn't exchange phone numbers. In these days of Smartphones had either of us used our brain when making these plans?

Once I park in Ingrid's driveway, I walk toward the front door with my tote over my shoulder and one hand feeling for Ingrid's keys. There has to be seven keys jingling on her key ring. Head down, I flip through them to a silver key. It fits, but doesn't turn the lock. After three more tries, a shove of shoulder finally opens the door.

Thyroid medication is on the counter next to the cat food. I set down my bag with a quiet thud. "Olga?" I search the usual cat hiding places, alongside the dining room buffet, underneath the couch, the bed, the basement. The house is huge. Olga could be hiding anywhere.

I open the can of cat food, clanging the cat bowl and rustling the dry food, but when the wall clock chimes, I throw my hands up and grab my clothes.

Olga scoots out of the master bedroom and down the stairs when she hears me coming. It's too late to catch her. In the bathroom I sponge a warm washrag across my arms and slip into fresh clothes. After closing all the bedroom doors behind me, I lock the front door. Olga shouldn't expect my return after my date.

I inch past a row of mid-size vehicles and SUVs looking for a space in the parking lot at the café. There's a black Hummer taking up two spaces— *I hope that's not my date.* Same goes for the Porsche—that one reminds me of the guy who pulled up in his sleek Boxster convertible, then filed bankruptcy right after he sold Dr. Bob a new software program.

Aaron is sitting in a chair reading the newspaper when I step inside the wainscot-paneled walls of the establishment. At least I'm pretty sure it's him. As Jeannie would say, he's easy on the eyes, but— *I can't help this—* I'm relieved that he's not as glamorous as his photo. *No waitress flirting with Aaron like they used to do when I was with Tim.*

Aaron gets up when he sees me and tucks the New York Times under his elbow. He's wearing dress pants, and his chest looks sturdy from the fit of his oxford blue shirt. An uneven bang shines with natural highlights from overhead lights, and my body makes an elevator stop when I look up into those summery blue eyes.

"Aaron? Hi, I hope you weren't waiting long."

"Hi Jill." He shakes my hand, but it's more like a hold. He's staring at my face as if I'm someone he recognizes, or pleased I look like my profile photos. "We should grab a table. This place can get busy."

My own anxiety downshifts the second he speaks. The slushy hint of a lisp reminds me of a boy in grade school who'd gotten picked on for the way he talked. Maybe that's why he was in a rush to meet before we spoke on the phone?

The hostess leads us into a dining room with bold colorful Art Deco paintings on white walls. The backs of my knees become silky with sweat knowing Aaron is right behind me. She seats us at a small marble table with a view of the neon marquis and the college theater across the street. The place is quaint, yet trendy—does this tell me something about my date?

"I've never been here, but the food smells great," I say.

"I eat here a lot," he says. "I've eaten at practically every restaurant in town, but this is one of my favorites."

Funny. Ingrid told Cancers have a close relationship with food.

"What's so funny," he asks, gently.

I feel myself blush that my emotions are so transparent. I adjust my seat and choose my words carefully. "My friend told me Cancer people have a fondness for food. Not that you look it." I clear my throat and try not to blush again. "So your profile mentions you sell homes?"

He reaches into his pocket and pulls out a business card: Hometown Realtors.

"Owwwh," I say, as if this is the most interesting profession I've ever heard of. I practically grit my teeth after my last experience with a realtor.

"I also deal in antiques," Aaron adds, "small stuff like paintings, home artifacts."

Sentimental about family and history, too, I'll bet, according to Ingrid. *Hang on to the past* is how she put it.

"What can I get you to drink?" our waitress asks.

"Do you want to order, Jill? I'm starving."

"Go ahead, Aaron," I say scanning the Special Entrees list on the table.

"I'll have the Champagne Chicken Pasta, and a glass of pinot, please," he says.

"And did you decide or would you like some time?" the waitress asks me.

"I'll have the House Salad with grilled shrimp and a diet cola. Thank you." I twist in my seat. *Damn Heidi Klum—still runway model thin after five kids.*

The busboy leans over the table to set a tray of flatbread and olives on the table.

"Have you been to the college theater?" I ask, pointing across the street. "They recently restored it. You don't see theaters with charm like that anymore."

Aaron rocks his body forward and his voice lifts in a boyish way that reminds me of being in puppy love. "Yes, I've been there. It's classic. Have you seen any 3-D movies?"

"Avatar. Twice. The scenery was beautiful. It's amazing what they can do with computer graphics."

The busboy refills my water glass and absentmindedly leaves another tray of bread.

"You were the only woman who commented on my poem," he says as if he's dying to recite it. "I guess you like Shakespeare, too?"

"Oh, no. Uhmmm, most of my college classes were in the sciences, so I didn't have time to read literature besides what was required freshman year." *Did I answer his question?* I start to reorganize the table.

"Tell me one of your favorite plays." I say.

"Well, my favorite quote is, '*Love looks not with the eyes, but with the mind.*'"

I fold my hands in my lap. He's blushing madly. "That's beautiful."

"Maybe you'd like to go to *Shakespeare in the Park* with me some Saturday night? They perform every weekend in August."

"Okay," I say wobbling my head because yes, I'd like to go with him, but no, I still don't like Shakespeare.

Aaron gives me what sounds like a quickie literature class. I'm bored with the conversation, but not with his looks—was this a shallow trade off?

I hope he doesn't ask me to share book titles I've read. Before out next date I'll get a list from Suzanne—her book club is better than admitting my last read was "The Horse Whisperer," and that was only because I loved the movie.

"Can I get you anything else," the waitress asks, jockeying dishes after she brings our meals.

"I think we're all set for now," he says, shooting a look my way to check in.

"How's your salad?" he asks.

With my mouth full, I give a universal approval sign.

"Good choice," he says, then a soft smile.

He shovels chicken onto his fork like he's mining for money. I still have three out of five shrimp left by the time he finishes his meal so I ask the waitress to wrap the rest.

She returns with my leftover box and brings two cappuccinos, a Tartufo, and two spoons.

Aaron slides it toward me.

What would Heidi Klum do?

I take the first bite. Food-sharing makes the date appear intimate, but I'm having an out-of-body experience— hovering over the table watching two strangers act like a couple.

"Our table is as crowded as the clearance table at the dollar store," Aaron says jockeying the china like chess pieces to chip away at the Tartufo.

"Oh, so you shop there too?"

"Great prices on cleaning products."

Domestic isn't he? Tim wouldn't have had a clue, unless the cleaning products were for vehicles.

"Hey, Aaron, what do you know about mortgages?"

I reach blindly for my cappuccino, which is in the delicate pedestal glass. My hand bumps the overfilled rim instead of the stem. *Mom didn't send me to dancing school as a kid because I poised. She sent me because I was clumsy.* My fingers retract from the hot coffee like a kitten taunting a mouse. Then foam splashes over the lip, and as the glass teeters, my hands play table tennis with the slimy mug. I lose. It makes a crash landing on my lap.

"I'm so sorry," I shriek, gripping my shrink-wrapped thighs.

Aaron hops to my side of the table and starts blotting my lap with his napkin. More than my leg is tingling.

"Please don't be embarrassed. I took a woman camping and she accidentally set the tent on fire. That was the woman I ended up wanting to marry."

I look up. Across the street, the movie must have ended because a crowd is gathered at the entrance. I feel as if I've walked out after a happy ending after watching a tense flick. Aaron is on the shy side, but there is chemistry brewing, unlike the accelerated reaction I had with D.J.

"I forgot to mention," I say after my legs, and composure, cool down. "I love that picture of your cat."

"I bought her for my ex-fiancé on our first Valentine's Day together. She always wanted a Persian. I kept Goldie because she couldn't take her when she moved." He shrugs and his face softens. "She still stops over to see her once in awhile. We're on friendly terms."

Friendly terms? How friendly? *Hang on to the past?* Was it crazy to think I felt a connection minutes ago? I can't imagine being "friends" with Tim. But why am I thinking of this on a first date?

Aaron pays the check and we walk outside together.

"How's your leg, Jill?"

"It feels like a Popsicle, but it'll be fine." *Nice that he's asked.* "I'll email you about the play next week." I decide not to give him my phone number—things might get confusing, dating more than one man at a time. I hit the clicker to unlock my car door.

Aaron takes his hands out of his pockets. I stand back for him to open the car door for me, but after my experience with D.J. I'm ready. I free my arms, I angle my body toward his. I tilt my chin thinking he's gonna kiss me. But my cheek ends up smooshed to his chest like a stuffed animal. *Love looks not with the eyes, but with the mind.* Oh, brother, I hope he can't read my mind, or see my face which must be maroon.

His hand slides down my back and to my car door handle. He leans down to my eye level after I get in.

"I'll be in touch," he says.

Did I say something back? I can't remember because 1000 volts of embarrassment short-circuited my brain.

I glance in my side view mirror to see if he heads toward the Hummer, but he stops beside a Volkswagen that looks as old as my car. *Okay, so his taste in literature is a bit high-brow. His taste in cars is just my type.*

By the time I creep inside and find Olga sleeping on Ingrid's couch, it's ten o'clock. She's an angel when I give her the thyroid pill and if I didn't understand cats as well as I do, I'd be totally perplexed by this behavior.

Before I leave, I add fresh food to her dish in the kitchen and set Ingrid's mail on the dining room table. On my way home, I stop at the grocery store. The date has energized me and I take longer than needed to pick out a picnic assortment of cheese, olives, tofu, Mexican dip— stuff that Aaron mentioned he likes for when we go to the concert in the park.

At home in my office, I blow out the scented candle I've lit. A wisp of beach walk fills my head with a memory of the night D.J. brought me that candle. By the end of the date, I knew he wasn't for me. With Aaron, there's something to look forward to— like the kiss that I sidelined.

My cats are lying in folds of comforter. I slip myself into the puddle of blankets and set my alarm for half an hour earlier than I normally do— a little extra time before work to swing by Amberfield.

~ 15 ~

Palo Alto, California

Dizzy greeted James with a snorty slobber when he picked her up at the vet hospital.

The surgeon handed a jar to James. In it was a smooth stone the size of a pigeon's egg. "She'll be more comfortable without this rock in her bladder."

"Thanks, Doc. I'll bring her back next week to have her sutures out." James slid his credit card toward the receptionist without reviewing the bill. He checked his watch. That last appointment with the department chief couldn't be cancelled. No time to bring Dizzy home, but she was no stranger to the university.

He walked slowly letting Dizzy sniff the crunchy gold lawn along the sidewalk outside his office building. It was a dry August. Like the song says, "it never rains in California." James took the alternate route inside the building, the one he avoided the past six months. Amy's name plate had been replaced by a new faculty member.

His gut clenched. If he had to do it over again, he would have ended things sooner between them.

He admired Amy, respected her. She accused him of stalling on marriage plans. Maybe he was. Ingrid had warned him five years ago, but he didn't want to face it. In the end, Amy's competitive edge wasn't a quality he could live with. Her new position at NYU was proof, Amy's career came first.

Ingrid had been right about her all along.

Well, it was a new year. Time to move forward. And yet, a weird premonition because of his uncle's phone call was pulling him back in time.

~ *16* ~

My body shakes after passing the dump truck hauling away chunks of blackened debris. I turn my car onto Meadowbrook Road.

The guy in the pay loader cuts off the atomic grinding sound and swings his body off the side of the hulking metal machine when I pull up to the house and walk toward where the barn used to be. At least part of the barn is still standing. As the pay-loader man struts closer, I take in eyefuls of damage as if I'm looking at the end of the world.

"Hey, you can't go over there, miss," he yells waving his thick arms like he's an umpire signaling a foul ball. There's caution tape across the driveway and I've crossed it.

"I'm sorry. I know I'm not supposed to be here," I say sweet and friendly. "I'm Jill Christie," I say, extending my right hand. His is sweaty and smudged with soot. "My friend and I played in that barn as kids. This was her family's home. I was hoping to retrieve an old keepsake."

"Hold on. I've got just the thing." He walks over to a pile of wide oak boards I recognize as part of the barn. Then he picks up a horse shoe and for a second, my eyes can't budge from the sight of it. It's small. The size a pony would wear. Maybe he'd lost it when he reared as they loaded the horses onto a trailer. That was the day Petal's mom had rested her pale forehead against mine. I was hysterical. "It'll be better this way, Jill. They're going to a good home. Someone to love them again."

My eyes are blurry, triggering a stutter from the demolition man.

"You can have it," he says, brushing dirt off the metal with the side of his fist. He holds it out to me like he'd do anything not to see me break down. "I was going to bring it home to my wife. She likes antiques and horses, too."

I take the horseshoe with both hands.

"This might sound silly, but my friend and I hid something in this barn years ago."

No, I hid it, after Petal died. I didn't want her father to find it after he told Petal's mom she'd "better get rid of it." I didn't want him to blame her for Petal. And I didn't want him to blame me, even though, *I did.*

He shrugs like it doesn't sound silly at all, even though he doesn't know what I'm about to say.

"We put it in the trap door of the floor. Do you think I could see if it's still there?"

"Oh, you can't get to the door. It's too dangerous. What kind of trinket did you hide?"

"It's not a trinket." I dig out one of Mount Pleasant Veterinary Clinic business cards as I explain to convince him that I'm not crazy when I tell him I'm looking for an old Ouija board.

"Sure, I know Dr. Bob," he says. "Nice man. Well, I can't promise anything, but I'll call you if I find that Widja board. My name's Joe."

"It has the word Ouija on the front of the box."

The pay loader thunders as I drive away. Why would this guy waste his time unless he's just nice enough to do it, or too afraid not to?

Jeannie is on the phone when I scoot past her reception desk Saturday morning. As soon as she sees me, she snaps the button to put the client on hold. "Just want to let you know Pam's here," Jeannie whispers with a dark grin. She thumbs in the direction of Bob's office.

How did I not notice Pam's Austen Healey convertible parked in the driveway? A client once mistook it for my car. I'd laughed. *My car?* I'd been raised in a family of practical car mechanics.

Bob's wife still treats me as if I am the kennel girl instead of her husband's associate. I hear that she hates that Bob's selling the business. I can imagine how she feels that he's holding the mortgage for me. It just might have something to do with the fact that Pam is about my age. And if that weren't bad enough, we attended the same high school before Pam transferred to a private school. I remember Pam before she had blonde highlights and contact lenses.

Poor Jeannie. She'd rearranged the office again last week. It's tidy and homey like Jeannie, but not what Pam had in mind when she and Bob remodeled a few years ago. Ultra glass block front desk. Cool pewter colored walls. If Bob had his way, the reception area would still have wooden park benches for seating and a Norman Rockwell painting (of a veterinary office, no less). I imagine Pam's face when she walked in today, a long hard look at Jeannie's décor before her curt greeting.

Admittedly, the modular design of our exam rooms, styled after some Seattle-based clinic, is quite an improvement. Each room has a dog or cat theme with a contemporary acrylic painting made by a local artist, a client who had to truly love animals to paint them with such realistic expressions. Jeannie insisted that "the white tile floor needed something to soften it up." It took little convincing that the dog clients would pee on the rugs and they'd need to be laundered each week. The thought of having to order extra laundry detergent was enough for Jeannie to decide that white tile floors were fine as long as she had great curtains.

"Hi, Pam," I call into Bob's room without breaking my stride back to my office.

"Jill?" I am almost out of ear-shot when I hear Bob call. *Damn!* I back track and tip my head inside the door to Bob's office. It looks like an upscale cigar lounge— carpeted floor, leather chairs and four grouped prints of hunting breed dogs. Bob is sitting behind his desk. Pam has one cheek up on the edge of it with her back to the door.

"Oh, hi, Pam."

"Hello." I know that her sniff isn't allergies like she pretends whenever she stops by the clinic, which is only after her hair appointment to get more highlights at the salon in town. Her Bichon is sitting on her lap. At least Pitou wags his tail at me.

"Pam and I were just talking about the building, Jill. The lease is up soon and it'll probably go up for sale in the next month or so if I don't give the landlord an answer." Pam swivels her body to face me leaning against the door frame.

Right, I think. This part isn't my business, and I don't want it to be. I shift my weight to my other hip and brush a bang out of my eyes. "Oh, already?" I hardly hear his comment because my busy mind has backed out of the conversation. "Hmmm. I need to check on the Cohen cat, Bob. I'll be right back."

I have no such intention. Talking about this with Bob will be hard enough without Pam figuring ways to sweeten the deal at her end. Especially today, I'm in no mood for Pam's phony persuasion.

As if the day can't get any worse, the second I enter the exam room, I choke on my cheery hello. The client who wanted to fix me up with her brother is standing before me. I hardly remember if I called him back. A stiff-lipped greeting tells me, *probably not.*

I hold out my hand and her Abyssinian cat approaches with suspicious sniffing. *Wonder if she put the cat up to it.* He licks my hands until they feel numb as my face. The owner opens her luggage-sized purse with her lacquered nails and takes out a list of kitty's latest neurotic behaviors.

The cat pokes his narrow snout in my lab coat pocket and steals a cat treat. *We're instant friends now.* Animals are so easy. *I should have brought in one of Jeannie's oatmeal cookies for the client.*

"I don't know if your brother mentioned that I called him back," I say as I grab my stethoscope from the shelf. "We haven't connected yet."

Thank God she mentions his name because I'd forgotten it.

"Oh. I thought maybe you didn't want to meet him. He said you left a message that you were busy." My nerves start effervescing.

The stethoscope is hanging from my ears. I hold up one finger so she'll shut up as I count the thump-thump of her cat's heart. I count a full minute instead of the usual fifteen seconds. By now the cat is doing the Cha Cha to wriggle out of my grip.

"Well, I'll tell him to call you again." *Thump. Thump.* My heart this time. "I'd love to have you come over our house, Dr. Christie. Do you like to play cards?"

Cards? No!

"A little." *I hate how my lip quivers when I fake-smile.* For the rest of the exam visit, my forehead feels like it's pressed into a vice. As soon as she leaves I reorganize the exam room, then I go back to my office and start there, contents of my purse, bookshelf, crumbs on my office carpet! Everything lately was out of my hands.

I do a quick check of my email. No message from Aaron, but there's several new ones.

I take the horseshoe out and lean it on the shelf against my textbooks. It hasn't brought very good luck to Amberfield, but despite being too Catholic to be superstitious, I'm too much of a Pisces not to believe in a little magic.

"Are we done for the day?" I call to Jeannie at the front reception desk after the last client has left.

"The phones are on service and I'm leaving. What a day. I didn't get to hear about your date. Promise you'll tell me Monday."

I promise, then I turn to go look for Bob now that Pam is gone.

I like this time of day when the rest of the staff has gone home, except for me and Bob.

Usually I don't need an excuse to stop by his office to talk. Today I need to force myself. If I don't, I might as well still be that kennel girl instead of his associate veterinarian.

I walk by Bob's office and peek in the door, but he isn't there. I continue to the back of the building where the stock room is located. It's more or less a huge closet, no windows with floor to ceiling shelves. I'd often catch Bob in there taking inventory, or hiding from the world.

I know how he feels the minute I see Bob's face, because I feel it, too. *Trapped.*

"I knew I'd find you here," I say with a weak smile. His eyes look tired and he looks pale. "Do you need any help?"

His cheerful persona dissolves with a heavy sigh. He's held it in until the last client walked out of the exam room.

"I don't know, Jill." His dull tone of voice sucks me into his dark mood. "There's never enough time for my family. There's never enough money if I don't work. And veterinary medicine gets more complicated every year. Not only the medicine, but running the business, keeping up with the latest equipment, new drugs. Expenses have gone up considerably and clients don't understand when I have to raise prices. Everyone thinks an animal vet should give their service away for free."

The knot of Bob's tie is pulled away from his neck and his shirt is unbuttoned to the ridge of collar bone. Times when Tim had looked like this after work, all I'd have to do was slip my arms through his and squiggle into his chest for a hug. *I can't do that for Bob.* It isn't shyness holding me back as much as the thought of how I'd feel if Bob did hug me back. *I'm not the kid he hired years ago.*

Yesterday when Pam called, I'd heard part of their phone call. There was no graceful way to be out of range of Bob's voice. It didn't take much imagination to figure out Pam's side of the conversation.

"Pam, Pam, I'm still at the office, Sweetheart. Can't *you* call the mechanic? Yes, Jill's still here, but she's trying to finish up, too. I can't leave now. It'll be at least another hour before I'm done checking animals and returning calls."

As we stand in the stock room now, the office phone starts to ring. Once, twice, three times. Bob shakes his head and rips his tie off of his neck. "Didn't Jeannie sign out to the emergency hospital when she left?" *Not one more thing to do* is raging in his voice. Jeannie usually never forgets.

I push away from the shelf I've been leaning against into a brisk walk toward the closest phone down the hall. I pick up before the fifth ring.

"Mount Pleasant Animal—"

"This is Pam. Is Bob there?" My mouth freezes open. Does Pam actually think she can pretend I'm one of the summer students? She saw me less than four hours ago.

"Hold on. I'll see if I can find him." I push the hold button and slam the receiver because the last thing I want Pam to know is that Bob and I are standing alone in a storage closet. Pam would never believe it is innocent, and Bob would be the one to suffer. If only Pam knew the sinful thoughts that have crossed my mind about her for the way she treats Bob.

"It's Pam, Bob." He slams the stock room door. As Bob slips by me, a whiff of sweat and spent aftershave passes like a humid tropical breeze. I'm glad he's too preoccupied to notice the effect it has on me. It isn't the first time I've fantasized about how nice it would be if I were married to another veterinarian. *To him.* We could leave work together each night, understanding how hard it is to tell that owner that her six-month old lab puppy has hip dysplasia, or that the family cat needs bladder surgery that will cost $1000. If Pam didn't make Bob so miserable, I would feel guilty. But I don't.

I sneak away while he's still on the phone. When I pass the resident pet room, the rustling sound of earnest whimpering connects my ears to my heart. I stop and open the door. A poodle that the staff named George Burns greets me with shiny eyes. I run a slow hand across his back, the hairless section of hide feels smooth as rubber where the dog had been scalded and left for dead. How could anyone do this?

Owning a pet should be like marriage, until death do you part.

Was it foolish to believe relationships like that exist? Lately, I'm not sure. And if there is ever more doubt about buying the business, it's now. I slip out the back door before Bob leaves and head over to Ingrid's to treat Olga on my way home. My nerves are jacked up. I need to know what's going on with Amberfield.

I could use one of Ingrid's talks. She should be home soon.

Later that night, the phone is crooked in my ear as I clean dishes— actually they're take-out containers for the recycle bin.

"I expected him to be taller." I tell Logan, referring to Aaron. "His profile said six feet tall. But I guess even Tim didn't appear to be 6'3" when I wore three-inch heels." I pinch my waist while I'm talking to Logan. My old trick of wearing a higher heel to appear thinner won't work forever if I don't get back to the gym. Logan doesn't hesitate to mention this during our conversation.

"He asked if I'd like to go see a Shakespearian play some weekend. There's only two more during the month of August. I never had time to read literature in vet school. I hope he doesn't think I'm illiterate."

"He wouldn't have asked you out again it he thought that, Jill."

I tell Logan about the *friendly terms* with his ex-fiancé.

"He said they were on friendly terms?" Logan repeats my words like a first grade reading teacher, as if anyone on friendly terms with their ex is having sex with their ex. "Have you set up any other dates yet?"

"I thought I'd see if I hear from Aaron. I bought a few picnic items for the concert."

"Jill, you've only gone on one date with him and you're already monogamous? You should be dating a bunch of guys. Just meet them and find out their sign later." I didn't need Skype to picture Logan pouting into the phone.

"I'm committed to finishing this zodiac plan," I say. "But I can't help thinking it would be great if I met someone and didn't have to."

After I end my call with Logan, I open my computer and find an email from Aaron.

Hi Jill. I had a good time. We'll do it again soon. Cheers, Aaron

Soon? I thought he meant next weekend.

I email back three men but politely refuse to meet them because two have used automated responses and one is from *KingOfHearts45* who looks older than Jeannie.

I have a young and gentle heart and know how to treat a lady like a princess. Please say you'll meet me. Prince Edward

Is he serious? Prince Edward? Though charmed by his noble words, there is over two decades between us! In his profile, he says he's a retired professor who volunteers at a clinic to help troubled teens.

Dear Prince Edward,

(I can't believe I'm writing this) *the world would be a wonderful place if everyone devoted their time as you have. Good luck. Jill*

I'm reading other profiles when he immediately responds.

Princess Jill, your kind words meant a lot. Prince Edward

Princess Jill! Well, would there be any harm to meet him for coffee? I scan his profile. Of course! He's a Leo.

I call Logan the next day with my dating update.

"I'm considering meeting him for fun, strictly platonic."

"He's a creep," Logan says. "Don't waste your time, Jill. He needs to find a woman his own age."

The next day Prince Edward sends me another message.

Dear Princess,

I am enamored by your photos and your profile. We match on several chemistry categories. I would love to meet you. Prince Edward

Several chemistry categories? Logan's right. *Chemistry* doesn't sound like he's interested in a platonic relationship.

HeartDoc50 has sneaked past my 20-mile distance limit, as well as my age limit. Even if he's in the great shape he claims, I can't imagine him at a Coldplay concert.

"There are people from all walks of life," I tell Jeannie. "It's kind of like that children's rhyme— doctors, lawyers, princes and beggars! It's getting ridiculous. Some of these guys are out of state. But the biggest turn off is erotica. I can't believe how many men check it as one of their Turn-Ons."

Jeannie may love reading sleazy tabloids, but only because it happens in Hollywood. "You're looking for a soul mate, not a bed mate. That's horrible."

"Maybe I'll give some of these guys a piece of my mind." *It's so easy to be bold when I'm anonymous.*

Later, I email a guy named *VisionQuestor.*

Sorry but I don't date men who check Erotica. I'm interested in a serious relationship. Jill

When I open the refrigerator to get some iced tea, I rearrange the items I've bought for the picnic date with Aaron. In high school I'd skipped out of the class discussions of Shakespeare and passed by reading Cliff Notes. I'll probably feel like an idiot next to Aaron. All I remember about Shakespeare is Romeo and Juliet, and that they both end up DEAD in the end— because of LOVE.

I Google Shakespeare. Most of it looks really depressing. So is the realization that my date with Aaron isn't happening this weekend.

Setting my drink on the desk beside my computer, I shift my mouse to the search bar. I notice Aaron's photo, with a message: **Online Now!** But what does that prove? I'm **Online Now!** too. I feel my body shrink back to my teenage self.

The next morning, I toss the rest of my tea down the sink. There are a few emails sitting in my Inbox. I choke when I see one from *VisionQuestor.*

My Dear Jill, many works of art might be considered erotic. It would be my greatest pleasure to show you if you'd visit me in New York. Your Admirer, Alejandro.

I write back a polite refusal, then he writes again. His inspirational words humble me. *Lesson learned.* Next time I won't treat a guy who's checked Erotica like he's a sex-offender!

At the office, I pull up a photo of Alejandro to show Jeannie and paraphrase Alejandro's elegant email to relay his story.

"He lost his brother to the violence of the streets, then convinced two gangs who were enemies to turn their lives around. He signed off as *Your Almost Soul Mate, Alejandro.*"

"Maybe you should take a trip to New York," Jeannie says. "What sign is he?"

"He doesn't list it, but he lives 100 miles away. I don't know how these men are slipping past the limits I've set. I'm getting over twenty a day."

"I don't believe you're writing personal messages back to everyone," Marlene says when she overhears me. "I never did that."

"Maybe people should."

I can't help but feel as if I am waving hello to one that has touched me deeply in another time and place, Alejandro writes back that night. Another time and place— yes I understand that, because even before the night Ingrid fell into her trance and confirmed a previous connection to Tim, I'd *felt* it.

Being "overly sensitive" as Mom calls it. Mom makes it sound like a disease.

~ 17 ~

Palo Alto, California

James had brought Dizzy to work with him again. He had that meeting at 6PM, and the pet-walker didn't do evenings. He ran his fingers through his hair. It was thick and wavy— no time for a trim lately either. He stared at the Post-it his assistant had stuck on his desk and leaned back hard in his office chair. The rocking helped him think. Of course he knew the number by heart. He had to call her back. It was just a matter of time.

It wasn't admitting he'd been wrong that bothered him. He wasn't one of those professors with an ego that put him above doing that. It's just that this visit would bring him face to face with his own mortality. He'd already lost one parent. And now this stirred up memories of the aunt that had remained a part of him even though he was a young boy when she'd died. Despite his research in cancer therapy, he never thought Ingrid wouldn't beat hers.

She'd only be on the west coast for one more day she said when he finally called back. Could she see him? Something important she needed to discuss. Property she'd bought. Someone she needed to tell him about.

For the time being, it sounded positive. Long range goals. Her future as bright as the green pastures she described to him as if it were one of the pastoral paintings he recalled hanging above the den fireplace. And then, the next day, at the little bistro named Sprout on University Ave, when Ingrid limped toward him, James faced the shock he feared. His uncle was right. His mother was not well.

~ 18 ~

Ingrid ended up being away for over a week, just as Olga began to warm up to the idea that I was her meal ticket. I show up at Paula and Eddy's Restaurant where she's meeting me for dinner. The brick-oven pizza place is located near the veterinary hospital. The same landlord owns both buildings.

The place smells of charcoal crust and sautéed tomato, but it looks different, and I notice there's no Paula. Eddy's replaced the red-checkered booths with black tablecloths and black café curtains, sci-fi-size photographs of eggplants, tomatoes and cucumbers are hung on stucco walls, smooth as the fresh mozzarella. There are new copper awnings and copper pots of pink geraniums. The sign on the awning has changed, too. It just says Eddy's Restaurant.

"The rent went up quite a bit since we reopened," Eddy tells me. His thick black hair has receded at his temples and his smile marks don't disappear when he stops smiling. "Paula baled out a few months ago. It's been tough without her. Ten years together is a long time."

Does Bob know that the landlord has raised Eddy's rent? We turn toward the door jingle and Ingrid walks in. I disguise my gasp with a cough at the sight of her frail appearance. Her complexion looks the color of a fading suntan.

"I bought you something," she says, her voice hoarse. After we embrace warmly, she hands me a collage of tissue paper. "It's for burning incense," she says when I unwrap a Cloisonné butterfly. Then she hands me another small box. The unmistakable piercing scent of cedar and eucalyptus gives the contents away. "I know you like incense."

"Thank you so much, Ingrid." Ingrid's silver eyes soften. "How was your trip?" I ask.

She smiles and inhales as if every muscle of her body is embracing the memory of wherever she's been. "I should have made this trip years ago."

"What are you ladies going to have?" Eddy yells from behind the counter. When Ingrid orders a salad, I do the same, since I'm the one who needs to lose weight.

"So how is the dating going, Jill?"

"Slow, but it's my own fault." I straighten up in my seat. "I'd written on my profile that I love dancing and horseback riding. Except it's been years since I've taken time for things I say I love."

Ingrid closes her eyes. *She feels it too.* The hair-feathering rocking gait of a horse and rider as they become weightless partners.

"There are other truths, too." I hesitate, "like having a baby." I bite my lip. "One time at Tim's sister's house, he disappeared and I found him sitting cross-leg on the bedroom floor building Legos with his three-year-old nephew. His sister's youngest, a colicky newborn, was propped in the crook of his left arm with her chubby face resting on his shoulder. I watched without him knowing, but I held back from going into the room, panicked that he'd hand me the baby."

Ingrid finishes what I am about to say. "And yet, for Tim, you would have had babies."

"Yes." My gaze drops.

Her hand covers mine. "If I'd had a daughter, I would have wanted her to be like you, Jill."

An overwhelming warmth swells to my eyes, like the time when Tim finished playing his first song in front of an audience, when his eyes searched the crowd and found mine.

"What would you say if I told you I was thinking of buying Amberfield?"

My mouth opens, but hardly a word comes out, and I'm glad, because my first reaction isn't kind. But then there was another alternative and I get the feeling Ingrid had read my mind the minute I realized she loved the place too. *If only I could live there,* I'd thought.

"Do you know you could forfeit property rights and pay less taxes. You would still own it, but the land would be preserved by the town," I say, talking faster than normal.

"You really did your homework, Jill. Of course, if you still wanted to buy it yourself—"

I shake my head. "It's a long shot, Ingrid." *As in my brother, Rob, winning the lottery.*

Two hours later, after Ingrid and I make a pact, Eddy shuts the kitchen lights.

When I get home I'm high on happiness, at least until I read another message from Aaron.

Aaron: *I worked in my vegetable garden this past weekend. Do you like to garden?*

Me: *Sometimes. I'm participating in a charity hike with the local animal shelter. They are always looking for more dog-walkers. Wanna come along?*

He never answers. Not even after the last curtain call for *Shakespeare in the Park.*

The bottle of Chardonnay that I'd bought for the picnic I never had with Aaron is sitting on my counter. I pull out my zodiac list and log onto Connect. As I scroll past the page with Aaron's profile, I notice the red caption: **Online Now!** beneath his photo again.

I twirl around in my office chair, clomp downstairs into my kitchen and swing open the refrigerator door. There is an assortment of gourmet cheese, tofu and black bean dip that I'd bought after our date— things Aaron mentioned that he liked. Things I hate.

I was *Lovely*, Aaron said the night he met me. And I was patient. Look where years of being patient ended up with Tim. I'm mumbling to myself. Package of tofu, *splat* into the garbage. Wilting celery sticks, one of those fluorescent yellow (expensive) peppers— Mom would probably tell me to make soup instead of wasting them, but what would I know—I can't even cook. I jam them with the heel of my hand.

Was Mom on to something with me? Was I too sensitive? No wonder she can't believe in me when she had a brother who committed suicide because he was *too sensitive* to handle the responsibilities of life. I clean off my hand and pull out my astrology list. *Gemini next.*

I know just who to choose. A Gemini man named Steve has continued to keep in touch. He seems witty and his words make a lot of sense. *When I reach out to too many people it gets to be self defeating, because it does not give any one relationship the chance. Often high hopes & expectations do not pan out.*

Steve works in sales and communications and travels frequently. Gemini traits, I've read, friendly people who are curious about everything and who often work with their hands or their mind. Ingrid is a Gemini.

Steve, as you had warned me, high expectations did not pan out. I'd love to meet.

I'm a Christie, not a quitter. And sometimes that's not enough.

~ *19* ~

"Oh, Jill, what's the matter?" Jeannie says when I call the office.

What does Suzanne call it— a mental health day? I clear my throat.

"Just run down. I haven't been sleeping well." It hardly makes sense to call out when this guilt makes me sick.

"You have looked tired the past couple of days. Oh, I have a call that came in for you from the service last night, but he said it was personal. Do you want it now?"

I sit upright and hug an oversized pillow to my chin. "Who is it?"

"Hold on. Let me get it." The other line is singing and so are the muted voices of owners at the reception desk— clients checking in dragging cat carriers, leashes, paws and shoes clacking across the tile floor. A dog barks— it's Barney beagle. Oh, I love that dog. Sixteen years old. He's probably looking for me. *I should go in.*

"Jill?"

"Yes. I'm still here." My fingers contract.

"His name is Joe."

My heart skips. "Joey Cannondale?" I shout, accidentally, recalling the name of the bike racer guy who wouldn't stop sending me mushy messages.

"How did he track me down?"

"I don't know I didn't talk to him. He left his number."

I scramble off the couch to grab a pen and paper. I scribble the number.

"Feel better, Sweetie," Jeannie says.

I press my cool phone case against my forehead like an ice pack for the headache I have now. Then I dial the number.

"Hell-o." The voice doesn't sound like the pictures of Joey the Cannondale guy—his profile photos are of a feather-weight nerd. The noise in the background is mechanical and rough, as is his voice.

"This is Jill Christie. You called the veterinary clinic asking for me?"

"Oh, yeah. I found that Widja board you asked about."

My shoulders sink back to normal position. Joe. The congenial demolition man. I forgot he told me his name that day at Amberfield.

"I can't believe it! Thank you so much, Joe."

"The box isn't in great shape. Looks like the mice got into it, but I didn't open it up." He talks like the spooks have gotten to him.

"I'll be down in an hour, Joe."

I pick up a few donuts and a cup of coffee. Joe looked like a guy that likes donuts.

I turn down Meadowbrook Rd and flex my clammy hands on the steering wheel. I'm a mile from the hospital where I've called in sick, and I haven't seen Amberfield without the barn yet.

Joe is beside the reconstructed stone wall in a mustard-colored backhoe that looks prehistoric. The black and blue cardboard cover I haven't seen since Petal died is leaning against the fence beside a thermos.

My feet freeze in place. Petal's miniature fingers were the last one to touch that box before I'd stuffed it in the barn floor.

I wave to Joe and leave the donuts and coffee. I carry the dusty Ouija board to my car as if it's a miniature casket, place it on my front seat and start my car.

Now I really do feel sick, especially when I pass by the street to the clinic. My lie to Jeannie is water-boarding my conscience. Tomorrow, I'll come clean. She'll understand. I just needed a day. Sitting beside me on my car seat was the closest I'd come to Petal's death in years.

I lock the Ouija board in my trunk when I get home. After all these years I can't shake its stigma, despite the weird peace of having it in my possession.

It's only mid-afternoon but I can't keep my eyes open. I'm in a twilight sleep on the couch when the phone rings. I instinctively grab the phone.

"Hello," I say clearing my sleep voice.

"Jill? What are you doing home? I called the office and Jeannie told me that you were sick." My body goes limp when I hear my mother's voice.

"I'm just a little tired. I've been working too much." I trace a clump of cat hair across the carpet with my toe. It's the same white fluff that I've ignored all week. Another rolled gracefully out of my path yesterday morning.

I can't bear to hear her say it again— "too much for a woman," when she means "too much for you, Jill."

"That big farm, Jill. You could buy a nice little condo for half the price."

Condo! Of all the things she could say, this strikes a nerve.

"I'm not like your brother, Mom," I snap.

I hear her exhale— a sound that I could recognize if I were standing on the other side of the grocery aisle.

"Sorry."

I hear the silverware clang. She's loading the dishwasher.

"I just don't want to see you get tied up and run down. I don't have to tell you, Jill. Depression runs in the family. Why would you want all that responsibility?"

I'm not sure I do, which is why Ingrid has become somewhat of an angel in my life. Her plan means I may not have to.

At work the next day, I blurt out the truth about Aaron to Jeannie and Marlene.

"Oh, Jill, it must be like being a kid in a candy shop for some of these guys. They're probably talking to a lot of girls besides you. I'm sure he liked you. Probably likes a bunch of others, too." She says, her voice low, and sarcastic.

Gemini69 writes back that he'd love to meet me on Sunday. I also add the name of a Pisces man to my zodiac list, and squiggle a black line through Cancer.

"I'll be riding my Harley," Steve says when we talk on the phone. "but don't think of me as a biker dude."

Biker dude? I can't tell if he thinks I'll be disappointed that he won't be sporting a skull bandanna, chains, and a leather jacket.

"You don't have to explain, Steve. My brother's had a motorcycle since high school. My dentist owns a Harley."

"Great. I'll look forward to meeting you on Sunday."

I laugh to myself, remembering that other "biker dude" that I refused to meet. The one who wanted to teach me to drive one. Little did he know, I already knew how.

Common Ground is located five miles from the vet hospital. I plan to swing by the office on the way to my date and pick up the sunglasses I forgot on my desk when I left on Friday. Not that I'm planning to get on Steve's bike. If I get on a bike, I plan to be driving!

Bob will likely be checking on the kennel help, but no worries about heavy talk. He's put things on hold after talking to Eddy about the landlord.

"What are you doing here today? It isn't your weekend is it?" Bob says turning toward my footsteps when I walk into the treatment room before my date. His tan brow ripples. He's the color of tea by this time of year and it makes him look fit and healthy, despite the cough he hasn't been able to shake. "Allergies," he keeps insisting.

"You mean I could have gone golfing this morning?" He's wearing khaki shorts, a navy blue sport shirt and dock shoes without socks.

"I'm on my way to a coffee date." I grab my sunglasses and slide them on top of my head.

"A coffee date? You mean a guy doesn't have to buy a woman dinner anymore?"

"You've been married too long, Bob. You're not in touch with the Internet dating scene."

"Pam would never have let me get off with a coffee date." He's partly talking to himself.

I do one of my snort laughs, then open blind Chrissy's cage.

"No wonder you still go to church, Jill. Those prayers must not be working. I don't understand how some guy hasn't married you yet."

I pet Chrissy's silky fur. I can't look at Bob. That comment makes me want to work for him forever.

"My grandmother used to pray I'll meet a man in church," I say.

"The synagogue maybe." Bob winks. I pretend to ignore him and massage blind Chrissy's chin. "It's a quarter past noon. What time are you meeting this guy?"

I glance at my watch. "I guess I should go." I fluff up Chrissy's cat bed and close the cage door.

"Be careful. Don't get in a car with this guy." His eyes look concerned, fatherly.

"He's driving his motorcycle," I say, before his tenderness is more than I can bear.

A man, whom I figure must be Steve, hops off his Harley when he sees me pull into the coffee shop parking lot. *Did he really think I could miss him?* The bike is painted the colors of a bumble bee, and unfortunately, he's dressed to match it. He tugs off his black helmet and yellow goggles. I'm at least a few hair layers in height taller than he is and that's including his spongy Brainiac curls. *Didn't his profile say he measured six feet tall?*

"I can't believe we're finally meeting," I say, gritting my teeth into a smile.

"It was a good day to take the bike out for a ride. Summer's almost over."

Summer is almost over, even if it doesn't look that way. There are striped umbrellas tipped over each table, white lawn chairs on the flagstone patio, and clay pots of pink impatience. But he's right. Even though I can still wear short sleeves and sandals, September is summer's last leg.

Inside the confectionery, there's a chalkboard behind the counter with a list of coffee concoctions that sound like ice-cream flavors.

"I'll try the Midnight Mocha latte," I say, my mouth watering for the pastry and chunky muffins staring at me from behind the curved glass case.

Steve pays for our coffees and we find seats outside at a sunny picnic table. I prop my feet against the wooden bench, put on my sunglasses, and settle back into the weak sunshine.

"So, you mentioned that you come from a big family, Steve?"

"Five kids, one sister. Wall to wall bunk beds in one room for us boys since my sister had her own room. It wasn't fun. I'm just glad everyone stopped calling me and my brother 'The Twins.'" He grins like the furniture salesman who tried to talk me into buying furniture insurance.

"Do you know Gemini is the sign of the twins?"

He swats at me like he's not the least bit interested in astrology.

"You said you recently started Internet dating, but were trying to only date one person at a time. What happened with that first guy?" Steve leans back and folds his arms with an adolescent smirk lighting up his face.

Before I finish telling him about Aaron, he's jerking his head back and holding his stomach with phony gut-splitting sneers. I pretend to be just as amused.

"Oh you're too sensitive," he says. "So you mean you *only* went on the first Meet with this guy?"

"The first 'Meet'?" He's getting to me. He's a caricature of the insightful guy he sounded like in his emails.

"It's a Meet, not a Date. I've been computer dating on and off for five years. Don't take this dating service too seriously. I've been dating two women for a year and I like both of them for different reasons. Both are smart and educated. One has her life complicated with her kids, and the other has little time for me due to her career." He folds his arms under his puny pectorals.

So he's dating two women simultaneously while hitting on me?

"You're involved with both women?" The tone of my voice is ten degrees cooler than my gushy hello. I'm fuming for two women I don't even know. *This was the nice guy who wrote that he was sincere about meeting someone special?* He'd told me he's "one of the good guys."

"Look. I meet a woman for coffee and things go well. I tell her I'd like to see her again. Then I go home and get an email from a few other women who are interested in meeting me. The temptation for a man is too much. It's like being a kid in a candy shop."

Ahhh, I understand now. *Kid in a candy shop— a child by his own admission!* Hadn't Jeannie used those *exact* words?

I sip my mocha coffee, trying not to burn my lips on the steamy liquid. Steve may have opened my eyes, but he hasn't closed my mind.

"I think some men are truly looking for a soul mate. I know there are guys who want to be in a committed relationship." I think of Alejandro and Prince Edward. Were they as disloyal as he was?

Steve adjusts his black frames from the side of his face with two fingers, like a jeweler positioning his eyepiece to inspect an imperfect gemstone. After weeks of corresponding with him, today we categorized each other in less than fifteen minutes—he into my "Player" category, and me into his "Hopeless Romantic" one.

My coffee is cold now, but I finish the last mouthful then see-saw the cup until the chocolate syrup settles in a crescent shape at the bottom. Someone else might not have bothered, someone else might have thrown the cup away, but I tap the bottom of the cup until I've coaxed out the last drop.

Steve's attention has drifted to the three teens in flip-flops and short-shorts.

"Well, I've got things to do and I don't want to take up any more of your time, Steve. Thanks for the coffee." I'm standing when he turns his attention back to me.

"Oh, okay. Good luck," he says, grabbing his helmet.

I walk away from him casting shadows of doubt that all men are as shallow as Steve. This date with him only fortifies my belief that he's not the right sign.

When Ingrid asks about my date with Steve when we meet again, I choose my words carefully.

"I know you're a Gemini, Ingrid, but it's as if he's a different person from the man I'd corresponded with these past few weeks."

She chuckles gently. "Gemini twins can be known to behave like two different people. But don't regard him as a generalization of the Gemini clan as a whole. Besides, friendship between signs can play out differently than what you might want in a romantic relationship. You still have nine signs left. No man is the wrong choice. Each one will lead you to the right one."

It sounds like a paradox, or a game. A game. When we walk to our cars I open my trunk, push back an old blanket and show Ingrid the Ouija board.

"I know this must sound crazy, but I've been afraid to bring it inside my house." The image of Petal's face in a glow of candle lights my mind, the two of us sitting cross-legged on the floor of her bedroom makes my arms tingle.

"I haven't seen one of those things in years," she says as if mesmerized by the sight. "It would be fun to try it, but we should have the right atmosphere— my great room on a full moon. I'll check my zodiac calendar to see when the moon is in a favorable position." Her voice is beaming and it lifts my spirits.

"What sign would that be?"

"That depends on what questions you intend to ask. If it's about home and family, I'd say Cancer, for work probably Aries since that sign is on your Midheaven, your career house."

"And for love? Should we plan for when the moon is in Leo?"

"Yes, Leo will never steer you wrong."

~ 20 ~

I turn my face away from the pillow, rubbing the tickle of whiskers with my wrist. "Okay, I'm getting up," I say, swinging both feet to the floor. Eight paws race me down the stairs to the kitchen. Not difficult for them with a four-legged advantage, but just the same, I've been dragging my feet long enough.

I spoon cat fresh cat food into two crystal bowls, then head to my computer.

I reread the first message Aaron had sent me. *Your natural beauty is lovely and your profile is interesting and thoughtful.* It isn't difficult to know why I hadn't deleted his message. Aaron had made me feel *Lovely.* But now it makes me feel *Lousy.* His tender concern over my scalded leg and invitation to a second date led me to believe he was sincere. Guess he's a kid in a candy shop too.

I zero the cursor over the DELETE button and *Click.* I check the tiny boxes next to the rest of my emails and they disappear into my trash bin like falling leaves.

The drone of my neighbor's lawn mower distracts me. It may be for the last time this season because the grass has stopped growing. Time is inching closer to Logan's wedding. Auburn leaves, then barren trees. I'm dreading this winter. *Maybe I didn't have to.*

I click over to flight search engines and type in San Francisco. Oliver. We were outsiders back in high school for different reasons— he was outrageously gay, and I was severely depressed over Petal.

Plus, there was someone else out in California that I had not seen in years.

I bring up a photo of the Pacific Ocean again at work—a white-sanded, horseshoe beach, red cliffs and a wind-bent cypress tree. I feel my body sigh. *I'm going. It's a done deal.*

Suddenly I hear Jeannie grilling the next appointment, because he doesn't have an appointment. "Walk-in appointments are at the hair salon down the block."

I cringe. Bob's asked her to be nice to walk-ins. She says it's hard to remember to do that. Jeannie will never change.

When I step inside the exam room, my attention goes straight to the trembling kitten wrapped in blue fabric on the client's lap.

"So, what do we have?"

The man gathers the soiled shirt and sets the kitten on the exam table. It's the size of a hamster, matted with sticky black fur. I barely noticed the client except that he's wearing hospital scrubs like Dr. Bob wears on surgery days.

"I found it on my way into work. It was cowering on the side of the road," he says. His baritone voice has a rich timbre, the sound of dark jazz. "I couldn't bear to leave it." I look up at him briefly because his words are so thoughtful. A glimpse of sadness darkens his expression.

I examine the kitten's eyes, ears, mouth, then palpate its empty belly and check four feeble limbs. "He's definitely undernourished, but he doesn't appear to have any injuries." I fit the stethoscope into my ears and press the drum to the kitten's chest.

"Your name is Jill, isn't it?" he says as I listen to the kitten's racing heartbeats.

My eyes slant toward him. Clients usually called me Dr. Christie.

"You were nice enough to email me back, even if you didn't want to go out with me." He smiles.

My lab coat feels like it's shrinking against my skin.

"Oh, I, ah—"

"It's okay. Tafari," he says as he offers his hand. "My mother was German. Guess that saying about a man looking for a woman who resembles his mother is true. You're as pretty as your pictures."

I feel heat rise to my face when I study his. That comment explains his great bone structure. Tim had those cheekbones too. But it still doesn't make me feel better that I refused his offer to meet. I'm about as comfortable as he is about picking up a strange kitten.

He stands and I look up at him. The stethoscope is still dangling from my ears. He pulls it away and leans toward me. "Do you think I could stop back for the kitten later? I've got to get to work. They don't cut us first year resident's much slack."

"Oh, of course." I am aware of my excessive blinking, but the rest of my body is numb. I would love to know what I said when I emailed him back. I just deleted all of my old emails.

I straighten my awkward posture from leaning over the kitten. "What specialty of medicine are you in, Tafari?"

"Neurology." He pauses. "I don't have the place to keep this little guy. I won't be around after next week. If you know anyone that might want him—"

I pick up the kitten and tuck him into the crook of my arm.

"Leave him here with me. I think we can get this one a home."

"Thanks. As I said, I don't have much time. I'll be spending my next year in Kazakhstan for a global health project."

I try not to let my blank expression give me away. Kazakhstan—I've heard of the place from Ingrid. It's when she showed me her necklace and she hinted I might go there one day. *Just coincidence.*

He pauses, searching my face, probably for weakness, I'm convinced, but not the neurological kind. "Cup of coffee and conversation once in awhile with someone nice and I'm happy. I noticed on your profile that you were a Pisces like me. I get along well with other Pisces."

"Me, too." I shuffle the kitten into a comfortable position, then struggle with my own comfort zone. *Not every date had to end up as a relationship.*

"Coffee and conversation, then, Tafari. I'd love to hear more about your work."

"Great. Call me later. I get an hour for dinner. You'll make my evening." He hands me a card with his long straight fingers after he writes down a number to reach him.

I don't breathe a word to Jeannie.

On my way home I meet Tafari at the Atrium Café. It's a cafeteria-type eatery located close to the hospital, a cold-looking place— lots of chrome and tall glass windows, dove gray laminate tables and marble floor— but Tafari is anything but cold. He escorts me through the cafe and greets the other staff with a genuine warmth I feel as well.

Tafari picks at his rice and grilled vegetables and tells me that Kazakhstan is bordered by Russia and China. He's involved in a global project to improve medical care in Third World countries. "I have a friend who's been there," I tell him. "I picture it being exotic, spicy, rich teas."

He chuckles. "I'm planning to take time to travel while I'm in Europe," he says. "Definitely Finikas— a beach near the northern tip of the Greek Island—clothing optional." His amber eyes beam in contrast to his ginger skin tone and tight black hair. They look anything but spiritual now.

He tells me he's "more interested in helping people than climbing the medical ladder." Ah, Pisces. Empathetic. I didn't need to read up on this sign. So he's bound to have a few secrets too.

"Can I ask you something, Tafari?"

"Of course. Do you want to join me in Kazakhstan?"

Someone so altruistic wasn't shy about getting his needs met. Why had I let that be so impossible to do with Tim? From the safety of the hospital comfort zone, I flirt back.

"How do you know you've made the right choice leaving everything here to start this project?" I ask in my most soulful voice.

He leans toward me over the table. "I don't know for sure. I just stopped being afraid to try."

My head tilts as if the scales of my subconscious are shifting. Could it be that easy to find the balance?

Then he says, "My mother had her hands full with me as a teenager. My father had left her. I got high one night and ended up in the hospital with seizures. The resident who was on duty changed my life. He cared about me, and it made a difference."

Every pore of my body tingles with the wisdom of his words. He'd cast off his demons like dead snake skin.

No coincidence that the words of another Pisces resonate. "I had someone who made a difference in my life too." I tell him about Dr. Bob.

He glances at his watch. "It's almost nine o'clock. I'd better run back to work, Jill. I'm sorry I have to leave now." He takes my hand in both of his and squeezes like he's not letting me go that easily.

For a moment, panic sets in. What more did he want from me? His hand massages mine, then he presses them prayer-like between his and his warm hands make the room around me melt. With my eyes I tell him I like this. At the same time this playful flirting would make me squirm if he wasn't leaving.

"When you come back you'll have to visit the kitten, or cat, that is," I say when Tafari walks me to my car.

"I'll send you my email. You can send me pictures, and I'll send you some."

"Cool. Photos from Kazakhstan— or wherever," I hesitate, "clothing required!"

Once I'm home, I set the cat carrier with my new kitten down on the kitchen floor. My cats slink by the cage to inspect their new roommate, their pupils dilate and noses press through the bars, their attitudes are out of joint.

Later, I add Tafari's name to my list next to Pisces. It'll be hard to follow-up on a more insightful date. He's made me realize what I'm looking for could be closer than I think.

"I'd like to treat you to a special place for lunch today, Jill," Ingrid says when we meet after I finish Saturday morning appointments. Ingrid flips back a strand of dry hair that perches on her shoulder like a broken wing. Despite her effort to keep up her health with natural products and a little sunshine, Ingrid does not look well.

The Health and Hatha Center is a spiritual retreat located at the crest of a mountain, less than an hour drive from the animal clinic. The Sleeping Monk is an obsolete monastery that was transformed into a yoga center in the 1970s. The building looks austere, a terra cotta brick structure with a healing garden secluded by rows of cone-shaped evergreens. In the center, weathered wooden meditation benches nestle between striped zebra grasses and a koi pond. In the hillsides are the grape landscapes that make the place famous— The Monk's Organic Juice.

We walk down the carpeted halls of the complex and stop at the little natural food store tucked in a corner of the first floor. Ingrid turns toward a shelf of anti-cancer herbs and spices while I browse New Age music discs, artists I've never heard of. She places turmeric, cinnamon, ginger and cayenne into her basket and two bottles of Monk juice, a purple concoction with a rainbow tie-dyed label.

From the store we walk into a spacious eatery painted the color of summer squash with bleached pine tables and chairs. A tasty humidity fills the air with simmering chicken stock seeping from brass caldrons.

"Smells, delicious in here, doesn't it?" Ingrid says.

"Mmmm." I inhale scents of parsley and basil in wooden bushel barrels. It reminds me of the breath of horses.

"The Monk's kitchen is known for their gourmet dishes. On the upper level is a yoga room where they have meditation classes, and healing arts from massage to aroma therapy." I can tell by Ingrid's voice that she's excited we're here together, yet I sense something is off.

New-Age Celtic music slides in hypnotic riffs as we seat ourselves beside the full-length windows. Outside, gardens bordered by snowfalls of baby's breath, are heaped with hostas, lavender spears, black-eyed Susan, papery balloon flower— perennials I'd planted at one time in my own yard. I used to love the mindless hours of watering my gardens. But they've faded away, like other things I've let go.

"So how's everything going?" Ingrid clears her throat with a slug of vitamin water.

"Well, I still don't have clarity if that's what you mean. Some people's lives follow a pattern, like a path they could find if they were sleep-walking. I never used to think that I wasn't one of them. Have you checked your zodiac calendar about a good day to use the Ouija board? I'm getting freaked out about storing it in my trunk, but I can't bear to bring it inside my house. My cats are in that house."

"I'll check my calendar," she says quietly. "Don't get discouraged." Then she looks away. "Let's get some food. There's something I need to tell you."

I'm hoping that includes an update on her plans for Amberfield.

We slide our trays along the rail rods bordered by an elaborate buffet, creative mixtures of ingredients and cultures.

"My sister would love this place," I say, thinking of Suzanne's trendy spice rack and cookware collection.

Ingrid picks at small portions of food when we return to our table. Her complexion looks milky, her lips look pale.

"I was in my forties when I first got cancer, only about ten years older than you are now." I feel faint like when Tim broke up with me. "I probably shouldn't have survived all these years. But it wasn't my time." She glances down at her hands, her fingers fan out across her lap. "The planets are showing me that now it might be."

A ripple of skin tightens at my temples.

"I've had a lot of pain in my legs. I thought it was arthritis. Dr. Bernard's pills have kept me in remission until now, but the oncologist tells me the cancer has spread. I'm leaving for Sweden Tuesday morning for an alternative medical therapy. I've found a little house that I can rent by the month. Adorable little A-frame with window shutters." Ingrid's smile quivers. "I'm not sure how this will go for me, Jill." She stares out at the garden.

I become immune to the taste of my food, deaf to the soothing music. It's one thing to predict love and career, but another if Ingrid can foretell her death. I'm stricken with sadness, and guilt that I've somehow invited this hell by digging up the damn Ouija board.

"By the time you're my age, breast cancer may be obsolete." It's not the least bit consoling that Ingrid's cancer has been a dormant time bomb. Since meeting Ingrid, I've gravitated to her like I had Petal's free-spirited mom. They were the purple Monk juice.

We finish lunch and climb the stairs to the upper level where the yoga classroom is located. Ingrid grips the handrail to lift her body with each step. We remove our shoes and enter the yoga room, shoe-polish white with skylights, starkly furnished with tropical floor plants, and plush royal blue wall-to-wall carpet that spreads into my bare toes. Ingrid lowers her body onto the carpet and shuts her eyes. Her pale green tunic flutters from the soft breeze of the ceiling fan. In the rapture of peace, the wrinkles in her face all but disappear. So does any hope for Amberfield. I came so close.

"Animals have a destiny according to their astrological birth chart, too," she says sitting up after the meditation. "I've had a little more time with Olga because of the treatments, but she's failing. I think it would be kinder to put her to sleep before I leave." Then her voice falters. "I've heard you and Dr. Bob make housecalls." Ingrid stops to give me a little nod. She doesn't need to explain.

The next day, I arrive at Ingrid's house with my medical supplies. Ingrid rests her hand on Olga, now a skeletal version of a feline. The cat blinks slowly, raising her head to meet the touch of Ingrid's hand as I inject pink solution after a mild sedation. Olga's diamond-slit pupils dilate to the size of shiny buttons and her body spreads across Ingrid's lap, limp as a cloud.

"She's taught me more about love than some people have," Ingrid says lowering her face one last time to kiss Olga. "I'll call you once I'm settled in Sweden, Jill."

She watches me wrap Olga's body in a bath towel as if her own arms have become useless appendages. I've done this before, but I feel numb as I hug Ingrid good-bye and carry Olga's body out to the car, but not the trunk. Only then do I cry.

Mass at St Francis' Church starts 9AM on Sunday. I sneak in seven minutes after the hour as the congregation takes their seats. I'm never on time, even for God. When I'd spent nights at Tim's place, I'd leave for church in the morning. Tim never went to mass, but he loved that I went, like his mom, Maggie. After Tim and I first split, I could barely concentrate when I looked into Maggie's face.

"How are you doing Jill?" Maggie asks today, words spoken by dozens of other people meeting in the vestibule. Maggie's nose, mouth and hair, even the way Maggie tips her head to look at me, are all Tim. She tells me with her lingering embrace, with eyes the exact color as Tim, that she had wanted Tim to marry me. I embrace her tightly to let her know I'm okay. I'm past wanting to see regret in her eyes. He's lost me now.

On my way back from church, I stop to read my horoscope, my

illogical combination of religion and superstition, I guess. I've kept one taped to my computer monitor, curled and yellowed like reproduction of The United States Constitution that Dad keeps hanging in his office since his army days.

PISCES: The saguaro cactus of the western deserts takes years to mature. During the day, bees enjoy its nectar and several bird species nest in them. You share many qualities with the unusual saguaro, Pisces, in your willingness to be of service to others. But sometimes you need to stand strong as the cactus.

I want to believe a message like that is timeless. I imagined I would feel so differently with each new man, like some women do a new dress or jewelry. But after meeting D.J., Aaron, Steve and Tafari, I feel more true to myself.

Later I meet Logan for lunch. I'm hoping she'll have info from Greg about Amberfield since the barn fire. Of course she's just interested in my love life.

"Wow, guess that Steve is dating his own zodiac of women," she says. "What did Ingrid say about him?"

"She said not to judge the whole Gemini clan by one person." I don't mention anything else about what Ingrid shared about her life— it's too private, too frightening.

Logan culls slivered onion from her salad greens. "You know, Steve's behavior isn't really all that surprising. You shouldn't expect that any man on this site is only dating you. After the first week goes by, I'd move on." Her brown eyes completely lack my rose-colored vision. "What about some of the others you were corresponding with?"

I take a bite of my sandwich and answer with my mouth full, give her the Reader's Digest version of D.J., Aaron, and Tafari. "It's complicated dating more than one person at a time."

"We're not in high school, Jill. We didn't have to worry about men being married or having ex-wives or children, or financial problems." She stabs into her plate, lettuce, tomatoes, olives, cucumbers, grabbing several vegetables into one forkful. "You're missing the whole point of dating. You should enjoy getting to know lots of different men."

"I have a list," I say, digging out the paper tucked inside my purse.

"So what sign is next?"

"Well, I met that Pisces named, Tafari, but there's another one that contacted me— *Pisces1*. His face keeps popping into my Inbox and what he wrote is," I stop to exhale deeply before continuing, "that he 'respects a woman who knows how to pick her battles, and behind every good man is a good woman.'"

Logan's face turns dreamy.

"Well," Logan says slowly. "he does sound, reeeally promising."

"He said he's not into the bar scene," I add. "And the sexiest part, he said he has 'two strong and gentle hands.'"

Logan sips her pinot and swallows hard. "This guy's good. So why haven't you met yet?"

"He's far. Niantic."

"Have him meet you half way."

"I asked him, but he keeps telling me how much he enjoys my emails, and then makes excuses why he can't get together. He said he works long hours and goes to bed by 8PM. Do you think he's married?"

Logan chokes on her breath as it races past her words. A tear squeezes out the corner of her eye. I'm not sure if she's crying until she bursts out laughing. "Did you say Niantic, and that he can't talk after 8PM?"

I can't imagine what I'm missing.

"The State of Connecticut Correctional Institution is in Niantic. I think this guy's in prison!"

We burst out in giggles until our muscles are so weak we can hardly sit straight in our chairs.

"My luck," I say, unfolding my list of connections to show Logan. "I wrote the user names of guys I'm considering dating next to their astrology signs." My list is circled and highlighted and starred in the order that I've decided to meet them. Four have a black line across their name.

Later, when I'm home, I log on to Connect and reread the profiles of each man on my list, paying close attention to any clues that Logan warned might be "Players, Married, or Losers."

I flirt with a few men knowing I'll never meet them. I think it boosts their ego to think that, if not for the distance, I'd date them. As I read each new profile, I ask myself if we have things in common, or if I would be bending my values like I had with Tim. One by one I search my soul before adding their name to my list, or before simply hitting DELETE.

How easy it is to see now how foolish I was. When Aaron said he was home "cleaning his basement or shopping for a good deal on a used car," I should have known he'd lost interest. I'll never know why, but I guess it's his privilege, as well as mine. It's the beauty of something as impersonal as computer dating. See a face, read their words, hope they were true, or like Mom suggested, "Sounds like he got that line out of a Nicholas Sparks book." Leave it to Mom to know. She's a sucker for romance novels, but she could tell a phony from fiction. A typical Taurus, she needs proof to believe, because as far as she's concerned, real life doesn't always have happy endings like the books she loves to read.

Mom's home when I call later. When I ask about Dad, she says "he's fine." She mentions their constant social agenda and that she misses seeing me. She doesn't usually say that.

I check the airfares to California before prices skyrocket for Thanksgiving. It's not the best time to leave. At least problems with the building have stalled Bob's plans to retire. When I show up the next morning there's a six-foot hole in the front entrance where Jeannie plants annual flowers and a small mountain of dirt. Three men are standing with their heads down watching an old oil tank being excavated from the ground. I'm sure one is the landlord. I look the other way.

I need that trip to California.

When I get inside Jeannie is spitting-nails mad over the mess the oil tank made of her garden, until I tell her I made a date with a new guy named Tom.

"I don't know one man named Tom that isn't handsome," she says in her Betty White voice. "Tom Cruise, Tom Selleck, Tom Hanks, my nephew…"

I pretend to ignore her, but then, I add, "Tom Petty."

"I happen to like Tom Petty," she says.

"Maybe back in the 70s," I add, rolling my eyes at an image of Jeannie in worn-out blue jeans, leather Water Buffalo sandals, and a halter top. "But have you seen Tom Petty lately?" Even Jeannie chuckles.

"This Taurus guy, Tom, has the same birthday in May as my mom. I hope he's not a clotheshorse like she is. Mom's jewelry and purse match every outfit she wears— I'm happy wearing tiny diamond-stud earrings all year round." Jeannie knows my boring attire is because I might be cleaning ear mites or anal glands at any moment.

"My nephew is a Taurus. He's good with money. He's been in finance for years," Jeannie says, giving me the sly eye.

"Good with money? I'd love it if I had a couple hundred thousand on hand to buy Amberfield." My temple throbs.

"What's wrong, Jill?"

Twenty years later, guilt rears up like a fist in my throat. "The day my friend Petal died I told her I forgot my helmet because I was too scared to get on her horse with her. She took off her helmet and tossed it to me, but I still wouldn't get on. Then she galloped off without me. Maybe if I hadn't refused that last ride with her, she would have been more careful."

"Don't think like that," Jeannie says. "Regrets are a waste of time."

I wasn't planning on wasting any more of it.

~ 21 ~

I tell myself that the Leo moon must mean something good as I step inside the Asian-Fusion restaurant. The rooms of the restaurant are dark as a wine cellar, burgundy walls draped in long sheer fabric that shimmers from track lights with iridescent lighting. I pass a romantic couple with intoxicated smiles toasting glasses of red wine and the woman is twirling her hair seductively. *Either they are lovers, or he is her gay hairdresser.* I should know this from my old friend, Oliver. *California.* I can stay with Oliver for the week. Rent a car. Do something I should have done years ago.

A waiter clears a table as I slink by him, his hair shiny from natural scalp oil. I remember that time in my life— pimples and PMS, losing my best friend, Petal, gaining another in Oliver.

My hips sway to the lively Salsa beat as I walk toward the dining area, but when I spot Tom, my momentum becomes less fluid.

"Can you bring an order of ribs, too? Thanks," Tom says to the waiter. "Hi. Are you Jill?" he asks.

I glance at my watch and give myself one hour. He's already consumed the bowl of crunchy noodles, now he takes the words right out of my mouth.

"I know I'm not this big in my photo, but I promise to measure up in personality."

"Okay," I say, sliding my stiff hips onto the stool across from Tom and squashing my smile into my fist.

"I hope you don't mind that I ordered. I wasn't sure you'd show up."

A harmonic sigh hums past my lips. I guess dating isn't easy from either side of the coin.

"Help yourself, Jill," Tom says. Before he grabs another fried dumpling, he unbuttons the top collar button on his shirt. The creases look like he'd just pulled the shirt out of the plastic wrapper.

"Your profile says you're a carpenter, Tom?" I say, though I can't imagine someone his size remodeling my bird-size kitchen.

"Carpenter? Is that what I called it this week?"

I should be annoyed, but I can't help but chuckle— that corny statement is something Dr. Bob would say. Besides, Jeannie would probably think Tom was adorable.

"I'm not very good with sheet rock or wood, but I did help my brother-in-law remodel his kitchen. And I made a tropical garden in my back yard using one of those pond kits." He's fleshing it out—the waterfall, leaves shaped like elephant ears, the lacy ground cover.

"Do you like houseplants, Jill?"

"I'm afraid my cats would eat them. My Mom loves them. She has her den window filled with all sorts of plants. She's kept a ficus tree alive since I was in college." A twinge of pride gushes out of me when I say this as I realize all the little things Mom does to keep her family healthy.

"So if you're not a carpenter, what do you do for work?"

"I'm a security officer at the university." His animated hands are coated in an earthy brown sauce that matches his shirt. I dig a Handi Wipe out of my purse and open it for him.

"Thanks, you remind me of my mother. She's always prepared," he says.

I crack my tomboy knuckles and help myself to a barbecue rib. "So what's your story? Have you been on many dates?"

"Not really. I was dating my girlfriend since college. We lived together for a year, but she wanted to get married."

I stop chewing. "So does that mean you never want to get married?"

He shakes his head. "I wasn't sure that she was the right one."

The *Right One.* I feel my date smile deflate.

I was *so sure* Tim was the right one. Was it different for guys? Was it a matter of timing? Did they only settle down when they were good and ready?

The rest of the date becomes a blur of superficial conversation.

Once I'm home, I toss the dangling earrings I'd worn onto the nightstand and unzip my slacks. I never ironed anymore, but I had tonight. My pants slide down my fresh-shaven legs and with mindless motions I drape them over the hanger and fold my sweater back into my drawer.

Un-hooking my lace bra, I have a moment of frustration at the clasp. Although I knew Tom wouldn't touch so much as a strap of that pretty bra, I couldn't help wanting to feel like when Tim had it off in seconds. Maybe I should act like some guys do. It didn't have to be the right one, only someone to have a good time with.

When I awake the next morning, I pull on a pair of jeans and a long-sleeved shirt, stuff my feet into the suede clogs Mom bought for me during her fall shopping spree. It's an old habit of hers that she hasn't stopped even at my age— the Labor Day back-to-school new shoes purchase.

I clomp downstairs to the kitchen and start to make coffee while looking out the window at my elderly neighbor as he walks to his mailbox in his slippers. He's been wearing the same limp sweat pants since his wife died two weeks ago. It's not like those two always got along. I'd hear their heated conversations blast through summer-screened windows and wonder if some people thought a marriage like that was better than being alone. My neighbor's head is down and his arms hold each other behind his back— he cried at her wake and told me how he adored her.

The new kitten sits waiting with my other two by the food dishes. He already knows the feeding routine like I know he belongs to me.

I scribble a line through Taurus like I have through Gemini, Cancer, Capricorn, and that soulful Pisces named Tafari.

"No one gets it right the first time," Ingrid had told me. "Lessons repeat themselves."

I have to make sure my life wouldn't become a vicious zodiac circle.

"Last patient," Jeannie says handing me a chart the next day at work. "You can go down to the first exam room to see Dr. Christie," Jeannie says to the gray-haired man in a dull wool sport jacket that smells like it came out of a cedar trunk.

"Here's my card. I'm sure we can sell the house for you. I've had good luck with that area," I overhear him say to another client in the reception area.

His dog, Waldo, starts doing 360-degree loops when he sees me.

"You can have one of my cards, too, Doctor, uh, Crisali." He stuffs the rest of his business cards in his pocket.

I give Waldo his much anticipated belly massage and can't help but notice that Waldo smells like his owner. I don't correct my name as I reach for his card. "Hometown Realtors," I say, noticing the familiar logo on the card. *Wasn't that where Aaron said he worked?* My blood pressure tells me not every trace of him has been deleted like his emails.

"I've heard of Hometown Realtors. Do you know a man named Aaron that works there?"

"No, I don't think so." He rubs his brow.

"Oh, unless you mean Scotty?" he says. "His last name is Scott, but his name is really Aaron. No one calls him Aaron at the office." He chuckles. "He was into all that Star Trek stuff. You know, 'Beam me up.'"

I feel giddy—*SCOTTY? A Trekkie?*

"He was my paperboy when he was a kid. I helped him get into real estate." He sounds like a grandfather talking about his grandchild.

Scotty the Trekkie doesn't sound like the sophisticated Aaron Scott that I met. The one with an ex-fiancé who is an English professor, the guy who loves Shakespeare. *And I was worried about being clueless at Shakespeare In The Park?*

I squat down to Waldo to administer the vaccine. "Waldo is all set for today."

"Okay. It was nice seeing you, Doctor, uh…. Well, see you next year."

It's a relief that he'll likely never remember to mention this to Aaron.

A while later, when I check my emails, I think about Aaron again. But now it's as if Shakespeare had spoken another quote meant for me—

"There is nothing either good or bad, but thinking makes it so."

Aaron had never tried to make me feel insecure. That was my issue. For all I know he'd gotten back with his fiancé… I could tell by the way he mentioned her, he still cared for her. I guess sometimes it's okay to go back.

And sometimes, it's not.

I walk back to the treatment area humming that old Led Zeppelin tune, "Going to California," about making a new start.

Bob is sitting at the microscope. I wasn't born yet when that song came out. He raises his head up when he hears the tune, smiles, then focuses the lens of the scope. I lean on the counter beside him as he reads the slide. Funny, I hadn't noticed the white hairs in his sideburns last month. Was that how it happened? One day you wake up and there's a wrinkle, or white hair. Bob backs his face away from the microscope and muffles another cough.

"Hey Bob, I want to remind you about my trip to visit my friend Oliver in California."

"Might as well go, Jill. There's never a good time. The pace isn't letting up. I haven't been able to take our usual trip to Vermont with the family. So what's in California?" He can't possibly read my mind about my college roommate, but my armpits get moist just the same.

"Well, I'm not having any luck with Connecticut guys, so I thought I'd try the west coast. I hear California guys are dying to marry a 'natural girl' like me." I make my voice silly to make him smile.

"Isn't your friend gay?"

"Oh, I don't mean Oliver. We're just good friends."

He stares at me for a moment and paralyzes me with fondness. In my mind, I've tipped my head to rest on his shoulder and he's put his arm around me. I straighten up before he can read my thoughts. And it's as if he does.

"So what else do you want me to do for you now?" he teases, forcing his grouchy voice as if he felt the fondness, too. We've played this charade before, stopping on the fringe of flirtation, neither forgetting he is married.

"It's Sherlock Woods. I looked at the x-rays. The cat's got bladder stones and needs surgery." Bob stands up and squeezes my shoulder.

"If you're up for being my co-pilot, you can set up the surgery."

Co-pilot. I love the sound of that.

"Dr. Bob, your wife's on the phone," Jeannie calls from the reception area. "Can you pick up now or should I tell Pam you'll call her back?"

I glance away when I hear him grumble.

"Can't I get anything done around here? Probably something else for me to do." He grabs the bottle of fruit-flavored Tums sitting beside him on the counter. His shoulders hunch and he plods back to his office, both hands shoved deep into his lab pockets.

"Sometimes I think he'd feel better if he said the SH—word," Jeannie says. "Passive-Aggressive," Jeannie whispers, thumbing her hand toward Bob.

"What does *that* mean?" I know, but want to hear Jeannie's interpretation.

"Someone who can't say SHIT to their wife!"

I stifle my laughter with my hand, then Jeannie starts to joke about Pam and Bob's sex life. She makes an obscene gesture, poking her finger in and out of her hollow fist and shaking her head. *No Chance Tonight, Bob.*

I choke back my laughter. Suddenly it's not so funny. Bob always comes through for patients, his family, and for me. And I'm planning to screw him.

It is nearing the end of Indian summer in Connecticut, and the setting sun is casting red-skinned shadows into dwindling daylight. In another month, amber leaves will toast and crumble, turning my yard to tarnished copper.

Instead of logging on to Connect tonight, I go to Expedia.com to check my flight to San Francisco. By now the sun has changed from Leo into the sign of Virgo. Ingrid would have told me why it was a good time for me to travel, and yet, after I've booked my flight, gotten time off from work and reserved the pet sitter, I don't want to go.

~ 22 ~

I lean on the pew of St. Francis Church, my forearms braced against the sturdy wood, but it's my mind that could use reinforcement.

Out of the corner of my eye, I follow triangular rays from the stained glass window. The likeness of a blue angel with violet wings and a halo is transformed into an artistic design on the back of a man sitting two pews ahead. He is tall with a fine blond ponytail nearly as long as mine.

The priest walks over to the podium to deliver his sermon.

"And now these three remain: faith, hope, and love. But the greatest of these is love."

I shift my weight. *That man looks familiar. Why does his auburn goatee and rugged skin make me think of the Grand Canyon?*

"Miss." The usher taps my shoulder and shoves the collection basket at me.

"Oh, sorry. I only have a twenty-dollar bill," I whisper. "Can I bring it to you later or—"

The woman in front of me turns sharply. "Shhhhh!"

"Sorry. "

Now the man turns around. His Arctic blue eyes meet mine. *I've seen those eyes before.*

At the vet clinic? The supermarket? An acquaintance of Dad?

I remember—an email conversation a couple of months ago when I set up my Connect profile. He said he wanted to see the Grand Canyon, but his ponytail, his love of Harleys, and a collection of old Playboy magazines, spelled *Biker Dude.*

"I'm not into bikes," I wrote back, "but I can understand why you love them." It reminds me of being on a horse.

"I'd be glad to teach you," he wrote back.

I left it at that, but now, I not sure I want to. *A man with a wild side who attends church can't be all that bad.*

When the service ends, I watch him pass by my pew.

"Are you getting out?" the woman who sat in front of me snaps before I'm ready. Trying to avoid a traffic jam in the church aisle, I step ahead of her to get out of her way.

Outside, I scan the church crowd with my purse propped on one thigh while pretending to search my pocketbook for my keys. Biker dude crosses the street, swings one long jean-clad leg over the chrome fender of a black and red motorcycle, and kick-starts the bike. I speed dial Logan.

"Logan, remember that Harley Playboy I mentioned to you from Connect.com?"

"Not really. What sign was he?"

"I don't think I checked. Hold on," I say as I search Connect.com to see if he's still on the site.

"I found him." I read through his profile about how he's looking for *The One.*

"He's a Sagittarius. Religion is important to Sagittarius, so is freedom and travel. Except I'm the one leaving for California next week."

"Email him," Logan coaches. "Guess he hasn't found what he's looking for."

"I never got back to him. Maybe it would be better if we meet at church."

"Like it's a sign?" Logan sneers. "There's nothing wrong with saying that you think you saw him."

"Right. I'll keep you posted."

In between appointments the next morning I tell Jeannie and Marlene about contacting the biker dude.

"Oh, it must be fate, meeting a man in church." Jeannie croons.

Marlene stares at Jeannie, then turns to me. "Jill, remember what I said about giving your heart away? When you're not looking for someone, that's when it'll happen."

"That's what everyone else says, except it's not what Ingrid said when she told me to look for Leo."

As I walk away, I overhear Marlene and Jeannie. "She's barely met the guy and you're picturing her marching down the wedding aisle. I don't trust a man with a ponytail."

One of them has to be wrong. I'm praying it's not me.

The night before I leave for California, I call Oliver.

"I'm coming in at 7:30PM, Oliver," I screech into the phone when he answers.

"I'll look for you at the baggage carousel. I hope you're rested, because I've got plans for us every day."

I have some plans of my own that I hadn't mentioned to Oliver.

I double-check the contact information I've packed—my old roommate from Tufts who'd become an equine vet and had a practice in northern California. Just looking at Andrea's name on the paper where I've written her name makes my mouth go dry. Andrea is so excited I'm coming to see her. But she doesn't know why I need to see her.

After I get off the phone, I carry two suitcases out to the car. But when I open the trunk of the car to put the luggage inside, I turn to stone. The Ouija board. I can't bring it inside the house with my cats. I tuck a thick blanket around the board, close the trunk, and dump my luggage in the back seat of the car.

Soon Ingrid will be home. We can get to the bottom of Ouija's message when it spelled out my own initials. Maybe, I will end up alone. Maybe my luck will change in California.

~ 23 ~
Palo Alto, California

Half Moon Bay was a surfer's dream, if that dream involved massive waves that could kill or thrill the best athlete. James left Dizzy at home with a plan for the pet-sitter to check on her twice today, just in case.

His feet burned in the sugary sand as he tucked the surf board into his armpit. The waves were ten feet and the surf was choppy. He needed this. The visit with Ingrid wasn't what he expected after he'd called her back. He only agreed to meet her since she said she was flying into San Francisco to visit an old friend. That had been a lie.

She was coming to see him.

Then it had started again over lunch. The astrology jargon. Any minute now he'd expected to hear Ingrid remind him how Amy's planets weren't right for him.

He'd exhaled and reached for his beer. "How are you feeling, Mom? Jake said you closed your practice. So what have you been doing?"

"I met a nice friend. A veterinarian at the clinic where I bring Olga. She helped her. We started getting together for dinner every week. I've grown quite fond of her, James. She's much younger than I am, but she has the same birthday as my sister."

If only for a minute, that had gotten his attention. It killed Ingrid to see him so sad. She was so sure she could fix that, especially when she saw a spark light in James' sullen eyes at the mention of the aunt who babysat for him before she died. The aunt he adored.

"What's her name?" James had asked, in conversation, rather than actual interest.

"Jill."

"Well, I'm glad you're not spending all of your time alone. She must be sweet if she was anything like my aunt."

"She is, James."

The serenity in her voice confused him because Jake was right. Ingrid did not look good. Her cheeks sagged from her facial bones and she'd grunted when she got up to use the restroom. But Ingrid's conversation about her new friend made it difficult to suspect the worst.

Then yesterday Jake had called to tell James that Ingrid called to ask him questions about "buying some property." He couldn't figure out why in hell she wanted to do that. But there was no talking Ingrid out of it.

"What kind of property?" James asked.

When he said it was an old horse farm, James figured there was nothing to worry about. His aunt had died from a horse accident. He couldn't imagine that Ingrid would want anything to do with horses again.

~ 24 ~

My plane ascends into the overcast Connecticut sky. It's late September, a Saturday morning. Oliver will be working most of the day at the hair salon. As the hours and miles tick closer to seeing him again, I recall when we met in high school after Petal had died. I didn't know he was gay when we first met, even though the signs were there—his preoccupation with fashion and hairstyles.

After six hours of flying, the plane lands in San Francisco. From the second I step on the runway to the gate, the harmonious evening temperature soothes me, and so does the sign, *Welcome to California!*

"Yes!"

A perfect stranger turns and smiles at my private cheer.

"Baggage claim," I chirp to myself, following another sign to the carousel, walking lopsided to balance the bulky carry-on slung over my shoulder.

I'm standing with the other passengers when my heart jumps.

"Jill, Jill!"

I turn to see Oliver descending the escalator, hair streaked copper and cappuccino. He's waving to me. "Hurry Darling, the limo is going to take you to your photo shoot. I told them to have your room stocked with white roses and chocolates, Godiva, of course, not some cheapy brand."

Oliver is wearing his Bahama shirt with the top button undone and despite his weight fluctuations each time I've seen him, today he appears to have squeezed into the same size shorts he'd worn when we were teens.

"We're going straight to the 42nd Street Club. Calvin is dying to see you."

"You mean your gorgeous *straight* friend?"

He leans in for a kiss and winks one marine green eye.

Nearby there is a small group of slight-built, businessmen speaking in a sing-song foreign language. Now the black suits form a semi-circle around us, aiming their phone cameras. We are the Hollywood couple no one will recognize.

Oliver gathers the rest of my luggage and shuffles past the phony hype he's created. "Run, Jill. Follow me. I'm parked illegally."

The top is down on his Jeep. He throws the luggage in the back seat and we slide into the front.

"Buckle Up," he shouts, swerving out of the Handicapped spot, and accelerates onto the highway.

"I forgot how much I love it here, Oliver." I shout over the radio. My voice sounds like a vibrato mix amidst the hum of speeding tires and hair-flapping tropical breeze. I snag a whip of my hair and hold it to my ears, but the rest dances into a tangled mess.

"Don't worry about your hair. I'll fix it for you later," Oliver yells.

Of course he will. When other couples in high school went parking, Oliver and I went to his parent's house to style our hair. It was a bad time in both of our lives but it brought us close together. I'd lost Petal, and Oliver had lost his virginity— to a priest at a local church.

"Why don't you move here, Jill? These California boys would love a sweet natural girl like you. There's so much plastic out here, everyone's got the same nose." Oliver pinches his nose between his fingers. "Not that I'm knocking someone getting a nice boob job. With your curvy figure you could find a California man in no time."

"Speaking of curves! Oliver, watch out!"

He stops short of a cactus landscape and Oliver's surfer friend. Calvin is an exotic blend of his Hawaiian mother and Swedish father. A delicious whiff of coconut suntan lotion lingers when he hugs me.

"I remember the last time you visited, Jill. I was in-between jobs and staying with Oliver," Calvin says.

"I remember. Practically every one of Oliver's friends has lived with him at one time or another. That's Oliver's Mi-Casa-Es-Su-Casa policy."

"So I'd say you're next," Calvin says with a flirty grin. It's what I need—to believe the surreal events of this coming week can suspend the reality I've been facing back home.

Inside the restaurant, I sandwich myself in the booth between them.

"How long are you staying?" Calvin crooks his arm across the back of the booth and brushes my shoulder.

What sign was Calvin anyway?

"I have to leave next Saturday." I don't look at Oliver after his comment in the car on the way over to meet Calvin—

"You should sleep with Calvin while you're out here, Jill. I hear he's—"

"Oliver, how do you know what he's like in bed?"

"I'm a hair dresser. People tell everything to a gay hairdresser. You haven't been with anyone since Tim, have you?"

No, I haven't been with anyone since Tim. And I miss that. "Intimacy," as D.J. mentioned the night I ended up driving myself home.

"Here, try this." Oliver slides over a goblet that looks like a Key West sunset. "It's called a *Tropical Moon*." It tastes as harmless as orange juice, so before we leave, I have another.

At home in Oliver's condo, I wobble over to the leopard-print sectional and flop down hard. "The place looks great, Oliver," my speech slurs. So do the hand-painted flowers in the Chinese-red foyer. His Gemini artistry defines every wall.

He makes himself another drink from an erotically-shaped bottle of rum. I stifle my dinner and try not to puke when he sticks one under my nose. My eyelids itch and my contacts feel glued to my eyeballs. This isn't high school anymore. I force myself to sit up.

"So are you dating anyone special?"

"I don't want a relationship. I've got too much I want to do with my life." His hand drifts back toward seven wall clocks, each clock set to a different world time zone including one labeled **Oliver's Time**, from which he has purposely removed the hands. Yet I'm hyper aware of the ticking clock Ingrid has set for my love life.

"How can you not want someone in your life?"

He shrugs one shoulder. "I don't care."

"You care—" The lingering effects my Tropical Moons render me incapable of finishing my sentence. I know how much he cared for his old roommate who'd left him two years ago. I feel myself drifting. I slide back into the couch and prop two cushions under my head.

When I awake, Oliver has shut the lights and covered me with a satin comforter. I wrap myself in it, letting it trail behind me like a bridal train as I hobble into the bedroom. But I'm not too drowsy to coo over the cat mirror and perfumed toiletries, gifts that Oliver has left in the guest room for me.

The following morning, my nostrils twitch to a buttery scent that makes me think of Mom's pancakes. I get up from bed, slip my toes into my flip-flops and shuffle toward the kitchen.

"Here, try one of these Hawaiian muffins." Oliver holds out a steamy mound. His hand is sheathed in a potholder shaped like a tiger's paw with boney plastic protrusions for claws. "I hope you like Macadamia Chocolate coffee. If not, there's some boring hazelnut or Viennese Pecan in the cupboard behind the Godiva. But don't get too full. We're going to the House of Zen for lunch. You're gonna love it—Sunset Salmon, Moonlight Mahi Mahi and Tiger Teriyaki rolls."

I have no idea what any of that is but Oliver makes food a sensual experience. I smack my lips from the tart pineapple. "Think I'll ever find a guy as fun as you are?"

"You can try while you're out here."

I swallow deeply, relishing the comforting flavor of muffin, and of our friendship. "Maybe I'll do a search on Connect.com and put your zip code in," I say, joking.

"You could stay with me until you find a place!"

"I'm starting to fall for this."

"Let me do your hair first."

"Nothing drastic, please, Oliver." I twist a swatch of my bed head.

"I'll put in some lowlights and trim a little to get rid of that Flower Child look." He scrunches my hair in his hands.

Balmy Santa Anna winds billow through the palm trees and bamboo shades on Oliver's balcony. Before I realize, I'm sitting on his bar stool with a towel around my shoulders as he trims away my dead ends, and it feels like an indoctrination.

The breeze is so mystical, so hypnotic, that I could forget I have a life back home.

Soon after I get back, Connecticut trees will become skeletal. Days will grow shorter and cold. Winter without someone special will be especially lonely now.

Sitting at Oliver's computer with my new hairdo, I log on to my Connect website and put Oliver's Palo Alto zip code in the Search bar. If I didn't know I was in California, I wouldn't have noticed any difference when the pages of California men appear.

"I don't know why I was expecting a bunch of surfer-looking guys. I wonder if their attitudes about dating are any different from guys back east."

Oliver looks over my shoulder. "One way to find out. Pick a guy and ask him out on a date. Or, if you want to see some really gorgeous men, try searching *Men looking for Men.*" Oliver's expression melts as if he's eaten one of his Hawaiian muffins.

What do I have to lose? It isn't like I'd fall in love overnight.

~ *25* ~

Sometime the next day, the moon slips into the sign of Libra, but only an astrologer like Ingrid would have known what it could mean for me.

"See you later, Oliver," I call out as my strappy sandals snap down the hallway.

"Don't forget what I told you about those pilots," Oliver says. "I want all the details when you get back."

I take the Caltrain to San Francisco, a forty-minute rail ride from Palo Alto which gives me a chance to take in the streaked tangerine and violet sky. "Your moon is in the sign of Libra," Ingrid had told me. "It's the sign of beauty, balance and partnership."

I choose Troy because he's a Libra, and was receptive to the idea of astrology matching.

Troy is standing at the far edge of the lounge. He doesn't know it's me yet, but his head weaves left and right tracking me through the crowded bar. Troy looks like his photo, except instead of a tee shirt and shorts, his trim physique is in a formal white shirt and navy pants.

"Jill? Sorry I landed off a flight from Chicago and didn't have time to change." His black wavy hair is meticulously layered and his chin is razor-clean as a U.S. Marine.

"You look great, Troy. My friend told me this place was casual." Oliver may have brought my hairstyle up to date, even though my gauzy melon-colored dress has a hint of hippy. Troy obviously approves because I have to turn to break his stare. "Do they have live music here? I see band instruments, but no musicians."

"Yes. You said that you liked music."

"You too, right? And dancing and incense?" I'm thinking kissing. He'd checked off kissing.

"I love incense—patchouli, musk," He stops mid-sentence with a smile that dimples his cheek.

So it is true that Libras have a dimple somewhere. I don't have to look far to see Troy's.

We find two leather bucket chairs beside the metallic bar. There are tasteful black and white photos of old aircrafts on navy blue walls and stainless ceiling fans that look like propellers.

"How often do you come to California, Jill? You mentioned you visit your friend here?" He chucks a handful of peanuts into his mouth and swivels back and forth like a restless kid, but his voice is as mellow as the Palo Alto evening. His slender eyes close a bit as he concentrates, warm brown eyes that conjure daydreams about doe-eyed children— even someone like me who thinks they don't want kids.

"I only visit once a year," I say, holding the connection between our eyes.

"I fly into New York at least once a month," he says.

I get the feeling he's letting me know more than his itinerary.

"So, is it hard to adjust to the constant time changes?"

"There are harder things to get used to," he says, his face more serious. "Being a pilot isn't that glamorous. There's a saying about flying— moments of terror followed by hours of boredom." Slipping an index finger along his neck, he loosens his tie and unbuttons the top of his shirt. He pushes aside his cap with a silver metal emblem, then reaches over to squeeze my hand.

"My friend warned me about pilots." I tease with friendly eyes. "He said that pilots have a girl at every stop."

Troy's shoulders round and he chuckles. "I won't lie. Some of the guys are like that. They have wives, girlfriends, kids. It's hard traveling all the time. It ruined my relationship four years ago." He sighs like he's said too much.

"Playing around is out of the question for me, now. I think if you find what you're looking for, nothing else matters. How about you Jill? I can't believe you're single, a sweet lady like you." Troy's mouth crinkles with a beautiful smile.

A sweet lady like you— even my décolletage blushes at the glance that exchanges between us. Then my eyes drift to the white-sanded bay outside the smoky window. "I thought I'd met the man I'd spend the rest of my life with." A tender laugh builds in my chest. "We loved going dancing and listening to music, too." I look up at Troy. "Then four months ago he broke it off, when we were about to buy a house together."

Troy takes a slug of his beer and repositions his seat, swiveling sideways.

I feel my hairline perspire, my smile melt. *What happened?* I stutter trying to back track. "I hope I didn't sound bitter."

"No, not at all. Sounds like you still love him." Troy's playful tone has vanished. "I'm jealous."

Why would he think this? Did my face turn dreamy talking about Tim?
"I'm over him," I say calmly.

He squeezes my hand again, but this time it's like my hand is a ball he's about to toss away. And unlike when Tafari had held my hand this way, I don't want to let Troy's hand go. I can't explain the reason for this the way Ingrid could— like a vibration inside of me, a song that sounds familiar, a puzzle piece that fits— was that what she meant?

The band starts to play. We dance to a slow song. I think the date's going okay, drinks and an appetizer. I excuse myself to use the ladies room.

When I return, Troy swings his navy blazer from the back of the chair and flips it over his shoulder. I feel frozen to the floor when I notice a five-dollar bill under Troy's water glass. He's already paid the check.

"I should get going. I need to get some sleep. I'm off to Miami in the morning. You're sweet and your pretty, Jill. You'll find someone."

Doesn't he understand that's the reason I'm here?

"Troy, I live very close to a small local airport. Maybe the next time you're on the east coast—"

He leans on the back of his chair and lowers his head. "I'll give you a call if I'm near the area." He bends to kiss my cheek. "We'll have dinner and you can tell me more about your exciting life as a vet."

Outside the restaurant window, a flock of gulls fly in criss-cross patterns. I lose myself in that pattern for a second, wondering why Troy made the comment about me and Tim.

Sure, I may always love Tim, but I've learned my lesson.

We exit the restaurant with barely another word and go our separate ways— two people who will find it easier to tell their friends when they ask how the date went, that they didn't feel a connection.

When I get back to Oliver's, his home is quiet and so am I. My kitties would have welcomed me with tails straight up like flags of friendship.

A note on the kitchen counter says: *Be back at ten o'clock.* I collapse into the sofa pillows and try Ingrid's cell phone, but I can't complete the call. It's too late to call Logan, so I call my home. After four rings, the machine picks up.

Hi this is Jill. Leave me a message and I'll get back to you as soon as I can.

I speak into the machine and tell my cats how much I miss them.

Within minutes there's rustling sounds on the other side of the door and Oliver opens it with his arms full of his green fishnet bag of peaches and grapes. He sets a wheel of cheese on the counter next to a box of crackers.

"How was your date?"

"It was alright, until he asked why I'd never been married."

"What did you say?"

"Nothing, really, except I mentioned Tim." I massage my brow and sigh. "He said he'd let me know the next time he comes to the east coast."

"He'll never call." Oliver's back is turned, untying red and white string from a box smudged with icing.

The grape I'd plucked into my mouth puckers my lips. *I already know Troy won't call, don't I?*

"Change out of that Orphan Annie outfit and let's meet my friends for drinks."

"It's 2AM in Connecticut and I'm still on east coast time."

Oliver mocks like a sad clown who's planned round-the-clock activities to make my vacation fun. It would be like giving our friendship the finger if I don't play along, even though his lifestyle apparently hasn't outgrown high school.

I refuse to drink at Oliver's local hangout, but he has a few. I'm relieved we're back home after a couple hours. Oliver turns on the stereo then passes out on the couch by the time I come back from the kitchen with our chamomile tea. *Guess Oliver isn't able to pull all-nighters anymore.* I pout at the sight of him, feet hanging off of the couch, his face half buried in a tiger print pillow. *Guess I wasn't cute the other night either.*

I leave him there and walk to the guest room, shut the door, take off my lace teddy and hop into bed. *Maybe I could have been in bed with Troy.* As if I ever would—I'd be miserable waking up beside a stranger— as miserable as sleeping with a man I love who didn't love me.

When I smell maple syrup and java beans instead of the fresh-cut flower-scented bedsheets, I hop out of bed. Before I find Oliver I check my messages—none from Troy. Or the man from church. I leave my note with the contact info of my old college classmate near the computer and head toward the scent of warm toast.

"I hope you slept well," Oliver says when he sees my groggy shuffle over to the coffeemaker. "Have some breakfast. Later we'll catch the Caltrain to San Francisco. One of my friends has a gallery." He hands me a book of dreamy paintings that reminds me of Alice in Wonderland, by an artist named Daniel Merriam.

"Daniel—that reminds me." D.J.'s called twice to let me know my neighbor's band is playing at the Wharf Restaurant again. I text him to let him know I'm in California. No harm in being friends, especially when he's my connection to Amberfield.

After the art gallery we eat at a Persian restaurant on a street with vintage architecture and funky clothing establishments. Around us are people who fit the neo-grunge scene. We dine on lamb, potatoes, saffron and flat bread sitting in a stark, slightly dirty and crowded room of college-aged patrons, reminiscing about how Oliver and I met in high school.

Before I leave California, it was time to revisit another old school friend. But that reunion would not be sentimental.

"It's Dr. A's day off," the receptionist says abruptly the next morning when I call the number of my college friend, Andrea.

"I'm an old college friend of Andrea," I say super sweetly.

She finally believes me that I'm not some conniving client, but still scolds that I should have confirmed the visit last week. What is it with these receptionists?

I leave my cell number.

"Too bad I didn't know what day you were coming, Jill," Andrea says when she calls me back. "I could have taken you skiing with me in Tahoe."

"I haven't skied since college. Besides, I'll have enough of winter weather soon when I get back to Connecticut. Any chance to squeeze in a visit tomorrow? Oliver will be working at the salon all day Friday."

"Sure. You'll need directions. I'll reconnect you with the front desk. See you tomorrow, Jill."

After I jot down the convoluted instructions, I receive a message from Suzanne. Dad's gone into the hospital for tests.

Oliver hands me the keys to his convertible the next morning. Armed with the GPS and a hand-written map, I head east toward Sacramento. I barely drive two miles and pull into the convenience store to pick up a bottle of water. My mouth is dry. *I'm really doing this, and Bob has no clue this is a big reason I've come to California.*

I park and as I squeeze past a car with the window down I side-step a snorting sound.

"Oh, I didn't see you!" I say in the baby-talk I reserve for my patients. I stick my hand inside the car and dodge the thick pink tongue pushing into my hand as I try to pet the bulldog strapped into the front seat of a BMW. "Aren't you a pretty girl," I say into the cow-like eyes brimming with adoration. "Dizzy?" I say, reading her name tag. "Well, Dizzy, nice to meet you."

I swing open the metal and glass entrance door and head for the cold drinks. When I turn around, I stop in my tracks. Déjà vu. Tall and lean, wet blond waves at the base of his neck, and sunglasses propped on his forehead. He's wearing a tee shirt and boat shoes.

I shake my head at the similarity. They say everyone has a twin.

The man pays for a Gatorade, walks out of the store, and drives away in the BMW with Dizzy.

I finally arrive after two hours. At the Copper Valley Equine Clinic where Andrea works, there are no pastel flowers planted along the terra cotta desert walkway to the front office. It's the equivalent of a shopping mall in comparison to Mount Pleasant Vet Hospital. Four receptionists are behind the front desk when I enter, but then I realize one of them is Andrea. She still looks like she should have been a ballerina.

"You look the same!" she says when we're close enough to feel the awkward distance of time. I suspect she's wondering if I've married Tim, and I'm wondering how much to tell her.

As Andrea finishes a call, I watch the front desk staff manage the multi-vet practice. I feel out of place. *Almost homesick.* I miss hearing Jeannie's crabby comments, the cozy sitting area with People Magazines neatly stacked for owners before they are called to take their pet into the exam room.

Andrea gives me a tour. The place is ultrahigh tech and everything is equine-sized. There are no exam rooms, just indoor/outdoor paddocks. Our laboratory and pharmacy combined at Mount Pleasant is smaller than their restroom.

"We can catch up on the ride, Jill," Andrea says when we exit the Employees Only area. "I'm sorry to start out like this, but one of the mares at Forrest Hill Farm is in trouble. After that we can head over to vaccinate the polo horses."

"Do you have everything?" I ask, scaling the dinosaur-sized vehicle with cabinets on the flatbed.

"Everything's in the truck. I won't need much in the way of supplies for the first horse call." She glances at me and I feel a lump in my throat.

"Syringes and euthanasia solution are in the cooler. We're doing this horse a favor. It's the only Premarin farm left in the state. There are still estrogen farms in Canada, but—"

She's still talking but I've tuned out, especially when I see the sagging cow barn not far from the clinic where these two horses are living. "My mom has been on estrogen since her hysterectomy, but I made sure her doctor prescribed the bio-identical kind."

"PETA has made a difference with drug companies about using horses. The last horse is being moved to our property so he won't be alone," she says. "The rescue project in Long Beach may take him."

"Sounds the same here as it is back at our clinic." *Our clinic.* I suddenly feel like a traitor. "We foster a ton of homeless kittens every year until we find them homes."

"Well, keeping a few small pets is a lot easier than keeping a horse with a life expectancy of thirty years," Andrea says as she parks her big truck near the barn. "I can't save them all."

"I think I'll walk outside," I tell Andrea when the stable girl comes out to help with the sick mare. I look over at the crater-size grave, the mountain of dirt, pre-dug with a backhoe because it's the cheapest way to bury a horse.

The scene hits me like a kick in the head. I slip on a pair of sunglasses to hide my onion eyes. *Why am I'm choking up? I've done this type of thing plenty of times.*

But there is something so sad about this, so opposite to the gentle way I'd done this with small pets, peacefully in the arms of their loving owner. Like Olga with Ingrid.

I walk over to the other horse standing in a barren paddock. He's a dull little chestnut with dirty white socks. He lifts his head and his empty look seems to say, "I don't care anymore." I slide one hand down his coarse mane and tell him with my hands that I do.

"You'll be fine, boy," I whisper, stroking his neck and backhanding my wet nose as I massage his velvet nostrils. His head arcs, his ears swivel toward the whinny of his stable mate. I can't bear to look over at the other paddock. "Good boy," I repeat, voice cracking. I hear the snap of his arthritic hips as he leans into me.

When we leave, Andrea drives to the polo barn. I'm quieter than usual, but it's been years since we've seen each other so Andrea doesn't notice.

A sleek thoroughbred probes my hand with his quivering muzzle. Even this isn't enough to make me ready for the company of horses again.

We grab lunch on the road and spend our last hour together traveling back to the clinic through the terra cotta desert and bluish-gray mountains, but I can't stop thinking about the sad brown eyes of the little chestnut.

The horizon bleeds like watercolors of violet and orange as Oliver drives me to the airport for my red-eye flight back home the next afternoon.

"You'd better come back soon, or I'll have to charter a flight with Troy," Oliver says.

I force myself to laugh. It'll be awhile before I come back and we both know it. My carry-on proves it. It's bulging with the Queen-of-California gifts from Oliver. The pilot standing by the cockpit wearing the same uniform as Troy doesn't help either.

I feel my body turning to sand.

I'm an hourglass and I'm running out of time. "Within one year," Ingrid had said.

I find my seat and throughout the flight I adjust my belongings like a neurotic canary that's been caged up too long. I want to get home. I browse the astrology app on my phone and read my prediction.

PISCES: Your life is like that scrapbook that you started years ago and never finished. It's time to write the ending. Let your free spirit lead the way.

Somewhere above the clouds I cannot see, I fall asleep.

It is 11:43PM when the plane lands in Connecticut. I've lost three hours from the time change. I find my car once I get out to the parking garage and slide my luggage onto the back seat. Ouija is still in the trunk. Any day now I'll see Ingrid.

I pay the parking fee and drive home to my real gifts— the unconditional love of my cats.

It is winter coat weather here now. A shiver reminds me there will be cold months ahead. I know now it would be impossible to leave the warmth of friends and family here in Connecticut. Like Troy had said, there are harder things to get used to. Sooner than I expect, there is.

~ 26 ~

Jeannie looks as if she's doing the funky chicken dance when she sees me come through the door. She opens her arms like she's about to fly, then embraces me like she's Mother Goose.

"Oh, Jill, I've missed you. How was your trip?"

"I have so much to tell you, but first, did Dr. Bob do okay without me?" I say this with the sorriest face.

Jeannie answers the phone, cupping it quickly in the middle of her greeting to answer. "He's fine, in fact he took a few days off. He hired a sweet temp vet, Dr. Bell." She thumbs her hand toward the back room, holding up her finger to continue. I can tell by the client's name that this phone call is going to be a long one, so I head for my office. I'll catch up with Jeannie later.

The door to my office isn't only unlocked, the door is wide open and there is a shabby L.L. Bean duffle bag on my desk. I sniff. It smells disgusting in here! Probably dirty fingerprints on my keyboard, too. I open my desk drawer with the Lysol wipes.

Too late—my foot shoots forward into a slide. I don't dare look. The welcome-back-to-animal-haven odor smacks me in the nose.

"Shit!"

Wow! Wouldn't Jeannie be proud of me! No passive aggressive behavior in that comment. My teeth are grinding. Where is this Dr. Bell?

I hobble out of my office to the kennel room sink, standing on one foot while I clean my shoe and try to compose my temper. *Shit!* Someone obviously let George Burns into my room. All the regular staff knows George Burns can't be trusted. I don't mind Dr. Bell using my room, but she could have at least respected my space. My heels knock the tile floor like engine pistons as I head to find her.

The vegan tech is standing in the treatment area with his pet rat named Twizzler on his shoulder, and beside him is another boy/man wearing a crumpled lab coat. I tilt my head. He's a strong resemblance to a younger Dr.

Bob.

"Hey, Dr. Christie," the tech says as both boys turn toward me. All one hundred and forty pounds of my fury are ready to be unleashed. But I feel my facial muscles deflate. George Burns. He's wearing a Nike tee shirt over his bald scars.

"Oh, my little Poody. Come here, beautiful." The dog doesn't come. "Georgie, what's the matter? I didn't forget about you." The dog hobbles over to the gurney, lifts his leg and urinates. It feels like he's given me the finger. He looks up adoringly at the boy/man and wags his stumpy tail.

"This is Dr. Bell. He's going to adopt Leo," the tech says.

My mouth opens to say hello, but all that comes out is "Oh." I don't know who to address first. I don't know why I assumed Dr. Bell was a woman. "Oh," again. I extend my hand with a shallow greeting. "Call me Jill," I say with a little more warmth, shaking his hand.

I'm gushing. Shit! What is it with me? I adjust my posture and zip the smile. "So, you want to adopt George Burns?"

"Yeah," Bell reaches down and fixes the tee shirt on George Burns. "I thought the shirt might make him less self-conscious of his scars."

I nod in amazement. The dog likes it and Bell is so sweet I can't bear to crab about the crap on my office rug.

Jeannie walks into the room. "Isn't it great that Dr. Bell, oh, I mean David—he said I should call him David when we aren't in front of clients—is taking George home with him?" Jeannie is gushing. So, Jeannie is in on this, too. I stare in amazement again. This is bizarre. Had I only been in California a week, or had I been hit in the head and out cold for a year?

"Yeah, I'm sorry about the accident on your carpet," Bell says. "I'll move my stuff and clean it up."

"Oh, no, that's okay. It's no trouble. I can do it."

"Oh. Okay. Thanks, Jill."

Jill? I feel weird calling this kid by his first name even if he does look like he's eighteen. And Shit! Why the hell did I offer to clean my own carpet? I suddenly feel like the senior partner and low man on the totem pole all at the same time.

Back in my smelly room, I clean the mess and give myself a kick in the pants— so much for not being passive aggressive.

Lowering David's duffle bag off of my desk, I suspend it over the soiled rug for a second before tossing it into the corner. There is a smattering of cinnamon cake crumbs on my desk. Jeannie was making muffins for him? *Traitor. Gushy traitor.*

Jealousy feels worse than being shrink wrapped with hot coffee. I should go back to bed, catch up on the sleep I didn't get last night after I got home. Plus, I'm worried. Still no message from Ingrid.

So, Welcome Back to your life, Jill. Where do I start? Work? Dad? Amberfield? Ingrid? Oh, and yes, my Fun dating plan. Not one date has panned out. And is it too much to ask to have expected a reply from Aaron, or a church guy, or honesty about being *About Average Size* from a man who has dated a woman for years and decides she's not the *Right One*? Even D. J. hasn't called back after I called him when I was in California. That's not like him.

And Bell doesn't help. Bob probably loves the kid. *The kid*— that's probably the way Bob thought of *me* when I finished vet school. Ten years later I'm in the same place— this place, the place I consider my second home, second family. The place I wanted to leave.

Sweeping the crumbs onto a napkin, I kneel to scoop and scrub the mess and try to start my day over. Jeannie leans on my doorframe, keeping her toes a good distance from the huge wet spot I've made on my rug, and cranes her head inside my office.

"I brought carrot cake for a little lunch celebration, Jill, since today is Dr. Bell's last day."

"Good," I crab with my head down.

"What?"

"Nothing." Luckily Dr. Bell is as temporary as my overrated expectations of dating.

When I get home I slip my cranky feet into my favorite slippers, the ones with the fur worn off at the heels that I'd never let Tim see me wear. The new kitten has unearthed a Q-tip from the waste basket and scuttles sideways like a crab until he notices the slippers. I walk like Frankenstein with him hanging onto to my feet like a chimpanzee. The two other cats are suspended in tiers of their cat tree. Rudy lifts his lazy chin from his paws at the sound of my laughter.

"Maybe you're the only Leos I'll have in my life," I say, extricating the kitten's Velcro grip from my slipper. Maybe Bob was wrong—

"You'll make a wonderful mother someday, Jill," Bob had told me, watching me with blind Chrissy. My face got hot. I still can't see myself with a real baby. Most men my age, I imagine, will expect a woman to want to have children.

Standing before the bathroom mirror brushing my teeth to get ready for bed, I turn my face left, right, then stand back to survey my body. I poke at my jaw, cup my breasts and lift. Then I smear cocoa butter beneath my eyes because Jeannie swears it works as good as the Estee Lauder stuff. I dig out my sports bra from my gym bag and put it on underneath my pajama shirt, smooshing my breasts into a uniboob—another anti-gravity tip from Jeannie.

While I'm in the shower, the phone rings but I can't grab it. It's a lawyer calling regarding Ingrid. He says he's leaving the office and will try to reach me again.

I lay my head on my pillow, smelling of chocolate and my breasts stiff as muffins. After an hour, I flip my pillow and stare out at my black walls to a vision of my mother in my college dorm asking me to promise to return home after vet school. That mother/daughter bond consumes me again, only this time the woman is Ingrid.

I bolt upright and rub both my arms as if they're flint sticks. *The furnace must be acting up again.* I flip on the light switch and check the thermostat that I thought I'd forgotten to set. but it reads 70 degrees.

My shoulders brace. Maybe it isn't the temperature. Maybe it's something Ingrid said the last night we had dinner together. "I probably shouldn't have survived all these years. But it wasn't my time. The planets are showing me now it might be."

~ 27 ~

"There's a call for you, Jill," Jeannie says, peeking her head into the exam room. "Do you want to take it now?"

My ears are attached to a stethoscope as I count the heartbeats of a deep-chested border collie. "Yes, Jeannie. I'll be right there." When Jeannie adds "it's in regard to Ingrid," my own heart starts pounding.

I finish up Jess' exam and exit the room with a sickening sixth sense.

"Hello, Dr. Christie. I'm Attorney Jake Chamberlain," the voice says when I pick up the phone. "I regret to tell you that I have some sad news. Our friend Ingrid passed away last night."

I back up to my chair, which squeaks painfully when I drop into the seat.

"Oh, no." My words sound like a hollow echo to my ears. My hand flies to cover my mouth.

"Ingrid told me you're a wonderful vet. She loved you like a daughter," he says.

I'm too paralyzed to speak. *Ingrid had mentioned him to me once— her friend the lawyer.*

"Ingrid came to see me before she left for Sweden," he says. "I tried to talk her out of traveling to Europe alone, but her mind was made up. She wanted to go for more than the aggressive cancer therapy. Her mother was born in Sweden. At least she made it to California before she died."

The clunky office receiver slips off my ear and I only catch part of his words. But I'd heard enough. If only I could lift my head off my pillow and none of this would be true.

"I'm very sorry, Dr. Christie." There's a pause.

"Thank you." I whisper the words as if they have no place in my life now. "Please, call me Jill." *Sweden. I had hoped it was Ingrid's miracle cure.* "Was she alone when she died?" I twist the phone cord around my fingers until the rubber tightens against my flesh.

"Yes, from what I was told. She must have gotten weak, because they found her on top of the bedspread with a bruise on her temple. The new chemo wasn't helping her diabetes. She would never have wanted to live like that. You know how she was."

I know. When I hang up with Attorney Chamberlain, my body quakes with grief.

After a few minutes, Jeannie's hard footsteps stop at my office door. *Appointments are starting,* her footsteps say. I blow my nose and try to stop crying.

When I shuffle back to the reception area, Jeannie is refilling the business card holders on her desk and fiddling with her sign: ***Payment is Required When Services Are Rendered. Thank you, The Management.*** Like Mom, Jeannie keeps busy when something is bothering her.

"Are you okay, Jill? You look pale." Jeannie studies my face with the intensity of a police dog.

A lump in my throat makes me choke.

"Dr. Bob can finish appointments. I'll tell him you need to go home." Jeannie doesn't have to know details. A lawyer calling about Ingrid, Jeannie surmised the rest.

I walk back to blind Chrissy and bury my face in his fur. At the sound of my whimper, he purrs.

"Why don't you take the rest of the afternoon off," Bob says, sweeping his hand across my back.

"Maybe I'd be better off working," I say, but his look tells me otherwise.

When I walk into the restroom and look in the mirror, I know why. *Not one of those pretty criers.* My nose is a blotchy red knob and my mascara looks like smashed mosquitoes beneath my dreary eyes.

On the drive home, cumulus clouds look Icelandic— silver, white and melon. The sun is shining through them like an aura. I hope Ingrid is there.

Later when it gets dark, I stand on my porch and look up at the sky for the stars. Ingrid claimed that the planets and stars mirror events on earth, and that they foretold everything that happened— opportunity, hard times, love, even death. Tonight, they are a mystery, offering no answer to as to why again I lost my good friend.

And now any hope of Amberfield.

~ 28 ~
Palo Alto, California

James had only packed his carry-on luggage. He couldn't stay long, but he had to go even though Ingrid wanted to be buried in Sweden. It would be a sort of closure for the sadness he now felt at losing the time he'd wasted being mad at Ingrid. He'd made sure Dizzy was set up. He promised his assistant he'd answer his phone whenever she called, but she would have to cancel all in-person meetings for the week.

A day with his uncle to discuss funeral and finance. A day to visit his old home. And maybe time to visit an old colleague at Yale. It wouldn't hurt to put feelers out, just in case the hole of emptiness he'd been feeling lately made him think about moving back east. Back home.

The plane ascended into the San Francisco sky. In twelve hours, he'd be sitting in Jake's office. Plenty of time to ponder something Ingrid had mentioned about the planets in his birth chart— how his "life was about to change."

~ 29 ~

A UPS package arrives at the office mixed in with four boxes of veterinary supplies.

"This one's addressed to you, Dr. Christie," the tech says, sorting packages and carrying the others to the stock room.

I angle the cardboard in the crook of my arm and run a scissor across the edge, prying open the box. Inside is an over-size textbook. On the cover is a rendering of the zodiac symbols. They form a circle that starts on the left with fiery orange horns of a silver and black Aries ram. The circle ends with two turquoise fish, swimming in opposite directions, the symbol of the sensitive, indecisive Pisces.

A card is tucked inside the book. On the front of it, a Monarch butterfly. In Ingrid's bold cursive script, the following note is written.

Dear Jill,

If you've received this, then I am gone. Our short time together changed my life for many reasons. I loved your attachment to the Amberfield property because I always loved that farm too. You also reminded me very much of the sister I lost from a horse accident like your friend. It was as if I were in her company again when I was with you, so you made the end so much less frightening for me knowing I would see her again soon. There is someone I never mentioned to you, but I couldn't just yet. It gives me peace to know you will have the chance to meet. I've done my part. Now, it's up to you. Stay true to what you love and you will find Leo. Love, Ingrid.

The letter's meaning is clouded by grief. And without knowing who it is that Ingrid never mentioned, I quickly dismiss the passing thought. I flip through the glossy pages and stop at my sign of Pisces.

Positive Qualities: compassionate, gentle, romantic, idealistic
Negative Qualities: gullible, indecisive, passive, tendency to escape
from reality with drugs, alcohol, or dreams
Careers: work involving the sick, animals, magic, photography, art, or
work behind the scenes
Ruling Planet: Neptune

This is nothing that I didn't already know. But there is a whole text book of people I have yet to discover. I slide the book onto my bookshelf between my psychology and vertebrate anatomy texts—where it will guide my mind and heart.

Now more than ever, Ingrid's death alone motivates me to keep trying.

"Marty Fisher's coming in with four of her 'Macaroni kitties,'" Jeannie says when I return from lunch. Each of Marty's kitties are as unusual as their names: Noodles, Ziti, Linguini and Pastina. Marty had found Pastina with her three kittens nearly frostbitten behind the Italian restaurant she and her husband own.

"Maybe we can get Dr. Bob to take one of the kittens for his daughter's birthday?"

"I think she's decided to keep all of them," Jeannie answers. "Marty said Meatball has taken a liking to them. I can picture that fat old dobe tip toeing around the kittens and letting them eat his food."

"What are you getting me to do now?" Bob says when he overhears me mention his name. His eyes focus on an oily slide under the microscope.

I narrow mine with a grin until all he'll see is a glint of blue-green iris and the honesty of my smile.

"How are you doing?" he asks. I know he's purposely let up on me with any decisions. It doesn't matter what he says. What matters is that he cares enough to ask. "I'm sorry for all my teasing about Ingrid. There was a nice article about her in the paper. I saved it for you."

I pick up the newspaper beside him and read about Ingrid's achievements. I avoid reading the obituary when I turn to a small article where I see something about the Amberfield property being sold. I can't bear to read any further.

I call Suzanne because I heard Dad wasn't feeling well and it's easier than asking Mom about medical stuff, or asking my dad about personal stuff. I immediately feel guilty for missing mass when after I ask Suzanne about Dad and she uses the words "Parkinson's. They don't know yet."

Before we end the call, I float over to my computer as if I'm having an out-of-body experience. I Google Parkinson's Disease then cross myself when I see the prognosis.

The vision of my father walking me down a church aisle flashes past my eyes.

~ *30* ~

I don't like the sound of neediness in my sister's voice.

"I'm driving to Connecticut on Friday morning for an ultrasound seminar. Can you meet me for lunch on Saturday?" Suzanne says.

"Is everything all right?"

"I'll explain when I see you."

I especially don't like her answer.

The last time I'd been to Health and Hatha was with Ingrid. My leg swings back and forth as I sit outside on the patio watching out for Suzanne. When I see her pull up, I jump up from my seat and wave. I know Suzanne will like this place. She's wearing her hand-made earrings of canary yellow beads with neon blue and emerald crystals. Her loose silky pants have a geometric Egyptian design in melon and fuchsia colors. Other Gemini's I know, like Ingrid and Oliver, also make some colorful artistic fashion statement, though none quite like the Gemini "Coffee Meet" guy in the bumblebee motorcycle gear.

"I thought you'd like this place. I came here with Ingrid," I say in a muse-like tone.

"Mom told me about Ingrid, Jill. I'm sorry." She rubs the blue-gray crescent of skin beneath her eye. How striking her Botticelli eyes are without those dark circles. Her mood matches the weather, a dark sheet of clouds in the sky, a hint of rain. Not even the organic aromas perk her up when we step inside.

"I talked to Mom yesterday. She said Dad's been achy and grouchy. She was busy packing for Florida," Suzanne tells me as we walk inside.

Achy and grouchy don't sound serious enough for Suzanne to plan a visit, and this is news to me that our parents are going to Florida.

Suzanne acts preoccupied as she stands in front of the smorgasbord of salads as if she can't decide. We find seats in the sunroom as a wink of sun returns to the sky.

"I was surprised when you called," I say, leaning back from the sudden glare to gauge Suzanne's reaction. My sister barely lifts her face.

Even her body language is holding back.

She props one hand to the side of her head, auburn curls squiggle to her shoulders like tendrils of tangled Coreopsis— she's *Thelma AND Louise,* a Susan Sarandon look that Suzanne has cultivated since high school.

"Yeah, there's been a lot going on at my house." She nudges pasta with her fork. Her lack of appetite is as unusual as her silence. Normally, Suzanne has every facet of her life under control, or at least on her endless "To-Do" list.

I slump back in my chair. I've never seen this Suzanne. All the years she's tried to shed those twenty pounds from her last pregnancy, until now, she hadn't succeeded.

I chew a bite of chicken until it tastes dry as a cracker.

There *had* been another time. It was a vulnerable time for all of us— for me, for Suzanne, and for Suzanne's husband, Lee. I never told Suzanne about the time Lee kissed me.

I flinch when a filament of lightening lights the clouds like paper lanterns.

"So what did you want to talk about, Suzanne?" I unscrew my bottled water and take a slug. My mouth feels air dried.

She opens up in increments, like prying open a fresh clam. "Lee's lost a lot of weight recently. Last month he had Lasik eye surgery. He didn't tell me until I asked him why he wasn't wearing his glasses. He's practically blind without them."

I bite into the calloused skin along the side of my fingernail.

"Last week he shaved his moustache."

My mind flits back to the night I'd let Lee spend the night at my freshman dorm on my couch. No moustache back then, he could barely grow one. Lee had driven from New Jersey to Boston when Suzanne broke up with him. He had been so upset. And drunk. I had never expected him to take my consoling as if it were affection!

I couldn't send him back to New Jersey from Boston when he was intoxicated, but I couldn't sleep. Early morning I'd walked into the living room and sat beside him to wake him. His glasses were on the coffee table. His eyes were still soft with sleep. He hadn't bothered to take off his clothes and they breathed with his sad drunken smell.

"You have to leave, Lee." He'd blinked like he was dreaming when he'd opened his eyes and saw me—

It was on the tip of my tongue to tell Suzanne the day it happened, but it was innocent. There was no point mentioning it after it was over, and it would never have happened if Suzanne hadn't started fighting with Lee in the first place.

"When I wasn't looking, Lee and I drifted apart," Suzanne says, her words jolting me out of the past. Her head is down, following the aimless motion of her silverware. "Our marriage is over."

The nerves in my gut slither up my throat. Their kids, the house, how could Suzanne let all that go?

"You can't mean that, Suzanne." My face feels warm. I force my focus from shifting back to the past.

Thank God Lee never came back to Boston again, and by Christmas, Suzanne and Lee were engaged. Would Suzanne have believed nothing happened if I'd told her back then? A little "drifting" doesn't have to mean the end of a marriage.

"I think Lee's seeing a woman that he works with. He moved into an apartment across town last week."

"Do the kids know?"

"Elanna does. She came home from her girlfriend's house last Sunday afternoon and found me in bed. I couldn't lie to her. She's upset. Aidan didn't say much. Lee told him, but you know boys. He doesn't talk to either of us much." She jams her fist under her chin.

"As much as sometimes I felt like starting over myself, I never did. Maybe Lee did me a favor. It might be nice to be with someone else for a change."

I shake my head. "Dating isn't like it was in college, like when you slept in a twin bed and ended up bonded together for the next decade of your life. Don't throw what you and Lee have away. Relationships are so superficial today. Everyone wants love so badly, but—"

"You and I are different, Jill. I wouldn't put up with some of the things you do."

I blink self-consciously. Was Suzanne referring to Tim? I thought my whole family loved Tim.

"I'm sorry, Jill. I should talk. I can't believe I didn't see it coming with Lee."

"You're right about me, Suzanne." I suck in a breath. "I did hang on with Tim." I crumple my napkin and flick at crumbs. "I'll bet if you tell Lee that you want to work things out—"

Suzanne is already shaking her head. "I work with a woman at one of the doctor's offices. She's seven months pregnant with twins and she's my age. Her husband left her four years ago after she told him she wanted to start a family. She found a nice guy on the Internet. I've never seen her so happy."

"Everyone looks like a great couple in public, Suzanne. But you and Lee truly are a great couple."

Suzanne's frigid stare entraps me in her sticky web, *but good family is like that, right?*

"I'll get us some coffee," I say to Suzanne. She's staring out window when I return with two mugs, black coffee for Suzanne. The wind has shifted from docile breezes to dizzy outbursts.

"I'd better get going soon. It looks like it's going to pour and I want be home before Aidan. He went to his friend's house for a few hours after school. Lee is coming over to talk about finances. It's strange. I used to take care of everything."

"I'll walk out with you." I get up in slow motion after we sip our coffee. Chimes of Celtic melody float around me, reminding me of Ingrid.

Suzanne and I linger in our embrace before she gets into her car—not our usual quick kiss on the cheek. She tries to smile when she reverses the Explorer, but her smile is lifeless.

On my way home, I click off the radio and ride in silence.

There are no guarantees that any of us won't end up alone. No guarantee for my old neighbor who'd lost his wife of fifty years. Possibly, no guarantee for Suzanne and Lee. No one is immune. It's a matter of fate, and a matter of choices, and maybe—the planets and the stars.

What would my life be like if I'd married young like Suzanne? Would I have still become a veterinarian? Would I have kids instead of cats? Or would I be looking for answers like I am now?

~ 31 ~

I've dated half the zodiac and am still clueless about Leo, yet each sign seems to tap into a different side of my personality.

"I'm using these next few dates as an experiment," I tell Logan. "Stepping stones as Marlene put it. *Classic60s* profile mentions he likes classic cars, and so do I, thanks to my family background. He's a Virgo like you are, Logan."

"That must mean something. We've been friends for so long. You know you're like a sister to me, Jill."

My gut flutters. Lately I feel a distance growing between us, and what Logan says next drives the wedge further.

"This wedding is getting overwhelming. I want it to be perfect. I wish my mother was alive. I haven't talked to my father in years—"

"It doesn't have to be perfect," I say, though I should know better than to say this to a Virgo.

"Jill, I was thinking of asking your dad to walk me down the aisle."

I've been multi-tasking while I've been on the phone with Logan, but now my focus becomes a laser beam. Dad's MRI showed advanced stenosis. He'll never be able to *walk me* down an aisle by the time I get married. My eyes must be turning moss green picturing Dad escorting Logan as a bride.

"I know he never got to walk Suzanne down the aisle since her and Lee didn't get married in church," Logan rambles when I say nothing.

"Yeah, well that's Suzanne's fault for eloping." My words taste sour as lemon juice. *It's Logan's own fault for not talking to her dad.*

"Do you mind if I ask him, Jill?"

Just Say No, Jill. Logan's father did kind of go off the deep end, dating every widow who'd go out with him in the bereavement support group he'd joined after Logan's mom died.

"Give him a call," I say nonchalantly, as if I don't care, when I definitely do.

On my way into work the next morning, I spot D.J.'s Silverado a few cars ahead of me. I've dodged his last call, but now I'm dying to talk to him.

I follow him through a Mount Pleasant neighborhood of adorable cottage-like homes with roadside mailboxes, shuttered windows and boxwood hedges. Shep's bowling-ball head is on the passenger side with his tail swishing back and forth inside the cab. The flatbed is loaded with lumber and taping compound that tells me D.J.'s headed to a job— *must be close to the clinic.* But at the last light, D.J. turns left onto Meadowbrook Road. *Amberfield? Why?*

I continue driving to work instead of following D.J., but I'm chewing my lip. A thunk against the inside of my trunk reminds me that the Ouija board is still in there and maybe my car, and me, will be the next casualty like the barn.

I turn sharply into the next driveway and turn my car around. My bumper scrapes the curb as I accelerate the slope backwards and speed off toward D.J.

His truck is already parked in the Amberfield driveway and as I hop out of my car, Shep spots me and lopes over. D.J. crooks his neck back over his shoulder, a six-foot plank strong-armed on one side of his body and the other toting a four-gallon tub of joint compound like it's a lunchbox. The simple blue-collar charm that infatuated me the first night I saw D.J. sets the clock back to zero hours.

"Hey, Jill. What are you doing here?" His mouth spreads to an eager smile.

"I could ask you the same thing." *I wouldn't have to pry like this if we'd been dating.*

"The new owner needed some work done," he says.

I feel my smile deflate.

"Oh, you didn't know it was sold?"

I guess I did but I shake my head, rubbing a fistful of Shep's soft ears. *Why didn't I expect this? I knew I'd never get that loan.* Logan never mentioned a word from Greg. Not that she doesn't have enough on her mind with her wedding. My shoulders slump, then a surge of fight or flight takes hold.

"You didn't pull out the cabinets, did you, D.J.?" The first thing most women might do is get rid of the old kitchen. Those old latches got stuck years ago when Petal lived there. "Is the pantry still intact?" That pantry was Mrs. Petal's favorite room, where she watched the horses while she cleaned vegetables from her garden.

I twirl Shep's ear and fire off another question. "So who bought the place?"

"I don't really know. I was hired by an attorney."

"The owner's an attorney?" My tone of voice makes D.J.'s face wince like he's stuffed a sore foot into a tight boot.

I glance at my watch, then at the pasture and feel heartsick. What if the attorney is remodeling the house and selling the land?

"I'm sorry, D.J. I should let you get to work." I glance at my watch. "And I'd better do the same." I sink my fingers into Shep's scruff again.

D.J.'s face looks wounded. "If the lawyer decides to pull down any woodwork, I'll let you know."

I nod. "Okay." My clogs scrape the gravel driveway until I reach my car and my brain shifts into high gear. It wasn't out of the question to make the acquaintance of a certain lawyer— after all, it wasn't as if some cozy family was moving in.

D. J. calls out to me as I start my car. I lower the window. "Hey, I should be here for a few weeks. Maybe we can get dinner after I finish work," he says.

I wave a half-hearted gesture because I know D.J. is too much of a workaholic to stop by later. But my addiction is Amberfield, and that means I'll definitely meet D.J. again.

Before I agree to meet a Classic60s guy named Barry, we talk on the phone because he lives fifty miles away. He tells me, "I'm not like a lot of other men on this dating service, but perhaps we can become friends."

Virgo and Pisces are polar opposites, and that can balance a relationship. Sort of a yin and yang—each sign has qualities the other lacks. Dr. Bob is a Virgo.

The first time I saw Barry's photo, I skipped by him. He was a few years older than me, but something about his eyes kept me going back to his photo. Barry's an artist who designs brochures for medical equipment, a self-proclaimed Renaissance man. I assume that means he'll be a gentleman.

On Sunday afternoon, I don't need to fake interest in Barry's 1968 classic Corvette when he pulls up at Starbuck's.

"Pleasure to meet you, Jill. You mentioned your family was in the car business, so I thought I'd take you for a ride in one of my favorites."

"If I hadn't gone to vet school, I probably would have worked at Grand Garage— I'm a closet gear-head." I'd learned my lesson after my date with the pilot, and don't mention how I used to help Tim fix his cars.

Barry pops the hood of his blue Stingray to show me the engine. *Maybe I laid the gear-head stuff on too thick.* Every detail matters to this man, right down to his polished cowboy boots. He folds his suede jacket and lays it in the back seat of the car. Then he adjusts his white denim shirt, fixes the belt of his jeans before he opens the passenger car door. I hop inside without any reservations and roll down the Corvette window. We cruise down the county road, unsure of where we're headed. He just said we would be outdoors, and that sounded safe and fun.

"I thought we'd take advantage of the fall weather, Jill. Have you ever been to the orchard to pick apples?"

"Not in all the years I've lived here." I guess it takes an artist to have more imagination than a coffee date.

The wind feathers Barry's tawny hair like the wings of a sparrow. Although he's almost forty, his age doesn't show. He's not a big man, but he's got the proportions right.

We pull into a dirt lot at the country store where a red pickup truck with wooden railings is parked. Ten other people are sitting on bench seats. Barry holds his hand out for me as I climb onto the flatbed, but it's hardly exciting having my thigh wedged against a pudgy grandmother.

The clutch grinds and the truck struggles uphill. At the summit of the dirt road, Barry and I veer off toward a grid of trees with plump apples.

"These Cortland apples make a good pie," Barry says, pitching one into my bag like a softball.

"I had no idea the kind of apples makes a difference to the taste of the pie," I say. I meander about thirty feet from Barry, picking out each apple with as much care as if picking out a puppy. The grass rustles beneath my feet, the tangy fragrance of fermenting fruit reminds me of potpourri. I pick three more apples and look back at Barry who is now standing on a stepladder, filling his bag.

"I hope they collect all these fallen ones so they don't go to waste," I yell. There's no answer, though I'm not sure he's heard me over the voices of children playing nearby.

Did I really expect picking apples to be romantic?

I cross over to the next aisle and stop short at the edge of a panoramic cliff. An auburn countryside sweeps across my vision, and so does the memory of cantering on Petal's fat pony. I'm lost in my daydream when I hear Barry's voice.

"There you are. How did you make out?" I turn my head to see Barry smiling at me.

"It's so beautiful here, Barry." I open my bag and proudly show him my four perfect apples. "Is this enough for a pie?"

He glances into at my bag and then into my face with a look so tender, I feel kissed.

"You don't cook, do you?" he says.

A warmth blossoms in my cheeks, not unlike times my Italian father pinched them affectionately when I was a child.

"I'm clueless when it comes to baking."

"That's okay. I have plenty of apples. Are you ready for lunch yet? There's a nice little country restaurant that I thought we'd try a few miles from here."

"I'm starving." *Maybe a mistake thinking this man isn't romantic?*

Barry pays for the apples, after he adds a few more to my bag, and with each kind gesture, he's growing on me. When we get back in his car, I glance across the console at his profile— his nose, his chin, slender, handsome. Maybe I *could* see myself with an older man?

After a ten-minute drive, he turns down a mile-long driveway into a golf course of smooth white sand pits and electric green lawns. The parking lot is empty.

"It doesn't look like its open. I'll go check."

His lips are pinched when he walks back to the car. He's removed his sunglasses and his hazel eyes are staring at the distant empty lawn.

"The place is only for members now," he says, scratching his temple. I'm touched how he's planned to make this so special.

"It's okay, Barry. I think there's a place down the road that has good food."

"Oh, that's right. The Hitching Post Inn. That's a great place too, as long as the name doesn't bother you?"

"I don't mind at all."

Barry starts to wheel the Corvette around in a neat three-point turn. I settle my head against the headrest anticipating a burst of muscle power onto the paved blacktop. But he crawls onto the country road like a Florida senior citizen. I bite my nails—looking back at the row of cars lining up behind us. *My mother drives faster than Barry.*

After he finds a parking space he likes at the Hitching Post, he double-checks the car lock and we walk toward the restaurant. At least he walks faster than he drives. He takes his hands out of his jacket pocket to open the entrance door for me, and stands patiently holding the door as the couple who look like they've been celebrating their 60th anniversary exits.

My heels echo on the dark wood as I step inside the foyer — silky golden grains running through wide boards like I'd stood on in my riding boots at the Amberfield farmhouse. I mention it to Barry as the hostess seats us beside the fireplace in a booth of burgundy and hunter green fabric. My cold nose warms instantly to the juicy scent of roasting meat and hot cider.

"So I thought your profile was cute," Barry says, and looks at me in his gentle way again over the menu. "The part where you described your home décor as Shabby *Sheikh?*" He's carefully worded the question even though he apparently knows the answer.

My expression must show him I don't understand.

"I believe it should be spelled *chic,*" he says.

I feel my face tighten. I'd misspelled the word *chic* as *sheikh,* and now it was posted all over the Internet.

Suddenly, one of Mount Pleasant's clients comes to my mind. Maryanne Romano was adorable when she misconstrued sophisticated words. No misconstruing my words now…I'm appalled, *not* adorable.

Barry reaches over and pats my hand.

"I thought it was cute," he says, like he means it, like I was cute, like he was sorry he'd upset me. "I have a membership at the Metropolitan Museum in New York City. I'd like to take you sometime."

His clever pivot from my faux pas tells me something about him that doesn't upset me in the least. This was a man who cared about my feelings.

The waitress takes our order. Barry asks about my hobbies, nothing too personal. I know he's divorced and has a teenage daughter because he mentions her name often in conversation.

"My daughter was born with a serious heart problem. She needed open-heart surgery when she was a baby. Every few years, she had to have more surgery." He lowers his storytelling voice. "One day when she was little, I took a few crystals off the dining room chandelier and put them in the brook behind our house. I told her it was a magic brook, and if she skimmed her hand along the top of the water she would be okay."

My sinuses feel like I've inhaled water.

"She's is perfectly fine today," he reassures me when I pinch back tears at the bridge of my nose. "She only needs cardiac testing every year. I'm teaching her photography. She took that picture on my profile."

That explains the loving look the night he popped up on my screen. "She did a great job."

"Hey, speaking of photos, I brought some of my wildlife shots," Barry says.

Over coffee, we sit side by side, looking at his portfolio of art and animals.

"Pardon me," Barry says politely when his knee brushes mine. He clears his throat and stutters to explain the next photo. Another man might have done it on purpose, and I wouldn't have minded. But I can tell he's not that man. On his profile he'd called himself a Renaissance Man— someone who is open-minded, who cares about a healthy mind and body, and lives for the experiences of life. It makes me wonder why he's uncomfortable with human touch. And it dawns on me— one's sun sign wasn't the whole picture. Dr. Bob wasn't like that.

After Barry pays the check and helps me put on my coat we step outside.

"It got chilly," he says, hugging his elbows to his ribs. We roll up the car windows and on the ride home a bittersweet scent of apples fills the air, much like our date.

"I had fun, Barry," I say when we get back to the parking lot where I've left my old Honda, now parked beside his ageless sports car.

"Yes, I'm sorry to see our time end," he says, stopping a few feet away from me. He reaches out to shake my hand. I make a split-second decision to hug him. His torso stiffens, and when I back away, he's blushing.

"I'm going to make a pie for you from these apples, Barry. My grandmother's family recipe."

"Grandma's pie? Wow. I'll look forward to that."

On the long drive home, I can't stop yawning. *Maybe this is the way a relationship should start?* Maybe Logan's advice, "Nice guy, but no butterflies," is a good way to judge a keeper?

At home later I email Barry.

I can't stop thinking of the magic brook! Thank you for telling me that story about your daughter.

What's that other saying about butterflies? *If it comes back, it's yours.*

~ 32 ~

Palo Alto, California

These were the sunny Sunday afternoons James loved as a boy. He drove up to his old home and pulled up the emergency brake on the sports car he'd rented. Toasty dried leaves scented the air as he entered Ingrid's garden and headed straight for the plaster birdbath where Ingrid hid a spare key. He knew it would still be there. Before he went inside the house, he walked around to the patio. He'd come back later to sleep here after dinner with his uncle, but he wanted to come while it was still light out.

His hands were in his pockets, his head was down, searching for the cement block with his hand-print. His aunt had shown him how the movie stars had done that on a sidewalk in Hollywood. She'd helped him do the same here. He remembered the way she smelled when she was near him, like fresh crushed violets, and he never forgot the gentle manner that she taught him when she took him to feed the wild ducks on the pond. He was too young then to know you can't marry your aunt.

The hand print was half the size his is now, and the grooves were shallow, but he could still make it out alongside his initials. J.C.

~ 33 ~

Even though D.J. works hard long days, he usually finds time to call me. It's odd that I haven't heard back from him.

Dr. Bob is trying to tie up loose ends again and finally I get the nerve to do something I've been avoiding for months.

That night when I get home I open my trunk and push back the blanket where I've tucked the Ouija board.

When I pull back the plastic cover, the cardboard releases a pleasant odor like fresh-raked earth. I sweep my hand across the old box and a few dusty pieces crumble off. They say Ouija can connect spirits of the dead. What if I could connect with Ingrid? Or Petal?

I dig out my old photo album and find a picture of Petal. *It would be nice if I had a photo of Ingrid.* I miss her. I realize I've stopped missing Tim.

Is all this dating making me less sensitive?

Maybe so.

And just in time to meet the most insensitive date of my life.

It is Halloween and nights are chilly— the sweater-less evenings of the Pacific west coast have spoiled me.

"I'm meeting a lawyer tonight after work, Jeannie."

"Well, you were dressed so nice I wondered where you were going. Ann Taylor isn't your usual style."

"It isn't, is it?" Was I changing to fit the profile of a prominent attorney, or have I changed?

"So what sign is this lawyer?" Jeannie asks.

"He's a Scorpio, like Tim was." I shrug one shoulder. "I thought it would be a good idea to date another Scorpio. Even two people of the same sign can be very different because of the other planets in our birth chart."

"How many signs have you dated so far?" Jeannie's expression looks frazzled. "I can't keep these guys straight," she says, fluttering her hands.

"Don't worry, Jeannie. So far I'll probably never see any of these guys again."

"Tell me again, anyway. Didn't you like anyone?"

I start to laugh. "I'm not sure."

She hands me a notebook.

"Well, hard-working D.J. is a Capricorn. The real estate guy that I had dinner with is a Cancer." I groan about Aaron and continue counting. "Tom is a Taurus-nice guy, but not for me. Steve is a Gemini, smart, but dumb enough to be intimately involved with two women at the same time." I stop to think about how so many people in my life are Geminis. Ingrid, for one, my siblings also. I continue, "Troy, the pilot with gorgeous dimples is a Libra. And Barry, who owns a medical company, is a Virgo, like Logan and Bob." I don't need to explain to Jeannie what that means. She's worked for Bob long enough to know that he is particular about cleanliness and order. I finally tell her about my date with Tafari, a Pisces like me.

"You mention Tafari like he's in the present," Jeannie says in her scratchy smoker's voice.

"He's somewhere in Europe," I say as if he's in outer space.

"A criminal lawyer should make for an interesting date. Speaking of lawyers, I meant to call Ingrid's attorney to ask if he has a photo of Ingrid. I didn't think to ask him the day of that awful call. It'd be a shame if they were thrown away. I'm sure no one else would want them."

Jeannie picks up the ringing phone but whispers to me before she answers. "I'll make sure you get out on time for your date tonight. That lawyer might be charging for his time!"

When I call the attorney, Vic Walters, to let him know that I'm running late, his voice sounds subdued, as if I woke him up, or he's hung over.

The parking lot is nearly empty when I pull into the diner where he suggested we meet. I park and walk toward the entrance, scanning the lot for a Beamer or Mercedes like the lawyers drive on television shows. All I see is a van and a few empty cars. I glance at my watch. This guy said it was a ten-minute drive from his home and it's taken me twenty to get here.

Where is he?

"Well, something told me you wouldn't disappoint me," a man calls out from his car window. His words resemble the hiss of a snake.

"Vic?"

"Who else would it be?" He slides out of a black Honda Civic, and starts talking to me across the hood —*so much for a Beamer or Mercedes.* "Hop in my car and we'll go somewhere better than this place."

I promised Mom I'd take my own car on these meets from now on. I approach slowly and glance inside his car. It resembles a filthy aquarium tank. Junk is cluttering the back seat, including a shiny green tie and one dull brown dress shoe big enough to be a sunken ship. There are manila folders and a thick black textbook similar to my veterinary books. The book looks legit with its bold gold letters that say Connecticut Criminal Law, although how would I really know? All I know is that this guy should watch some television shows. Lawyers on television know how to dress. He's wearing a maroon V-neck Izod sweater vest over his striped dress shirt and a gold chain I haven't seen the likes of since the Brady Bunch.

"Come On. You can trust me." He slides his long legs back into the driver's seat, leans over and opens the passenger door from the inside. Ironically, the respectful morality that made me promise Mom I won't ride with strangers is the one that, out of politeness, makes me get into his car. "Besides, you look like a big girl. I'm sure this isn't your first date."

I'd just clicked my seat belt. My brain shifts into emergency mode. I loosen the seat belt across my lap. *No fear.* I think of the Rottweiler I handled so smoothly last week, his marble eyes bulging from a bowling ball head. My pretense of Alpha cool worked with the dog.

As Vic drives up the road we pass a sign for the next town. *If it had been dark out already I wouldn't have done this.* I slip a finger into my purse, probing for my cell phone.

"There's a place across from the town green," I say, pointing when I think he's driven far enough. "The prices are very reasonable." Judging by his economy car and his comment that he "didn't like to waste his money going to the movie theater," the place should appeal to him.

His calculating eyes connect with mine, not the way Barry's had. They are eyes trained to view the world with suspicion. He pulls into the parking lot. Finally, I unfold the crab-like posture of my upper body, at least until we near the restaurant.

I keep a one-foot distance from him. It was so different when I'd walked into a place holding hands with Tim. It didn't matter if Tim was wearing a pair of worn jeans and I was wearing a dress and heels. People would say we look like we belonged together.

The restaurant is full when we step inside. Vic places his trench coat on a chair and his hands on his hips, scrutinizing the other patrons like he's in a courtroom of criminals. *He's the one who's guilty of misrepresenting himself.* Some women might find him attractive, stately even, but I don't. He didn't have that ugly bushy moustache in his photo, and his hair looks like he's had a perm.

"How long is the wait?" Vic asks the hostess. He his loafers scuff the tile floor with the patience of a hit man.

After he approaches the hostess for the third time, she grabs two menus and escorts us to a small table. As she hands me a menu, his vulgar stare switches from her legs to her chest. Watching Vic size-up the hostess is as nauseating as finding an insect in a half-eaten salad.

"Hi, can I get you some drinks to start?" Luckily a waiter, not a waitress, comes to our table. Vic orders coffee. I order diet soda. At least we have something in common, even if it is only caffeine.

"So how long have you been on Connect, Vic?"

"I told you on the phone that I broke up with someone three months ago." He doesn't look up from the menu when he speaks. I drumroll my fingers, then slap the menu closed.

"I don't think you mentioned you'd recently broken up with someone, Vic. We didn't talk that long on the phone." His face changes, as if puzzled by who he spoke to on the phone recently. I feel my insides turn with a smile.

"Well, I wasted three years with this last woman I dated," he says, adjusting the chain around his neck. The young male waiter returns with our caffeine. At this point I'd be better off drinking liquor. Vic's behavior jacks up my nerves a little more every time he opens his mouth. "Bring us this appetizer sampler," he barks before the waiter asks for the order. "So you said you were into this astrology stuff. What does it say about you and me? I think after a few dates it's time to get intimate, don't you?" He backhands my thigh. The waiter's mouth drops open. He leaves the menus on the table and scurries away.

Although I was careful about mentioning Tim again on a date, I'm determined to do this now. "I was with someone that I thought I'd be with for the rest of my life, and he was a Scorpio, but—"

"So you like Scorpios?" he says, cutting me off.

The waiter returns with our fried food, timidly placing it before Vic. I turn my head as his manicured fingers grab a spring roll.

"Have some," he says, nudging the plate.

"Thanks. I'm not hungry."

He takes a bite of food, jerking his head with each crunch like a dog with a bad tooth. "Look, I don't want to hear about your ex-boyfriend. I'm talking about you and me."

You and me? Is he serious? If he thinks he can intimidate me, he doesn't know me. But how can he? I'm not sure I know what I'll say next!

"I plan to get to know a lot of different people, Vic," I say sharply, "and learn something from each person I date."

He stops chewing and stares at me.

"But you're the rudest person that I've met yet."

He drops his mangled roll onto his plate and throws his napkin on top of it. Then he tips his weight back until his two front chair legs rear off of the floor.

"Get me my check," he yells across the noisy room. He stands up and paces until the check comes, then slaps ten dollars on top of the bill. I slant my eyes towards the other patrons as he grabs his coat, praying no one noticed his tantrum, or recognizes me.

Vic speed walks ahead of me. His head is hunched and his trench coat is billowing like he's some giant bird of prey. Once we reach the car he gets in his side and leans across the front seat to open the passenger side like he'd done earlier. I stare down at his car aquarium again, and at bubbled paint along the edge of the door. The rust looks minor, but I know from Dad, it has probably rotted the car's frame to its core.

He rolls down the window. "Are you going to get in?" he says, looking up at me standing at the curb.

"Not with you." I back away. "I'd walk the mile if I hadn't worn heels—although right now I could sprint the distance barefoot." I lift my cell phone, turn my back and dial Lucy's Taxi.

In fifteen minutes flat, Lucy pulls up with the pink unoccupied light glowing on the roof of her white Ford Taurus. *Thank you, Lucy, for being a woman who followed her dream of owning her own cab business.*

Ingrid had told me that Pisces could be like this — gentle as a gold fish, or powerful as a whale.

It is dark when I speed down my quiet street. Tomorrow neighbors will go about their Saturday morning business—moms in their minivans, husbands raking leaves, teenagers with hands stuffed in their pockets as if time's only purpose is meeting friends at the mall. In ten years, they might be in my shoes.

Once home at my computer, I click the Block Sender option and enter

Vic's user name, *CourtlyLove*. I've experienced Scorpio's sting twice now. The date wasn't a waste of time after all— but I wouldn't let Vic's personality, or my final days with Tim, erase all the things I once loved about a Scorpio.

"So did you meet anyone special yet?" Marlene, the office accountant asks when I pass by her office the next day.

"Not quite, but you were right about finding out what I don't want. I had the worst date of my life, and the guy was a lawyer."

Marlene's head snaps up from her work, her expression stunned like the day the U.S.D.A. agent showed up at the office to investigate an ex-employee who'd stolen a controlled drug. "What happened?"

What did happen? I never expected to act so bold. "I don't know," I start to say. "He was rude and I let him have it."

Marlene's face brightens like a painted pumpkin.

My fiasco becomes an adventure when she pumps me for details. Marlene cackles and gives me the high five when I tell her and Jeannie how I refused to ride back to the diner.

"Women love a good story about men behaving badly," Jeannie says.

"Hey, what ever happened to the guy at church?" Marlene asks.

"Never saw him again."

"He might show up." Marlene winks.

"I'm past magical thinking, at least regarding dating. With three signs left before Leo, I don't expect the world to change."

In my office I call Attorney Chamberlain's office about the photos. *I wonder if Vic knows Ingrid's lawyer.* My stomach grinds at the thought.

"Hold on, Jill," the legal assistant says.

I slouch into my chair and sift through the pile of lab results while I'm holding for Attorney Chamberlain.

"Funny, you just came to my mind this morning, Jill."

My arms tingle. "You know what Ingrid would say about that. Did you find any photo albums at Ingrid's home? I'd love a photo of her."

"Well, I shipped everything off to James, but I'll ask when I see him."

"Oh." I pause to think of names Ingrid might have mentioned to me. "James?" I ask.

"Ingrid's son, my nephew." He chuckles. "I guess Ingrid never mentioned him to you."

"I'm confused," I say. "Ingrid has a son? So you were more than Ingrid's friend?"

"Oh you didn't know, did you? She was married to my brother."

"And so—"

"Ingrid kept her maiden name. My brother passed years ago when James was only a teenager. That's when she started having problems with James. It's too bad. He's a very nice guy. About your age, I'd say. He works at Stanford University. They were estranged for years, then Ingrid made her peace with James before she left for Sweden."

Her trip to Colorado and Texas, I remember she also mentioned California, but never that she had a son.

"I'll see what I can do about a photo. I have something else that I want to talk to you about. It's about the Amberfield property."

My stomach somersaults.

"Listen, Jill, give me a call in a week or so."

I hang up in slow motion. So Ingrid has a son who lives in California. "And I just got back from California!" My shrill of laughter sends Jeannie flying into my room.

"What happened?"

I'm standing with my hand over my mouth. "Something good," I say. I open my desk drawer and grab the newspaper article that Dr. Bob had saved for me with the article about Ingrid. Jeannie comes to my side, fidgeting with excitement though she has no idea why. Still she checks her watch and lets me know we have ten minutes until the next appointment. I have the paper open to the article on the sale of Amberfield and scan for the name of the buyer. Even before I see it I know who it is. James Chamberlain.

During the first week of November, I get a message from Barry. His dad has gone into the hospital and now Barry is traveling thirty miles to visit him each day.

Jill, I'll look forward to a piece of that pie. You might have to keep it in the freezer until we can meet again.

The less I hear from Barry, the less I think of him. *I'd never felt that way about Tim when we were together.* If absence was supposed to make the heart grow fonder, maybe my indifference was telling me something.

Like when D. J. leaves me his last message.

"Hey Jill. It's D.J. I got your message about Amberfield. Haven't met James Chamberlain yet, but don't worry, the old kitchen cabinets you love are still there. My brother's band is playing at the Wharf this weekend if you're interested." There's a little pause before his tone softens. "I can't dance with you this time. I, ah, started dating your neighbor."

I smile when I hear D.J.'s message. My private rooting for D.J. makes me realize that he and I were never meant to be more than just friends.

I haven't talked to my sister to see how things are going with her and Lee. But when I call Mom to ask how Dad is feeling, she says, "the doctor gave him pills for his pain. They can't find anything else wrong. They referred him to a neurologist."

"A neurologist? Why?" She mentions the word Parkinson's as if it is arthritis. *She doesn't understand.* The last time I was with Dad, I noticed the odd way he held his fork. But I'll be able to see for myself when we spend Thanksgiving Day together. At least, I'm hoping we'll be together, because the holiday won't be the same if Lee isn't there with Suzanne and the kids.

On Sunday when I walk into church, I admit to looking over at the pew for the man with the blond ponytail. Instead I see Tim's mom, Maggie.

"Hi Maggie. How are you?" I stoop to hug her tiny frame.

"Oh, everythins good, Jill," she says in her Irish lilt. "But Tim left his job with his father, and he's teachin' music, or somethin'." She says it with a wave of disapproval.

"Well, that's good that he's trying something new, Maggie."

"He doesn't know what's good for him. He left you." Her upper lip crinkles like skin does at women her age, but her eyes are bright as star sapphires.

Tim often talked about a music career, except he could never bear to disappoint his dad. Or me, I guess. I'm not sure I'd know this Tim now. *Have we both become different people?*

I wonder if that's occurred to Mom as we await results about Dad? I know that "no news is good news," didn't apply to medicine. I know the longer Dad goes without a diagnosis, the more baffling it'll be to find one.

~ 34 ~

It's difficult to cross Barry's name off my list. He sends an email every week, but never asks to see me. This time I don't worry it's personal.

On an unseasonably warm November Sunday afternoon, I glance at the clock on my dashboard and lean on the gas peddle. Not the smartest thing considering my next date's a cop.

It was his idea to make our "first meet" an athletic activity, and I got the impression that staying out of a coffee shop or a bar was my Aries date's way to make sure I'll measure up to his standards, not to mention his ripped rhomboids.

I park and walk over to the park entrance where we're supposed to hike. My hair is clipped up stylishly bed head, strands dangling along the side of my face. I've worn a slimming pair of fitness slacks with a powder blue stripe down the side of my leg. I bought a yoga jacket to match and I'm toting two cool neon-blue water bottles—the second one is for my date.

I prop by backside against a sun-warmed boulder and watch hikers and joggers pass by, including one of my clients on their weekly bird-watching hike with their mixed breed collie that has little interest in anything but a cookie, preferably coated with chocolate. I do a quick check for ticks on wiggly Peppermint.

"Thanks, Dr. Christie. Are you meeting someone?" they ask.

"Yes. He should be here soon." The wife winks, then the couple resumes their hike. I double-check my phone for messages. *I expected a cop to be on time.*

After thirty minutes passes, I feel as if I'm the canine crossing guard. I'm dressed like a hiker who never breaks a sweat, yet I suddenly do, because it starts to sink in. He's not coming.

I don't understand this— I'd given him my cell number— I had no reason to believe that he wasn't a cop (and I'd done some detective work to make sure).

Maybe I'm in the wrong spot?

I start down the obscure path that leads to a pond where Dad had brought us when we were kids. The pond is so much smaller than I remember. The last time I'd seen it Petal had come with us, too.

I pry one flat stone out of the mud and angle my body like Dad had taught us. Then I flick my wrist and let the rock fly. It slaps the surface and plops to the bottom. Dad had made it skip two, maybe three times. I feel this avalanche crumble inside me. Dad used to be so agile and fun.

What are the doctors missing? He'll never make it to walk Logan down the aisle next spring, let alone me someday. Mom said Dad choked up when Logan called to ask him. He told her he'd "be honored," then went to bed and slept through half the next morning.

I leave the other two rocks I'd collected on the boulder. Then I turn to leave.

Before I drive off, I check my phone one more time. No messages. *Face it. You've been stood up.*

On the way out of the park, a few fire fighters are standing on the exit lane, collecting money for Thanksgiving turkeys for charity. They're dressed in navy trunks with reflective yellow vests and navy tee shirts. I slow down and dig one hand in my purse, fishing for a few dollars to toss into the Buck-in-the-Boot donation.

I lower my window as I approach the handsome guy smiling at me who happens to resemble my brother, Rob. I stop beside him. He sips his coffee and sets it on the ground. When he tips back his blue cap, his brown eyes fixate on mine.

"How are you today?" he says smoothly. He rests his arm on my window frame and leans on my car. His face is less than ten inches from mine. A few other guys are standing in the background calling out to other cars. I count out four dollars, slowly. He leans close enough to smell coffee on his breath when I hand him my donation.

"Thank you, Honey. Have a nice Thanksgiving." he says.

I feel my face light up with a smile that starts in my gut.

Then I notice the band on his left ring finger.

"You, too," I say. As I coast away I tip my head and glance back in my side view mirror. He's waving and doesn't take his eyes off my car until I exit the park.

When I get home I text Logan. "Donating money for a turkey turned out better than meeting some turkey!"

I get a text apology the next day from Mr. Aries who says he "was playing racquetball and lost track of time."

I learn all I need from his insincere message and decline his offer to meet again. Yet, if I believed all Aries were inconsiderate, I'd have to include my father, and that would be dead wrong. Later, I squiggle a black line through Aries. For the third time this weekend, Dad crosses my mind.

"So how is it going with Barry?" Jeannie asks between appointments.

"I promised him a pie from the apples. It's probably the only thing that makes it out of my freezer before it expires!"

Wednesday night I drive to meet Barry at a café located half-way between our homes. I've brought the pie that I made him and I can tell he's sincere when he says he "really likes deep dish pie." But I feel shallow sitting with him today. I need more than a story about a magic brook from Barry.

I need to find the magic I had once— not with a man—with my whole life.

Last week there was an old Volvo like Ingrid's parked in the clinic lot. A client mistakenly thought it was my car and had left a note on the windshield, *Sorry I missed you.*

I never heard back from Attorney Chamberlain about Ingrid's photo. Did she think I wouldn't find out about James? Or was that who she meant in her letter, when she said that was up to me after she was gone? Yet, there was no service planned for Ingrid, and James lives in California.

If dating has taught me anything, it's that it takes time to get to know someone. *Do long distance relationships ever work?*

"Within one year," Ingrid had said I'd find Leo. Much as I hoped she were right, I can't help wonder if that old Ouija Board might end up being true when it spelled my own initials, because within one year is now only a matter of months.

~ *35* ~

A young family of four that includes two irritable children slides into the pew ahead of me the following Sunday morning at St Francis' Church. As the mass starts, the toddler jangles a fistful of keys and drops them under the pew. I bend down and fish blindly, jingling the key ring with my pinky. Another couple turns around at the fuss. So does a man with a blond ponytail a few pews ahead. He locks eyes with me, expressionless, then turns away.

I try to convince myself I don't care, but my reaction tells me I do.

In zodiac speak, Sagittarius with Pisces forms a relationship that would be challenging. Except I know from Ingrid that the other considerations of a person's birth chart were important as well. *And a little bit of tension isn't always a bad thing.*

After mass as the family gathers the baby's belongings and exits the pew, I decide our paths should cross. I'm determined to handle my introduction smoothly, though I can't say the same about my damn keys. If I was capable of doing something like this on purpose, I would have been smart enough not to do it with him.

My palms are moist. I'm clumsier than usual. My key chain of bobbles and nametags of every cat I ever owned crashes on the floor with the tinkle of breaking glass. The young mother stops for a second and turns back.

"I'm so sorry," she says, unable to free her arms of the wriggling baby.

"It's okay. I can reach them," I say. I kneel and sweep my arm under the pew. The shuffle of parishioners fades into the vestibule as sandy unknown elements nestle beneath my fingernails and get the best of me. I jerk my hand back when it meets with slimy rubber— I'm hoping a toy dropped by that baby. I'm extricating a snag of my hair from one of the pew bolts when I hear a male voice talking above me.

"Here are your keys," he says. I knock my head on the seat and glance up at my broken cat charm and the rest of my keys.

I rub my forehead and pop up from my knees.

"Thanks," I say holding out my hand. He plops the keychain into my palm like a wet octopus. "I haven't seen you here in awhile," I say fondling the broken cat. My lip is damp and it's November. "You contacted me months ago on Connect."

He looks at me intensely but says nothing.

"I saw you a couple of months ago and I emailed you. My name is Jill, not that you'd remember, I'm sure you talked to a lot of people, and …"

"I was away," he says bluntly. "My name's Sam."

Finally, after all these months, I learn his real name. He's prickly— I expected fun-loving from a Sagittarius, playfully affectionate like my brother-in-law.

I clench my keys so tightly they imprint on my palm. *I guess that's that. He doesn't like me.* "Well, have a great day," I say, and turn to leave.

With each step I feel more ridiculous about how I'd sat in church wanting to meet him. *To hell with him.* I don't like him. *But damn.* For some strange reason, my body is sending signals I do.

Now that I've seen him up close, he isn't that good-looking, not in a traditional sense. His face is sunburned and slightly pocked by old acne scars. How I hated sometimes that Tim was so good-looking. I never let on how it felt when I'd use the Ladies room only to return to find the waitress at our table flirting with Tim.

He starts to follow me as I walk out of the church. When we reach the sidewalk, he's walking beside me. Okay, maybe it isn't my imagination.

"So did you ride your motorcycle?" I say as I reach my car.

"It's too cold for that. You know, Jill, I do own a car. In fact, I own quite a few." His thin lips melt into his manicured beard.

He points to an older model car with a dealer plates. It's nostalgic. Sunday rides with Dad and Suzanne, when Mom sent him to buy bread for dinner and Dad bought us ice cream cones at Dairy Queen.

"My grandfather had a car exactly like this when I was a kid. 1968 Electra, right?" I say, panning its clunky metal hood ornament, the long vinyl back seat. Sam squints at me.

"Most men couldn't have guessed the year or model of that car. You're close."

"My family is in the car business. I wondered why I didn't hear back from you," I say, changing the subject.

"I've been down in New Orleans working with Habitat for Humanity, rebuilding houses. No computer access most of the time, so I didn't check email once I left Connecticut. Besides, there are a lot of game players on the site."

"I'm relieved to hear you say this." I was afraid he might be one of them. "You said in your profile that you'd answer everyone back."

"Did I say that? I must have meant everyone except women who believe in astrology. And women who like cats."

I snuffle a snort-laugh. So he does remember me. "Don't you believe in astrology?"

"No."

I can't read his expression. Is he joking? Or honest, as in confident? Tim may have had looks in his favor, but confidence was something Tim didn't have. In the end, it came between us.

"Coffee?" he asks.

"Sure, but I'll have to follow you. I promised my mother I won't get into a car with men I don't know. You never know, not even about a church man." His straight white teeth break the ice when he smiles.

We drive in separate cars to the diner where I'd met the lawyer. When it comes to good food and great coffee, one bad experience can't leave a rotten taste in my mouth.

"Hi Carmella, hi Effie," I say to the ladies who make the place sweet as their pie.

"Hi Honey. Pick a table. I'll be right over to get your order."

We walk to the far side of the diner.

"I'm thinking of moving out west," Sam says sitting sidesaddle in the seat, one elbow propped on the back of the chair. "Maybe take some time off and visit the Grand Canyon. I've always wanted to see it." His dramatic round eyes follow the waitress' footsteps back and forth, minus the vulgar gawking like Vic. But he's also avoiding my face when he talks, his gaze off in the distance as if he's making plans as we speak.

"You're lucky you can take time off," I say.

His head hangs as if he's got a problem with the word "lucky."

"I'm not sure how long I'll stay here. I come to church each week looking for answers, but…" He finishes his sentence with a mysterious expression and wrinkles his auburn chin hairs.

I get the feeling he knows what he wants but hasn't found it.

"I like your name," I say, referring to his Internet handle, *Freedom#1*.

"I think it scares some women away," he says blandly.

It doesn't scare me, but maybe it should have scared me. He's my age, but his sun-beaten skin appears older, tougher. After coffee, and a few long looks from Carmella, we leave.

I keep my distance as we walk to the exit, but when his calloused hand brushes mine, I know it's no accident. His coldness doesn't fool me. He's searching for something all right. And I get the feeling it could be me.

"See you at church next week," he says, when we reach our cars. He arranges his king-sized frame behind his steering wheel.

"It must be fate, meeting a man in church." Oh Jeannie, could you be right about this?

As much as I want to believe there's a good reason I finally met a man at church, something about Sam doesn't feel quite right.

~ *36* ~

Thanksgiving is two weeks away. I'll be able to see how Dad's doing once he and Mom are back from Florida. Much as I thought I might have had a date by my side by this time, Dad is more concerned than I am that I haven't seriously dated anyone since Tim. Normally I wouldn't give it a second thought as to why he's in a hurry for me to pair up with someone. Now I do.

Sam and I have met for coffee a few times and once for a ride on his Harley. He doesn't dress like Steve, the Gemini who showed up on his yellow and black bike in a matching outfit. He doesn't wear a helmet, though he makes me wear one. But he doesn't sport a tee shirt, or a tattoo for that matter either.

He'd worn a tailored long-sleeved striped shirt over clean blue jeans the first time. The Harley had sent vibrations from the soles of my feet to my spine. The rest of my body was falling for the vibration of being close to Sam.

His silky hair had blown butterflies across my cheek each time the bike accelerated. I wasn't the least bit afraid, though I'd pressed myself close to his ribcage as if the speed terrified me.

Sam had stopped at a deserted park and we sat on fallen leaves near the pond. That first kiss lasted hours. After that, we talked every night on the phone, and teased each other about where this was leading. I'm trying to think with my head and not follow my heart. I have two signs to go, and I don't want to stop now. Besides, Sam still travels a lot. I'm not sure why. Sometimes I feel as if he's fitting me into his schedule. Usually it happens on the spur of the moment, and at odd moments in the day that he'll ask to see me when he knows I can't break away.

Tonight when Sam arrives to pick me up for dinner, it's totally different. He's wearing a navy sport jacket and jeans, and he's holding a bouquet of pink carnations. His cologne is a spicy blend of cloves and rum that he said he bought in Aruba.

"You look nice, Sam," I say, admiring his presidential appearance. I pet his trimmed goatee and lift up on my tiptoes to hug him.

Sam reaches for my hand, presses his lips to my palm as if we're in slow motion.

"The reservation is for 7:30, Darlin. Are you ready?"

I look up at the blonde highlights framing his broad forehead, those ice blue eyes. I feel weightless when Sam touches me again.

"Unless you want to stay home and order take-out."

"She offered herself to the big bad wolf and didn't scream when it took its first bite." Where did these freaking feelings come? That weird line from the *Wintergirls* book Suzanne read to me just popped into my head.

I grab my purse and we walk out to his car. It's a Mercedes this time, not a make and model that only the daughter of an automobile family would know. Most women would recognize this car. He opens the door for me, and it closes with a plush thud.

I look over at him when he slides in. His interesting face has become less complicated, and more that of a man I trust.

"Did anyone ever tell you that you look Scandinavian, Sam?" I say when he puts the car in reverse. His head twists to face me, but although his eyes meet mine, there's a delayed reaction as his mood shifts.

"Why do I look like a Viking pirate?" he asks.

It's not like I asked if he were adopted. Then he laughs, a high-pitched howl, and glances at me as he reaches over and raises the radio volume. Soft rock. The mood is like that.

So family background is off limits. Maybe he doesn't have a family? Maybe he doesn't want to have one. There was a way to find out.

"Do you have plans for Thanksgiving?" I ask.

His eyes don't budge from the road. "I'm leaving for Colorado on Tuesday to spend Thanksgiving with my sister."

I swivel toward him. "You never mentioned your family before. I was going to invite you to spend it with mine."

He flexes his hands on the steering wheel.

"Sorry, Darlin. I can't. You know I like having you all to myself anyway." He smiles. A wolf's grin.

I smile back but it's a mask for my disappointment. I won't be with someone who can't share me with family.

He pulls the car into the lot and parks. We walk into the restaurant holding hands. His touch is all I need to dismiss his odd reaction. Sam has his arm around my shoulder as a hostess leads us to our table. He orders a scotch and water as a waiter rushes by.

"I'm going to miss you, Darlin. Will you wait for me when I'm away?" he asks, working his hand back and forth across my silk blouse.

"Sam, I'm still on the dating site and I know you are, too."

The waiter returns with our drinks.

He shuffles the ice in his cocktail and swallows half the drink. "Maybe we'll change that."

My feelings for Sam are not ambiguous like they have been with the others. Despite the caution tape across my mind, I can't deny that the rest of me is tempted to cross it. It's been six months since—

"I'll be here when you get back," I say coyly. "How long will you be away?"

"I'm not sure." He's looking at his empty scotch when he answers, and orders another before dinner. "Would you bring another soda for my girlfriend, too?" Sam says to the waiter.

Girlfriend—the word is synonymous with significant other, exclusive. Intimate.

It's barely ten o'clock, when we leave the restaurant. By now he's had four drinks and polished off his 16oz steak like it was a slider. I'm tearing the skin of my thumbnail on the ride back to my house.

"Do you want to come in, Sam? You should have some coffee before you drive home."

He glances at his watch as if it's past his bedtime. "I guess that'll be okay."

I open the front door and walk in with Sam following me. "This is it," I say about the tour of my small living room and dining room. Bedrooms are on the second floor, so I skip that part.

For a moment my mind drifts. I could have been standing in the Amberfield house and saying *it's mine.*

I take a box of chocolate-striped cookies out of the kitchen cabinet and arrange them on a plate while Sam studies my eclectic paintings— the Renaissance fairies hanging on the mustard-colored walls of the narrow hallway. His broad shadow lingers at the bleak Wyeth of a freed slave in a vivid green pasture that hangs in the dark corner of my living room. When he turns around and looks at me I realize I'm as conflicted as those paintings. *So am I the fairy or the slave?*

As the aroma of steamed ground roast seeps from the coffee maker, I become aware of Sam watching me, and my skin radiates with innuendo of his touch.

I lift up on my toes to reach two coffee mugs from the top cabinet.

Then Sam reaches over me to grab the cups. His arm brushes mine, the tingle unravels down my spine. I lean into him, his body heat like a warm bed in winter. *This is difficult to turn off.*

The explosive hiss of the coffee maker squeezes the last drops of water out of the reservoir. The room becomes fuzzy when Sam wraps his arms around me. His lips cover mine, his fingers find the corner of my blouse and suddenly I feel them cross my naked flesh.

"No, Sam." My arms fold back to hold his.

"No? I think you mean yes."

I start to hyperventilate as he tugs my hair. I twist away playfully.

"You're sending mixed messages," he says sternly.

"I don't understand your sudden change of heart, Sam. You're constantly traveling. I didn't know you had a sister. How am I supposed to get close to you?" I reach for the coffee pot and spill half pouring some into a mug. Maybe it isn't Sam's heart that I don't understand.

"Maybe you should leave before we get in deeper than we should." I'm aching for him to touch me again, slowly.

A chuckle whistles past his straight white teeth, then he kisses my forehead. "Kissing is enough to hold me over until you're ready. I'll call you when I get to my sister's place."

The minute he says this I'm disappointed that I resorted to being defensive. My body is bristling with wounded pride. *He expects me to wait for him after only four dates? Does he think I'm desperate? Was it obvious that I'm falling for him? Or is it possible he's falling for me?*

He grabs a cookie and heads for the door.

"Bye," he says with a sly smile.

I fold my arms tightly against my chest, my last chance to hold onto the passion.

Once Sam leaves, I turn on the television and eat every cookie on the plate. But coffee, chocolate and contemplation turn out to be a bad combination. I'm running out of reasons not to give in to Sam. I have only Aquarius left before Leo.

I'm still sitting in front of the television when the phone rings at midnight. *Must be Oliver calling from California. He's likely stoned and forgotten the three-hour time difference.* I lower the television and pick up the phone.

"Jill?" a woman's voice is barely audible. I hear a cluck as she clears her throat trying to catch her breath. Then I recognize the diminished voice.

~ *37* ~

"It's Bob's wife," she says. The last time Pam called my home was to invite me to Bob's surprise birthday party. Jeannie was sure Bob knew about the party, because that's the only way Pam would have invited the entire office staff.

"What's wrong?"

I slap my heart before I hear her answer.

"Bob's been rushed to the hospital with a heart attack," she says, in a faltering voice.

The office pace has never let up like it does this time of year. Bob even postponed his family Thanksgiving trip. I should have realized something was wrong with his frequent bouts of indigestion, but I've been too damn busy trying to avoid him.

A younger Bob's face flashes in my mind— the day that I'd first met Bob as a teenager.

"This is Jill, Dr. Bob," Jeannie had said. "She's going to be helping us here during school break this summer."

"Jill Christie, Hmm? Doctor Jill Christie sounds like it would make a nice name."

I would still be a vet assistant instead of a veterinarian if not for Bob. Holding the phone, my torso crumbles into my lap, like my world surely will without Bob.

"He woke up this morning with a pain in his left arm, but he thought it was from playing racket ball yesterday," Pam says. There's a drawn out silence. I can feel my heart knocking against my ribs.

"Pam?"

She whimpers. "I'm sorry, Jill, I need to get a tissue."

The phone clunks when she sets it down. Her hiccup-like gasp fills me with spite, remembering times Pam called the office each afternoon to find out when appointments ended. I hated seeing Bob rush out of the building at the end of the day as if he were being clocked to drive home.

Often we'd hear Bob squawk into the phone. "The animals need their evening treatments, the staff needs to finish mopping the exam rooms, and clients are expecting a call for lab results. I can't leave for another hour, Pam." Pam didn't understand what it was like, dealing with clients that ramble from their pet's bum leg to their own.

There is a static sound as Pam picks up the phone. "Bob said he felt nauseous tonight and he didn't want to eat dinner." She sniffles and coughs. "He said he was going to lie down. Then I heard a crash upstairs and, uhhh, I feel faint myself now."

My mouth goes dry. "Is Bob okay?" I don't mean to shout, but it comes out that way. At least it scares Pam straight through the next bit of information.

"The EMS came and rushed him to our local hospital, but they shipped him to another hospital by helicopter because he needed some special surgery on his heart."

"He's in surgery?" I'm trying to make sense of this bad dream.

"The doctor said Bob's got four blockages. I don't remember anything else the doctor said. Bob used to take care of everything." Pam's voice trails off into a series of sighs.

Life Star helicopter? *Bob is so physically fit. It's hard to believe he's old enough to have a heart attack.* Pam's silly suspicion of my relationship with her husband, pressure for Bob to get home in time for dinner with their children— I'm seething. Sure, a heart attack is possible.

I could always tell when Bob and Pam had been fighting the minute he came into work. He'd walk through the clinic door, an obvious strain in his face from holding back on losing his temper. He never did though. He'd slam a door or end up spilling coffee on his shirt, then act as if everything was fine by the time he saw clients.

"I didn't know who to call, Jill. I don't talk to Bob's sister, and Bob's mother is starting with Alzheimer's. Besides I didn't want to call them at this hour. Bob, Bob thinks the world of you, Jill. He says you're so smart and good with clients."

My head drops. *Compliments from a woman I thought hated me.* It completely defuses my anger.

"Do you need anything, Pam?" My words sound distant and cliché, but I mean it. I've known Pam for years, but I hardly know her. Who was I to judge when I didn't know the whole story of being the spouse of a dedicated veterinarian?

"I don't know what I'll do if he doesn't make it," Pam says. "I never finished getting my nursing degree. I haven't worked since having kids." Pam's voice cracks. I'm speechless, and frozen with fear that Bob could die. In some ways, Pam and I are in the same situation. I'd never worked for anyone but Bob.

"Don't worry, Pam. He'll be okay. I'll take care of everything at the office." I say it because I have to believe it.

I hang up the phone and press the corners of my eyes, the bridge of my nose, my temples, but my head feels ready to explode. Right now I don't feel one bit as smart as Bob made Pam think.

The next morning, I'm in work by 7:30AM. Jeannie usually arrives at the office before me, so Jeannie has to know something is wrong when she pulls up to see my car there, and not Bob.

I'm on the phone, stuttering-talking to someone when Jeannie walks in. My usual smile is flat and I can tell this makes Jeannie panic. "Okay, thank you," I say as I look up with wet eyes.

"Jill, what's the matter?" Jeannie slams her lunch bag on the counter.

"Dr. Bob had a heart attack last night. Pam called at midnight. I talked to the hospital and they gave me a room number in the Cardiac Care unit, so at least he made it."

The color fades from her face. "That's terrible. Terrible, oh this is terrible. Tell me what I should do, Jill?"

I've never heard Jeannie sound so helpless. She's always been the strong one, but come to think of it, that was only because, like all of us, she had Bob to fall back on. Now that her backbone has crumbled, she seems fragile. And she's looking to me to show her the way.

"Okay. Let me think. Why don't you reschedule any non-urgent appointments?" She grabs the appointment book as if she's ready to get right on it. "And Jeannie," I add on the way to my office, "give Dr. Bell a call to see if he can help us out." I smirk to let Jeannie know it's okay to smile.

In my office, I put in a call to Pam to see if she's heard from the doctor.

"Pam spoke to the cardiologist," I yell out to Jeannie. "Bob has three cardiac stents to open his blocked vessels." Jeannie's office chair squeaks as she gets up and comes to my office door. We stare at each other, as if our brains locked on the same thought—even if Bob gets back to normal, everything else here is going to have to change.

~ 38 ~

Palo Alto, California

James pulled the ribbon on the FedEx envelope and removed a cream envelope with a University logo. A formal invite. He'd already agreed to speak at the faculty meeting next semester. This time he'd plan to spend more time back east to check out the old Amberfield property Jake couldn't talk Ingrid out of buying before she died. He knew his mother. She was eccentric, but she wasn't crazy. So he'd plan some time to meet the woman Ingrid liked so much—the woman Ingrid made James promise that she would lease the farmhouse.

There really was no need to meet her. Uncle Jake would take care of everything. After all, he was trying to simplify his life, not complicate it with a property that had liens and now a renter. But he couldn't help but be a little curious now that the heartbreak of Amy's rejection had cooled. How could he not wonder after what Ingrid told him? Jill shared a birthday with his beloved aunt.

His childhood home—the big house at the edge of Red Rock park— invariably triggered images of the aunt he had loved. He knew Ingrid must have purposely planted that seed. That was taking on a life of its own— was she anything like her, or as beautiful? And since she had died in her twenties, he still remembered her long, light brown hair, the thick brows and fleshy lids of her Eurasian eyes. As a boy he had a crush on her.

He dialed Attorney Chamberlain's cell.

"James, I didn't expect to hear from you so soon. Are you in town?"

"Not yet. I was wondering if you've met the veterinarian that's interested in renting the farmhouse?"

"I've only talked to her briefly on the phone. Why?"

James cleared his throat. "Well, I wasn't sure whether I should keep this property. I've got a lot on my plate. I'm not sure I want to be a landlord, too."

"Why don't you let me meet her. You know I'm a good judge of character."

James didn't want to sound foolish. He had to word this the right way or his uncle would be all over him about moving back to Connecticut. "Ingrid happened to mention a few things to me about her."

Jake was no dummy. "Mary brings her dog to that vet," Jake said, referring to his right-hand woman, Mary. "Says Dr. Christie's a sweetheart. Pretty too. In fact, Mary once told Ingrid that she'd be perfect for you."

James cleared his throat to disguise the soft sound of longing that escaped by surprise.

"I'll have Mary set up an appointment with her as soon as we finalize a few details. Call me when you're in Connecticut."

When James got off the phone he jingled the leash for Dizzy. She toddled into the kitchen, tipping her chunky head in confusion. This wasn't time for her walk. James had just gotten home from work. It had been months since he hadn't been too tired to do anything but nibble on some almonds and cheese and fall asleep on the couch in front of the Nature channel. But tonight he had put on his jogging sneakers. Dizzy let out a gleeful whine.

It put James in a great mood, one that had started when the phone call to Jake ended. For the first time in months he was excited. He'd hated that Ingrid had been right about his old girlfriend, but that made him realize that Ingrid might be right about Jill. There was a reason Ingrid went through so much trouble to make sure he'd meet her.

~ *39* ~

Two days after Bob's procedure, I leave the clinic and drive to the hospital. I creep softly into Bob's room, expecting to see oxygen tubes sticking out of his nostrils and I.V. bags hanging beside his bed. I guess I watch too many medical television programs.

Bob is sitting in a chair reading the newspaper, clean-shaven, with every hair slicked back in place, as always.

"Hey," he says, and I feel my eyes fill. "Pam just left." I peek out the thin blinds of the thick window to hide my tears and spot Pam in the distance leaving the hospital. She's dressed like a store mannequin as I catch a glimpse of her opening the door of a pearly BMW that Bob had bought for her birthday. Things are back to normal for Pam.

I choke on my words when I hug Bob and try to talk.

"There's a One-Day-Only-Sale at Nordstrom's. That's Pam's therapy," Bob jokes. "I'll have to start cardiac rehab in a couple of weeks. At least my therapy is covered by insurance and cheaper than Pam's." He is smiling one of his "Aaaargh" smiles, as if his own peace of mind depends on ignoring Pam's spending addiction.

"I'll take care of things at the office, Bob," I say. I can't stop thinking about what Pam told me Bob said about me. It makes me want to take care of everything for him. Except surgery. I can't. And he definitely notices.

"Dr. Silver said we could refer any difficult surgeries to him, Jill. Clients will understand."

My hands curl into fists. I know it's something he would only do if he had no other choice— to refer his patients to another hospital when they trusted him for years. He folds the newspaper and tosses it aside, leans his head back and looks up as if weighing my reaction.

I'm failing the man who is always there for me.

"Dr. Bell's doing a great job keeping up with dog and cat spays." I tell him as if it doesn't kill me to admit this. My insecurity over Bell makes me want to crawl under the chair, but I make a joke of it. "Jeannie's been bringing in fresh baked goods every day to make sure he stays." I realize I'm not fooling Bob. If he is entertaining ideas that Bell might be interested in his practice, he doesn't let on.

A hospital aid dressed in a flowered top slides a tray down on the rolling table that Bob is using as his desk. "Here's your lunch," she says lifting the gray cover. "You were supposed to order from the lo-salt menu." Bob grumbles a goofy insult about how lo-salt food is for sissies. I watch him dissect a bland turkey sandwich.

"I'd better get back to the office," I say checking my phone after an hour.

"I'll call you later to make sure everything's going okay," Bob says.

"You'd better not or I'll tell the nurses to put a muzzle on you. I can handle things."

No sooner that I leave, I count each floor tile as I walk toward the elevator leading to the parking lot. The white slivers of my fingernails are bitten to the flesh. Being here reminds me that my own father isn't well. If a young guy like Bob could come so close to death, what about Dad?

On my way to my car, I call Mom and Dad in Florida. Between the sunshine and orange juice and playing cards with their friends with their jars full of pennies, Mom thinks Dad feels a little better. I'm not buying it. Dad gets on the phone and tells me he misses his Sunday walks in the woods with the neighbor's mutt. No woods in Florida, too many palm trees. No mutts, either, only lap dogs who don't get their feet wet unless they're at the groomers.

Before I start my car, I check my messages and find one from Attorney Chamberlain. Hopefully he's calling about the photographs, which means he's talked to James. And that means news about Amberfield.

And James.

I work at least twelve hours a day the next two days, even with Dr. Bell helping out, I'm feeling the pressure. Maybe it's because of Dr. Bell.

"So I heard you might be buying the clinic, Jill," he says, leaning on the door to my office where I'm sitting with my textbook in my lap. A cold coffee and unopened lunch is on my desk with a stack of charts, beside a foreleg splint that I removed from a kitten and a new shipment of Amoxicillin. He's tossing a roll of bandage material from hand to hand like a softball. I can see it from my corner of vision without looking up from my textbook.

"Maybe." I still don't look up.

"This is a nice practice. I've filled in at a lot of places, but I like this place."

"Uh hum. So, do you like doing relief work?"

"It gets old. I'm starting to think about finding a place. You know?"

I feel my teeth press together. "Yeah." I take a swig of cold coffee. "David, would you make sure the tech finished x-raying the kitten?"

"Sure." He pushes off the door frame and swaggers toward the treatment area. So he's cool. Nonchalance doesn't cut it when it comes to running this business. If he ever had to run a busy practice like this, it would fold in a year. *Yeah, he'll buy this practice over my dead body.*

"If the fracture's healed, you can send the kitten home," I yell from my desk. "The owner's waiting to hear the results," I say a little louder. "Please write up the discharge instructions and put the charges in for Jeannie." Then I force denouement of my bossy voice. "Thanks, David."

"The heart doc said I can start back to light duty in a few weeks," Bob says when he calls me later. "I'm not supposed to lift anything over ten pounds and I don't have use of some of my left fingers. The cardiologist says it's unusual, so he isn't sure when the sensation will come back."

I don't let on— the thought of Bob not being able to do surgery makes me numb.

~ 40 ~

I don't like what I see when I pick up Mom and Dad at the airport. Dad struggles to lift the luggage (I don't offer because he'll refuse) and he's lumbering like he's an elephant when I can tell he's lost weight.

"What have the doctor's been saying?" I ask. Of course, he hasn't been back because they gave him a three-month subscription of NSAIDS. "But you need to call and tell them they're not working. If you were a dog, your owner would be on the phone blasting me."

I stuff down part of my cold hamburger and warm potato salad at the semi-fast food place off the highway on our drive home. Mom and Dad have used the international airport rather than the local airport next to my home. Can't blame them, cheaper flights. None of us eats much. Mom is dieting, Dad isn't hungry, I'm sick with worry. He was always hungry, though he could eat for two and not put on a pound. I drop them off at their house and head back to my home. At eleven o'clock. I remember I never called Ingrid's lawyer back.

When I drag myself into work on Friday, despite that the scare of Dr. Bob's heart attack is over, my stomach is too knotted to sip much else but water for breakfast. It's not from the restaurant food last night. Today was one of those days every veterinarian dreads. I open the door to the exam room to see Mandy, the cocker spaniel, sitting in her owner's lap. Her stubby tail rustles against his jacket when Mandy sees me and I want to throw up.

"We've tried everything we can," I try to explain again, examining Mandy's milky eyeball and avoiding the confused expression of her elderly owner. "Our only choice left is surgery to remove Mandy's eye."

"How much it cost?" he asks in choppy Yiddish English.

I hate to say the numbers so I knock off a few hundred dollars. "About a thou—, maybe eight hundred dollars."

He shakes his head while I'm holding the face of his spaniel and trying to focus my own blurred eyes.

"I'm on pension." His fingers worry his frayed baseball cap. "She's old as me. Neither one of us live much longer now."

After signing the authorization for euthanasia, he nestles his bald head into Mandy to muffle good-bye. The tech comes in and carries Mandy to a cage in the back ward because he doesn't want to stay. Much as I encourage owners to be by their pet's side, I don't push it when he wobbles with grief, holding on to me as he leaves the room.

I go back to the dog ward and open Mandy's cage. I tuck a comforter under Mandy's round belly, remembering my playful scolding I gave her owner that beef stew wasn't helping her diabetes. Now I would love to see Mandy eat the treat I've offered her, hoping to quell her anxiety, and mine.

I wipe my nose and don't care that it's swollen and red when I go into the next exam room. I draw a Lyme titer and prescribe antibiotics and NSAIDS because I'm pretty sure already that this is a classic case of Lyme disease when I see how much pain the dog is in. "She's even refusing her food," the owner says. "She's never done that before."

"Hmmm." I tune everything else out as my brain reviews the symptoms, first of my patient, then they switch to Dad— the walks in the woods with the neighbor's dog, the sudden onset of fever, debilitating pain that was not relieved by pain killers. Fatigue, loss of appetite—my mind starts racing now.

As soon as I finish appointments I run back to my office. I look up Dad's doctor and ask him to call me. The nurse gives me a hard time about HIPPA privacy. Of course, but I'm not in a patient mood. I call Dad next and tell him to make an appointment with his doctor so he can be tested for Lyme disease. This week, if possible, or else I'll be down to the house to draw blood for a Lyme test myself! He promises to call the doctor. It may be a long shot, but it'll be one less thing to worry about in my life if all this time Dad's been sick it was because of Lyme disease. From now on I tell Dad to walk the neighbor's dog on the sidewalk!

Bob comes up behind me as I walk out of my office, sighing. I'm as shocked to see him here.

"What are you doing here? Aren't you supposed to be resting?"

"It was just a couple of cardiac stents. I just need to take it easy. Most people go home the next day. I'm going crazy staying home." Jeannie told me he's been calling every few hours.

I shake my head at him, then swallow hard, remembering Mandy and what I need to do next. But Bob knows me too well.

"Listen, I'll get the technician to put Mandy to sleep," Bob says.

I feel the color drain from my face.

"If my hands weren't so shaky, I'd offer to do the eye surgery as charity. I haven't gotten my coordination back in my hands yet." He pauses, as if choosing his words carefully before he says them. "You could do this Jill. The skill that you lack isn't in your hands, it's in your head."

I sniff back tears so hard that a pain shoots through both sinuses.

All these years I'd confessed my insecurity to dozens of furry ears when I thought no one was listening. I can't look at Bob's face. Guilt over having to put Mandy to sleep is killing me. My face feels swollen and hot as I turn to hang up my exam coat then run out the door without saying good-bye to Jeannie. I barely unlock my car door before I erupt in a cry that shakes me to the core.

That night, I'm so haunted by the crumbled expression on the old man's face, the forlorn look as I'd shut Mandy's cage door, the words of Dr. Bob, that I pretend not to hear the phone ring when Jeannie calls me to make sure I'm okay.

"I know you can do this," Bob has said to me so many times. But all I think about is the lifeless white body of my pet rat, lying in a bloody cage at the research lab when I was in college—my first surgery attempt that went horribly wrong.

My eyelids are puffy when they open to sunlight the next morning. I have no idea what time I fell asleep on my couch, but I become startled by my own laughter, dreaming I'd performed Mandy's surgery and had been rejoicing with her owner when he came back to see Mandy.

My head is down the minute I see Bob's car in the office parking lot when I pull up. I understand why he needs to come to work, but I walk toward the building with sheepish reluctance. At least Dr. Bell isn't here. When I open the back door of the clinic, Jeannie avoids looking at me. Then I see Bob. He nods with a stern look I've seen before. My face contorts from holding back tears as I race back to the kennel room where I'd left Mandy yesterday. The cage is empty.

Bob's voice startles me when he walks up behind me. "I gave Mandy a sedative and asked the technicians to prep her for surgery. I'll be in the scrub room," he says. When I snap my head back to look, he's already entering the operating room.

I don't have time to think of excuses. Bob's no-nonsense attitude sobers me into action. I follow his tracks toward the sterile room. As I unwrap a surgeon's gown and stare at the green rolled fabric before me, the steamed cotton odor from our old autoclave makes me gag. I swipe my greasy forehead and tuck stray wisps of my hair under a snug surgical cap.

Bob opens the door and peeks in on me. He's already gowned and gloved. His cap and mask are on and his eyes are talking, but they're not saying what D.J.s eyes had said to me the night we were on his couch. Bob's eyes are saying *it's now or never, Jill.*

I tie a mask behind my head, fumbling as if a clown's hands are dressing me. It sucks back into my face and feels suffocating until I take my mind off my breathing and start to scrub my hands.

I'm trembling on the other side of the door to the surgery suite. I look the part. I just don't feel it. I float inside the surgery room and stand beside Bob, feeling nauseous and light-headed. My body temperature feels like its three degrees hotter than normal when I look down at Mandy. She's draped for surgery, her chubby body covered with four overlapping cloth squares so all I can see is that one part of her face where I need to operate to remove her diseased eye.

Bob leans over and whispers, "You aren't the only vet to ever lose and animal, Jill, and you won't be the last." I get the feeling Bob's telling me something he probably hasn't told anyone before.

"There would be none of us left to do this work if we all quit because of a mistake," he says.

I look up unable to blink. He's holding his elbows tucked close to his ribs, hands away from his chest to keep them sterile. They are clasped above his heart like a priest holding a chalice.

"My disability is in my hands, but yours isn't, Jill."

His words are framed so eloquently. After eight years of veterinary school, those words move me more than my diploma.

Pearls of wisdom? Yes. And major stepping stones, too.

For the next hour, Bob walks me though surgery. He's manipulating my mind as I manipulate the assortment of miniature instruments. When I finally sew Mandy's eyelid shut and pull back the surgical drapes, she looks like a sleepy stuffed animal.

I turn when I hear the whoosh of the surgery door open and Bob disappear behind the soft thud of door closing between us. I didn't need him to hold my hand anymore.

"Mandy's owner is on the phone," Jeannie says after lunch. She looks at Dr. Bob. "He can hardly speak, he's so grateful." My heart *blossoms* with joy.

"You can handle the call too, Jill." Bob winks at me, then he walks away.

On the way home when I stop to get gas, my feet feel like boulders. A winter weather advisory is in effect and the air has a sickly chill. Maybe it was partly the way I was feeling. I grab the local newspaper on my way out of the store and read the astrology column.

PISCES: Life goes in cycles and every so often, hardship turns out to be a blessing in disguise. The light is at the end of the tunnel. Keep walking toward it. Clarity is closer than you think.

Except I was still in the dark about Leo.

~ *41* ~

Sam has called twice to say he misses me, and once to say his plans changed and he won't be home until late December. Now I have no reason not to finish my zodiac plan.

"I'm not waiting around for Sam," I tell Logan. "I'll be at my parent's house for Thanksgiving dinner. Why don't you and Greg stop by?"

Suzanne and Lee won't be coming. They're pulling it together to spend the holiday with her in-laws, or so she said. Suzanne hasn't let on to Mom that she and Lee are separated.

My brother, Rob will be at Mom and Dad's house for the holiday, and Mom tells me he's bringing "a friend." She used to call Tim "my friend" for the longest time, as if calling him my boyfriend meant she'd seen us having sex.

On Thanksgiving Day I'm shocked as hell when I arrive at my parent's home and Rob steps out of their living room. My eyes drop to the pizza dough he's carrying around his midsection. As we hug, an attractive blonde walks up and hovers beside him— she's got chocolate chip cookie-maker written all over her face.

"This is Melody, Jill," Rob says with a flattering gaze at his new honey. I've never seen my brother this smitten. In fact, I swear I see a look of matrimony in his eyes.

"Hiiiiiye. I've heard all about you and your lovely family from your handsome brother. It makes me miss my family so much. I'm from Georgia, ya know, and I feel so blessed to be spending this day with ya'll."

"We're glad to have you, Melody. Looks like you're taking good care of Rob, too," I say, a visual sucker punch aimed at Rob's gut.

"Hey, I heard your boss had a heart attack a few weeks ago?" Rob says. The sweat on his upper lip is a clue he wants no part of my teasing.

Even if his little blonde sweetie isn't proof of my brother's finesse as a smooth-talker, the switch is. I pretend not to notice how he turned the spotlight on me.

"Yes. He's doing great now, but he doesn't have full use of his hands. We did eye surgery together. Well, I did with him guiding me. The owner was going to have to put his dog to sleep." At the thought, I shut my eyes.

"Is that right? That must have made you feel good."

"Like being shocked with ten volts of happiness."

Mom is standing at the stove, stirring hot liquid in an aluminum pot. A ceramic cup of flour and water is on the counter beside her and she's skimming warm juice into the cup to make a roux.

My mother's eyes dart toward me. "I hope you aren't still thinking of taking over the business, Jill." Her hair is a little lighter, a little shorter. She's changed it again, but she never strays too far from her usual style of what it's been for years, short layers and champagne blonde.

Mom turns back to the stove wildly clanging the spoon against the sides of the pot. I don't answer. I know she's worried for me. Unlike her brother, I wasn't about to ever kill myself from the stress, though it isn't hard to see how Bob ended up with a heart attack at his age. For weeks now while Bob continues cardiac rehab, I've carried the weight of the business. I've kept up with payroll and paid every vendor from antibiotics to vaccines. I've ordered a new line of pet diets that target diabetic animals. I proved I can do it if I want to.

Dad lifts the roasting pan with ease from the oven and sets it on the counter. His doctor started him on doxycycline when his titer came back positive for Lyme disease.

"You look like you're feeling better, Dad. Did your doctor happen to mention you've got a smart daughter?"

Dad moves closer, bringing with him the faint scent of meat musk, the warmth of the oven, and of himself. He places two stainless carving knives in front of me and though I can see his hands are better since he's been on the right medication, he motions to me like Bob had the day I finally performed surgery. "Here's your chance, Jill. Show us those new surgery skills. Nothing stopping you now."

Throughout the day, Melody's Southern sweetness is a constant reminder how much Sam loves the south. I glance at my phone expecting his call, but he doesn't call like he said he would. Despite what I told Logan about Sam, I miss him.

Mom sets the chocolate cake Melody made on the table. It looks as rich as the three sticks of butter she said she used to make the frosting.

Then Rob stands up at the table beside Melody and raises his glass.

"I know we don't get to see each other very often, and I wanted Suzanne and Lee to be here, but I'd like to make an announcement."

Most of the time, I'm hardly aware of my breathing, but I am now.

I like Melody, I really do. But I'm not ready to hear that my younger brother is ready to marry a girl he met five months ago on the Internet.

"I've decided to move back home," Rob says. He smiles at Dad. "Melody is going to move to Connecticut, too. We're going to look for a little house."

There are times when family is the most important thing in my life. This *should* be one of those times. I freeze before I can blurt out "Congratulations!" I lean over and wink at Melody. Rob is hiding behind his coffee mug.

Buying a house. Nice. With whose money I wonder? He never acknowledged that he still owes me—that his mistake cost me more than the $8K he borrowed. I guess I really haven't let this go.

We all knew Rob had left Connecticut because of issues he needed to sort out alone. Was it failure that made people turn back to their roots, or in Rob's case, was it finding someone special to share his life that made it possible to turn his around?

Here I am, Rob's older sister, and I'm still unsure of where I'm headed. Spending the day at the horse farm with Andrea made it clear that being an equine vet is out of the question. Would I be putting my tail between my legs if I stayed to work for Bob, or would it be wise of me to remain in the successful practice I know so well?

It wasn't the money Rob borrowed—I was mad at myself for not knowing what to do.

When it's time to leave, I say my good-byes to my parents and Melody. Then I whisper to Rob, "Take a walk outside with me."

I walk out to my car with Rob following me carrying a doggie-bag of left-over turkey, sweet potatoes, corn pudding, stuffing, and a big piece of Melody's five-layer dessert. He hands it to me when we get to my car, then he looks down at the ground and shoves his hands in his pockets.

"I'm sorry I haven't paid you back yet, Jill. Thanks for never mentioning any of this to Mom and Dad." He slouches back against my car.

"It's okay. I know you will. That's not why I asked you to come outside."

He straightens his posture and cocks his head.

"Rob, can I ask you something?"

"Sure. What's up?" His expression sobers, spoiling the fluid grin he's worn all night.

"How did you know with Melody? I mean, it's easy to see why you two are great together. But ..."

My brother's eyes don't blink as I struggle with my question. We'd always teased, never confided on an intimate level—I never knew Rob was capable of a mature relationship, until Melody.

"Was the timing right with Melody, or is there a feeling that you have with her that you've never felt with other women?"

Suddenly Rob's face melts. It looks serene in the glow of streetlight. Even nightshade can't hide the glimmer of joy in the eyes of a smitten lover.

He puts his head down as if he's giving his answer a lot of thought. I'm hoping to hear something profound.

He nods his head side to side, then he says, "I had to be ready. I wasn't before now."

I feel diminished with disappointment. Rob obviously notices my face pout. He stammers, as if he's reaching deeper. "That had a lot to do with it, but so did this girl. But the way I *really* knew," the expression in his voice intensifies, "was by the kiss."

By the kiss.

That's how he knew?

I would have still thought my brother was shallow, if I didn't know *exactly* what he meant.

The heart-to-heart with Rob puts me in an introspective mood. On the drive home, the moon shines down on the leafless trees turning them into silhouette dancers stretching to the stars.

I get off the highway, but I don't head home. Instead when I get to Meadowbrook Road, I drive to the end of the street. I hesitate at Amberfield's pebbled driveway, then I shut my headlights and coast. The road crunches like thunderclap under my slow tires. My hands steady the steering wheel but it's not the chilly air that makes them numb. I reach over and blast the heat up in the car, but can't get warm. Every light is extinguished inside the farmhouse. Obviously no one has moved in yet. The house looks lonely.

I look up to the window that used to be Petal's bedroom. Twenty years ago, two pre-teens in pajamas huddled cross-legged on her bed with a candle on her nightstand. They ate Mrs. Petal's homemade cookies and played Ouija. One of them was me.

I remember my confusion when the Ouija board spelled my own initials, *J.C.,* the time I asked it who I'd marry. We shrugged it off and put the board away when Petal got her answer.

Was it possible I'd get the same answer if I asked my question today?

Dr. Bell is working this week and he's brought George Burns with him. George looks so proud wearing his new tee shirt. I'm starting to like Bell.

In between appointments I check my phone and find a new voice mail message.

"Jill, this is Attorney Chamberlain. It's important we speak. Please call me."

My thoughts misfire like an overloaded computer. Did someone report me for trespassing on the property last night? *It is Black Friday.* Half of the world is out shopping today—the other half is using their day off to come to the vet!

I call back Attorney Chamberlain before the next appointment.

"Can you come in next Friday?" he asks.

"Okay. Were you able to get a photo of Ingrid?"

"Not yet. I want to talk to you about the Amberfield place, but it's a little complicated, so I'll see you next week, okay, Jill." He hangs up before I give him my answer.

~ *42* ~

Attorney Chamberlain's assistant calls Tuesday.

"Hi Jill. I need to reschedule your appointment."

"Is everything okay?"

"Oh yes. He's been called out of the country. Can you come next week?"

Do I have a choice?

She schedules another appointment. However, I do have other choices.

I've dated ten men in less than six months. From time to time my Connect pen pals email me. I have genuine fondness for a few, even though we haven't dated. *Thought I'd say hello*, they write. I know they're checking up on me. But the details we've shared with one another make them feel like friends.

Aquarius is the sign of friendships, the humanitarians of the zodiac. My last sign left before Leo. After scanning a ton of profiles, I find the perfect guy for the part. He's got fifteen photos posted and not one in which he isn't smiling, or hugging somebody.

As soon as I send off my email, he emails back and tells me to call him. His name is Vinny Valentini.

"Sounds like a cartoon character," Logan says. I assure Logan he isn't.

"His face could land him a part on the soaps," I say. Logan's face turns young and restless as a desperate housewife.

I can barely hear Vinny when he answers my phone call. People are yelling in the background, but he tells me he's home.

"I'll meet you Sunday at noon at the Panini Express at the mall," Vinny says.

I'm looking forward to being in the mall for the holiday season more than I thought I would without Tim this Christmas. Maybe it's because of the cheerful music, maybe it's the elaborate sparkle of the décor. *No, it's definitely because I'm meeting a guy who looks like Vinny.*

As expected the kiosks are shimmering in colorful lights, a mouth-watering scent of baked cinnamon and chocolate waifs through the corridors, and leather handbags and silky scarves are hanging everywhere I turn. But Christmas still isn't as special without someone special to shop for. As I walk towards the entrance, I can't help but think of Sam.

It is a shivery thirty degrees outside, but I warm up as soon as I mingle with the mob at Panini's. (Who doesn't love hot bread on a cold Sunday?) The establishment has a trendy mosaic tile floor and swirled blown-glass light fixtures hanging low over each table. It's noisy and crowded, but I have no trouble spotting Vinny. He's dressed like he was in one of his pictures, all black which accentuates his Mediterranean features. When I offer my hand to shake, Vinny steadies me and plants a noisy kiss on my cheek. I'm a little shocked, a little smitten. *He's gorgeous.*

"So you're a pisan, Jill?" Vinny says, staring at me with dark playful eyes.

I smile and tell him only one side of me and he tells me "he knows which side." I catch him checking me out like a horse dealer at an auction— eyes, legs, ahem…rear end.

Vinny spots a table and drags me by the hand to get to it before someone else grabs it first. He pulls out a chair for me and slides his seat close to mine. I clasp my cold hands under my chin, elbows propped on the table. He reminds me of one of my fun cousins, and that makes me instantly like him.

"So what do you do for work, Vinny? You didn't mention your profession on your profile."

"I work for my father. So do my three brothers and sister. My grandfather started the family business, V&V Electronics," he says. Even if he hadn't told me about his big Italian family, this would have been a clue. He unzips his leather bomber coat and helps me peel off my long winter coat. "I'm not an electrician—yet." He says it like it's a curse.

"We have relatives who are in the same boat, so to speak," I say, tucking one side of my hair behind my ear. "My grandfather started our family car business, although my brother didn't follow tradition." *Until now, I think.*

"Speaking of tradition, my mother thinks I'm too old to be a bachelor. And my father's worried I'm gay when he doesn't see me dating. They think I'll change if I find the right woman." He's talking to me at the same time he's snapping his fingers to hail down a waiter. "Sometimes I like to play with them to keep them quiet. You know?"

I laugh at his logic. "My best friend is gay," I say.

"No problemo. So's my cousin. Hey, it's been ten minutes. Where's this waiter?"

I turn to look at the crowd still piling in. "This is a busy place," I say. "The smell of that bread is making my mouth water."

"Come on. Let's get out of here. I have a better idea." He grabs my hand and throws both our jackets over his shoulder, then we head for the exit.

In the parking garage, Vinny stops beside a low black vehicle that looks so modified I can't tell what kind of car it is. There's a bumper sticker on the trunk that says: *Talk to your cat about catnip before it's too late.* I shake my head and snort-laugh. That sticker is almost enough for me to trust him.

"Maybe we should take my car, Vinny."

"No problemo," he says and shrugs, then opens his car door and swoops in to grab a pair of rollerblades on his front seat.

"What are those for?"

"They can steal my car but I don't want anyone stealing my blades."

I study his face and for the only moment in this comical afternoon, he's totally serious. When we find my car in the snowy parking lot, he tosses them onto the back seat and hops into my passenger seat. When I start the car, he changes my radio station and raises the volume, which I can't say I mind because his seat dancing is contagious.

I drive fifteen minutes before he tells me to slow down as I head down a street of older but well-kept three-family dwellings, many with Christmas-tree type or cubed shrubs along the front porch, and one with a nativity set on the lawn. "Pull over," Vinny says when we reach the house painted green on the bottom floors, and white on the top half.

"See that window?" he points to the top floor. "I live right up there."

We climb the stairs to the porch, but instead of the third floor, he shoulders open the first floor door. It isn't only the temperature change that warms me.

The house has a familiar smell— baked bread, tomato sauce, Italian cooking spices. It lasts only a second then dissipates inside my clothes and hair, the fragrance as much a part of me as it has always been. I inhale and more than my taste buds feel the longing.

Vinny walks before me into the living room and kisses a blue-haired lady on the cheek, ducking before her hand makes contact with his head. He leaves me standing there with his grandma staring at me through silver cat-eye glasses. She throws up one flappy arm and mumbles "Bella…." The sentence is half in English, half in Italian, but I recognize one word.

"This is Jill, Mom," I hear Vinny say in the next room over the scratchy sound of crumpling paper. He is unwrapping a loaf of crunchy bread and standing beside a buxom woman when I step into the kitchen.

I know what I'm in for now— his comment earlier about how he likes to "play" with his parents. I start to pray that his mother doesn't ask me about kids and getting married.

"Finally, a pretty one, Vinny, instead of those girls with the crazy earrings everywhere," Mrs. Valentini says, coming toward me for a closer look just to make sure. Her dark brows and eyes are a female version of Vinny, and they are surveying me from my shoes to my hair. I feel bamboozled and lightheaded from hunger.

"She's a vet, Mom." He raises his voice when she squints at him like she doesn't understand. "A dog doctor. You know, like where we take Butchie." The silver Elkhound standing beside the counter cocks his wolf-like head, then his rolled tail swishes across his back. Mrs. Valentini pinches Vinny's cheek until Vinny yelps.

One by one the rest of the family shows up for dinner, like they do "every Sunday at one o'clock," Mrs. Valentini tells me. All four brothers look so much alike that standing side by side they could have been quintuplets. I meet Paulie, Michael, and Frank, Paulie's wife Denise, Michael's wife Janet, and Frank's third wife Tina. A bald man that I assume to be Vinny's father, Vinny Sr., comes out of the bathroom buckling the belt of his pants that look as though he's shrunk three inches from when he'd bought them. He doesn't look the least bit embarrassed when he spots me. Instead, he raises his brows at Vinny and points his finger at me.

"So is he treating you good?" he asks me. "He better," he says before I answer. "Have something to eat," he says taking his seat at the head of the table wearing a white sleeveless undershirt that exposes his pale shoulders. But I'm not the least bit appalled. My father does the same thing. Mr. Valentini teases his grandkids seated beside him at the folding table. The place is chaotic until all the food is on the table and they stop for six seconds to say grace.

Vinny's niece and nephews are making toys out of every utensil on the table. Their mother, Vinnie's sister, Donna, shifts her hips and looks my way. Donna's eyes and lips are painted like a makeup counter attendant and her hair is wild as wisteria.

"I can help if you ever want nail extensions," she says, splaying her fingernails over the meatballs. They're dotted with gems that sparkle like the holiday brooch on grandma's sweater.

"Oh, thank you, Donna, but I don't think I'd be able to work with long nails." I hide my stubby fingernails with my palm, but I feel as though I've been bestowed high honor of approval from Vinny's little sister.

"Okay. If you change your mind, I do a nice job."

Vinny tousles his nephew's hair, walks behind me and kisses the top of my head. He sits beside me, butters a thick piece of crusty bread and sets it on my napkin. I am captivated by his innocent affection. This feels so different from Sam.

Mrs. Valentini leans over the table and drops two more raviolis in my plate. "We don't want you to leave hungry. We want to make sure you want to come back. Right, Vinny," Mrs. Valentini's voice booms as she glares at her son.

"No problemo."

"Vinny, bring the picture to show Jill, the one of me and your beautiful mother on the day we were married," Mr. Valentini says, pouring another glass of Chianti. I cover the mouth of my wine glass and decline politely when he gestures to pour me more. I've only choked down a few sour sips. In fact, I haven't had a drink since I was in California with Oliver, and I don't plan to end up on the Valentini couch!

"Mmmm, beautiful," I agree looking at the photo. Mrs. Valentini's waist was the size of a pinky finger. When we finish dinner, I help Mrs. Valentini and Donna swap dirty dishes with a whole set of clean ones. Tina makes coffee, expresso and regular. Denise brings out a tray of Italian pastry, and Janet carries a plate of Rice Krispie treats to the kids. Grandma sits in a corner next to a crystal ashtray smoking cigarettes. No one says a word about the smoke.

By this time, I'm stuffed with food and my ears ring from the arguing and yelling. The tablecloth is stained with coffee and wine and sauce, the kids are watching television, the grown-ups are falling asleep. But I can see the love between them. I'd forgotten how my family used to spend Sundays together. Everyone has gotten too busy to realize how much it matters, how much it's a part of who we are.

Before it's time to leave, Mr. Valentini pushes his wine glass aside and picks up a walnut from the teak fruit bowl on the table. He looks at me and crushes the walnut with one hand. Everyone left at the table stops and watches with hardly a whisper. Then he reaches across the table and sets the handful of walnut bits before me.

From across the table, next to Mr. Valentini, I hear a quiet, "yay." My eyes rise slowly over my lower lids and lock onto Mr. Valentini's fist. His knuckles have rivulets like the shell. He raps them on hard wood and shakes one fist at Vinny, talking to him with his eyes. I have no idea what all this means, all I know is that it means something.

"You're in," Vinny whispers into my ear. "He likes you."

At the end of the night I'm sure I'm falling in love— with Vinny's family.

"Jill, there's a man on the phone asking for you," Jeannie says as I place blind Chrissy back in his cage at work Thursday morning. "He said that you've treated his pet skunk before?"

"That Vinny. If he wasn't so cute he'd be corny." I'm shaking my head as I pick up my office phone.

"Hey, Jill. My friends are having a party. Wanna go with me?" I hear munching and the crackle of a chip bag.

"Sure, Vinny. Are you bringing your skunk?"

"It'll be past his bedtime. I'll pick you up at 9:30."

"Tonight? You mean tonight? It's Thursday and I have to be in work eight o'clock on Friday morning. I can't stay late."

"No problemo, Jill."

I shake my head. What would it be like being married to a guy that thinks problems are only for grown-ups?

Vinny shows up at 9:45PM wearing jeans and a tee shirt with tour dates of a band I've never heard of. I'm wearing strappy sandals and a paisley silk top.

When we arrive at his friend's apartment, the first thing to greet me is the rancid odor of beer cans in a garbage bag in the foyer. Vinny opens the unlocked door to a hallway which is dark for good reason. Upstairs the only light in the room is from cigarettes and candles.

"This is Jill, everyone," Vinny yells above music as obscure as the band on Vinny's tee shirt. Vinny weeds past three young women huddled like sparrows. They barely look old enough to drink, but at least someone is dressed like I am.

A guy puffing a smoke nods when he sees Vinny.

"This was my college roommate," Vinny says, over the woof and tweeter of speakers. It's too loud to talk, or hear. The guy waves one finger at me, the rest of his fingers still gripping the neck of his Budweiser. *I should have taken my own car.*

"We don't have to stay late," Vinny whispers.

It's okay, I say with my eyes, but I don't mean it. I haven't been to a keg party since college. Never mind the pot plants under a black light on the kitchen counter. Guys making nature calls off of the back porch wasn't cool with me even when I was in college. And after two hours, the lack of any meaningful conversation leaves me feeling—well, older. By the time we leave, I've ingested more nachos, salsa dip, and brownies than I've eaten in the past five years.

"I'm going to Miami to visit my cousins for Christmas," Vinny says on the ride home.

Miami? As in college break and twenty-year-olds hanging out on the beach in bikinis?

"Aren't you spending the holiday with your family?"

"My mom's mad, but she'll be okay." I have the car door open and one foot planted on the sidewalk after Vinny pulls up to my house. His thick wavy hair matches his eyelashes and brows and his eyes are too big for his face. Yep, he's about as unattractive as a baby seal, which makes squirming out of his good-bye pretty tough.

I kick off my heels as soon as I'm inside my door. That ankle still gives me problems when I'm dumb enough to stand too long in strappy heels. *No more weekday dates when I have to be in work in six hours. And definitely no more keg parties.* It's not that I've outgrown them. I've never liked them.

I toggle the buttons on my alarm clock and set the wake time. The appointment with Attorney Chamberlain tomorrow afternoon pops into my head. I'm exhausted. I'm over-tired. I'm awake for hours wondering what he will say.

~ 43 ~

Palo Alto, California

James sat at the bar watching the bartender fill his beer mug. He turned quickly when a large hand slapped his shoulder.

"James, what are you doing here? I haven't seen you here in quite a while."

"Yes, well, things changed." *Amy.*

"Oh." He lowered his voice. "Sorry, bud. Join the club." He started to slide into the bar stool beside James then stopped. "Are you meeting someone?"

"No, please, take a seat."

"So what's new? I hear the department has a new chief. Does that affect you in any way?"

"To tell you the truth, I haven't noticed. My mother died recently. It was unexpected, and things are a little complicated right now with her estate."

"Sorry for your loss," he said, the way people often did out of conversation rather than compassion. But James couldn't say he felt Ingrid's loss when they'd never been close. What he did feel was the loss of something that was always a part of him. The home he never quite found in California.

"It makes you think, you know?"

The man's face sobered.

"I'm thinking of moving back east. I'll be on sabbatical next year. Plenty of options there if I decide to stay," James said. It would be lonely starting over again in Connecticut, but living back home for a while would help him to decide. He could do many things with his career, but there would never be another home for him like the one where he grew up. For someone who spent his days striving to improve the health system for the lives of Americans, he owed it to himself to do the same for his own life.

~ *44* ~

"Jill, can I talk to you?" Bob waves me into his office when I arrive. He's back to work full time now. I'm floating from a Venti-sized Starbuck's to offset my lack of sleep. I lower my tote bag from my shoulder and lean into his doorframe.

Bob rubs his fingers together like the sensation is coming back.

"You aced that surgery on Mandy's eye last month. You're going to do great here, Jill."

My fingers press into the wood door frame.

"How would you like to take the afternoon off?"

"You're joking, right?"

"Do this housecall for me at the Morgan's and you can call it a day. Eight Shepard pups need to be vaccinated."

"No problemo." The words gush out of me.

Bob squints at me like I'm an alien.

Did I really talk like Vinny?

"Do you have a doctor's appointment today?" I ask, watching Bob squeeze a blue rubber ball that the therapist gave him to do hand exercises.

"No. I'm dying to get in a few holes of golf with this break in the winter weather."

My posture stiffens. Is he pushing this a bit? "Bob, do you think that's okay for you to do that so soon?"

"I'll be okay, doc," he jokes. "Go have a nice afternoon."

I hope I can. At four o'clock I have an appointment to see Ingrid's lawyer.

I check the carrying case of medical supplies for the housecall. The technician stocked it with alcohol, syringes, and vaccines. I've made sure I've packed my stethoscope, a nail trimmer, thermometer, otoscope, and enough puppy records. When I open my car door to set the case on the back seat before I leave the office, I notice that Vinny has forgotten his rollerblades and gear in my car.

I pull one out and look it over—size 9. Vinny has a pretty solid physique, but he isn't that tall and his shoe size isn't much bigger than mine.

"Are you coming back today, Jill," Jeannie asks when I go back into the office before leaving.

"No, but hopefully I will tomorrow if I survive. I think I might try to rollerblade. Vinny left his pair in my car. I'll be right near the bike trail with this housecall."

The kennel boy is standing nearby. "That's cool, Dr. Christie. My mom can blade eight miles in an hour."

The December weather has turned to an unheard of fifty-five degrees. I look at him and swallow. *I have to try it now.*

On my way to the housecall, I stop to buy a heavy pair of socks to make up for the extra room inside the rollerblade boot. The client's home is located in the area of Mount Pleasant where the homes are like Southern plantations. An abandoned railroad splits through the woodsy edge of the properties, and there is a paved walking trail in place of the old tracks.

When I arrive at the Morgan residence, I'm greeted by pitchy yapping from taut-bellied, stubby-legged pups. We mark the pups with colored collars as I vaccinate and examine each one.

"Oh, one more thing," I say after I've answered all questions regarding the bitch and pups. "Can you tell me where the entrance to the linear trail is located?"

"It's right down the road, Dr. Christie. That's where I walk Spock and Sheba."

They let me borrow a bike helmet when they hear what I'm about to do.

There are a few people walking dogs on the asphalt trail and a lone cyclist who passes by. The grounds smell clean as rain. I slip my foot inside the rollerblade, snap three buckles, and secure the wrist and knee guards.

I boost myself to a sliding-standing posture gripping my open car door as if it's a rudder. *Thank God I borrowed the helmet.* I fit my iPod ear plugs and adjust the strings of my hoodie.

It's now or never, Jill. I let go of my car door and push away as I shove the door closed. The skate wheels spin past wheat-colored brush, transporting me to where Dad took us for Sunday adventures. My childhood whizzes by as the black top vibrates beneath the balls of my

PATTI CAVALIERE

feet. Suddenly I'm ice-skating on the dairy pond with Dad. He'd skate
backwards and pull me like his caboose until I learned to skate on my own.
I stroke the pavement with long glides, lean forward over my hips and
push my face into the breeze. To think, I'd forgotten how holy this feels.

At the entrance of a sand-colored cubed building later that afternoon is
a sign with the name *Chamberlain Estate Law*. My chest feels like it's a
bursting butterfly cocoon. I take the elevator to the top floor. Outside the
glass window the sun has left the sky. Magenta and violet watercolors fill
my view. It reminds me of the day I saw Ingrid sitting in her sunny great
room before we took the walk down to the lake. So much has happened in
six months.
    "Hello. I'm Jill Christie," I say to the receptionist. "I'm hear to see—"
    "Oh, yes, Dr. Christie. I'll let him know you're here."
    Attorney Chamberlain isn't how I pictured him. I had Alfred
Hitchcock in mind when he'd called about Ingrid, but he's trim and
distinguished, wearing a charcoal suit that looks stunning with his white
hair and blue silk tie. His eyes are gray and business-like. He offers his
hand and I shake it.
    I follow him to his office and sit in the leather chair facing a long
walnut desk. Attorney Chamberlain seats himself behind it. He tosses a
few manila folders aside, opens another and starts to sift through some
documents. I sit, silently admiring the rich décor of the paneled room, the
mahogany cabinets with brass pulls and rose-colored halogen lighting
along the ceiling. One abstract acrylic painting hangs frameless behind the
oval conference table.
    "Can I get you some coffee or tea?" the assistant dips her head in the
room to ask.
    "No thank you. I'm fine." I lie. My fingers are cold as popsicles, but I
know it's not the room temperature.
    "It's a pleasure to finally meet you, Jill. You had some connection to
the Amberfield farm years ago?" It's a question, but I can tell he knows
the answer.
    "Yes, I did." My breath quickens.
    "I remember when that little girl got killed. That was a shame. Let me
tell you where I'm going with this," he says.
    He tells me about Ingrid's family who once owned a lot of property in
Mount Pleasant. "Ingrid was quite the equestrian in her day," he says. "But
her sister was killed in an accident involving a horse. Ingrid told me you
have the same birthday that her sister had. She felt a deep connection to

you."

"I saw a picture at Ingrid's house, a girl with a pony. She never told me that's how her sister had died."

"Ingrid was touched by your similar misfortune with your friend, and your passion for horses."

His chair swivels sideways toward the full-length windows and he appears enchanted by the sunset, or of the world beyond it, as I do.

"Ingrid mentioned how torn you were about not being able to buy Amberfield. She knew she was dying at that point and figured the best way to preserve a town she loved was to save its last natural landscape. She told me she'd discussed this with you."

I nod in a way that conveys my sadness, and a little confusion. "What will happen to Amberfield now?"

"Well, that's why it was so important for Ingrid to reconcile with James. At least she used it as an excuse. I know she missed him terribly."

Our eyes meet and his soften as does his tone of voice. "She became very fond of you in the short time she knew you, Jill."

My throat tightens from holding back tears.

"Ingrid's stipulation with James was that he'd never demolish the farmhouse. At her request, I'm in the process of giving the town property rights after the barn is rebuilt so that the land can never be developed. Her second request was to let you live there."

My eyes erupt with juicy tears. "I can't believe it. I love that place. I don't know what to say."

Attorney Chamberlain hands me a box of tissues, then the lease for Amberfield. "Ingrid knew how much you loved it. You can move in as soon as the plumbing repairs are finished," he says.

"I can't thank you enough."

"You don't have to thank me. It was all Ingrid's idea. James officially owns everything, and of course I don't know what his plans are for the rest of the property, but—"

"The rest of the property?"

"Oh, don't worry. There's plenty."

My mouth starts to quiver. I can't have him think I was ungrateful, but I'm sick at the thought that *any of Amberfield* would disappear. If James could just see it in the summer, the way a full moon illuminates the fields like a Renaissance painting, or how the clouds appear lavender on a damp morning trail ride, the menthol scent of white pines on hot afternoons. If only I had the chance to show James before it's too late. Luckily, Attorney Chamberlain can't tell the difference between my tears of happiness, and sheer panic.

I start to get up. I'll see Amberfield again soon. And it will be like going back in time.

I grab my pocketbook beneath the chair.

"Oh one minute, Jill."

I can't imagine what he'll say next, but I perk up until I watch him frantically shuffle the stack of papers in the manila folders.

Then my heart turns to marshmallow.

"Darn it! Mary! Mary did we get that stuff back from the clerk's office? On the Amberfield property."

His legal assistant stands in the door with her hand crooked at her waist. Mary's lush Italian hair is styled with a gray streak sprayed into place. One of Jeannie's perturbed expressions is on her face. *Guess I know who runs this office.* "I told you I was having a problem. There's a bunch of liens on the property. Guess the guy hadn't paid the taxes in years."

Petal's father. I try to swallow but my throat is dry. "So is there any problem with me moving in? I'd like to let my landlord know as soon as possible."

"You'd better hold off until you hear back from me, Jill. I'm sorry."

I flick my hair off my sticky collar. My one-year lease was up in March. The landlord was counting on me leaving. I'd already promised him last year that I'd be moving out.

On my way home I call my landlord.

"Hi Mr. Premkumar. Would it be possible for me to stay another month or so? I could pay up a little early." I'm practically whining.

"I'm sorry, Jill. My daughter and her husband need a place while they're building. Why can't you move in with your boyfriend?"

I try to swallow but pride is like a walnut in my throat.

~ 45 ~

In Sympathy On The Loss Of Your Father. I stare at the three sympathy cards in my hand after reading through at least a dozen. They all say about the same thing: *May fond memories of your loved one comfort you at this time of loss.* Fond. Loved One. Comfort. Not one word fits. But since I can't bring myself to go to the funeral, I pick the purple card. Tim loved the color purple.

Maybe it was the brain aneurism that made his father mean. It's not the reason I won't go to the funeral. It would be uncomfortable if his new girlfriend is there. The same friend who called to let me know about Tim's father, hadn't failed to mention her.

As I write my note of condolence, it goes deeper than I expect. I no longer think of Amberfield as the place I lost because of Tim. I forgive him for breaking it off so abruptly. He was finally true to himself.

And so was I.

Next week I give Vinny a ride to the airport since its right by my home, and I still have his rollerblades in my car.

"I'll call you from Florida, Jill," Vinny says. He drops his luggage on the sidewalk in the middle of a crowd of pedestrians to kiss me good-bye. "Be careful on those blades."

"Aren't you taking them?"

"Merry Christmas. They're yours."

I blow him a kiss as the glass door slides open. "Have a good Christmas, Vinny," I yell over the cold air that screeches inside the warm terminal.

"Ditto, Jill."

"I will. I'll be with my family."

My family. Something I used to always count on. Maybe not all of them anymore.

I wonder about Suzanne and Lee.

After I leave the airport I drive down the highway to the mall so I can finish, *or start*, Christmas shopping. It isn't much of a surprise when I bump into a shopaholic like Logan.

"Logan!" I call out when I spot her and Greg exiting a shoe store with a boot-sized bag.

"Hi Jill," Greg says warmly. "It's been awhile since I've seen you."

"I know." *I'm dying to tell them about Amberfield.* "I've been so busy and you'll never believe—"

"Jill, I can never reach you. I've been dying for an update of your zodiac dates."

My head snaps back. I have been out of touch.

"Are Greg and I going to meet one of them for Christmas? How about that guy Vinny?"

"He just left for Florida. Vinny is just a friend." My optimism fizzles at the mention of Christmas. First one in years that I'll be solo.

"What about the walnut thing?" Logan asks, referring to the gesture of approval from Mr. Valentini.

Greg shakes his head and chuckles.

"Did I say something wrong, Greg?" Logan's tone is sugarless.

"It doesn't matter how nice, or smart, or great a woman is with a guy's family. A guy's got to be ready."

Before Logan asks, "Like I am," he says, hugging Logan as if he's her bodyguard.

"Sorry we never made over to your parent's house on Thanksgiving, Jill. Let's get together for dinner this week."

"Okay. I was going to tell you something about Amberfield…" Greg is twisting his lip. "…but never mind."

"Sorry I wasn't much help on that," Greg says. He gives Logan's shoulder a brisk rub like he's ready to leave. Logan is on her own trajectory, backing away toward Victoria's Secret.

"We need to catch up. Call me and let me know when." She turns back to me and exaggerates a wink behind Greg's back.

Greg's comment about how "a man has to be ready." That's the second time I've heard that. First Rob, now Greg. What about women? What about me?

As preoccupied as I am by Greg's comment, I'm just as curious about Logan's gesture.

I start and finish most all my holiday shopping in two hours.

Sometimes Obsessive Compulsive Disorder works to my advantage. Later, at home I sip hot chocolate while sorting wrapping paper and ribbons and bargaining cat toys for Christmas bows with the kitten who's hiding a stash of them behind the refrigerator.

I send an email to Tafari and thank him for sending pictures of a dog he's rescued. I attach the picture of the kitten I've named Kaz, for Kazakhstan.

I haven't heard from Suzanne in weeks. *I wonder if she's dating.* For kicks I put Suzanne's zip code into the Connect.com Search bar.

I click on a few pages, then my hands draw back from the keyboard. *Is that who I think it is?*

I move closer to my screen and stare as if I'm in a bad dream. *Lee!* Suzanne's Lee.

And it's a family photo with me in the picture! There's a second photo that *I had taken* the time I'd visited Suzanne and Lee, of Lee standing with their dog beside his minivan.

My eyes are frozen on the photos. A great guy like my brother-in-law will be hit on by dozens of women, minivan or no minivan.

I tap my keyboard to advance to a photo of Lee in his bulky team jacket when he coached Aidan's soccer last winter. There's another of him in swim trunks by a lake. My mouth goes dry. Suzanne was there. She probably even took the photo!

I have been in a committed relationship for many years but if you know how lonely life becomes when you become invisible to your partner then I'd like to hear from you.

I can't read anymore. Suzanne is a good wife, a good mother. I click away from Lee's profile, but even when his words disappear from the screen, they worm their way back inside my head. How am I going to handle this? I'll have to talk to Suzanne eventually.

I navigate back to my Home page to check for messages and then, I see that ridiculous caption.

Look Who's Viewed You. Answer Them Back Now!

I slam my laptop shut. It's only a matter of time before Lee receives the message that I did: **Look Who's Viewed You. Answer Them Back Now!**

I start to pace. How will I console Suzanne when there is no denying how devastating it feels to be replaced? It's like getting a new pet too soon after the beloved one dies. It's hard to imagine ever caring about the second pet as much as the one before it.

But then it happens.

I know because I was fine with losing Tim—until his friend told me Tim had a pretty new girlfriend.

~ 46 ~

Due to the holiday slump in appointments, Jeannie and I have time to catch up.

"So what's been happening with the dating?" Jeannie asks holding out a coconut-pineapple muffin.

She's baked one of her specialty muffins—just for me. No Dr. Bell in sight.

"New recipe. Pina Colada. Have you seen the church man again yet?"

"He emails." I'm as stingy with information as Sam is with me. There's no lack of sweet nothings, now that he's over 1000 miles away. But I haven't been able to pin him down for New Year's Eve.

Jeannie's paparazzi eyes zoom in as if her island flavor is some kind of truth serum.

"Delicious," I say, accidentally spitting a few crumbs and looking over my shoulder to make sure Bell wasn't called in today without me knowing.

"Do you mean my muffins or the church guy?" Jeannine asks. She shifts from Betty Crocker to her Angela Lansbury personality. "Sam does an awful lot of traveling doesn't he? Makes me think of that television movie about that guy that had two wives."

"He's not married," I say, flicking a few crumbs. "But I'm not sure Sam and I are at the same place in our life."

"I thought you told me *everyone* on that dating site was *seriously* looking for someone."

Ouch! I get it. "Guess I was pretty naïve when I started this. Here I am eleven guys later and I haven't seriously connected with anyone."

I hope Lee's not one of the "serious" ones. I need to talk this over with someone. And I know exactly who to call.

That night I meet Logan for Thai—light dinner, heavy conversation.

"Logan, I have some things to tell you, but you go first. What was that wink for when I ran into you and Greg at the mall?"

She smirks behind her hand then lets it drops to her lap. Something is off but I'm not sure what it is.

"I think you'd better talk first," she says, chopsticks poised over her Pad Thai in the square white China dish.

I lean over the plate of dumplings for no particular reason, but Logan does too. (We must look like spies.)

"I'm glad you're sitting down." I breathe deeply and sigh hard. I'm not usually this dramatic and Logan's eyeballs pop open wider.

"The other night I saw my brother-in-law, Lee, on Connect.com." I back away from the dumplings to check Logan's reaction. Nothing. "Well, how am I going to possibly tell Suzanne?" My shoulders hunch up to my earlobes.

"Jill, didn't you tell me that Suzanne and Lee are separated?" Her chopsticks are in the poking position.

"Yes, but—"

"Jill, *some* people need to move on. He's not doing anything wrong. Maybe Suzanne's on it too. Did you check to see?"

I'm preoccupied by Logan's looks, but I shake my head as if I'm still only following the conversation.

"Why don't you ask Suzanne if she's dating?" Logan asks. It's no wonder why Logan patronizes me, but didn't she understand how upsetting this is for our family?

"If I know Suzanne, she's not wasting time," she says. "Speaking of which, what's going on with you?" She finally lowers her weapons into the Pad Thai and does one of her eye rolls.

Finally, I narrow mine and move in for a closer look.

"Logan, did you do something to your eyes?"

"Eyes, brows— Botox and collagen fillers," she says.

"But why? We're not even forty!"

"It makes me feel better." She puts her chop sticks down. "The reality is that I don't want to be alone either, Jill. And until Greg and I walk down that aisle, I can't be sure."

An invisible curtain falls— a rock like Logan acting unstable about a relationship I considered to be so solid.

How will I ever recognize solid again?

On my ride home I speed dial Suzanne. "How are things going?" I ask when she answers.

"Lousy."

My jaw clenches. Luckily, she can't see my face. "What's wrong?"

"I give you a lot of credit," Suzanne's sarcasm softens. "Dating is hard."

My tires swerve to the side of the icy road. "What? When did you start dating?" My cheeks pinch back into a smile.

"If you can call it dating. I've gone on a couple of coffee meets. No one calls back. They're irresponsible, or immature, or broke. None of them interest me."

I bite my lip.

"Lee was over to take the dog to the park with Aidan the other day. He broke it off with the woman he was seeing. He actually acted a little depressed. This might sound strange but I forgot how good-looking he is."

My shoulders inch down when she says this. *I guess I haven't totally given up on love.*

"So weren't you supposed to be getting married soon according to Ingrid?"

"I don't think she meant marriage." I tell Suzanne the good news about Amberfield. "I started a yoga class on Tuesday nights and I've been thinking of taking horseback riding lessons again."

"That's great, Jill. Listen, I'm sorry to cut you off, but Lee walked in. I want to catch him before he leaves."

"Go ahead. Don't let him go." I pause a second. "See you at Christmas. I love you, Suzanne." I'd never said this to my sister before, but it slipped out so easily. Why had something so simple taken so long?

Maybe finding love wasn't as hard as I was making it out to be.

~ 47 ~

Palo Alto, California

The university was closed for the Christmas break. James drove to the office daily to settle affairs before his sabbatical started in January. At home, he finally took out the box of photos his uncle had sent after Ingrid had died. Now that Dizzy was better, he needed to look through those photos, pick one or two that he could send to the young woman who'd requested one of Ingrid. James appreciated Jill's apparent sincerity, that the fondness his mother had for her wasn't one-sided.

He picked out three photos. Then he kept sorting the pile. This was the first Christmas without anyone he could share it with, and finding the photos of his aunt made him realize how empty that felt. Amy had been in his life the past four Christmases, and now he didn't even have Ingrid. Somehow, though they hadn't spoken in years, Ingrid was like a beacon, the place in his childhood that he could go back to when he wanted. Now it was up to him to keep that big old house from falling apart. It would be ridiculous to try and rent it. Who would rent such a monstrosity in the midst of middle income suburbia? Sure he could find a few college students, but that was out of the question. At age thirty-five, it wasn't that long ago. He remembered what college students could be like.

Yet it was time enough to know that without a partner in his life, soon he'd end up with no family. Many of his colleagues already had a wife, one or two kids. Someday he wouldn't even have Jake.

He drew out a piece of stationery he'd picked up at the campus gift shop from his desk drawer. The note was the first thing he'd written in months that didn't have anything to do with his research, or Amy. He was tempted to say more than he did, about how glad he was that his mother had met such a loyal friend. The image of a woman he barely knew began to build in his mind. Maybe he wasn't ready for possible disappointment?

Maybe this wasn't a good idea?

The next day he stopped at the post office to mail back some documents to Jake, but for now he left the package with the note and three photos sitting on the backseat of his car.

~ 48 ~

I call back Attorney Chamberlain to ask if the plumbing repairs are finished so I can move in to Amberfield. In my heart I know this move is final. Sure I could always move if I want to, but down deep I know it will forever ground me to Connecticut. I was almost thirty-three. It was time to dig in, establish my career. And after my trip to California in the midst of Dad's medical scare, I've decided this is where I want to be.

Mary, the law assistant picks up the phone. The delays have "nothing to do with the plumbing" she tells me. She doesn't hide the irritation in her voice when she tells me "it has something to do with James."

I've had no trouble losing those five pounds I'd put on from the stress. Saturday afternoon after morning appointments finish, I duck out the back door a little early. All the animals are stable. Everyone has a dry blanket to curl up on, fresh water and kibble. I'll stop back later to give the diabetic dog her 6PM insulin shot.

I cruise down country roads, my tires bucking over the bumpy road that snakes its way to a long driveway lined in white fences. The smell of manure is absent this time of year, although the stable grounds haven't frozen yet. Four horses in the paddock watch my car pass by them, their sleek shine of summer replaced by fuzzy winter coats.

As I drive by the horses, I remember how the breath of Petal's pony had warmed our fingers. I recall mornings at Amberfield in the quiet kitchen after sleepovers with Petal. Finally I'll see it again.

At the front of the barn, I park my car on the gravel drive. Then I grab the dusty riding boots I'd dug out of my closet from the back seat. The boots are tight and cold as I wrestle to put them on. They slide past my calf with a sucking thump that makes me blink.

The riding instructor waves to me when I enter the Olympic-size indoor arena, zipping my fleece jacket like it's a bullet proof vest. The group lesson is ending. He holds back one gray horse. I shove both fists into my pockets to stop my hands from trembling as I walk toward them.

"Hi Jill. Ready to ride?"

I nod. My elbows are clenching my ribs to steady them. "What's his name?" I ask.

"Dansin. The boy's a good jumper, but we'll start with basic equitation today."

The Morgan gelding sniffs my gloved hands. He has no clue as to his 1000-pound weight advantage over me.

The instructor looks at his watch.

I need to get on.

I climb the steps of the mounting block as if my knees are made of tin. Then I fit one foot in the stirrup iron and swing the other leg over the saddle. The leather creaks as I grasp Dansin's mane, my thigh muscles turn to jelly the second my butt hits the seat.

"Ask him to move forward," my instructor commands.

With a squeeze of heel to Dansin's ribs, I flex my back and he walks.

"Riding is a relationship between rider and horse. It's a give and take. Tighten your reins, Jill."

After I circle the ring a few times, I position my body for Dansin to trot. His head rises as he changes gait. My calf muscles mold to Dansin's sides.

After thirty minutes into the lesson, the instructor yells, "Now ask him to canter." I freeze at the trot and circle the riding ring again.

"You don't have any contact with his mouth, Jill. Your leg is sliding back and forth. You need to be guiding him, not the other way around. Make him trust and respect you and he'll do anything you want. Show him your fear, and he'll be afraid too."

"My disability is in my hands, but yours isn't," I hear Bob's words the day he tricked me to perform eye surgery.

I squeeze the inside rein, press my outside heel behind the girth. Dansin arcs his neck and plants his inside hoof on the ground, bursting into a rocking canter. My smile grows stronger with each revolution around the riding ring. So does something more important.

Make him trust and respect you and he'll do anything you want. I used to think riding was only a matter putting my body in the right position. But riding, like so many other things, was about confidence.

After my lesson I walk Dansin until his chest is cool and he blows out a snort of relaxation. Feeling the same, I lead him into the barn.

Make him trust and respect you and he'll do anything you want.

When I arrive home from the stables, my cats run to me, then abruptly drop their nose to sniff my soles. I straddled the stairs to my bedroom as if I'm still on Dansin, then I fall on top of the bed with two ice packs across my thighs and fall sleep.

I zip up my maroon wool coat and pull my knitted hat down to bushy un-plucked brows. My twelfth birthday is coming soon. It is nearing springtime--a tease of longer days is in the air. The horses can feel it. Their nostrils flare and they twist their torso into sudden bucks. The new horse is alone in the field. He stretches his neck for me to pet him. Then in an instant, he whirls around, stinging my face with a splash of dirt as he gallops away.

I try to roll out of bed, but my legs feel like boulders. The melted ice packs have left a wet spot on the sheets. I run my fingers across my forehead to rouse myself from another dream puzzle. Later I see the text from Sam that he'll be home soon and "can't wait to see me."

He stretches his neck for me to pet him. Then in an instant, he whirls around, stinging my face with a splash of dirt as he gallops away.

When I see Sam I'll either have to remember what Ingrid taught me about trusting my instinct, or be willing to go for a wild ride.

~ 49 ~

"What happened to you, Jill?" Jeannie asks when I hobble into the office.

I wince when I try to laugh. I'm walking like a duck from the pain shooting down my butt.

"I'm old."

"I should be so lucky," Jeannie says.

"I went riding yesterday. I don't know what's harder. Riding horses or dating men."

"Women," Bob says as he comes up to the front desk.

Jeannie says, "You know I saw an article that said 34% of woman would choose their dog as their boyfriend if they could."

"Or their cat," Maryanne Romano says, lugging a carrier full of her 25-pound Maine Coon into the reception area.

"Come into the second exam room with Whiskers," I say to one of my favorite clients. I have a ton of favorites, but Maryanne is also a favorite of Dr. Bob's.

She is dressed in her usual attire, leopard-print leggings that match her Maine Coon cat, and a tight sweatshirt with big blue cat eyes stretched across her voluptuous chest. Her eyes are lined in thick pencil, with little commas at each corner. I glance over at Bob and catch him eyeing Maryanne as he walks by.

"Ya know, Doc," Marianne says to me. "Whiskers has been coughing for awhile now, but I ain't seen no hairballs. I brush him every day so he don't get matted." She's picking at her coiffure so it sticks out in peaks as if trying to resemble Whiskers. "But the cough is kinda like a wheeze, like he can't catch his breath, and his *resuscitations* ain't right."

Marianne teases a knot on Whiskers' chest using her pointy nail tips like scissors. I smirk when she misuses her word and think of Barry. It's cute on Maryanne. I feel silly now that I was humiliated when Barry pointed out my *sheikh verses chic* mistake in my profile.

When I lean over to position the stethoscope on Whiskers' chest, I instantly detect cigarette smoke on his fur. Maryanne leans closer to me.

"His heart sounds good, but he does have rales," I say.

"Rales? What's that?"

I'm careful to spare people's feelings, but not when it comes to the safety of animals.

"It's the sound of breathing nicotine." I loop the stethoscope around my neck.

Maryanne's mouth opens wide, like she inhaled a golf ball. "I didn't know cigarette smoke could affect my Whiskers like that. I told Lenny he better quit smoking those cancer sticks. He was just sayin' that he felt heart *propagations* the other day. Wait 'til I tell him this. He loves this cat."

My own heart feels like it's palpitating from stifling my laughter.

"Animals are as susceptible to second-hand smoke damage as we are," I say.

Maryanne's eyes water, her charcoal commas now smudged beneath her eyes.

"I think Whiskers will be fine, but tell Lenny we're going to have to lock him up in a dog crate if he doesn't quit smoking."

"Don't worry about that, Doctor Christie. That Lenny's gonna be in the dog house tonight."

I catch Bob peeking at Marianne again before she leaves. She obviously does both our hearts some good.

After seeing Maryanne Romano this morning, that night I decide to call Barry to wish him a happy holiday. I'd never gotten his address to send a Christmas card and he's shut down his profile, but he did call to tell me how much he enjoyed the pie that I'd made for him for Thanksgiving.

"Maybe he's got things settled with his father by now," Logan says when I call her. "It might be nice to get together with him for the holidays. You said he mentioned a membership to the Metropolitan Museum."

Logan must be preoccupied with wedding plans to advise me to call a man. But between my conflicted feelings for Sam, and this whole dating thing coming full circle, I have a lot of unanswered questions about why a responsible man like Barry never wanted to see me again. It's the men I haven't dated, like Alejandro and Prince George, who continue to keep in touch. Every one of them has made a stab at revisiting our relationship—everyone, except Tim.

Barry's home phone rings three times. The answering machine picks up. Then, his voice message leaves me reeling.

We can't come to the phone, so leave us a message. Bye. The dainty voice is that of a young girl. I end the call quickly and toss my phone on the counter so hard it bounces. How could I have been so gullible?

So Barry's got a family — probably a young wife, another child. His daughter with the heart problem wasn't old enough to have children or her own, so the child can only be one of Barry's. No wonder he didn't have much time. He probably *never* had an ailing father.

An hour later, I'm curled up on the couch watching television when the home phone rings. I don't bother to reach for the phone. **Hi, it's Jill. Leave a message after the beep and I'll get back to you. Beeeeep.**

"Hi, Jill. I saw your number on my phone when I got in from visiting my dad. I was so happy to get your call."

At the sound of Barry's voice, I grab the receiver.

"Hi Barry." I steady my voice. Self-control. Cat spit. Self-control. "How is your father doing?"

"He's adjusting to the assisted living center, but he's not happy about it."

I listen to his answer, but the child's voice on his answering machine is replaying inside my head.

"Barry, you told me you had an older daughter with a serious heart problem when we went out on our first date and you told me that magic brook story." My shoulders drop, recalling the touching scene of Barry and the shimmering chandelier crystals. "Does your daughter still live with you?"

"Yes, I see she left me some dinner on the stove." I hear his gentle laugh and struggle to continue interrogating this soft-hearted man.

"There's a young child's voice on your machine." I say, softening my tone.

He chuckles. "That's my daughter when she was six. After all these years I can't bring myself to erase that message. I still love hearing it."

My twisted posture unfolds. This is a man who had invented a magic brook to ease his daughter's fears. This is an honest man.

Yet I know it wasn't the stick shift, or miles, or spans of time that has kept us apart.

"Barry, can I ask you something?"

"Of course," he says.

I swallow air. "Are you dating other people? Of course it's none of my business, because I've been dating. It's just that I thought our date went so well, but—"

"I honestly haven't dated anyone in a year besides you, Jill. If my father wasn't sick and we didn't live so far from each other, it might have turned out differently. I guess I'll always be one of those people with too many things to do."

Too many things to do? How do people put love on hold because they have too much to do?

"If a man wants to be with you, he'll make time," Logan had said.

Perhaps we can be friends I remember Barry said to me the very first time we spoke. Perhaps I should have listened more closely.

~ *50* ~

There's a long pause on the other end of my office phone on Christmas Eve day when Jeannie tells me to pick up a call from Florida. I have no doubt who it is.

"Hi Vinny. Merry Christmas!"

"Who's Vinny?" My head rears back at the sound of Sam's perturbed voice.

"Sam! Oh, my Gosh, how are you?" I chuckle but he doesn't sound amused.

"So who's Vinny? You sounded happy to hear from him."

I feel my face flare, first from being caught off-guard, then for letting Sam make me feel I've done something wrong!

"Oh, come on Sam." I'm unaccustomed to possessiveness, and it makes me act the same. "I thought you were going to Texas. What are you doing in Florida?"

"I'm visiting my parents."

Parents? "You never mentioned your parents before."

"I was calling to tell you that I missed you and that I'll be coming home the week after New Year's." So he isn't planning to be with me on the biggest night of the year. Not that I was holding my breath for him. Vinny has decided to fly home to surprise his mother for her birthday in January, and that means there's bound to be a party.

"Well, have a good holiday Sam, and thanks for calling."

"I'll call you again, Darlin. Stay away from that Vinny."

I have no intention of doing anything of the sort.

On Christmas Day I stop by the clinic on my way to my parent's house. It'll be a quiet dinner of three since my brother is spending Christmas with Melody's family, and Suzanne and Lee took their kids skiing in New Hampshire.

The kennel staff has left already, as there are only a few boarders. I never minded being alone with the animals on holidays when I was the kennel girl. It gave me time to think things over. Like now, with only one sign left.

As I sit at my desk and look over my choices I have no clue which Leo man to choose. I thought that dating eleven other signs would help narrow my search. I thought I might have had a special connection with at least one man. But since I don't, I'm more vested than ever in Ingrid's advice to look for Leo. Leo ruled the heart. It was the sign of love.

I just need to make sure I choose the right man. If I've learned anything from my astrology experiment, it's that no sign is an ironclad mold. Free will and life lessons create our personality.

Just to be sure, I decide on two very different men and send both an email.

"Dr. Bell offered to take call on New Year's, Jill," Bob tells me at work on Monday.

"Why?" I surprise myself when I hear my voice become defensive.

"I don't know. I thought you might have a date."

"No. I don't. I can do it." I start to walk away.

"Oh. Okay, I'll tell him," Bob says. He scratches the side of his head.

"Why did he offer?" I snap. Why would Bell offer to work New Year's Eve?

"Well, to tell you the truth, Jill, he's expressed some interest in buying the clinic."

My body feels vacant as a ghost.

"Jill, I realize I've pressured you and I'm not sure this is what you want. You'll find someone, get married, start having a family before you know it."

It takes a few seconds before I blink. Everything Bob said flashes by me as if it's my past, instead of my future.

"Does David have the capital to buy a practice?" I can't bring myself to ask what I'm thinking: *Please don't tell me you made Bell the same offer as me, not a kid fresh out of college that you hardly know.*

"Evidently." One brow rises above the rim of his glasses. "His family's in Chicago. Bell Oil Company."

Bob obviously notices I'm panicked because he holds out his empty hands like he's at a loss on what to do with me. "Jill, you know I'd give you the shirt off my back."

"I can't work for Bell," I moan. "I'll do it. I'll buy the practice."

I see my future flash by again, but not one with a husband and family. I see myself stopping by the hospital on *every* New Years because we give the staff that day off. I see myself spending summer days indoors from morning until night, a syringe in one hand, stethoscope around my neck, a half-eaten meatball grinder on my desk.

Then I picture the time I'd come home from the office after saving the police dog that was shot, when Tim had turned away from the computer to hear me retell the story. "That's great, Jilly," he'd said in his deep voice. Except I won't have Tim's support to keep me going on those long days.

Bob sighs like he's worn down from trying to figure me out. "Okay. Don't discuss this with him. He'll be filling in again in February when I go on vacation."

I've lost him. I've changed my mind so many times he can't trust me on this deal, and I'm scared to think what will happen if he loses faith in me.

After I leave the office, I spend New Year's Eve night on the couch with my three kitties and a lot of food I've decided I shouldn't eat anymore. There's comfort in knowing I'm not alone when I get emails from all my regular pals at midnight, which tells me they don't have a date either. And at 2AM, I get a text from Sam. "Hey Darlin. I miss you."

I write back. "I miss you too," but I've heard back from one of the Leo men.

I don't let on to Sam that I'm planning another date.

Vinny surprises me at work with a stuffed skunk animal when he flies back from Florida for the weekend to celebrate his mother's birthday during the second week of January. *Who does he think he's kidding coming home after less than one month.* After my quiet Christmas, I thought I could use a day with Vinny and agree to take a ride to the casino. He's driving this time and blasting a CD of a hip-hop group he saw in concert. I plug my ears and count the minutes to our arrival.

"There's more costume jewelry, orthotic shoes and oxygen tanks here than a nursing home," I say, while Vinny tries his luck at the blackjack table. But I kind of enjoy my chat with a stiff-haired granny on a handicapped vehicle parked at the slot machine.

An hour later when he's bored and hungry, he forks over a twenty for two Ben and Jerry's sundaes, and we walk toward the specialty shops. He's hell-bent on spending the few hundred he's won. He buys a bomber jacket with a satin Elvis on the back and an Elvis key chain for me. I don't have the heart to tell him I'll never use it because I'm sure he's seen my keychain with the nametags of my cats.

"The keychain is enough, Vinny. I won't use a purse with an Elvis face."

The young woman at the register is giggling at Vinny's corny jokes as she checks him out, literally, but Vinny is oblivious to her adoration. It was part of his charm, actually, that he's not the least bit conceited about his looks. But spending time with such an immature man makes me feel older by the hour.

"Come back to Florida with me. I'm having a party next week."

"I can't get the time off, Vinny." I'd rather be alone than the chaperone at a keg party.

Vinny makes a sad clown face. I don't fall for it. He'll be over my rejection by the time he reaches Florida, which won't come soon enough when I bring him back to the airport on Sunday night.

"My mother's been bawling her eyes out. I probably shouldn't have come back." I understand why Vinny's parents can't support him for moving away from the family business, from family. But I understand why Vinny needs to find his own way. I'm splitting myself down the same path.

On Sunday night I drop Vinny off at the airport again. He has the personality of a puppy. But he's not all that shallow.

"Listen, take care of yourself, Jill. I know you might think you can trust that church guy, but if he really liked you, he would have been with you over the holidays."

This time when he hugs me, it feels like he's like my brother.

"Promise you'll visit me, Jill?"

"Okay." I can't bear to say the word "promise." I know it's probably one I won't keep.

"You know, Vinny, you taught me a lot."

"No problemo. Ditto, Jill."

I stop myself from getting sappy when Vinny turns and disappears into the crowd because I know better. This won't be the last time I'll see him.

~ 51 ~

I start packing my belongings in preparation for my move. One way or another, I would be leaving. Where I was going was still a mystery.

Although Mr. Premkumar had given me a little more time, he was too nice to hold him up any longer. Premkumar. *Love and affection.* He'd told me that's what his name meant. And all the years I'd known him, he'd lived by that name.

I stop and sit back on my heels to look through the astrology book from Ingrid. I stopped reading it after meeting Sam. I didn't feel the need to read up on Vinny. He was easy to figure out. Unlike my life. I couldn't stall any longer.

I pick up the phone and dial the number I've been carrying around in my purse.

"Clerk's office."

I swallow. "Hello, this is Dr. Jill Christie." I almost never pull the doctor card, but this was one of those times.

"Dr. Christie! This is Micki's mommy!"

Bingo!

"Oh, hiiii. How is she doing?"

"She's great since you put her on antibiotics. No more peeing in the sink."

Bingo, again!

"I'm so glad." *Now maybe you can help me?*

"How can I help you?"

Yes, but was this legal? "I hope you can. Do you know the Amberfield property?"

She moans. *No Bingo.*

"Ohwwww, yes. I'm probably not supposed to say this, but there's a ton of liens on it. That guy never paid his taxes. The lawyer's assistant is driving me crazy. Calls every day."

Definitely, no Bingo.

"Okay. I'm glad Micki is better."

"Okay, Dr. Christie. I hope that guy isn't holding *you* up for money."

"No, not money." *Something more precious.*

I reach over and tap a key and bring my laptop to life. All I've had until this point is a series of dates with eleven men. There are messages in my Inbox every day. The words of some hit home like fresh wounds of my own rejections each time another one says they are resigning their Internet dating subscription because they're discouraged.

There are so many phonies, one man writes. *One woman that I dated went back to her old boyfriend after she'd told me how badly he treated her. I really liked her. I hope you have better luck than I have.*

I haven't, but that doesn't mean it was a waste of time. The two biggest dates of my life are still to come, and if neither turns out right, I will at least have succeeded in learning that there is a part of everyone in me.

At three o'clock, I enter the exam room where Doris Keeley is holding her dog, Pixie. Doris' skin has a violet sheen, her cheeks are tight and round— both her full face and the behind that she's stuffed into jeans.

"How's Pixie today Doris?" I ask when she sets her miniature pinscher on the exam table. First she removes both their coats. "Has she been coughing since we started the Lasix? If the ultrasound looks good, I can lower the dose so she doesn't urinate as much."

"No problems, Girlfriend. Everything's good. You know how I LOVE this little dog." Doris bellows like a sexy saxophone.

"And how's your love life?" she whispers, watching as I listen to the rhythm of Pixie's heart. Doris has raised two daughters after her husband left her for another woman, so when the subject changes from dogs to men, Doris is the one with the expert advice.

"It could be better, Doris." I shine a light in Pixie's eyes to get a closer look at her cataracts, then lift her lip to check her gums. "Maybe I need to let my feelings catch up with some of these men." I am intentionally flip. Pixie's lip twitches with a snarl.

"Catch up? Honey, if you don't feel anything right off when you're with a man, your feelings are *never* gonna catch up." Her black eyes look wildly nocturnal. "You got to *feel* him. You know what I mean?"

My face feels like it's the color of Doris' painted lips. Doris had a way of making everything sound juicy, whether it was the way she felt about her dog Pixie, her bar-b-q cooking, or making love to a man.

Before Doris leaves, she gives me a tight hug. Yes, I knew what it was like to *feel* a man. I'm a little worried I'll never find it again— and I'm a little worried that I feel it again when I see a text from Sam.

He's finally coming home tomorrow and tells me that he's cooking me a special dinner. Finally, I'll get to see where he lives. *Riding horses.* I remind myself of my horse trainer's words as I lock the door to my office and head home for the day. My relationship with men had to be more like riding horses. *Make him trust and respect you and he'll do anything you want.*

I pull up to the front of Sam's cottage-like home, then re-check the address to make sure I'm at the right place. There are flower boxes under the windows and flower pots on the brick steps, although at this time of year, they are decorated with multicolored holiday lights and sprigs of pine. I'm surprised— it's cozy and cute. Shutters border two small pane windows and the house looks like it is smiling. It makes me think of kindness and children. I never thought of Sam this way before.

I knock with my free hand, holding a bottle of wine in my left, my nostrils lifting to meet a juicy beef scent seeping through his closed door. Until now the brief affair we've had barely lasted as long as the pink carnations he'd given me. Yet hearing his voice again sent my head spinning back to the last time he kissed me and left me with a plate of chocolate-striped cookies, and a mouth wanting more.

As soon as he opens the door, the distance between us these past months evaporates, and the gut-erflies I had the first day I met Sam come fluttering back.

"Mmmm, smells good Sam," I say stepping inside. "I didn't know you were such a good cook." His blue eyes soften when he looks into mine.

I lift up on tiptoes to give Sam a peck on his cheek, but he pulls me close for a kiss that turns my complexion inside out.

He frees my hands of the bottle and kisses me again. "I missed you," he says. The musky aroma of his cologne lingers on my cheek as he leads me into his small living room. It's subdued by tawny light and there's a velvet sectional couch—tasteful and clean for a rugged bachelor.

"How was Florida?" I ask, sinking back into the pillows.

"Beautiful, but hot. I was glad to get home." He walks over to the stereo and picks up a plain brown package. "For you."

He doesn't have to touch me now to feel his affection. I see it in his face. Inside the bag is a spiral coppery piece of metal with one-inch crystals hanging from it. The crystals are translucent, but turn rainbow colors when I hold it up to the light.

"I love it, Sam."

"I think it's some sort of dream catcher," he says proudly.

It's a wind chime, but I don't correct him.

"It looked like something you'd like. Something to make you dream of me when I'm away from you." He sips a cocktail. "Or maybe make you want to travel with me."

I slant my eyes toward him. Is he playing with my feelings? I'd have to be in a pretty committed relationship to travel with him.

Sam combs my hair back with his fingers and starts to kiss me again. He tugs my hair gently, then takes my hand and pulls me toward the stairs. My body is a powerless dingy floating behind a ship.

The bedroom where he leads me is cottage-like and tiny. Two windows are draped with brown sheers and streetlight is streaming through them. In the twilight, Sam's hands twist the blinds closed.

He guides me toward his bed. I sink down onto the water mattress and my hair spreads across his pillows. Then he slips off my shoes and leans over to kiss me. As his beard brushes my collarbone, it tingles like pins and needles. My waist flinches as his fingers inch up my ribcage and he slides his barefoot leg beside me. Succulent kitchen aromas surround us. The slosh and slap of the waterbed is the only sound. My back sinks into the warmth of it as his massive torso settles against mine.

Then the clink of his belt buckle echoes and breaks the silence, and something more. But I wasn't sixteen, or even twenty-six. My life was ticking away, and I hadn't been with a man in over six months. Yet, my gut registers a different sensation now than when he opened the front door. I shove Sam's hand away.

"We've hardly dated, Sam. I can't."

He raises his head, now buried below my neck, and stares at my face. *This is too soon*, I say with my eyes.

He slips his hand from his belt buckle and braces it alongside me.

"It's okay. We can hold off until you're ready." His voice is mellow, his eyes so much kinder than the man I did not know months ago in the photo on his profile. *If only I didn't have a conscience.*

"Let me go check that roast. I don't want you to think I'm a bad cook. Take your time and come down when you're ready." He rolls away from me and rights himself on the edge of the bed to slide his shoes on. All six and a half feet of him tower beside me for a second. *If only he would lay here for a second.*

I prop myself on my elbows and slide closer toward him, but he never turns back. After a few stunned moments, I slide my bra strap back onto my shoulder. The waterbed shifts me when I try to stand up. I'm barefoot and carrying my shoes as I descend the stairs.

Sam is standing by the stove with his back to me, head crooked into his cell phone when I walk toward the kitchen. At first he doesn't hear me. Then his eyes dart toward me and he ends the call abruptly with one hand. With his other hand, he quickly hands me the ice-melted glass of soda he's poured.

"Thanks, Sam," I say taking the glass. But his hasty gesture with the phone stops me cold. It reminds me of the amateur magician game Dad had played on me as a kid— a slight of his right hand to distract me from the hidden penny in his left hand. I was good at that game.

Vinny's warning, *"if he really liked you, he would have been with you over the holidays."*

I slide into a chair at the dining room table, set with china and silverware, a scented candle, but it doesn't feel as romantic as it looks. Sam turns back toward the oven and continues to baste the roast.

"Sam, can I ask you something?"

He turns around but his eyes can't focus on me.

"Do you think you'll ever settle down someday?"

He carries a platter of asparagus spears and lamb to the table and sets it down between us.

"Maybe."

I couldn't argue with "Maybe." Sam's cards were on the table It was my move now. I catch a ghost of my reflection in the china platter. The sight of rare carved lamb makes me gag.

I am so glad I didn't sleep with him. Makes it easier to let him go.

Of the two of us, I wonder who is more elusive — a man like him who can't keep his feet in one place, or a woman like me who is learning she's strong enough to stand alone.

More than ever, I need to date a Leo.

~ *52* ~

"Wanna walk with me at lunchtime?" Jeannie's voice is soothing as hard candy. "We can walk around the lake. I'm trying to lose a few pounds. Mine don't come off as quickly as yours did. You're getting too skinny."

"I guess it's because of the stress. Let's walk." I've noticed Jeannie is wearing a little make-up. "I like your new glasses, Jeannie." I give her a sly look. "You're not holding out on me are you? Are you dating someone?"

"Listen, I'm not too old to look." Jeannie rubs a tan spot on her bony hand.

I coo to myself at her comment. *Had I given Jeannie the incentive to find love?*

After our walk, I head back to my office to catch up on veterinary journals. Bob is on a skiing vacation with his family, and Dr. Bell is filling in again. It's never the same here without Bob.

"I've done a lot of thinking, Jeannie, and I finally made up my mind."

Her face droops. "You're not leaving the clinic, are you, Jill?"

Suddenly I'm the summer student and Jeannie is introducing me to Bob for the first time. *"Jill Christie? Dr. Jill Christie sounds like a nice name."*

"No," I tell her, but now that I say it, I'm not sure I really mean it. So much of my life was still up in the air. And there was still Leo.

That night I stare at the two names I've written next to Leo, rapping my fingernails on my desk with the precision of a metronome. Now that I've reached the end of my zodiac plan, I'm not sure I want it to end.

If only I'd had the chance to ask the Ouija board who I would marry when Ingrid was alive. *What would it mean if I got the same answer I did twenty years ago?*

I pick up my cell and call Logan.

"What's up?" she asks. Logan lowers the radio volume on the satellite station she loves, a psychologist who offers free relationship advice.

"Do you remember what I told you about the Ouija board?"

"You aren't serious?"

I hum a sigh. "What if I don't pick the right Leo?"

"Jill, the whole idea sounded hokey, but at least it got you to start dating."

Hokey. Logan is still talking, but I've tuned her out until I hear her mention "Sam."

"Have you seen him since he invited you over for dinner?"

"He asked me out for dinner on Valentine's Day." My voice grows distant. "He accused me of sending him mixed messages. 'Absence makes the heart grow fonder' works in reverse for me when it comes to Sam. It's more like 'Out of sight, out of mind.' At least until I hear from him, then these crazy feelings for him start over again."

"There's something wrong with that logic, Jill. I always miss Greg when we're not together."

"Something is wrong, but I'm not sure what."

"My wedding is two months away. Are you going to ask him?"

I wasn't sure. I plug my phone into the charger after I end the call with Logan. *Speak of the devil.*

"Hey, Darlin, I have to leave for Florida, tomorrow. We'll have to postpone dinner. I'll stop by for a Valentine kiss."

My contact lens dislodges from my eye. "Don't bother coming over, Sam. I'm tired of your games." I hang up, but he follows up with a text.

Something came up with my parents. Things will be different when I get back. I promise. I've decided to close my profile.

My thoughts are stuck like the color wheel of my iMac when I need to install an update. Sick parents—that struck a nerve. How could I not understand?

"You said you needed me to close my profile before you could be exclusive, right?" he says when he calls back.

I sigh in place of an answer. Is that what Sam needs to feel bonded?

"I've given this a lot of thought, Jill. I need to see you before I go."

"Don't expect anything more than a good-by kiss, Sam," I say. Maybe that's what he needed, but there was something that I needed. I won't wait even one week for Sam to come home.

Hard snow crunches beneath Sam's snow boots when he stops over the next day. He's bundled in a turtleneck sweater with a red vest and blue jeans. When I crack open my back door and see him, my body feels like a Dove Bar—a hard chocolate coating, a silky vanilla core.

"Want some coffee?"

"No, I had some," he says, slamming his car door shut. "I had to see you before I left. I hid my profile," he says after he kisses me, pressing his cold cheek to my face. "How about you?"

"I need to think about it, Sam."

He wraps his arms around me as we back inside the warm kitchen. "It's so cozy in here. I could stay here with you forever. I promise we'll get together as soon as I'm back."

"Please be careful driving, Sam." I haven't said it to anyone since Tim. Mom says it every time I leave, as if she's blessing me, protecting her loved one. It slipped out with Sam.

He puts the car in reverse and waves good-bye. Now more than ever, I need to finish my zodiac plan before he returns.

I need to rule out every last man before closing my profile for Sam.

After he leaves I look over my zodiac list with the starred and checked user names. It looks like my checkbook after I've balanced it. Only Leo is left.

I've chosen two men with totally different looks. Wayne is rugged, all-natural picture of masculinity, dressed in a corduroy shirt and work boots, with black hair, dark brown eyes, and a beard. The charm of his appearance is that he's more like a Teddy than a Grizzly bear. And I love what Wayne's written in his profile about fireflies around the campfire and watching a *smoking band*.

On the other hand, Jay's intellectual side appeals to me. He's dressed in a business suit and I can practically smell Polo cologne looking at his photo. Not an unruly side to him, except for the wildlife at the high school where he teaches.

These two guys are bookends to what intrigues me about Sam. Maybe a date with each of these men will help me to see why that's so. Or, maybe they will completely turn my feelings for Sam around.

~ 53 ~

Palo Alto, California

Without having to go into the office, James' life revolved more and more around Dizzy's schedule—breakfast, walk, dinner, play, sleep.

He also found himself reaching out more to old college colleagues on the east coast— and not necessarily networking about health policy.

When he passed his assistant's desk that week, he dropped off the manila folder he'd been carrying around in his car. He'd forgotten it until he threw his luggage into the back seat. The only thing James hated more than the lines at the DMV was the post office. They didn't allow dogs.

He left a sticky note and five dollars on the package addressed to Dr. Jill Christie, and he left his key to his office, just in case someone needed to get in while he was away on the road trip he'd planned down the Pacific coast, then to the high desert area Ingrid had told him she enjoyed during her last visit. Suddenly, he felt the need to see as much of the west coast before he made his final decision to head east.

He'd booked his trip east in March, and those two months were like an eternity now that he'd started his sabbatical. Dizzy, of course, would be coming too. As of now, he hadn't booked a return flight.

~ *54* ~

Wayne, Leo #1, suggests we meet on Friday night at a chain restaurant, a log cabin-like structure with red and white-striped awnings, cozy booths and prices that won't put a strain on his wallet. Friday night. *Pick-Up-Date-Night* my friends and I used to call it. Come to think, in all the time I've known Sam, he's never taken me out on a Friday night.

Inside the establishment, I notice a guy wearing a worn brown jacket with fringe sleeves the likes of Daniel Boone. But his woodsy appearance doesn't turn me off at all. It has the opposite effect.

"Wow you *do* look like your photos," Wayne says when he spots me. He's a big man with magnetic eyes and a hug that feels tremendous.

"Two?" the hostess asks us. *Yes, I think. Two.*

As we start towards the booth, Wayne's phone rings.

"Excuse me, please Jill. I promised my daughter that I'd call." He tosses me a wink. "Hi honey. I just got here." His tone of voice is soft as flannel sheets on a chilly evening. The way he brackets his words with endearments lowers my pulse. I can't help but smile.

"I'll be home in time to help you with your project, Honey, don't worry." He rolls his eyes and winks at me again.

He snaps his flip-phone shut. "That's my little girl. Six years old going on twenty-six. I can only stay an hour. She has a project due on Monday."

It's already seven o'clock.

"Oh." *Silly guy. I had this all figured out for him.* "Why don't you do homework tomorrow? There's a band playing at the pub down the street. I was going to ask if you wanted to go."

His face looks as if I'd just pinched him.

I haven't been out to listen to live music since I met D.J. last summer.

A medley of songs has been in my head all day. Suddenly I don't hear the music.

"Friday night's tough. Start of the weekend. I try to get school projects finished before the weekend starts. Saturday afternoons she's in the Lucky Lanes bowling league. I usually hang out there for a couple hours so I don't have to go back to pick her up." He's talking with hands big and soft as a catcher's mitt. "On Sunday I bring her to my parent's house for pancake breakfast so I can do laundry and food shopping before I pick her up in the afternoon. I never married her mom. She's not even in the picture."

I nod as if I understand when I can't imagine my life like that.

He's fidgeting with a ring of keys as he talks until the waitress comes and takes out her pad. "I'm good with coffee," he says. The waitress scowls under her breath as she grabs Wayne's menu. It's a busy Friday night. Dinner hour. Two cups of coffee won't add up to much of a tip. She starts to grab my menu.

"I'll have a hamburger platter," I say. "As long as you'll help me eat the fries, Wayne."

"Sure." He gives a sheepish nod to the waitress. "So did you find this place okay?" Wayne asks.

"Yes. You gave me very good directions." Pride sweeps across his face as if it's been awhile since someone has complimented him. "So you mentioned that you have a dog?"

"Yep. I brought him with me." He thumbs toward the Jeep parked on the lawn near the parking lot. "Because you said you worked for a vet, right?" He crosses his forearms on the table and leans on them.

"Yes. I love animals." I never told him I'm a veterinarian. "So what do you do for fun, Wayne?"

He tells me movies are too expensive since he can rent DVDs from Redbox for one dollar. Concerts? I ask. He chuckles.

Rollerblading, skiing, travel, museums? I don't have to ask. "How about television?" Of course. "The Family Channel."

"I pretty much watch whatever my daughter watches." My sad realization is that he actually likes watching children's programs.

"Hey, by the way, if you know of anyone that needs their floors sanded, my prices are reasonable."

I don't ask about the *Some College* he mentioned on his profile, because it doesn't matter at this point.

He sips his coffee when our waitress returns and I angle my plate so he can help himself to my fries.

"This is the first night I've been out in a while. I only had two dates last year," Wayne says, relaxing back into the booth, one arm over the back of it. I picture his daughter crooked inside it like a puppy.

Two dates in a year? My eyes flick to meet his. He shrugs as if he's content with two dates a year. With a young daughter to care for alone, maybe he has all the female companionship he needs.

After Wayne finishes coffee and my fries, I wrap the rest of my burger for him to give to his dog that he brought in his car. When we walk to the car and he opens it, a rambunctious brown and white pit bull hops over the back seat and shimmies against my legs for my affection.

"I don't have much time to work with Vyla," he apologizes when her tongue slobbers my chin.

"I can see you don't have much time for yourself."

He shrugs his shoulder. "When I'm with my kid, that's doesn't matter."

It occurs to me that this is Wayne's strongest quality, and I admire him for it.

"I had fun tonight, Jill. Give me a call if you ever want to get together again," Wayne says cheerfully.

I'm glad he had fun. I hope he'll do it again. With someone besides me.

~ 55 ~

I tote an empty green basket down the aisle of Whole Foods supermarket the next afternoon and head for the frozen food aisle. While squinting through the frosty pane of the freezer case, I sense someone hovering— a woman is leaning over the handle of her shopping cart, staring at me.

"Oh, I'm sorry," I say, backing away from the desserts with my quart of ice cream.

"No, no, it's okay. I was trying to see if it was you."

I feel my face twitch. I don't recognize her. She smiles one of those nervous smiles, but her plump face looks cheerful and we *are* standing before a delicious assortment of sweets. There has not been one animal mishap at work. No disgruntled client *that I am aware of.*

"Umm. You attend mass at St. Francis, don't you?"

"Yes, I do."

A flutter crosses my face like the dangling pink hearts slung across the card department for Valentine's Day because something about her question makes my sixth sense flash *"Warning!"*

She fiddles with the flap of a cereal box. "This is none of my business, but I saw you and that guy, Sam, together in church a few times."

My thoughts jump to the icy road conditions when Sam backed out of my driveway. I don't think I've blinked since this woman started her sentence.

"Even though I don't know you, I know people at church who do."

I think of Tim's mom, Maggie.

"I'm not sure I understand." *Just spit it out.*

"I guess you don't know." She hesitates. "Sam's married."

Married. Married. Married. I feel my expression melt like my cherry ice-cream.

"I'm sorry." She looks down for a second. "My husband cheated on me. When I saw you sitting next to Sam in church, I couldn't stand the trusting way you looked at that creep."

"Are you sure about this?" Blame my humiliation for blurting out the opposite of what I think. *Of course she is sure.*

"My friend knows him from that dating website. She went out with him last summer. His wife lives in Florida and he comes up to Connecticut and stays in his sister's house while she's trying to sell it. Obviously his wife doesn't bother to check on him. Or doesn't care."

I can barely look her in the eyes, but even if I could, my vision has become a blackout.

"Thank you for having the courage to tell me." I say robotically. "My name is Jill."

"Tammy." The blotches on Tammy's cheeks fade. "Well, I better get going with my shopping. The kids will be wondering where I am." She ducks her head with a shy grin.

At the self-check-out lane, I pay for the ice cream and leave without anything else. My hand slips when I try to put the key into the ignition. Anger and self-pity are knotting my intestines.

I should have trusted my intuition about Sam. I have a stranglehold on my steering wheel as I drive home.

His claim of travel to locations "without Internet access," no Friday night dates, the abrupt phone call when I came into his kitchen. Intuition? No, this is EVIDENCE.

For reasons that probably only the stars can explain, Sam had me totally off balance.

Well, not any more.

Once home, I toss the pint of ice cream into my freezer, then I scale my stairs in double leaps. I log onto Connect.com and click the Registration tab.

The complicated scheme I've dreamed up has nothing to do with intuition.

As I create a new fake profile, I'm amused by how easy it is to create identity theft of myself. Still, I've never been so devious. I hesitate before submitting the phony profile and dial Logan.

"Please don't say anything until I get this all out," I blurt. Logan doesn't interrupt once when I tell her what happened. "I know this sounds crazy, but I have to know for sure, Logan. Maybe Sam and his wife are separated." It even sounds shaky to me. "I'm setting up a fake profile and I'm going to see if he takes the bait. I need proof that he'll hit on another woman when he's trying to sleep with me."

"Can I talk now? Go for it, Jill. Use my photo. Pick a good name and call me as soon as he bites!"

I snort-laugh and snort-cry with relief.

When I get off the phone, I feel oddly cool, my reluctant feelings regarding Sam these past weeks finally validated with one word. *Married.*

I need to set up this profile for my own sanity. It will be nothing like my other profile. This will be short. This will be *Sexy*— pictures of Logan in a slinky red dress and a sappy story about her recently moving to Connecticut after a bad experience with a man. This little lady needs a strong shoulder, and maybe the back of a Harley, to cry on. Just the girl for Sam!

From my computer photo file, I pick out two pictures of Logan when we were fooling around with wigs last Halloween. Laughter trickles down my cheeks.

User name? *No problemo.*

Vinny had called last week pretending I'd won a trip to Florida. But his voice was not pretending when he told me Sam was probably "a Player." Funny how serious men are with a woman they consider their friend.

I slide my fingers through my hair. All I have to do now is watch to see if Sam will take the bait— *TammyBabe*'s juicy email.

The next day I get an email from Alejandro and *LesMakeADeal* on my *Butterflies303* account. There's also one from the other Leo man, Jay, asking me to join him Saturday night. Sam isn't due back until Sunday.

But my forehead turns to concrete when I search for Sam's profile. Like he promised me, he's hidden his profile.

I stare at the screen trying to make sense of it all. What if Tammy was mistaken about Sam? What if he is falling for me after all?

My insides feel balled up like wet rope as I lay in bed, checking the alarm every hour before it goes off the following morning. I walk past my computer twice before I get the nerve to check my new *TammyBabe* account. My heart races. Then curiously the knot inside me unravels like the mystery of Sam.

Hi TammyBabe. Don't know how I missed a little Darlin like you. I'd take you for a ride on my Harley, but it's too cold for that now. I promise to keep you warm if you want to meet me. I hope you look like that hot picture you posted. You won't miss me. I'm 6'4" with long blond hair. Call me. Sam

And there it is. Sam's cell phone number.

I print out *TammyBabe's* email and read it over again and again when it spits out of my printer. My fingers curl into fists imagining the day I will rip out his *long blond hair.* I'll read the email back to him when he shows up at my house for a cozy get-together after his trip, the showdown timed with the precision of a jungle cat.

Little does he know I have quite a night planned when he returns to see me.

~ 56 ~

After work, I do my laundry, pay bills, go shopping at Pet Depot and T.J. Maxx— anything to kill hours and take my mind off confronting Sam. But I don't say a word to Jeannie, sparing myself a lecture about getting my throat slashed.

"My boys are here visiting this weekend," my next Leo man, Jay, says when I call him. He speaks in the proud tone of a great dad. "But I'm free Saturday night. My ex-wife is dropping the kids off Sunday morning. Usually I drive two hours to pick up them up in New Jersey."

I'm getting a whopping dose of parenting from these Leo dads.

"Why don't we meet downtown at the blues café," he says. "I'll be sitting in on a few sets with a local band, friends of mine." I don't let on how I love the place, how I'd been there at least a hundred times with Tim.

"Sounds fun," I say.

Jay tells me he used to pretend he was on stage from a very young age. He plays harmonica and sings. *At least he doesn't tell me he wants to be a rock star.*

As I walk toward the dim red bar lights outside the old brick establishment on Saturday night, I get a sinking feeling. Despite that months have passed, it doesn't ease my nerves that I came here with Tim.

I told Jay I'd wear my white ski coat so he'll recognize me. Jay looks away the second he sees me enter. And I should have turned around and left the minute I spotted him.

Jay's hair is shocking white. White, not prematurely graying like he said, or brown like his photo. *He can't be thirty-four years old.* Tonight I'm not in the mood for even a little white lie.

"Hi, Jill. Thanks for coming," Jay says when the song ends. He shakes my hand then he pretends to inspect the harmonica he's holding. "Can I get you a drink?"

"No. Thank you. I ordered a soda."

"Okay. Next one is on me."

If I'm still here.

"I'll have some time to talk during the break," Jay says, apologetically from where he's standing on the makeshift stage in the corner of the room.

He looks like he's dressed for work. He's wearing dress slacks and a bulky cable knit sweater over a dress shirt. Business casual is a bit professional for the jean crowd that frequents this establishment. But I forget about all that once he sings. Jay has quite a soothing voice.

At the break, he pulls a chair next to mine. His deep-set eyes can barely look at me. He scratches the side of his face. I can tell he's embarrassed.

"I didn't expect someone who spends his days doling out detentions to have such a beautiful voice," I say to ease the tension.

His brown eyes soften. "Thanks, Jill. That's very nice. So what do you think of the band?"

"I'm glad I came. The band is good and I love the mix— classic rock, pop." I swallow. Neither Jay or the music are enough to erase the memories I've had here. "I hope you don't mind, but I might leave before the next break." *Before Tim walks in with his new girlfriend and spots me sitting alone.*

"I understand. We'll do this some other time when I'm not singing."

I look away. *I don't think so.* "So you said your boys are visiting with you tomorrow?"

"Yeah. I love seeing them." His shoulders wiggle like an excited child. "But it *ain't* easy meeting people when you have kids. You're pretty, Jill. No baggage. Why do you need a dating service to find someone?" His raspy voice has sexual appeal. "Just get out. Come listen to music." He makes it sound easy, like it's a song and he's conducting my life.

"Maybe you're right," I say. But it's not that easy. I'd come so close with Tim, and now I've dated every sign of the zodiac and come up empty.

"Listen, I'm sorry, Jill. The next set is starting. Please stick around."

When I remember Jay after I leave here tonight, I won't remember his eyes, or the clothes he wore. I'll remember what he sings, because it's a Sting song about galaxies and mysteries and love. Suddenly, I feel like I'm in outer space.

I slip out of my chair feeling invisible in the dark bar, and walk out the side exit. It had started to snow and the street and sidewalks are shimmering like sand dunes. I raise the hood of my white down coat and disappear like the snow angels I used to make when I was a child.

No matter what Jay may think, trying to find someone *ain't* easy. My gullible mind and soft heart has pushed me past anything I've imagined I'm capable of. When I get home I stare at the proof of what I've done, the email from Sam to *TammyBabe*. It's taken the heart out of me. Not to mention that this last date with Jay, the date I'd anticipated for over seven months to meet, is a slap in my face. This was like searching to find that perfect outfit, only to learn that it was discontinued.

"Tell me I did the right thing," I ask Logan when I call her. "Should I confront Sam, or is it enough that I beat him at his own game?"

"You're doing what every woman who's ever been cheated on probably wants to do. Call him."

~ *57* ~

I consider how I'd dress to meet Sam as *TammyBabe* when he returns home. *Hot little red dress?* But I'm like a horse frothing at the starting gate. I can't postpone this any longer.

First I forward Sam a copy of the message he'd sent to *TammyBabe*. Only this time I'm emailing from my real email. When he shoots back a squirmy *"I wasn't serious about Tammy"* email, I tell him to *never* contact me again. No surprise when my home phone starts ringing, and when I don't answer it, he switches to my cell.

Finally, I pick up.

"Don't ever call me again, Sam. I thought of confronting you, but I can't stand to see you. You're a liar and a loser!" I drop my phone on the desk and push away from the computer.

I walk into my bathroom hearing the phone ring again and let the thunder of bathwater drown it out. After I fill the bathtub and light a scented candle, I submerge my body into the steamy water. My flesh rises like tiny mountains, then my skin equalizes like the temperature inside me.

Self-respect was all about finding balance. *It's really not hard letting go of something I never had.*

In the distance, my phone keeps ringing. But I have to treat Sam like he's a bad dog. Giving him any more of my attention will only encourage him. Every pitiful apologetic email from him over the next few hours feels like another victory.

"People will come into your life to help you through a time of transition," Ingrid had said.

These men weren't changing my life. I had changed my life.

Later I open the astrology book and read what Ingrid had written. *I know you will find what you're looking for as long as you look for Leo.*

With my legs tucked up to the side of the couch, I prop the book on my lap and slip my finger into the page of Leo.

Leo is ruled by the Sun. It is the essence of our identity, our very self.
Key words: confidence, leadership, strength
Body part ruled by Leo: The Heart

Ingrid's message to look for Leo appears to have new meaning. *It's up to you now*, her note had said. This wasn't the end, it was just the start of something, someone, better.

Sunday morning instead of church service I drive to the Sleeping Monk monastery where I'd come with Ingrid for yoga and meditation class. Pachelbel's Canon is playing softly as I walk barefoot across the room and lay prone beneath four skylights in the corpse pose, Savasana. I feel sacred. I feel spiritual.

The past seven months flash across my mind, the zodiac cycle of men, Dad's illness, Suzanne and Lee's split, my visit with Oliver and the horse farm in California, the fire at Amberfield, the death of Ingrid, the near loss of Bob. His heart attack was a life-changing event for both of us.

But now for this one hour, I need to think only about myself.

"Take a deep breath," Kali, the yoga instructor says. Kali looks as frail as a praying mantis. She folds her legs in the lotus position, fingers tipped upright like spires to the temple of her heart. Ten students lay on the floor, face up, eyes closed, barefoot. Each one of us is like an island, separate yet connected by the royal blue carpet beneath our bodies.

"Imagine that you are walking into a forest, carrying a basket," Kali says. "In the basket are three heavy rocks. As you walk down the path, remove one of the rocks and leave it at the side of the path." My breath moves like a tropical breeze in the warm room. "Feel the weight of this rock as you release it from your hand. The basket is lighter now." As Kali continues the meditation, her voice softens.

"Walk farther down the path and remove the second stone. Drop it at your feet and step past it." She pauses to let the music finish. Her body mimics a violin bow when she stretches her slender arms over her head. As the symphony plays the final note of the song, salty tears pool in my palate.

"Finally," her voice is serene, "when you reach the center of the forest, remove the last stone and leave it behind."

A fishnet of lights intersects behind my closed eyelids. I take a deep breath, exhaling the weight of my body into the floor.

"Continue your journey until you arrive at a pond." Kali is standing over her sea of students. "Kneel beside the water and run your hand over the surface. It is the temperature of your body and feels like silk. When you are ready, gaze into the pond."

My misty reflection appears in my mind as an aura of blue-green light. My torso feels as if I'm levitating, yet my arms feel glued to the floor. I wiggle my fingers and toes. My lids flutter open. Then I sit up and fold into a position that looks like a tee pee.

"Amazing how powerful our mind is," the instructor whispers. "All you have to do is open it."

One by one the students collect their shoes in the adjacent room. I am the last to leave the studio. There is a mural of clouds painted on the walls—cream and gold pillows against a powder blue sky. Across the middle a quote is stenciled in italicized script.

The most attractive people I have met are those who have learned the secret of making themselves happy.

It's dark by the time I pull up to my mailbox at the end of the driveway. After pulling out bills, fliers and envelopes, I carry them inside the house and slide them onto the counter. There are boxes in every room where I've started to pack up my belongings for my move to Amberfield. **Amberfield!** I've written on each box, as if I can't believe it's happening. Just in the nick of time.

I scoot past one of the boxes, but an odd premonition stops me from heading upstairs. I backtrack to my pile of mail and shuffle through it like I have many times before, only to discover a letter from an old friend who happened to pop into my mind, or a bill that I had been anticipating. This time I see a manila envelope post-marked from Palo Alto. If it were from Oliver, it would have had hand-drawn balloons or stars or flowers on it. A chill drizzles down my arm. I know who this is from.

When I tear open the envelope, I find a note and three photos. One photo is a black and white copy of the one I'd seen at Ingrid's home. It's a young girl dressed in equestrian clothing and seated on a pony. On the back is written, **Ingrid— Age 7.**

Another photo is in color, a barefoot child standing beside Ingrid. I figure the child must be James because he has Ingrid's angular face and elongated eyes and his reserved smile is a reflection of Ingrid's.

The last photo, larger and in color, is of Ingrid standing in front of a stone building on a cobblestone street. In the background are shuttered windows and tail lights of a foreign vehicle. It appears to be a European city. Ingrid is grinning as if posing for someone—she looked about my age. She looked happy.

On the front of the note card is a picture that I recognize from the gift shop at Rodin Gardens in California.

Dear Jill,

I hope you like the photos. Mom thought a lot of you. Possibly we can fill in the missing pieces of each other's time with Ingrid. I'll be in Connecticut next month. Lots of memories that I'd like to revisit, and as I get older, I realize how fortunate I was to live there. I will look forward to meeting you. James

I look at the photo of James again. There is a cake with candles on the table. A birthday party. I squint to read a date stamped on the photo. August 7th. The month of Leo.

~ 58 ~

Bob looks especially handsome today, not that he ever looked bad, even during his medical scare. He's wearing the yellow Polo shirt Jeannie and I bought him as a get-well gift. Not much bothers him lately, even when I'm late he doesn't complain like he used to. I kind of miss the teasing.

"How's it going, Jill," Bob asks after appointments finish and he's about to head home early.

"No Leo, if that's what you mean." I snicker as if it doesn't matter, but he doesn't laugh. He sighs and it feels like a hug.

"That Tim doesn't know what he's lost." He leans back in his leather rocker and rests his head against the pillow of the chair. To hear him mention Tim after all these months has a paralyzing effect on me.

"I'm okay with that now," I say. "My subscription is about up, so I'm done with Internet dating, at least for now."

"I thought you were having fun, except for that lawyer jerk. And that other guy from church." He scoffs, "Married. I can't believe he thought he'd get away with that." He shakes his head.

"That isn't the only reason I've decided to take a break. Maybe it's better to let it happen."

"It will," he says, like everyone else.

"Maybe it will. I think Ingrid's message went deeper than she let on. I should have realized, knowing Ingrid wasn't a superficial person."

"Guess she saw what I've known about you all along."

My eyes start to tear.

"I'm heading out, Jill. I'll see you tomorrow."

I'm counting on it.

On my way home, I stop at Home and Gardens to look for a frame for the photo of Ingrid. I find one exactly as I had pictured in my mind—

scrolled metal inlaid with mother of pearl. When I get home I set the more recent photo of Ingrid into the frame and tuck the older photo of James and Ingrid into a book at my bedside.

Since it's a little late to start cooking a real meal, I scramble two eggs and stir them into seasoned broth and noodles. The small pot of soup starts to boil when there is a knock at my back door. *It's probably one of the neighborhood kids looking to sell overpriced school gifts again.* Of course, a softie like me always buys.

When I swing open the door, the smile I'd put on my face is torn apart. The walls I thought I'd built around my heart are fragile now.

"Hi, Jilly." Tim's cheek twitches, unsure of my reception. It was an expression that used to always work after a late night out drinking, or crawling into bed smelling of cigar night with the guys. His eyes taper like almonds when he smiles.

My heart is pounding as if it has outgrown the place that kept it safe. After I'd sworn to everyone that I was over Tim, now I'm not so sure.

Tim brushes a chunk of blond hair out of his eyes with the back of his hand and I remember when his big hands had brushed my hair out of my eyes. He'd never been one to say, "I love you," so many times, I'd let his hands speak for him. Gestures used to be enough. I can't let them be enough ever again from anyone. My eyes meet his eyes.

"Tim— I'm surprised to see you here." My words have no bearing on my feelings, because, I guess all along, I knew this day would come.

"I was in the area, and...," he shrugs. "I wanted to see you, Jilly. Sorry I'm a mess. I was working on one of my cars and I started thinking about some of our times together."

He leans against the open door, bracing one hand against the woodwork. I step back, sit down in a chair and stare at him as if he were a pair of worn blue jeans that I could never bear to throw away. He glances at my face then looks away like he used to, like I loved him so much but he didn't deserve it.

He's wearing work clothes, navy blue with mechanic grease smudged from knees to thighs. I look at his waist, belt cinched a notch or two smaller. He's lost weight. How could I have thought once that it would make me glad to see him need me? I get up and go to the stove to lower the flame beneath my soup.

"Your mom told me you quit your job."

"Yeah. I started teaching engineering classes at the trade school and giving guitar lessons on the side." He looks away as if he's worried about my reaction.

"You were always good with kids, Tim." I sense myself doing it, building him up before I let him down. My eyes are drawn to the red letters of his shirt label: *Tim Ireland* spelled in cursive script. There was a time, Mrs. Jill Ireland meant more to me than Dr. Jill Christie.

"My mom turned sixty in February," Tim says. "We threw her a little party. You know us Irish," he says. One cheek dimples with half a smile.

"Yes, your mom mentioned it when I saw her at church." It made me heartsick the day Maggie mentioned the party. She'd stammered in her lilt about the date and time and place. God love Maggie for trying, but the last thing I wanted was to show up if Tim hadn't invited me.

"I kept hoping you'd walk in, Jill. I wanted you there more than anyone." This is the last thing I expected to hear. Didn't he have a girlfriend?

I glance down at my palms and finger the deep creases. Whether my Line of Life or my Line of Destiny, one of those intersecting lines is Tim.

"I'm sorry I never called you, Jill. I wanted to." His head drops, hands set deep in his pockets. "I made a mistake, Jill. I love you. Everything started happening so fast—buying the house, pressure to get married." A tick of regret crosses his face. "Not by you," he adds. "I needed time to find myself."

My thoughts shift to find the right words to follow the perfect ones he just said to me. He's saying the things I've wanted to hear for so long, but they are asking too much of me now.

"It's okay, Tim. I needed to find myself, too. I just didn't know it." *But Ingrid knew.* I cradle my hands in my lap. Then I look up at him. It feels good not to be mad at him anymore.

Tim juts his chin. "I got a little band together. We play down the pub once a month."

"You did?" my voice lifts, then his.

"Yeah. You know how I always talked about it." He swallows and hesitates because Tim's too polite to say what I know he's thinking—

He did talk about it, but I never took him seriously. I was afraid to. Tim playing at clubs with girls in short skirts and high heels hanging around the band? I couldn't handle it. Yet, how many times had Tim told me how much he wanted this? And I *never* encouraged him.

"You did it, Tim. That's great."

He backhands his glistening cheek.

There was a time, we could talk with our eyes, so it killed me the night he let his fall away from me the last time I told him I loved him. This past year all I thought about was how he'd let me down. Turns out, I had done the same to him. "I never realized until now that I held you back from something you love so much. I'm sorry, too, Tim."

He clears his throat. "Why don't you come to see the band play sometime, Jilly?" His cheek quivers again. He holds his hand out to me.

He is inches away. A voice inside my head is saying, *take him back, take him back.*

"I do still love you, Tim." I reach my hand out to him but my heart is breaking— opening to let him go. "But we can't go back and start where we left off." Was it possible to outgrow someone I once loved so much? Or was I afraid to lose myself again?

He squints like his eyes are burning as he stares at my face. "I was afraid you'd say that," he murmurs. He releases my hand and it drops to my side.

Tim turns to walk out the door and my chest tightens. Was this all a test? Had Ingrid meant for me to realize Tim is the one?

"Tim."

He turns his head back slowly.

"Hold on a second." *I needed to know if my brother Rob was right.*

Tim lowers his chin as I approach him. I lift my head and feel his breath on my face, his wet lashes on my cheek as I kiss him. Losing all sense of time and place, for those few moments we slip back into the best of our past.

Yep, Rob was right. It's in the kiss, isn't it? *"You both needed time to grow up and you would never have been able to do that if you'd stayed together."* Ingrid's validation of my past-life connection to Tim isn't difficult to believe, but would our timing ever be right?

"I heard about you and Amberfield," he says, still holding me. His chin juts again as he masks his pain. "If you need any help moving in or fixing anything, I'll help you, Jilly."

Wasn't this where I thought we were nine months ago?

"Well, I better go." No smile, no light from his blue eyes.

I grab his sleeve. "Tim, I don't have anyone in my life either."

He stares at me for a few seconds as if my kindness will haunt him forever.

From the window where he can no longer see me, I watch Tim back his car out of my driveway. I'd measured my worth through Tim's eyes, and lost sight of my own.

Finally, that's changed.

~ 59 ~

There is a little shop I love to visit when I need to find a special gift. Jeannie's birthday is in a few days. Like me, Jeannie is a March Pisces.

The following evening after work I drive down the highway and head to the shopping mall. After I park, I enter the mall through the card store where I stop to buy one for Jeannie. I end up reading every single one of the Coffee House series before I choose. Then a teal-colored card catches my attention because it's in the wrong slot.

It has a pink psychedelic butterfly on the cover, and this quote.

Just when the caterpillar thought the world was over, it became a butterfly.

-Anonymous

I purchase it with the birthday card I've picked out for Jeannie.

At the top of the escalator is the boutique with pottery displayed in the window— turquoise, rust and plum metallic glazes like Suzanne uses. Wind chimes ring faintly like distant bells.

The air is thick with smoky incense as I walk inside the shop and sandalwood perfumes the air. Inside the curio cases are winged dragons and wizard figurines, another has miniature car reproductions and another glass paper weights. Along the wall is a shelf of ceramic cats and dogs and burled wooden sculptures. Dream catchers and crystals are dancing from the fan blowing a soft breeze. Stuffed animals of every breed and color are bunched together on floor to ceiling shelves.

When I see the case of handcrafted jewelry, I reach up to the necklace Tim had bought me.

"Can I show you anything?" the clerk asks. When she walks toward me, the base of her maxi skirt waffles like waves. She rearranges the display with bell-shaped sleeves and tiny fingers adorned with silver rings.

"I like this necklace."

Her earrings tinkle like a tambourine as she leans forward to unlock the case. She slides the chain out and hands it to me. It's a delicate braided metal ring attached to a string of jade pebbles There is also a blue topaz crystal, and a teardrop-shaped amethyst. It reminds me of the seven yoga chakras.

"It's called 'Morning Star.' The artist imports semi-precious stones from all over the world." All Ingrid had needed to make a statement was a jagged coal rock from Kazakhstan.

I pick out a pair of tiny stud earrings for Jeannie and a peach-scented candle that smells like warm pie. I carry them to the register with the necklace.

When I get home, I unclasp the necklace from Tim. I open my bureau drawer and open a black velvet box that looks like a jewelry casket and lower Tim's chain inside it.

Then I sit on the edge of my bed and reach into the bag with Jeannie's gifts. From the tiny white box I lift Morning Star around my neck and clasp the lock.

Before I hop into bed for the night, I check my phone for messages. There's a number I don't recognize.

"Hey, Jill. James Chamberlain. I have a few things of mom's that I think she'd like you to have. Call when you can— I'll be up late—I'm still on California time."

With my heart beating fast as a sparrow, I dial back the number. As James's phone rings, an image of him takes shape in my mind from the birthday photo of him and Ingrid. Would he resemble her today? Would he be wise and kind and spiritual like she was?

When James answers, his mellow voice sets off a chain reaction of emotion.

"Hi James. It's Jill," I say, like I've said this to him a hundred times before, because somehow, I feel I have.

"Oh, Jill, I was hoping you'd call. I feel a little lost here after all these years."

A giddy wave of excitement swells inside me. "I was so happy to get the pictures, James. I don't know where to start."

"I've got time," he says with a soft laugh.

It's 2AM when we get off the phone. I should be exhausted, but sleep is the farthest thing from my mind. James has asked me to meet him this weekend.

I look again at the photo he'd sent. And his birthdate. *Leo.*

"Oh, my gosh, Happy Birthday, Jeannie," I blurt the next day when I walk into the office. I lean into Jeannie for a side-to-side hug, my arms stiff from holding a gift bag and small cake. I'm in shock as I back away to get another look at Jeannie's new hair color.

"Tell me the truth. Do you like my hair?" Jeannie asks, plucking the flame tips at the crown of her head. "It's so easy. My stylist said it makes me look ten years younger. Do you think it's too red?"

I have never seen this side of Jeannie. She never asks for anyone's approval, unless she was sure of the answer.

"It's totally you. I love it. Who says we have to look older on our birthday."

"Oh, Jeannie I didn't know today is your birthday," Dr. Bob says when he comes into the reception area. He twists his head for a double-take at Jeannie's hair. "We'll all go out for lunch later to celebrate."

Jeannie and I look at each other. He's never done this in all the years Jeannie has worked here.

She lifts her cheaters to the bridge of her nose.

"What a unique necklace, Jill. I've never seen it on you before."

"I bought it yesterday at a new store. I got you something there too." I set two decorative packages on the front desk. (Though I'm feeling a twinge of pre-gift anxiety that the opal studs will be too conservative for her now!)

"Did I tell you that I decided to sign up for a dating service? They're running a free special this month, so I've been trying to think of a name. Thought I'd call myself something with the word 'Flame' in it. You know, like an old flame, because of my last name, Sparks."

"Well, it goes with your hair color!" I swallow back tears. It's scary to see Jeannie so vulnerable.

"How's the dating coming along? I haven't heard you mention anyone lately."

"I've decided to take a break." The crinkling sound of gift unwrapping stops. "I've met a lot of nice men that I'll keep in touch with. We exchanged our real email addresses."

"Do you think you'll ever meet that Alejandro in New York?"

Jeannie shows more interest in these men than usual now.

"Probably not. He's dating a woman now. If only they could all find someone." I sincerely mean this, except for a few. "I had to block Sam's emails after his incessant begging my forgiveness."

"Nothing like rejection to make a guy think he loves you," Jeannie quips. I think of Tim.

"You know, although I didn't meet anyone special, I've met a lot of special people."

The office assistant, Marlene, comes out of her office. Jeannie swivels in her chair opening her gifts.

Marlene's advice to let each man be a stepping stone— what would she say about coming full circle with Tim? What would she say if I told her he stopped over and I didn't take him back? I'd felt so free walking that path during the yoga meditation.

Later, when Jeannie and I are alone, I tell her Tim stopped by my house.

Her eyes widen like open arms. "And?" She looks like she's expecting a good ending to a sad love story. She knows I'd loved Tim like there was no hard bed.

"I don't know yet."

Jeannie has a sad look on her face.

"So does that mean you don't believe in soul mates anymore?"

"Oh, I'll never stop hoping. But he'll need to love a woman who hates to cook."

Her smile puckers as if she's worried for me.

"Jeannie?"

Jeannie tips her head back to look me in the eye.

"I talked to Ingrid's son, James Chamberlain, last night. He's in Connecticut."

Jeannie's mouth parts open.

"He isn't the least bit stuffy like I imagined after meeting his stern uncle about Ingrid's will. James invited me over Sunday night. He has some antiques he thought I'd like for the farmhouse and asked if I'd go to dinner with him. We talked for two hours last night. He ran the Honolulu Marathon last year and takes his bulldog, surfing with him in San Diego." I feel the corner of my mouth twitching to smile.

"I'm silly with joy for you, Jill." Her hands fly around her spiky red head, until my face clouds.

"What's the matter?" Her brow scrunches like a Shar-Pei pup.

"I was excited too, until I got off the phone."

"Oh don't worry. It'll be fine. And he must be handsome if he looks anything like Ingrid or the attorney. It sounds like you'll have a lot in common."

After Jeannie hands me the next appointment chart, I scribble a note to myself on a Post-It. *Email Prince Edward about Jeannie.*

I walk toward the exam room counting floor tiles with my footsteps, reluctant to tell Jeannie why I'm really nervous about meeting James. After talking to him, I finally got the nerve to use the Ouija board.

Now, more than ever, I need to know the real truth.

My favorite patient greets me (although I say this about quite a few of them). Mandy is looking for me with her one good eye, and I know she's expecting a treat. Mandy's owner looks excited to see me as well. He has brought me a treat too—Hungarian poppy seed roll with powdered sugar that he baked for me.

After lunch, and after appointments are finished, I walk into Bob's office. He has his back to me and he's reading a veterinary journal. He looks like one of those gentlemen that old movies portray smoking a pipe, only he's stopped sneaking cigarettes from Jeannie and he's sucking on an e-cigarette. Vapor fills the room with the scent of Carmel Latte.

"Bob, can I talk to you?"

"Of course. What's up?" he twirls himself around in his new massage office chair that Pam bought for him.

"I'm leaving a little early to go to a concert tonight."

"Who are you going with?" He lowers the magazine.

"I'm going by myself. I've wanted to see this group for years, so I bought a ticket."

"Well, maybe you'll meet someone."

I shrug one shoulder. "It would be nice, but it doesn't matter." I clear my throat. "I was also thinking of taking some time off after Logan's wedding in the Caribbean."

The lines around Bob's mouth flatten. I remember his face from years ago before the lines were there. I've been with Dr. Bob longer than any man alive besides my father.

"You're going to the Caribbean alone?"

"With my parents and some friends that I haven't seen in years."

"Oh, good." His eyes blink back from papa bear to animal doctor boss. "So how long am I going to have to do without you?"

"I thought I'd give you enough time to miss me. Maybe three weeks? I'm moving into the Amberfield place. There's a bunch of painting and cleaning I want to do." My shoulders scrunch up, squeezing myself into a hug.

"Geez! You're excited about a ton of physical work?"

Every muscle flexes with enthusiasm. "It's the closest I've come to owning Amberfield." Then my voice gets shaky. I can't look at him. "I don't think I can buy the practice, Bob."

His chair stops squeaking and his eyes turn reflective. "Before my heart attack, I might have tried to convince you, Jill. You'll always have a place here with me. I'll make sure of it even if I sell the business. To tell you the truth, I'm not sure I want to. I'm too young to retire. I think I'd miss the animals and clients. And I've been thinking of something else. Maybe I'll expand the practice, have you do a little equine on the side. But I'd have to have David Bell fill in. It might work out best for us all."

I lean over and hug him, then I turn my face and kiss his cheek like Italian families do—a kiss of respect. Wasn't that what love should be after all? Physical chemistry was a start, but without respect, a relationship would never amount to much.

Bob rubs the wet tip of his nose and blinks hard. "Hell, who was I kidding? I can't stop working as long as Pam keeps shopping."

"Thank God for Pam," I say and mean it. For as long as I live, I know Bob will always be in my life. I hope he lives forever.

~ 60 ~

Suzanne and Lee are driving up from New Jersey to celebrate my birthday at Mom and Dad's house. Logan and Greg said they'd stop by. I'm sure Oliver will call from California, and Vinny, from wherever he is these days. I wouldn't be a real Pisces without at least one or two ex-boyfriends keeping in touch, though I hear Tim reconciled with his girlfriend after the night he stopped by to see me.

As Mom would stay, "It's for the best."

In the morning I stop by Amberfield to drop off a few boxes now that Attorney Chamberlain's office sent me the key.

I turn the key in the lock and feel my heart slide up my chest as I crack open the newly-painted door. There's a familiar smell when I enter the kitchen, maybe not what I'd try to describe because it wouldn't sound so great. It's the sweetness that a heart senses when it revisits a fond memory, even with eyes as blind as Chrissy—slivers of shellacked oak from the old rocking chair that Petal and I squeezed ourselves into, microscopic bits of dried flowers that Petal's mom hung in the sunny window. They've comingled with desiccated drops of chocolate milk that seeped from our giggly mouths onto the linoleum floor, musty air from the dirt basement where we swore the spooks lived, and maybe there's some butterfly wings that we found sealed in the crevices. It feels like I've come home. Maybe I just imagine it that way because of Petal.

I turn the glass knob on the bedroom door and look out the window overlooking the pasture. The small barn that D.J. is building is almost done and I picture a chestnut gelding with white socks standing beside it. I've already called Andrea to see if she still had that sad little horse that I'd met when I visited her. They're waiving the adoption fee. It's only a matter of working out details with Copper Valley Equine Vet to get him transported to Connecticut. I'll keep his name. Chippy.

I check the pilot light on the gas stove, pull the chain of the overhead fixture, even though the room is already saturated with natural light. A warped floorboard in the dining room creaks when I step on it because James has left the structure pretty much untouched. I'll probably wish he'd replaced the leaded glass cottage windows that are in every room when I have to heat the house this winter, but they are one of the most romantic features— oh, except for the painted white stone fireplace in the bedroom and the built in bookshelf in the den where my cats will take naps. And the French doors in the hallway, the ivy-draped terrace off of the dining room, the low ceilings, antique paisley wall paper in the back bedroom— I wrap my arms around myself. This feels like love.

Before I leave, I unpack the antique sugar bowl Mom had given me as my early birthday present. She's kept it in her hope chest for years.

"It was grandma's," she had said, her fingers smoothing the patina of antique china. "The gold trim is 14-carat. They don't make china like this anymore. It belongs with you and the Amberfield house." I find a hundred-dollar bill stuffed inside it. "Buy yourself that cute little kitchen table you showed me."

"I love it, Mom," I'd said, cupping it in my hands.

"I want you to know, we're proud of you, Jill. I never doubted you. I just felt bad you were on your own."

"I know, Mom. But I never would have known I could stand on my own if Tim had stayed in my life." I guess Ingrid knew that all along.

I open the cabinet and place the sugar bowl on the shelf until I buy the table. I'll make sure to tell Mom again how much I love it— how much she means to me.

It is one of those March days when nature is erupting like teenage hormones. A lukewarm current whistles through the leaky storm door. I'll have to have D.J. fix it. He's still dating my neighbor. In fact, he and Shep are moving in to live with her in my old neighborhood.

I put my down coat back on and lock the door. With a bag of raisin bread on the car seat beside me, I drive down the highway to the beach. It is deserted this time of year, except for a few dog walkers and the constant gulls.

When they see me with my bag of food, they start screeching and circling, their wings floating in sharp displays of aerobics. But as soon as I'm out of bread they disappear like fickle lovers.

I walk down to the water's edge and slip off my shoes. It's unbearable, sinking my toes into the cold sand. Quickly, the imprint disappears, washing back toward another shore. In my daydream I imagine it reappearing on a California coast.

But James Chamberlain is in Connecticut now, and the chill through my bones is only partly the freezing water, partly nerves at how I will feel when I meet him tonight.

I haven't told anyone about the night I finally used the Ouija board. I'd lit a candle and sat on the carpeted floor of my empty living room. That candle grew taller and taller, then began to flicker madly. The air had filled with a pleasant sulfuric fragrance.

I didn't think Ouija would work alone, but it did. My hands shook on the plastic pointer as it started to slide across the letters. It circled the letter "L" over and over again. My fingertips remained stiff as a wooden mannequin. I pressed my tongue against my front teeth and stared in disbelief at the heart-shaped planchette as it zig-zagged across the board.

When it stopped, I felt immobilized. I floated back in time to the night I'd slept at Amberfield with Petal, when she asked when she would die and it circled the next year. I believe now that what happened to Petal was a terrible coincidence to what the Ouija predicted. As for me, it all makes sense now.

Ouija simply tapped into my own subconscious mind when it spelled my own initials— proof I needed to find my own heart. Ingrid's message to look for Leo was simply her way of helping me find myself. *Leo is ruled by the Sun. It is the essence of our identity, our very self.*

Or did Ingrid have her own agenda?

Using a sea stick, I carve my initials, *J.C.* into the sand. J.C. Jill Christie.

It is also James Chamberlain's initials.

Underneath my initials I write the message the Ouija board spelled out that night. It was without a doubt a message sent from Ingrid. In the sand I write *LEO IS LOVE.*

When I return home my message machine is blinking. I press the play button expecting to hear Oliver. Then an elevator of emotion rises and falls inside me.

"Happy birthday, Jilly. I'm glad we're friends. If you need any help with the farm, let me know." I stare at the answering machine in disbelief. My solar plexus somersaults at the sound of Tim's voice. After meeting a whole zodiac of men, not one made me feel like Tim does. Not yet. But sometimes coming full circle is the only way to move forward. I finally have.

Upstairs at my computer, I click onto the dating website. The counter in the corner of *Butterflies303* page shows that my profile was viewed over three thousand times.

There is one last email inviting me to renew my subscription before it ends. My pointer finger hesitates over the *Hide My Profile* button. This is more difficult than I expect. I click on a few profiles of my pen pals. It is bittersweet to see them, still hoping to find someone. It's as if we were *Almost Lovers*. What free beautiful words.

Should I tell them? *Look for Leo.*

The cursor is hovering like a gull over the button. I stop one last time to look at the list I've compiled of my special friends' personal emails. I know all their real names now.

I open the local entertainment newspaper I've picked up at the market on my way home and turn to the astrology column.

PISCES: Despite your sometimes childlike heart, you were born a very old soul because Pisces people are a blend of all other eleven zodiac signs. In this way, Pisces, you've got the world at the tip of your fingers.

After I shower and change out of my jeans, I drive down to my birthday celebration dinner with my family, all of them, together. There's nothing I want more in my life, except for finally meeting James later tonight.

It's only 7P.M. when I leave Mom and Dad's with three doggie bags of penne pasta, Mom's meatballs, and Suzanne's coconut cake. Suzanne and Lee had left early to drive back to New Jersey with Champ, his coat lush and shiny on his hypoallergenic doggie diet that I had suggested.

My forty-minute drive back to Mount Pleasant is a blur.

I pull up to the front of Ingrid's beautiful Victorian and sit there for a minute letting a tidal wave of anxiety subside. A subdued light emanates from the second-floor bedroom window, mirroring that of the creamy full moon. It's as if that big house is alive again.

The next thing I notice is Ingrid's Volvo. It's parked in the circular driveway instead of the garage where Ingrid had kept it. I shut off my car engine, get out and bump the car door closed. Then I walk toward the front entrance past Ingrid's garden. There are no flowers this time of year, only lumpy black mulch where inches below the surface, new life awaits. My heart is blossoming with anticipation.

At the familiar whine of the front door hinge, my head snaps up. The door swings open and a stubby bulldog gallops towards me with her tongue dangling from her mouth. I stoop to rub her belly when she flops at my feet. *Dizzy?* I look in disbelief at the collar I'd seen in California.

Then I notice James.

I knew he would look like this—casual and collegiate, a mild degree of athleticism in his easy posture. He tilts his head back and smiles, feathering his bang away from his forehead like he's a little nervous, too.

"He's very handsome. A kind face."

As I stand up, he walks toward me, bringing the aroma of lime and musk. A translucent sheen of beard tells me he's just shaved. First, he extends his hand to me, but we both know, that's not enough.

Although we are strangers, after our phone conversation the other night, there's a bond between us. It only takes a second before he hugs me. It's the feeling I'd longed for all year.

James lets out a soft laugh when he lifts his face from my shoulder. Fresh shower lingers on me from his sweater. Then he brushes tears from my cheek with his thumb. "I couldn't wait to meet you, Jill." His eyes are shining with emotion.

"Me, too." We hold onto each other for several seconds as if our bodies we are made of sand.

"I want to show you something," he says.

A magnetic current closes the distance that has kept us apart as he takes my hand and walks me to the back yard.

"It's a full moon tonight," I say. "It's in the sign of Leo."

James stares at me as if he's heard this many times before, but not in a long time.

"That's something that Ingrid used to say." He stares with a sad fondness, then he bends down when we reach the patio and brushes leaves off two stones set side by side in concrete. "My aunt liked to paint and sculpt. She taught me to draw. One day we carved our sun signs in the cement when the masons were pouring the patio."

He takes out his phone and aims the light beam so that I can see the image carved into the stones. One has a looped scroll that I recognize as the symbol for Leo. "She told me it would last forever to remind me she would always love me. I was too little to understand why she never came to see me anymore."

He shines the beam on the adjacent stone and I gasp, awestruck by Ingrid's promise. There's a symbol of two fish swimming in opposite directions—the symbol for Pisces.

"I have the feeling she just came back." His eyes look the way Ingrid's did when she told me I had the same birthday as her sister. My eyes blur with joy.

"Come on, Jill. Let's go inside. There are some things Ingrid wanted you to have for the Amberfield house." With one arm around my shoulder,

James calls for Dizzy to follow us.

"I'll bet you like incense right?" he says.

"How did you know?"

"I had a feeling. A good feeling."

The last nine months of my life are winding down like the end of a romance novel. But it's not the end, it's the beginning.

Yes, Ingrid. I understand now.

The End

ABOUT THE AUTHOR

Like the main character, I am a Pisces. I love animals, dreams, home, music and people, not necessarily in that order, as Pisces often live their life in peaceful chaos.

This novel presents a superficial representation of the astrological personalities for entertainment. Each sign has positive and negative traits and each person is unique in their own right. Although our date, time and place of birth define the blueprint of our life, circumstance and free will play a part in who we become.

Some of you may read this book looking for romance, some out of curiosity about the zodiac. I hope I've satisfied each of you.

I live in Connecticut with a one-eyed cat named Jonny, and a recovering feral named Mickey that thinks he's a Pit Bull. By day I work at Yale University for a wonderful group of doctors, and spend most of my free time with my beautiful thoroughbred named Epic Romance, Romeo.

Please visit my Website http://patticavaliere.wixsite.com/author

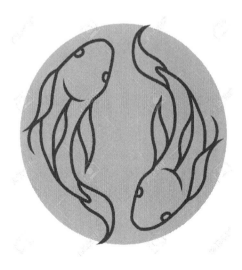

PATTI CAVALIERE

BEHIND THE SCENES OF LEO

I used my experiences as a veterinary assistant as the backdrop for this story, and my fascination with astrology as the framework. It took several years for the deeper theme, the main character's attachment to an old home, to emerge. That, too, was drawn from my own life.

In 1980, I was newly married to an architect and we bought our first home in Newtown, Connecticut. It was a tiny mustard-colored ranch house that sat on four acres of flat pasture well-suited for horses. Across from our country road, there was a trail through woods darkened by tall trees and cabbage leaves, ending in a grassy clearing. It was the edge of a rolling hillside estate owned by Dr. Brian Silverlieb, a veterinarian in town. Within a short time, our lives crossed at a social equine event.

Brian's home was in disrepair when he bought the dove gray and white cottage-like dwelling from two artists. I remember the gold-embossed dining room wallpaper curling at the seams, water-stained ceilings, the drippy white enamel kitchen sink, English ivy snaking through a crack in the window frame of the China-red foyer. But there was something charming about the house with its leaded windows and stone fireplaces. It even had a carriage house, and a room where the artists painted murals, some of which were purchased by Jacqueline Kennedy.

Before Brian remodeled the home, he took immense pride in transforming the grounds. Meticulously-manicured perennial gardens— islands of them— popped up amidst the yard's natural landscapes of fruit trees and evergreens. I was enchanted by the idyllic beauty of this property, especially when greeted by Brian's three yipping Shelties. Once he bred a litter of them, and when I visited, it felt as if I'd stepped through the Hunter green door and into the world of Lassie. Of all the magnificent homes I have seen, this image remained in my memory, even years after I relocated forty miles away from the quaint town.

In 1986 I was hired at a veterinary clinic in an English Tudor-style building in the section of Hamden called Spring Glen. The Arts and Crafts bungalows of Spring Glen served as the location for Mount Pleasant Veterinary Hospital. Some of the pets I came to know during my days as a veterinary nurse and pet-sitter are immortalized in this novel.

For the twelve years that I commuted to work, I drove past the elegant historic mansions that border East Rock Park. The panorama of 1900s Colonials—Greek, French, Spanish, Neoclassical, and especially Georgian, styles situated in the area between 240 and 510 Livingston Street in New Haven became the inspiration for Ingrid's estate.

Yet, in all their grandeur, none compare to the home Brian owned and named Amberfield. Sometime in the 80s, Brian remodeled his farmhouse into a gentleman's showpiece. He took care not to compromise the romantic features like low, sloped-ceilings, French doors to a den with a book-cased wall, or the cozy bedroom with built-in drawers and a stone fireplace. In 2004, Amberfield was included in Newtown's Historic Home & Gardens Tour. By then it had a sunken living room with a floor-to-ceiling thin stone fireplace, two atriums with exotic Zen-like themes, an enormous white kitchen with vaulted ceiling beams, and a Master bathroom with a Jacuzzi tub overlooking his grazing horses and lush gardens of lilies, lilac, pear trees and hostas. The pool on the terrace was designed to mirror the pond in the lower pasture, and the barn was built with a royal flair—lacquered pine stalls with brass nameplates. The interior of the home was artfully decorated with Persian rugs, framed prints, wall hangings and furniture that chronicled Brian's world travels. And of course there were portraits of his beloved animals.

Brian owned a menagerie of cats, dogs, horses, sheep, and goats—mostly rescues of some unfortunate fate of which he himself could not escape. After Brian passed away, the young thoroughbred he had bred was given to me as a gift. He'd named him Epic Romance. I learned to ride again and the bond we developed rekindled the secret of horses that I knew as a child—the almost spiritual, intuitive connection with these gentle animals. Some of this passion is expressed in this novel. Romeo is my treasure, and the best therapy next to writing. Our photo can be seen on my website or Facebook page.

A picture of the real Amberfield is also on my website, with thanks to the lovely young couple who now lives there. The real estate agent who sold Brian's house told me she used to sit on the stone wall to feel the magic. It's much too strong to be unaffected by all that beauty.

As far as the secret to find love, I'd be lying if I didn't admit parts of the novel are true, but I wrote the ending I wish I'd had. In time I found there are many roads to happiness. I hope as you read this novel, you will also find your Leo.

Made in the USA
Columbia, SC
23 June 2018